Adam Armstrong was born in 1962. He lives in Norfolk. His first novel, *Cry of the Panther*, is also published by Corgi.

www.**books**at**trans**world.co.uk

Also by Adam Armstrong

CRY OF THE PANTHER

and published by Corgi Books

SONG OF
THE SOUND

Adam Armstrong

CORGI BOOKS

SONG OF THE SOUND
A CORGI BOOK : 0 552 148121

Originally published in Great Britain by Bantam Press,
a division of Transworld Publishers

PRINTING HISTORY
Bantam Press edition published 2001
Corgi edition published 2002

1 3 5 7 9 10 8 6 4 2

Copyright © Adam Armstrong 2001
Map © Neil Gower 2001

Set in 10½/12pt Sabon by
Falcon Oast Graphic Art Ltd.

Corgi Books are published by Transworld Publishers,
61–63 Uxbridge Road, London W5 5SA,
a division of The Random House Group Ltd,
in Australia by Random House Australia (Pty) Ltd,
20 Alfred Street, Milsons Point, Sydney, NSW 2061, Australia,
in New Zealand by Random House New Zealand Ltd,
18 Poland Road, Glenfield, Auckland 10, New Zealand
and in South Africa by Random House (Pty) Ltd,
Endulini, 5a Jubilee Road, Parktown 2193, South Africa.

Printed and bound in Germany by
Elsnerdruck, Berlin.

For Kim
with my love

ACKNOWLEDGEMENTS

A special thanks to Greg 'Gib' Gibson, my friend – who said he wouldn't go.

My thanks also to Lance Shaw, Ruth Dalley, Jimmy Sheard, Andy Williams, Essie, Pam, Liz, Stoney Burke, the Marine Studies Centre at the University of Otago, Southland District Council and Fiordland Travel. The extracts from Thomas Musgrave's diary which appear on pp. 168 and 402 are reproduced by kind permission of the Southland Museum, Invercargill. *The Wake of the Invercauld* by Madeleine Ferguson Allen, referred to on p. 402, is published by Exisle Publishing Ltd, Auckland, New Zealand.

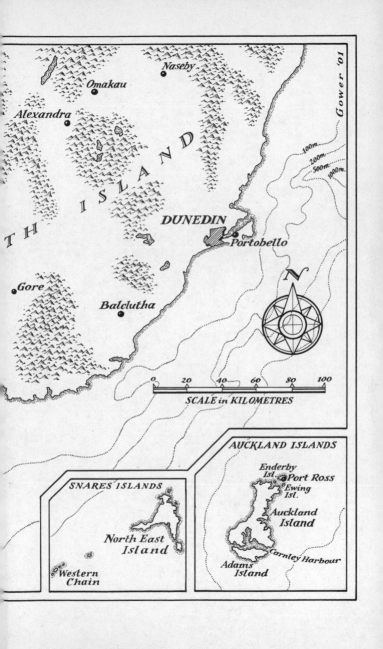

Gower '01

Naseby

Omakau

Alexandra

TH ISLAND

100m.
200m.
500m.
1000m.

DUNEDIN

Portobello

Gore

N

Balclutha

0   20   40   60   80   100
SCALE in KILOMETRES

AUCKLAND ISLANDS

Enderby
Ist.   Port Ross
        Ewing
        Ist.

SNARES ISLANDS

Auckland
Island

North East
Island

Carnley Harbour

Western
Chain

Adams
Island

PROLOGUE

1970s

John-Cody knew they were FBI agents as soon as they walked in. He sat behind the bar tuning his guitar and listening to the sounds of laughter coming from a group at a corner table. Saturday night in Hogan's Hotel in McCall: he was preparing to play the first half of his set. Hogan always made him tend bar for the first part of the evening, then play a twenty-minute set to get the drinkers in the mood for a party. After that, he would tend bar again till the second set. That was fine by John-Cody; if they liked the way he played, the tips between sets were enough to pay his rent. This week had been slow, however. There was too much snow on the ground, notwithstanding the cabin fever that usually set in by February.

He stared at the two FBI agents in their sharply cut suits, both with grunt haircuts. They stood out a mile in a cowboy bar. For a moment he wondered why he had come back here at all: they were bound to catch up with him at some point. He hadn't meant to stay, he had just wanted to pick up his guitar and get going again. It had been Hogan who persuaded him. Hogan liked to have a male bartender as well as Nancy and

11

Lisa whom he employed on alternate nights of the week. John-Cody was swift and thorough and he'd been lying about his age since the days when he was fronting his blues band in New Orleans. He had just turned seventeen when he headlined for the first time and he had been as sure as a gulf coast storm he was on his way to the top. But that feeling had been well and truly dashed the day of his eighteenth birthday.

'Hey, Gib.' A cowboy from a ranch on the South Camas prairie rattled an empty bottle at him. 'Set me up, buddy. I can't wait all night.'

'You bet.' John-Cody slid off the stool and put his guitar down. He took a cold bottle from the refrigerator and snapped the top off.

The cowboy peeled a dollar bill off the roll he had tugged from his pocket and slapped it on the counter. 'Change is yours.'

John-Cody rapped the wooden bar with his knuckles.

Lisa moved next to him. She had dyed blond hair and pink-painted nails that he could never quite decide were false. She poured a shot of whiskey into a glass and topped it up with 7Up, the gaseous liquid crackling over chunks of ice. 'Hogan wants you on that stage, Gibby,' she said. 'You best get to it.'

John-Cody felt the little tingle in his palms that he always felt when he was just about to play live: a hint of nerves that gave him the edge to play as well as he could. To say the presence of the FBI agents accentuated that feeling was something of an understatement. So far they hadn't approached him, but once the set began his identity would be broadcast. He looked towards the door but the crowd barred any thoughts of an exit route. The back way was locked and double bolted and he knew they would have some deputy sheriff covering it from outside.

He was calmer than he had thought he would be, given the circumstances, and he put it down to the fact that he had known they would come the moment he let Hogan convince him to stay. He was a fine guitar player and word got round quickly. Complacency and familiarity: he should have moved on like he had planned. He brushed against Lisa, catching a whiff of her perfume: it was too sweet for his tastes but feminine in an in-your-face sort of way. He could smell the burnt quality that the dryer left in her hair and a faint hint of female perspiration. One of the FBI agents leaned on the bar and looked him right in the eye. He was in his mid-twenties, with sharp blue eyes and a button tip to his nose. 'How you doing?' he said.

'Howdy.'

They looked at each other for a long moment. 'My name's Muller.' The agent nodded to the guitar. 'You best play if you're going to. We don't want a riot on our hands.'

'I've got two sets.'

'Not tonight you don't.'

John-Cody picked up his guitar, stepped through the gap in the bar and made his way to the stage.

Louise was going to sing with him tonight. She was three years older than he was and had been singing the local circuit for a year and a half. Her father made the best ice sculptures in town. People carved them in their yards when the first snows hit and by the time the winter was over the sculptures would be hardened to a stone-like quality by the cold. Her family lived off the main highway heading for Cascade and they had an ice model of Apollo 11 right there in the front yard.

She was having a drink with her redneck boyfriend who liked to stare John-Cody out whenever he was on stage. He did that to anyone who got within ten feet of his girlfriend; it was his way of letting you know that she was his property. He didn't dance or clap his hands or sing along to anything, but just kept those little drill bores on John-Cody. At first it was unnerving, but after eighteen months of prison John-Cody figured he could handle a cold stare. He touched Louise on the shoulder and she nodded. He went up to the stage and waited for her to disentangle herself from Billy, who would much rather she didn't get up there at all. John-Cody plugged in and played a little riff then broke into some New Orleans guitar blues he had composed while playing that year on Bourbon Street.

He picked at the strings again, another tune, along the lines of James Booker but his own composition. The bar was as crowded as he had seen it and he wondered if there was any way that he *could* sneak past the FBI agents. Cowboys stood in their winter gear drinking beer from the bottle and townspeople hogged the barstools and milled between the tables.

John-Cody played, waiting now while Louise rearranged her clothing at the mike stand, and he watched the two agents standing at the near end of the bar. Their air of controlled composure was all too familiar and he felt his heart sink as the front door opened and the sheriff stepped inside. If there had been any chance of getting away it was certainly gone now.

He played his heart out one last time, head bent, imagining he was with his own band kicking butt on

Bourbon Street. He wore dark glasses so nobody could see the fear in his eyes and whenever he looked up the two agents were watching him.

He launched into the first cover, Janis Joplin's version of 'Bobby McGee': Louise plucked the microphone from the stand and moved across the little stage as she sang. John-Cody glanced towards the bar and the two agents in their long coats were still watching him. Cold all at once, he missed a chord and only the strength of Louise's voice saved him. Closing his eyes, he let the breath hiss from between his teeth, thinking again how dumb he had been to get stuck here. He had crossed the state line three months after they released him, having been unable to find work in Washington, which was as far as they would let him stretch his neck. Hogan had given him his old job back and he knew people in McCall. They seemed to accept him notwithstanding the reason he had been plucked from their midst in the first place. The parole officers in Washington had gone out of their way to obstruct him. They were friendly with the sheriff and the state police and as far as they were concerned his crime was as bad as it got. With no work he could not get by, so he had played them at their own game and skipped over the mountains to Idaho.

Everyone seemed to be staring at him now, the crowd pretty quiet. Louise was into a slower song and he was plucking the strings with his thumbnail. The two FBI agents sat on stools at the bar with their coats hanging open, Muller's jacket barely covering the bulge at his armpit. They seemed to be enjoying the show and Muller grinned wickedly as their eyes met. He tapped a finger to his temple in mock salute and John-Cody felt sick. The blood seemed to slow in his veins. The set was coming to an end and he had no way out of here except right past the bar and out the front door. The two men seemed to sense the timing and Muller got up and moved towards the handful of people dancing in front of the stage. John-Cody watched him and the man looked right back, a big smile on his face, pacing slowly and taking care not to step on anyone's foot. His partner sipped Coke at the bar and fastened a button on his overcoat.

John-Cody finished the set. Louise replaced the mike and the clapping echoed across the barroom. One drunken guy at the back whistled badly and Louise stepped off the stage to where Billy was waiting for her and eyeing the FBI agent as if she was the object of his attention. John-Cody set his guitar on the stand and ran his fingers over the frets. He hoped Hogan would look after it for him like he did the last time.

He straightened up and looked Muller in the eye. The agent was tall and muscular under his clothes and he looked at John-Cody out of those chipped ice eyes.

'You're John-Cody Gibbs.'

'And you're the FBI.'

Muller showed him white teeth, fingers jangling against metal in the pocket of his coat. 'You violated the terms of your parole.'

'All I did was cross the state line. I had no choice. I couldn't get a job in Washington.'

The man made a face: he didn't care about the reasons. Why should he? He was only doing his job. He retrieved the noisy hand from his pocket and showed John-Cody cold metal handcuffs. 'Turn around.'

16

People were watching now, people who knew him, people who appreciated his guitar playing. John-Cody wondered how long it would be before they realized there would be no second set tonight. He looked the agent in the eyes, sizing him up, but he knew there was little point. Muller was big and well trained and even in jail John-Cody had never had a fight. Exhaling heavily, he turned around and offered his exposed wrists. There was a sudden silence in the bar, and he heard the cuffs snap to and felt them pinch his flesh where it was thin across his veins. The agent wheeled him round again, glanced at his buddy and nodded. He didn't say anything to the crowd, but took out his shield and set it in his breast pocket so everyone could see what he was and figure out what they might or might not want to do about it.

John-Cody cast a roving glance over the faces of the crowd, wondering if anyone would say anything, stick up for him, intervene in some way. But they didn't. These were very calm, very assured government agents and even the most ardent redneck would think twice before getting involved. He was marched through the people he knew, all of them falling back until he was at the door and the hand of the second FBI agent was resting on his shoulder.

'That's it,' he said. 'Nice and easy.'

John-Cody paused as Muller opened the door and the wind bit into him. 'I'm going to need my coat.'

The agents hesitated, looked at each other and then Muller asked him where the coat was. John-Cody told him it was behind the bar and he moved to the counter and asked Lisa for it. She looked slightly stunned as she passed it over. Muller thanked her and as he moved back to the door Lisa's eyes met

John-Cody's. She looked puzzled: he shrugged, then he was out on the sidewalk with the wind cutting his flesh.

Their car was right out front and he was bundled into the rear seat. He sat on the handcuffs and winced, the metal twisting against his flesh. He thought about asking them to take the cuffs off or at least secure him in front, but he knew from experience they wouldn't.

Muller climbed into the passenger seat while his partner got behind the wheel, started the engine and let the wipers clear the snow that had gathered on the windshield. He let the engine idle for a while. 'Maybe we ought to just put this guy in jail tonight. Go north in the morning.'

John-Cody listened for Muller's reply, sitting there in the back while they talked about him as if he wasn't there.

'I guess we could.' Muller peeled his sleeve back to inspect the dial of his watch. 'It's only nine thirty,' he said. 'I think we should get some miles under the wheels. Once we're on the highway the ploughs will have most of this stuff cleared.'

'Where'd you guys come down from?' John-Cody spoke for the first time. Muller leaned his arm over the back of the seat.

'You say something?'

'I wondered where you came down from. I figure the road between here and Lewiston is only fit for a four-by-four this time of night. You didn't come down from Lewiston, did you?'

Muller cocked an eyebrow at him. 'You want to spend the night in jail?'

'I'm going to anyway. One jail's much like another.'

18

'You trying to be a smart ass?'

'No. I just—'

'Button it.' Muller turned back to his partner. 'Let's go.'

The driver levered the column shift into drive and they pulled away from the kerb.

John-Cody shifted around in the back: McCall to Lewiston, that would be six hours at least in this weather. Then they would have to turn west and head for the coast. That's if they were taking him straight back to McNeil Island. He was supposed to see his parole officer once a fortnight in Seattle so they might be taking him there instead. Either way he'd end up in prison.

The two agents talked in low voices as they headed out of town, past the snow sculptures that lit up people's yards in the moonlight. The driver swore under his breath, the wheels skidding slightly as they started down the hill. Behind them John-Cody sat on his hands and watched the backs of their heads, Muller's face in profile when he turned sideways to talk to his partner and the scraped, reddened flesh of the driver's neck under his marine-style crew-cut. He tried to adjust his position to make the journey more comfortable but he knew that no amount of shuffling about would help. By the time the cuffs were taken off, his wrists would be chafed raw and his hands numb through lack of blood. Prison again after nine months of being out. He thought about the first eighteen months of the three-year sentence the judge had handed down. In the state penitentiary there had been no lightweight farm duties for him; it had been jail-time and hard and he had no inclination to go back.

Outside the vehicle the country flashed by as the driver grew more confident. The fields unrolled in white to the lunar grey of the mountains. The road was better than he had thought, but the temperature was well below freezing and there would be patches of black ice in the more exposed areas. He thought about the valleys and the high mountain passes between here and Grangeville: assuming they made it that far, it was Winchester and Lewiston then the rain-soaked coast road all the way to Seattle.

The two agents talked quietly as they drove on and he could barely make out their words. Their voices became just a murmur and he slouched in the seat, trying to keep the weight off his hands. The Plymouth was new and the smell of polished vinyl was thick in his nostrils. His mind drifted back to the bar and the faces of the customers: the cowboys, Louise and her oversexed boyfriend. Vaguely he wondered why a girl like Louise went out with such a redneck in the first place. She had soul, she appreci-ated good music and understood what it took to combine rhythm and lyric in a way that picked at the senses. He doubted Billy had read a word since high school that wasn't written on his pay cheque or in a sports bulletin.

He thought about leaving Hogan in the lurch again. The old man had been there the first time the FBI caught up with him, the two of them together on the sidewalk outside the bank after paying in the cash from the weekend. Hogan had just stood and gawped as two agents cuffed him then bundled him into the back of a car. He had been tried in Lewiston and sentenced to three years at McNeil Island. He had asked them to parole him back to Idaho, where

Hogan would stand surety for him, but they wouldn't. Perhaps that was just another indication of their vindictiveness. Hogan had never asked one question of him that first time he showed up and he didn't ask any when he saw him again eighteen months later. He just gave him back his guitar and his job and pleaded with him to stay.

Recollections of prison revisited him, images, memories, smells and sounds that he had put to one side the day he walked out the gate. Now they fairly flooded his mind and a sallow feeling like nausea settled in the pit of his stomach. McGuire's thin and crooked features, Dallallio, and Mamba, the big black brother from Mississippi who had killed three state troopers in California. They would still be there, along with all the others, those who delighted in intimidating him, trying to get him alone so they could rape or maim or murder him as and when they chose.

Somehow he had survived eighteen months without being defiled and without getting into a fight. The bulls had allowed him access to an acoustic guitar and that was probably what saved him. He had been playing guitar since before he could walk and had the kind of memory retention that allowed him to reprise any song he was asked for.

Saturday afternoon in the yard became something of an impromptu jamming session. Mamba liked the music, as did Dallallio and McGuire. They were the three meanest men in his wing and they made it clear that as long as John-Cody played guitar he was under their protection. Everyone in the place was scared of Mamba, and when the word went out John-Cody's life improved dramatically.

21

They would still be there, but the chances of his being put back in their wing would be slim. The bulls knew the deal with Mamba and the others and something told John-Cody that spite would play its part in where he ended up. The thought appalled him and the sickness grew in his stomach.

Two hours into the drive they came to Cascade and pulled over in the parking lot of a diner. Muller yawned and stretched, then he looked over his shoulder and told John-Cody to sit still as he was not going anywhere. The driver got out, stamped his feet in the snow and made his way up the rickety wooden steps to the diner. He came back with some coffee in styrofoam cups and passed them through the passenger window. Neither agent looked in the back, neither of them said anything and John-Cody had to sit there and smell the freshly roasted coffee.

'I'm going to the john,' said the driver.

Muller sipped noisily, gagged and blew on the liquid. John-Cody's hands were completely numb now and they throbbed at the wrist where the feeling stopped at the metal. The agent took out a cigarette and snapped open his Zippo. The smoke drifted in John-Cody's nostrils and he turned his head away, thinking of the crumpled pack of Lucky Strikes in his pocket.

The driver came back, stamped the snow off his shoes and climbed into the car. He shivered and worked his shoulders, then took the top off his cup while Muller went to the toilet. The driver looked at John-Cody. 'You want a sip?'

'Thank you.' John-Cody worked his way forward while the agent held the cup for him.

'Don't you be spilling it now, I don't want my fingers burned.'

John-Cody sipped at the coffee and it scalded the back of his throat. The agent set the cup down again and squinted at him.

'You should've just done the time.'

'I did.'

'You know what I mean.'

John-Cody pursed his lips and shrugged.

'You want me to get you some coffee?'

'I got money.' John-Cody smiled. 'I got cigarettes too.' He looked over his shoulder at the loop of the door handle. 'What say you unhook me in back? Much more of this and my hands are going to drop off.' He gestured with his chin to the handle. 'You can hook me up there with one hand. I still won't be going any place. It's hours till we get to Seattle.'

'How d'you know that's where we're going?'

'That's where the parole officer's at.'

The man nodded. 'I tell you what. You sit tight till my partner gets back and we'll see.'

When consulted, Muller looked through the windshield then sighed and swivelled in his seat to check the quality of the door handle. 'All right.'

He opened the back door and steered John-Cody out into the cold. He stood in the snow, which climbed above his ankles while the agent unlocked the handcuffs.

'Now don't try anything stupid. Because I tell you, partner, it's that damn cold I'd just as soon shoot you and be done with it.'

John-Cody stood shivering while Muller brought the cuffs round in front of him, then pressed him back into the seat and secured the loose cuff through the door handle. John-Cody was grateful when the door was closed again and the breath eased in his chest. The driver had stood on the steps to the diner and watched to make sure all was well before he went inside and bought more coffee. Muller was back in his seat, the engine still idling and clouds of exhaust fumes rising from the tailpipe. The driver came out with the coffee and John-Cody was able to sit in relative comfort and sip it as they headed north through the night.

They were climbing steadily now, easing up onto the high plains where the weather could turn in a moment at this time of year. Snow started falling around late November and it did not stop till May. The snowploughs worked every day to keep the main highway clear but invariably there was a layer across the blacktop. It would bank up at the sides, sometimes eight or ten feet, and when the wind blew a horizontal storm would ensue, causing a total whiteout. If you did not know what you were doing you were dead.

Something told John-Cody that these two agents did not know what they were doing. They took it in turns to drive, pulling over hurriedly to the side of the road to swap positions, each driving as quickly as the other and laughing when the back end slewed out of line now and again. Their easy manner bothered him. John-Cody didn't know, but he figured they would be from the Seattle field office, which put them in rainy country. It was a land of low-lying fog and that dank drizzle that came off the Pacific in winter, nothing like the high plains of Idaho. He wanted to tell them to be careful, especially when they cut through the mountains south of Grangeville, but he knew they wouldn't listen to him. Joe Fulton drove a delivery truck from

24

Boise to Lewiston and travelled this road most days of his life. Only this evening when he was propping up the bar in Hogan's he had been telling John-Cody that the road was treacherous where the county workmen had been blasting. It seemed like they had been trying to make that road wider for years.

They climbed higher still, the road snakelike and switchbacked now, but the two agents seemed more relaxed than ever. Muller lit another cigarette and shook the pack at John-Cody.

'We're driving through the night then,' John-Cody said.

Muller squinted at him. 'What do you think, buddy? You don't stretch to a motel room.'

John-Cody drew on the cigarette and exhaled smoke. 'You might want to take it easy over the next bit. This road can be a bitch in the dark.'

'Hey, fella.' The driver looked in the rear-view mirror. 'You just sit there, OK? We drove this road yesterday.'

'It wasn't snowing yesterday.' John-Cody sat back, smoked his cigarette and looked out at the whitened high country, falling away now as the hillside dropped to their right.

He felt the back go almost before they did: then the driver was frantically spinning the wheel and John-Cody saw the world in a spiral of white. Brakes squealed. Somebody swore. He could smell the fear in the voice, then the car was at the edge of the road and flipped over and John-Cody heard metal shear and glass splinter and he was upside down, his hand almost wrenched from his arm where it was fixed to the door.

All was black and pain thudded at his wrist. He

could smell something odd like the invasion of a dream and he didn't know what it was. Then he must have opened his eyes because he could see a beam of light casting the snow yellow across the hillside. Hillside and snow. He remembered then: the car, the two FBI agents and prison waiting in Seattle. He felt the sudden cold in his bones and saw that the windshield was gone and the two men were motionless in their seats. The car seemed to be upright but tilting badly to the left and he worked at the window with his free hand, smearing the condensation from the glass till he could see the pit of the valley floor three hundred feet below.

Still he sat there, not quite sure what to do. Then he realized that the door he was hunched against was buckled and the handle loose where the handcuff was attached to it.

'Hello.' The word popped out of his mouth. 'Are you two still there?'

Nothing. He leaned forward, his wrist caught him and instinctively he tugged: the handle gave and he could move properly now. The interior light was out, but the headlights reflected back off the white of the snow and he saw blood on Muller's face. Feeling at his neck, he thought for a moment he was dead then he got a pulse and looked to his colleague. Again a pulse: both were unconscious but alive. All at once he realized he was free, but then the smell took definition in his head. Gasoline. The tank had ruptured and was leaking gas into the car. Very carefully he eased himself across the back seat and opened the far door. Now he stood in the snow, thirty feet below the road, where the car had been caught and wedged by a tree. The trunk was fractured but still there and that was all that kept the car from falling into the valley. The cold snapped at him like an animal and he was shivering uncontrollably. Instinct took over and he began to plough his way up the bank till he stood on the road. For a moment he could not get his bearings, but the night was clear and crisp and the moonlight edged the snow in a silvery grey wash. He figured which way was north then recognized where he was on the road, maybe ten miles south of Grangeville. Still he stood, trying to work out what to do, looking back down the slope to where the two men sat unconscious, strapped into their seats. They would die if he did not get someone to help them. And still he stood there: this was his moment, his time to get away. With every mile his misery had been heightened, cold sweat working its way into his bones as he considered confinement all over again. The day he walked out of that penitentiary he had vowed he would die rather than be locked up like that again. Now he stood here, freezing by the roadside, with freedom a possibility. He felt as alive as he had ever felt. Yet those two men would die down there if he just left them. So what? What were they to him? Human beings, his father's voice muttered in his head. Doesn't much matter what a man does for a living, son: everybody's got to feed his family. A man's still a human being no matter what. And then he heard the grinding of gears way down in the valley and looking beyond the peak he saw the glow of headlights.

He stood in the middle of the road as the truck worked its way round the bend and began the climb to the ninety-degree right-hander where the FBI agents had shot off the road. John-Cody had his coat

27

zipped to the neck and the handcuffs pressed up his arm so he could hide them under the sleeve. He waved both arms above his head and the driver eased down a gear and then another and the lights washed over him, hurting his eyes. The driver stopped without hitting the brakes. John-Cody heard the hiss of the emergency brake and stepped up to the door as it opened. The driver looked down at him: a big burly man wearing a heavy woollen cap, with a thick black beard clutching his jaw.

'What's your problem, partner?'

John-Cody told him about the wreck and the driver jumped down, grabbing a flashlight as he did so. He panned it over the car still caught by the tree on the lip of the ravine.

'You were in that wreck?'

John-Cody nodded. 'There are two other guys still down there. They're unconscious. I was in the back. I guess I was lucky.'

'I guess you were at that.' The driver scratched his head. 'Come on. It's ten miles to Grangeville, we can holler up the sheriff when we get there.'

John-Cody nodded and climbed up next to him. The driver ground in the gears and tugged the handle on the emergency brake and they rolled gently round the ninety-degree bend and down the far side of the hill. From there it was one more hill and then the Camas prairie took over where the whiteout would hit when the wind began to blow. Tonight was still, however, just very cold and the freshly fallen snow had hardened to ice underfoot. The driver wore a hunting jacket and thick waterproof boots and the cab of his truck smelled of cheap cigar smoke. John-Cody glanced at the girlie pictures he had pasted on the ceiling.

'Where you from?' the driver asked him.

'McCall.'

He held out his hand. 'Merv Clayton.'

'John-Cody Gibbs.'

'Who are the other guys, those two in the wreck?'

'Just two fellas. They gave me a ride from Cascade. Guess they didn't know the road like I thought they did.' John-Cody paused. 'I could smell gasoline when I came to down there.'

The man nodded. 'We'll be in Grangeville in just a little bit. As long as no sparks are flying that wreck'll stay right where it's at. You can tell it all to the sheriff, son. He'll take it from there.'

He eased the truck to a stop outside the sheriff's office on the main street in Grangeville, telling John-Cody he needed to be in Lewiston in the morning and had to press on. John-Cody thanked him and stood for a moment on the sidewalk, looking up at the lighted neon sign of the sheriff's office, acutely aware of the irony. He shook his head, blew out his cheeks then thought of the two FBI agents freezing to death in the twisted wreckage of the car. He walked into the office and told the deputy behind the counter exactly what he had told the truck driver and exactly where the wreck was. 'You can't miss it,' he said. 'It's right on the bend where the county's been blasting the road.'

'You just sit there, son.' The deputy pointed to the bench beside the water cooler. 'I'll need you to come along with me. Just let me call up Search and Rescue.' He stepped back into the inner office and John-Cody hovered for a moment, knowing it was now or never. He went out into the night and disappeared down the alley alongside the building. Carefully and quietly he worked his way up to the main road junction, where the big Amoco gas station was situated. He stood in the lee of the motel complex as the deputy's truck took the corner with its strobe lights flashing and headed south on the road to McCall. He waited while the Search and Rescue vehicles followed, then he crossed to the gas station with the diner attached and inspected the truck he had hitched the ride in. The driver was obviously stocking up on the calories before he headed for Lewiston. John-Cody found him at the counter drinking coffee: he sat down alongside him and the waitress poured him a cup. He held it in his uncuffed hand, the other in his pocket, letting the steam play across his face. The driver looked round at him.

'Find the sheriff, did you?'

'Yessir.'

'Didn't want you along then.'

'I told the deputy where the wreck was at, but I got to get to Lewiston same as you.'

The driver dabbed his mouth with the back of his hand. 'Well, it's a long night and cold enough to kill you,' he said. 'Figure I could do with the company just to keep me awake. Come on, I'll give you a ride.'

Two days later John-Cody was in the port of Bellingham, sitting on a bench which overlooked the harbour and eating a sandwich out of waxed paper. There was no snow here but a damp winter wind blew in off the Pacific and found the tiniest gaps in his clothing. Trawlers lined the harbour walls, inshore and offshore vessels all tied together in a chain of rusting iron. They bobbed on the harbour swell and the bells tinkled on their masts and the copper-coloured cables groaned hoarse as the dredges strained in the wind. A lone gull cried above his head, swooped low over the water then headed out to sea. John-Cody finished his sandwich, folded the waxed paper and put it in his pocket. A worn metal sign flapped in the breeze outside a ramshackle fishermen's bar across the deserted road.

John-Cody could smell rain in the air and the urgency of the wind told him a storm was building out on the horizon somewhere. He had no idea what had happened to the two FBI agents, but he hoped the deputy made it to them in time. Luck had been with him and now he stood here at the western edge of the country that had hounded him without mercy. Laughter broke from the doorway of the bar and he was reminded of Hogan's. He thought of his guitar and hoped Hogan would look after it properly.

He was not much of a drinker, technically too young anyway but nobody ever carded him, especially after his jail time when he must have come out with that particular weary look in his eyes. He turned up his collar and checked his wallet for the handful of dollars he had left. He had not even had time to collect his tips from the glass jar by the cash register. He looked at the few crumpled bills and figured that the bar was warmer than here and a shot of whiskey in his veins might keep out some of the cold when he bedded down in the open air again tonight.

The bar was noisy but not crowded. There was plenty of stool space and he shuffled onto one and laid a dollar on the counter. A surly-looking bar-tender with a Mexican slant to his eyes laid a towel over one shoulder and looked at him.

'What do you need?'

'Old Crow straight with water back.'

The bartender slapped a shot glass on the counter. John-Cody shook a Lucky Strike from his battered pack and lit it, then looked at his surroundings where various ships' wheels adorned the walls along with sections of fishing net and a mural of old-time whalers in open long boats. John-Cody sipped the whiskey and listened to the howl of conversation at the table under the window. Five men sat there and one of them, a fat guy in his fifties with little bits of hair poking out from under his cap, was holding court. He had a tall glass of beer at his elbow and a glass of dark rum next to it. He was gesticulating with black-nailed hands and his eyes darted with flame in their piggy sockets.

'Where the hell is Gonzales?'

Nobody answered him.

'Did he quit or what?'

'I think he had a fight with his girlfriend,' somebody said.

'That damn Mexican. When's he going to get his life sorted out? We sail in two hours. The skipper is going to roast my ass over this one.'

John-Cody sat and listened and as he did so an idea formed in his mind. 'What's the deal back there?' he said to the barman.

'Crew of the *Hawaiian Oracle*,' the man muttered. 'They're a man down.'

'Where they headed?'

'I don't know. Hawaii, I guess.' The barman shuffled away and John-Cody downed his drink and picked up his cigarettes. He moved over to the window table and stood in front of the mate.

'What're you looking at?'

'Bartender told me you're a man down.'

The mate screwed up his eyes and looked John-Cody up and down. 'Are you telling me you want a job?'

John-Cody held his gaze, trembling inside but not letting it show. 'I'm telling you I want *his* job.'

'You been to sea before?'

'I can knock the dredge pins out without killing anybody.'

A couple of the crew laughed and the mate nodded to the empty chair. 'Sit.'

John-Cody did as he was told, still looking the man in the eye. He knew nothing about sea fishing: he only knew about dredge pins because he had watched them being scraped of rust at the dry docks in New Orleans.

'Let me see your hands.'

John-Cody held them out and the mate arched his eyebrows: John-Cody's hands were rough and yellow from hard labour in prison. The mate looked him in the eye once again. 'You look awful young,' he said.

John-Cody signalled to the bartender for another shot of whiskey. 'I am awful young. What's that got to do with anything?'

Again the crew laughed and John-Cody stared at the mate. 'You sail in two hours and I make you a full crew.'

The mate thinned his gaze, head slightly to one side. 'I can't promise you a full share.'

John-Cody looked back at him. 'We can talk about that,' he said.

ONE

TWENTY-FIVE YEARS LATER

The flight attendant poured more wine and Libby stared at the video screen, reflecting on all that had happened: how quickly things had moved on once she received the offer from the Marine Studies Centre. Bree was asleep alongside her, the headphones from her Walkman dangling around her neck.

The job Libby had left at the sea life centre in France had been only part time and they had been aware when they employed her just how little they were paying and how much her talents were under-utilized. The dolphin watch team were also sorry to see her go, but she could still liaise with them from her new position in New Zealand.

Libby glanced at Bree. They had spent almost a year in France and Bree had been just about settled: no wonder her silence was so complete when she was told about the new job. Libby regretted having to move her again so soon. The location in Vimereux, near Calais and two minutes from the sea, had been ideal for Bree and one of the few benefits she had seen in moving to France. Come the weekend she and her friends would be at the beach, using their house as a changing room and eatery. Her school was only fifteen minutes' walk up the hill: it was perfect in so many ways. But what Bree didn't know was that the rent was exorbitant, and what Libby earned from the sea life centre and the dolphin watch programme combined still wasn't enough to keep them. She had taken the house because it *was* so perfect for Bree and she had slipped into the new life beautifully, notwithstanding the language barrier. But things had got difficult, the rent hadn't been paid for three months and then letters from the landlord started falling through the box. Libby shuddered at the thought: Bree would never know just how close they had come to being homeless. It was why she had had to take the New Zealand job when it was offered.

Gently she touched Bree's hair. Bree twitched and moved her head and Libby sat back again, thinking about the dolphin watch group and their concerns over a pod of bottlenose that inhabited a stretch of water between Poole Harbour and Guernsey. A team of volunteers kept a visual check on their movements from the coast with telescopes, particularly after the introduction of a high-speed ferry service. Professor Tom Wilson headed up the programme, and he had contacted Libby when the dolphins suddenly disappeared. Wilson was an expert on cetaceans, the order of mammals that included whales, dolphins and porpoises. The dolphins had vanished after the ferry started running and Wilson was concerned that the noise from the boat had disturbed the acoustics of their territory. Libby specialized in dolphin and whale communication and he wanted her opinion.

She was not sure about the acoustic damage. She had considered the possibility that the pod were all

35

males and had formed a mating alliance with others in the Channel. If that was so, it might explain their sudden disappearance. But when they did not show up again she began to wonder.

An old fisherman she knew from Boulogne told her he used to see them regularly, but now all he came across was a lone dolphin. Single dolphins always intrigued Libby. They were by nature social animals and generally part of a pod. Single dolphins were probably pod members who went off by themselves now and again or visited other pods, possibly to mate and keep the gene pools healthy. Sometimes, however, they were just loners, those who had left the normal social structure to find their own way. Why they might do that was open to conjecture: life for the lone dolphin was far more difficult. Hunting for food became a solitary occupation, which meant that the hunter no longer benefited from multiple sonic pulses to locate their prey by echo.

Libby closed her eyes, aware of the flight attendant removing her dinner tray, and recalled again the moment she told the directors at the sea life centre that she was leaving for New Zealand. Diplomacy had never been her strong point and Pierre had been visibly shocked. Poor Pierre, she felt for him. He was a marine biologist, and it was largely down to him that Libby had got the job in the first place; the centre was exploring the possibility of building a dolphin enclosure and they had asked her to evaluate it for them.

She had just returned from a year in Punta Norte, Argentina, where she had been studying orca, the killer whale. She needed something permanent but had already been contacted by Tom Wilson with regard to the dolphins in the Channel. She and Wilson had been at Cambridge together but had not seen each other since. Libby had worked for Greenpeace for three years before dragging Bree to Harvard while she studied for her Ph.D. She had written one of the best theses Wilson had ever read on cetacean communication.

The dolphin watch programme could not pay her what she was worth, but with what she earned between that and the sea life centre she thought she would have just enough to make ends meet. As it turned out she didn't, but by then they had moved to Vimereux, she had enrolled Bree in yet another school and it was too late.

Poor Bree, six schools already and she was only twelve: six schools in six countries and three different languages. The trouble was the world of cetacean research was a precarious one and it meant going wherever the work was, which could be in some very far-flung places. Somehow Libby had managed to keep body and soul together without recourse to her parents.

Pierre had been very distressed when she told him she was leaving. They had worked closely together and initially it was merely a working relationship. He was thirty-eight, in the throes of divorce but had his two daughters living with him, the elder of whom was the same age as Bree. It did Bree good to have some company her own age. The girls got on well. There was no catty behaviour or jealousy and Libby found that she was spending a lot of weekend time with Pierre and his children. Bree liked him and she seemed more composed when he was around. She had never had a male role model in her life, at least not a permanent one, and it showed when Pierre was with them. He was a big, affectionate Frenchman who was always hugging and kissing his daughters. He hugged Bree when they were together, and at first Libby had been unsure, but Bree seemed happy enough to be treated as one of the family.

Libby had been single for over two years. Her work station at Punta Norte was remote to say the least and she had been tempted to take up her father's offer of putting Bree into an English boarding school once and for all. But ever since Bree had been born her parents' disapproval had plagued them.

Bree was the product of a one-night stand at a Los Angeles party twelve years previously. It had been one of those gatherings when people brought other people whom nobody really knew, a classic Californian beach party with lots of tequila and beer and hashish, skinny dipping in the breakers and sex round the camp fire. Libby had got drunk on tequila and ended up sleeping with a man whose name she didn't even know. She only vaguely recalled the incident in the morning, and was off to Mexico anyway. Two scientists had chartered a boat to study the grey whales that migrated from the Arctic every year to breed. Greys had the longest range of any ocean-going travellers in the world and Libby was interested in observing their navigational skills at close hand. She was in the research year of her first degree and in demand: she did not even know she was pregnant till she finally went to a doctor when she'd missed her third period. She had missed periods before and she had always meant to go on the pill to keep regular, but had never got round to it.

None of this had been kept from her parents.

Brutal honesty had been her policy ever since she realized her father's job was to train dolphins to be used in warfare; maybe it was a case of the more she could hurt him the better. When Bree was born, the very last thing Libby wanted was some kind of grandparental indoctrination. Bree was her daughter, unplanned and unlooked for but her flesh and blood, and Libby loved her with a vengeance.

The hardest place had been Punta Norte, where she had had to educate Bree herself as the nearest school was in a tiny village thirty miles away. By the time they got to France they'd only had each other for company for ages. Bree was delighted to get some friends of her own age regardless of the fact they were French, and Libby, lonely for some male influence, sort of hooked up with Pierre.

Pierre had fancied her from the beginning. She could tell from the way he looked at her, the way he smiled, made bad jokes, stood close to her while they were working, the way he always seemed to turn up where she was. She didn't mind. He was not unattractive, he was fun and outgoing and was always suggesting things to do. They started leaving the three girls at his house with his housekeeper/cleaner to keep an eye on them while they went out. Libby found herself watching movies in French, eating seafood in lots of different restaurants and enjoying the best social life she had experienced in years.

They became lovers one Saturday night when she had already arranged to stay over with Bree. Up until then Libby had always slept in the spare room, while the three girls insisted on all sharing a room right at the top of the house. That night, however, Libby and Pierre had a lot to drink and ended up in bed together. Libby had been unsure about it in the morning, as shades of the past came back to haunt her. Pierre was great but she was not in love with him and she knew, even then, that if she was not very careful he could get really hurt. She had contemplated cooling it off but it was difficult after they had slept together. Then one night, completely out of the blue, Pierre asked her to marry him.

They had been eating dinner, overlooking the coast at Cap Gris Nez. Pierre had picked the best table, outside on the veranda with the sun in the west so it was not in their eyes and the hillside green and chalky beneath them. Below was the rock-strewn beach where breakers in green and blue burbled between the stones: no cloud, the end to another perfectly beautiful day. Pierre sat opposite her and dipped crusty bread in juice from the mussels.

'What're you thinking?' he asked her.

'Oh, just that it's been another gorgeous day. How many is that now, ten in a row? It's lovely but not normal, Pierre.'

Pierre sat back, his face reddened by the sun and not yet turning to brown. He wore a short-sleeved shirt and his arms were tanned and covered with blond hairs. Libby watched him watching her and was suddenly self-conscious. He had this habit of roving her face like a traveller, seeking new paths and avenues. It wasn't intrusive so much as slightly unnerving, as if he thought he saw things that she had no idea were there.

'Pierre, please don't stare at me like that.'

'Like what?' He looked suddenly pained.

'You know what I mean. The way you take over my face. I've told you about it before.'

He laughed and sat back, arms across his chest. He was just beginning to spread, to get that belly which all men vowed they wouldn't but which most eventually did. Libby could see a little square of flesh exposed by a stretched button at his navel.

'I'm just admiring, Libby. You're very beautiful.' He sat forward again, a loose smile on his lips. 'With your dark eyes and dark hair and your perfect skin . . .' He reached over and stroked her forearm with his fingertips. 'Not a mark, not a blemish, beautiful.'

Libby pulled her arm away and placed her hands in her lap. 'Stop it, Pierre. You're embarrassing me.'

Again he sat back. 'English girls – they can never take a compliment.'

'If it bothers you, go out with a French girl.'

There was a tension in the air and she did not really know why: his words were innocent enough, words spoken when a man is involved with a woman. But she could sense his mood and given what she was already thinking her defences were suddenly up. She looked beyond him to the sea, flecked in bony waves of white now, mottled grey in places. Gulls cried and swooped for scraps dropped by walkers on the beach. She heard the crash of the surf and was reminded of the shingle beaches of Punta Norte where killer whales charged out of the water after the seals. The first time Bree witnessed the act she had screamed.

'Libby.' Pierre had her hand in his now and was looking earnestly across the table. 'I'm sorry. I didn't mean . . .'

'It's all right.' Libby squeezed his hand. '*I'm* sorry, I'm too snappy. Just ignore me.'

He nodded to the waitress and indicated the wine bottle. She brought another and Pierre poured fresh glasses. 'Do you like working at the centre?' he asked her. 'I mean, your skills are hardly used but there is scope, don't you think?'

'That depends on whether you get any dolphins.' Libby looked him in the eye then. 'And it depends on why you want them. I've never been keen on trained dolphins, Pierre. The thought of them jumping through hoops doesn't exactly inspire me.'

'Your father.' Pierre sat back again, toying with the stem of his glass. Libby had told him about her father's role with the British and US navies, strapping sticky explosives to dolphins' backs so they could place them on the hulls of 'enemy' vessels.

'Our dolphins won't jump through any hoops, Libby.'

She looked at her plate. 'I know they won't. I didn't mean they would. The centre's a great facility, Pierre, don't get me wrong. I'm just not sure it's the place for dolphins, that's all.'

'Well, we'll see. That's partly why I wanted you with us in the first place. To figure out whether or not there would be any scientific benefit.' He emptied his glass and poured himself another.

Libby arched an eyebrow. 'Shouldn't you go easy on that? You're driving, remember.'

'Don't worry.'

'I'll worry if you crash the car. I'll worry if my daughter's an orphan. She only has a mother. I'd like to make sure she still has me at least.'

'Libby.' Pierre was frowning.

Libby knew she was doing it again, being argumentative without really knowing why. Over the past couple of weeks Pierre had started to get a little more serious. She had sensed it; there had been small changes in his behaviour and the odd irregular sigh, often when they were in bed together. He seemed to look more longingly at her when she was in the shower or soaking in his bathtub. It unnerved her: she did not know what was coming but she sensed something that disturbed her. Her work at the centre was not very satisfying, her talents were wasted and she knew it was unlikely to be a permanent position. She had no money and she missed whales. The last thing she needed was any more complications.

Working with dolphins was fine, but she would rather be studying the big baleen whales where communication research was still in its infancy. She had studied northern rights in Canada and southern rights off Tierra del Fuego. She had spent a year analysing hydra-phone data gathered from migrating blues in the St Lawrence Seaway, after the US government allowed her access to their underwater listening network set up to monitor Soviet submarine movements.

That had been the one and only time she had called on her father for influence, got him to phone up some of his old NATO cronies in America. To be fair, he had come through. She had been allowed a computer link with the hydra-phones and had listened to the largest creatures who ever lived talking to one another at distances of sixty miles. It never ceased to amaze her: what did they say? Was it conversation or was it simply to help them navigate the ocean?

She considered the elusive pod of dolphins Wilson was concerned about. Nothing had been picked up on the hydra-phones for nine months now. What had happened to them? Had the noise from the ferry interfered with their communication frequencies, driven them from their territory?

'Libby.' Pierre's voice snapped her attention back to the table. 'Where were you? Your mind's all over the place.'

'I'm sorry. You're right, my mind *is* all over the place. But I've always got so many things to think about.'

'Like Bree, you mean,' he said. 'You feel guilty about her, don't you?'

Libby stared at him, not replying right away. She did feel some guilt about Bree: the fact that she had never been able to tell her what her father's name was bothered her, but she wasn't guilt-ridden like a lot of people thought she should be. She had been a teenage single mother, but had never contemplated an abortion and worked ceaselessly to feed, clothe and educate her daughter.

By the time she knew she was pregnant she was in Mexico, which is where Bree had been born, and the two of them were back on the research vessel within a couple of weeks of the birth. Libby had had no choice, Bree had to be clothed and fed, and the project was her only way of making any money. There had been no time to retrace her steps, find out who was at the party, what the blond-haired guy's name had been.

Pierre looked across the table, seeming to guess her thoughts. 'You can change things, you know.'

She wrinkled her nose. 'What, look up her dad after twelve years, delve back into the guest list of a beach party there was never a guest list to? I'm not

44

proud of it, Pierre, but all I remember is he had blond hair.'

'Like Bree.'

'Yes, like Bree.' Bree was twelve and gawky, a stick insect still, having grown up but not out, got her first smattering of spots and the tiniest buds of breasts which just about showed through her bikini. She had long blond hair, which she plaited in the same style as her mother, but that was the only resemblance. She was fairer-skinned and had blue eyes and a little turned-up nose. She was just as bright as her mother had been and certainly as pig-headed.

'I didn't mean change it like that.' Pierre sipped wine.

Libby felt in her bag for a pack of Camels. She found them semi-crushed and lit one from the candle burning between them on the table.

'What did you mean then?'

Pierre let the air escape from his cheeks, hollowing his mouth into a little tunnel as he did sometimes when he was considering what to say. Libby felt her heart suddenly pound so that it echoed in her chest like an alarm bell ringing.

'Libby.' He took her hands in his and looked her in the eyes again, with that earnest expression she had witnessed more and more of late. 'I want you to marry me.'

Libby stared at him, mouth dry all at once. She didn't blink and his words seemed to resonate in her head. *I want you to marry me.* Not *will you marry me?* I want you to. There was a difference.

For a long time they sat in silence. Pierre's face was redder than usual, as if he was suddenly self-conscious. She looked beyond him then, watching the sea. The cliffs at Dover were clear and topped with green against the horizon. She heard the surf lapping at stone then drawing back with a sound like a suction cup. She saw Pierre's face, featureless at the blurred edge of her vision.

'Libby.'

She looked back at him, then at her cigarette burning into nothing in the ashtray. The smoke suddenly irritated her. Bree was always telling her to quit. Bree, that's what Pierre meant. Bree needed a father, or at least Pierre thought she did. Libby wasn't sure whether she did or not: the two of them did not actually talk about it very much. Ever since Libby's mother told Bree how she had been conceived and what had happened afterwards the subject had been somewhat taboo between them. Libby had never quite forgiven her mother for that. It was something between herself and Bree: a subject to be broached when she, Libby, felt the time was right, not to be muscled in on by an overzealous and disappointed grandmother.

'It would work, Libby. The three of us and my two girls.'

'Pierre,' Libby said gently, 'you're not even divorced yet.'

'I will be. It's only a matter of months. The papers are all in.'

'And you think it's a good thing to be talking about a second marriage when you're not even out of the first one?'

'Libby, that's over. It's history. I love *you* now. We could be so good together.'

Libby held up her hand then: this was too much, too much and too soon. 'Please, Pierre. Just let me think.' She stood up. 'Let's walk, shall we.'

Pierre flung a bundle of notes on the table and emptied his glass. Libby was already walking along the cliff path away from the restaurant, the sun on her shoulders weak now but still warm on the skin. No wind came off the sea.

The drone of the engines broke in on her thoughts and Libby opened her eyes: she saw that Bree was awake, headphones plugged into her ears, gazing out of the window where the clouds formed a thick white carpet under the sky. Libby knew she had been right to turn Pierre down. She would have done it regardless of her mounting debts and the job offer in New Zealand: she had told Bree about his proposal before she finally said no. Bree had been nonplussed, but then that was Bree these days. It was so difficult to know what she was thinking. She internalized so much, kept her own counsel: a real heart-to-heart between mother and daughter was such a rarity it seemed normal for things to be this way. Maybe it was: they had always been close but never demonstratively so. Libby was honest and open about everything, far too open according to her parents who even now tried to convince her that an English boarding school education would be the best thing for Bree. Her father offered to pay. It was as if they wanted to rectify the mistakes they had made with Libby through their granddaughter. Libby thought about that then. She was the youngest of six children and the only one not married and settled in some conventional middle-class role. Perhaps her parents wanted things settled for themselves before they passed on?

Bree took her headphones off and looked at her mother. 'Can I get past please? I want to go to the toilet.'

Libby smiled and moved into the aisle. Bree avoided her eye, one hand on the back of the seat in front of her as she slid out. She stuck her headphones in her ears and joined the queue for the toilet. Libby sat down again with a sigh: she'll come round, she told herself. Give it a few months and she'll be just fine.

She knew Bree blamed her mother's ambition for the move: but that wasn't the reason and it wasn't Pierre either. Bree had no idea just how tight money had been while they were living in France. The job in New Zealand had been nothing short of a godsend.

Flicking through the *New Scientist*, Libby had come across an advertisement for a two-year posting. It was not working with whales but it intrigued her because there was an obvious connection with what she had been doing in the English Channel. The University of Otago, together with the Department of Conservation, had established a research programme in Fiordland, in the south-west of New Zealand's South Island. They believed that the most southerly pod of bottlenose dolphins in the world was resident in Doubtful Sound, but for a number of years fishermen and tour operators had sighted bottlenose in Dusky Sound, which was further south still. The two bodies wanted a scientist to identify whether there actually was a pod as far south as Dusky. They also wanted to begin assessing the level of environmental damage that might be inflicted on dolphins by the provision of marine mammal viewing permits for tour companies. A significant part of the research would be noise-related as the fiords would provide a unique environment for study. As far as Libby was concerned she was the person best qualified to do that research, so she applied for the job. Very quickly she heard that she had been selected for interview at a hotel in London.

The interview had coincided with a conference given by the World Wide Fund for Nature which she had wanted to attend anyway. The venue was a Docklands hotel, which she thought was a little grand, but WWF were trying to raise their profile and this conference was fundamental to the future of the Southern Ocean blue whale. Research scientists from around the globe were gathering, as well as environmental journalists and students. Libby recognized a number of people, some of whom she had worked with before and some she had come across on the Internet and at various other conferences. She had discovered long ago that the academic world demanded a certain amount of visibility if you wanted to be considered for worthwhile jobs: talent and reputation were not enough on their own.

She had dressed well. Normally jeans and a sweat-shirt sufficed, but that day her face was made up, accentuating the height of her cheekbones and the blackness of her eyes. She wore the only suit she owned, a navy blue two-piece with the skirt above the knee. Her legs were bare and waxed and her feet crammed into a pair of court shoes she had not worn in years. Her black hair was scraped back in a French plait and she knew she looked good. Bree had been adamant that she must look good for the conference. What Bree had not known, however, was that her efforts were for the interview and not the conference, and if those efforts were wasted they would both be on the street.

Her interviewer was Dr Stephen Watson, and he was there primarily to give a lecture on the numbers and distribution of blue whales in the Southern Ocean. Libby watched the composure and ease with which he delivered his address, using a computer-prompted slide show and bringing some new data to the attention of the assembly. Smallish, with sandy hair and a moustache, his blue eyes behind steel-framed glasses, he interspersed the serious passages of his address with the odd joke here and there. Libby had known of him for some time although they had never actually met, and he was one of the few so-called whale experts she respected.

He was due to see her after lunch and she wondered how many others in the gathering he would interview. She suspected that there would not be that many because the salary offered was not brilliant and most people wanted far more security than a two-year contract. She wondered why the department had not just plumped for a Ph.D. student and she asked Watson as much when he sat down at her table during the lunch break.

'The interview's this afternoon,' he said.

'Yes, but the conversation is now.' Libby looked him in the eyes and he smiled.

'We've not been formally introduced,' he said. 'Steve Watson.'

'Liberty Bass.' She shook his hand. 'So why not the student route? It's normal in these circumstances.'

Watson nodded. 'If it was just down to the Department of Conservation, it would be.' He picked up his fork. 'The identification – establishing whether or not there is a pod in Dusky Sound – is pretty straightforward, although a similar study lasted three years and not the two they're planning here.'

'Carsten Schneider in Doubtful Sound,' Libby said.

'You've done your homework.'

'Of course. It's allegedly the most southerly pod in the world. Their breeding habits must be fairly radical.'

'They are.' Watson hunched forward in the chair. 'As I said, the ID bit's not the problem. DoC wanted a Ph.D. or masters student, but I managed to persuade them that if they really wanted to look at the tourist implications then an acoustics expert was needed.'

'You obviously didn't tell them how much acoustics experts usually cost.'

He laughed. 'You still applied.'

'I did, yes.' Libby looked evenly at him then. 'But I doubt you'll get many people with my qualifications coming forward.'

'So do I.' He put down his fork. 'Marine mammal viewing is big business in New Zealand, Liberty. We depend on tourism of all kinds: it's a massive part of our economy. So far we've only conducted a few studies on the effects of tourist activity. You probably know about the sperm whales off Kaikoura.'

'I've read about them, yes. What sort of results have you had?'

'We don't really know yet.' Watson looked at her. 'But this dolphin watch you're involved in intrigued me.'

Libby fisted her hands beneath her chin. 'We go out once a month and monitor the changes in activity between Portsmouth and Bilbao. There are over thirteen different species of whale in those waters. Amazing when you consider whaling pretty much started in the Bay of Biscay.'

Watson sat back then and nodded to the waiter for water. 'What's happened with the dolphin pod and the Channel Island ferry?'

'It's still early days, but I think the impact could be serious. The pod has been gone for almost a year. It could be frequency interruption, we don't know yet. It could be that they're all male and looking for mates. We've never been able to sex them.' She lifted her shoulders. 'It's like everything we study, Steve. It's ongoing research.'

Watson nodded. 'There are big plans for Fiordland. It's still a wilderness area but more and more people want that wilderness experience. Milford Sound is swamped on a daily basis. More people than ever are going into Doubtful Sound. The next obvious one is Dusky. We need to know what the environmental impact is going to be before all the decisions are made on a purely economic basis.' He made a face. 'There's a lot of pressure from above. Like I said, the country depends on tourism but we need to manage it properly.'

Libby looked at him again then, resting her chin in her palm. 'Steve, there's nobody in the world better qualified to look at cetacean communication than me.'

'I know.'

'So do I get the job?'

Watson sat back and laughed. 'Everything they said about you is true.'

'They?'

'The global academic establishment.'

'None of it good, I trust.'

'That depends on how you look at it.' Watson leaned on his elbows. 'As far as I'm concerned, the job's been yours ever since I received your application. I just don't understand why you want it.'

Bree sat down on the toilet seat at the back of the plane and took paper and pen from her bag. Resting the pad on her lap she began to write.

Dear Dad,

It's been ages since I wrote, I know. Well, a couple of months, but that seems like ages. There was nothing to say for a while, but there is now. Can you believe I'm writing this in the loo on a plane to New Zealand: we're stopping in Singapore, but we're going to New Zealand. I can't believe it, Dad. I was so happy in France. School was working out OK and I made some friends finally. I first thought they liked me because I was English and a bit of a novelty but now I think they really did like me, which was cool. You know what my schools have been like with Mum dragging me all round the world. Often nobody wanted to hang around with me because they thought I wasn't staying long or they just didn't like me, I don't know. Anyway that doesn't matter now because she's done it to me again. Does she love me? She never thinks about me. I'm so unhappy I could cry. I have cried. I cried when she told me. I cried at the airport in England when we said goodbye to

Grandma and Grandpa. Mum didn't know because I washed my face afterwards. I was so happy in France, Dad, and now she's done it to me again. I'd only just made friends and now I've been made to leave again. No wonder no-one likes me, I'm never there long enough. I just breeze in and breeze out whenever Mum gets a new job. And it's not even a good job. I heard her talking to Pierre: that's the guy I told you about, the one she wouldn't marry. He said the job was rubbish, only two years with nothing at the end of it. At least we had a cool house in France. Mum says we're staying in a homestay in New Zealand. I don't even know what a homestay is.

What am I going to do, Dad? I wish you were here, you'd sort it out. I'm trying to be cool but it's hard, Dad. How am I going to make new friends again? What if I hate them? What if they hate me? I'll die if they call me a Pom.

God I wish you were here now, this is really awful. There's another thing – Mum is going to study dolphins in a place called Dusky Sound. I've looked on a map and you can't get there unless you take a boat or fly or something. There are no roads and we're supposed to be living in a place called Manapouri, which is miles away. Is Mum going to leave me there on my own or will she dump me on someone while she's off swimming with dolphins?

I'm so fed up I could die. What shall I do, Dad? I don't know what to do.

Love you always, Bree

TWO

John-Cody woke up on the couch in his office and wondered where he was. Bad dreams clung like bats to the inside of his head and he lay there for a few moments just concentrating on his breathing and looking at the map of Fiordland above him. Mahina had made it: she had bought all the largest-scale sections and pieced them together to form one huge canvas, which she then pinned to the ceiling. When people came in to ask about boat tours she encouraged them to lie on the floor and study the area that way.

John-Cody rubbed the heels of his palms into his eyes: outside he could hear the breeze and the patter of rain on the corrugated iron roof. He realized this was the first night in a year he had not slept on the boat. The pain was fierce, worse than ever, and there was so much to be done: a year to the day and Mahina's wishes must be honoured. He stepped outside the sliding door and stood for a moment on the wooden porch looking out across the little wetland they had planted together: the Lake of the Sorrowing Heart lay quiet save for thin tufts of water scuffed by the wind. The Keplers stood tall and shadowed against the sky running west to the Tasman Sea. Before them, flatter against the horizon, lay the silence of the Cathedral Peaks. John-Cody closed his eyes and saw Fraser's Beach and the dead eucalyptus tree and Mahina's favourite thinking stone that was half submerged in water the last time he'd been down there. It had rained a lot this spring and according to the forecasts it would rain some more before it was done. The breeze licked at his hair, long and silver and hanging below his shoulder blades. They had cut his hair when they put him in jail all those years ago and he had let no-one near it since, save Mahina who used to spend hours brushing it for him.

The pain crushed his chest as if someone had kicked him: for a full year he had woken to this broken emptiness and today it was as bad as it had ever been. He bit his lip, steeled himself and with shaking hands took tobacco and papers from the back pocket of his jeans. He had half-promised her he'd quit, save his lungs and heart, but he had failed. Carefully he rolled a cigarette now and sat down on the porch to smoke it.

The first tui of the morning called from the tree line across the road, where the dirt track ran to the beach. Mahina had put little bird tables all along the porch, and on the little bridge they had built she'd placed strategic nails for apples which bellbirds licked clean. The giant fuchsia tree outside their bedroom window had been the birds' favourite haunt first thing in the morning.

He got to his feet, looked at his watch and pursed his lips. Twenty minutes till Tom fired up the Z boat and took the diggers over to where they were tunnelling at West Arm. He needed to be on that boat, but first he had to go to the house. Flicking away the stub of his cigarette, he walked up Waiau Street with the lake on his left. His footfall seemed slow, weary. Yesterday he had been on the boat at Deep Cove, dreading today; not sure what he would feel, how he would deal with it and terrified of what would come after. For a year all he could think about was diving the Gut and not coming up again, but he could not do that. He had made a promise and today that promise would be fulfilled: perhaps it was the thought of what was possible afterwards that terrified him.

One year ago to the very day, the fire was burning low and he dozed in the reclining chair. He slept little in those days, always watchful, always aware of what was going on, as if he was at sea where the slightest movement, sound or smell would prick him into consciousness. If something altered he was awake and attentive, right there by the bed. Yet she asked for nothing save the morphine that had been prescribed and to be able to lie outside even in cold weather. She told him to go skipper the boat and let Alex handle things, but in the last days he cancelled every tour they had and lay by her side on the bed of bracken he'd made between the fuchsia and the mountain beech.

She would look at the sky and see things he had never seen, point out the faces of the gods, tell him over and over the tale of Rangi and Papa and how their son Tane Mahuta pushed their coupling apart to form the world between them. How the rain was

Rangi's tears for the loss of his love, Papa the earth. Mahina would point out the cloud formations and remind him of the north-west arch, grey and white cloud blown up by a nor'wester so that it looked as though God had taken paint and palette to the sky during the night.

That last night, though, he had been dozing: Mahina had commented on the greyness in his face, the great black hollows beneath his eyes, his skin ravaged by fear. She had cupped his cheek as he gave her morphine and her eyes rolled and the smile played about her lips and she joked about dying more often so she could get high on the drug.

'You're not dying,' he told her.

She touched his cheek and her fingers were thin and fragile and the flesh hung from her arm. And he recalled her in his mind's eye as she had been only a few precious months before, when they knew nothing of this and she was as vibrant and beautiful as the day he first set eyes on her. He thought then how quickly the disease had taken hold: how frail the body was and yet how strong and utterly indomitable the spirit.

Mahina knew she was dying and she fought it for as long as she could. Then, aware the fight was futile, she calmly told him her time was up. The spirits of her ancestors were whispering across eternity and it was her appointed moment to join them. The wine had dried in his mouth and he stared at the fire with his jaws clamped together, not wanting to show her his fear and not wanting to believe her, but knowing that she was right. One look at her face told him she was right. Gaunt now, she looked, and so pale, the skin of her face thin and seamed like withered parchment suddenly brought into light.

She told him she'd lain in bed feeling strangely weightless under the blanket. The window was open and there was no rain now, just the pattering of possums' feet on the roof from time to time. As she lay there she heard the cry of the morepork owl in the trees that bordered their garden. The sudden stillness was all-consuming; her senses heightened, she could smell the sweetness of manuka with last night's rain on the leaves. She could feel the bark dropping from the fuchsia and in her mind she witnessed the saucered ovals of darkness as the possum blinked from its branches. Her breath was light in her chest, almost as if it were not hers. Then she heard the morepork a second time and quietly she waited, fingers gripping the green teardrop stone, the tangiwai she had picked up from the bay at Anita when her mother was alive and she and Jonah were young. And then she heard the morepork a third and final time and she stared at the ceiling before she eased herself onto one elbow, amazed at her own weightlessness.

'John-Cody.'

He heard her call him from where he dozed in the chair. She didn't need to raise her voice or call a second time: he was there, gazing at her through the glow of the firelight in their open bedroom doorway.

He stood on the corner of his street now and peered through the gloom at the darkened walls of the house. Single storey, they had built it like a cabin before Mahina decided to divide it in two so they could offer some self-contained bed and breakfast accommodation to travellers. That was before they began the charter business; he was still a fisherman, supplementing their income with trapped deer for the newly formed venison farms.

Tree and shrub dominated the front aspect of the house and he could make out the flax and the skinny, naked lancewood tree. So many memories, they seeped into his mind like ether: Mahina's face in laughter, her aged, thoughtful father and Jonah, her wild-eyed Waitaha brother who'd asked if he could crew on the *Korimako* just to be close to her memory.

The moon moved between the clouds to cast the gravelled road in silver. Soon the dawn would come and Tom would be waiting for him down at Pearl Harbour. Crossing the road, he walked down the drive to the left of the house and came round the back where the dark curtainless window of their bedroom dominated the wall. Before him the garden was a labyrinth of arbour and bush and building, the hut where his guitars were stored, the shed and the broken-down caravan the two of them had travelled the South Island in when they were young.

He had been in New Zealand for twenty-five years now and he had been with Mahina for twenty-two of them. Night after night, day after day, they had only ever been parted when he was at sea. Until last year, when the pains in her back grew to an unbearable level and finally the specialists in Invercargill told them she had lymphatic cancer and her chances of survival were nil. She had lasted only six months, the deterioration savagely sudden, wiping the vitality from her so quickly she cried for release.

John-Cody looked at her through the bedroom

doorway and she held out her arms for him and he knew then that it was time. She had always told him she would know and she would be ready. She looked ready now. There was a calm about her features, the lines were flatter in her face and, although she was frail and thin and weak, her beauty was intact.

'Carry me outside,' she whispered. 'I don't want to die in my bed.'

She showed no fear. He could not show her any: he smiled and as he bent down his hair fell into her face and she caught up the ends in one hand and breathed in his scent.

'I always loved the way you smelled, John-Cody. I'll carry that much with me.'

He lifted her easily. Light as a feather, she was so much skin and bone. Outside, the first scratching of dawn unravelled like thread. John-Cody paused by the wooden seat and table where they used to sit at night and talk. Mahina moved against him: arms about his neck so her lips brushed his cheek and her hair was light and fuzzy against his skin. He carried her to the main road and across Waiau Street where Lake Manapouri, the Lake of the Sorrowing Heart, lay black and still in the darkness.

His boots crunched on the gravel as they made their way down to Fraser's Beach, Sierra running ahead as soon as she could smell the water.

'It's so still,' Mahina whispered.

John-Cody did not say anything: he was not sure of his voice, the lump in his throat already threatening to choke him. He picked his way carefully between the beech trees so that the fingered ends of branches didn't scratch her. As he set foot on the shingle she was so quiet he thought for a moment he'd lost her. Then she stirred and shifted in his arms and looked towards Pearl Harbour where the gum tree stood tall and white and naked, its branches stiff like petrified limbs against the gorse and scrub and the smaller black-barked manuka.

'Look at the eucalyptus,' she breathed. 'See, there is magnificence in death.'

'Don't say that.' His tears threatened to fall, but she gripped both his cheeks between her palms and squeezed until his mouth puckered.

'Don't you go sentimental on me. Not now: not when I'm about to go on the journey of a lifetime.'

'You're not going anywhere.'

Still carrying her, John-Cody walked along the shore, the stones damp and sucking at the soles of his boots.

'You're right, I'm not,' Mahina said. 'Not right away anyway. I want to watch over you, make sure you're OK.' Again she gripped his face, deliberately squeezing hard. 'Not just you but my father and Jonah: take care of Jonah, John-Cody.'

'You take care of Jonah. He's your brother.'

They were at her thinking stone, pure white against the shingle but dappled grey in the half-light. The sun was rising but had not yet climbed above the Takitimus to the east, and the lake reflected the night.

'I won't be here to take care of him. You'll have to do it for me.'

John-Cody sat on the stone. This was where she came most days, quietly on her own or with Sierra. She always sat here with the blue gum tree to her left and the lake stretching before her to the Cathedrals and Kepler Mountains.

'You'll still be here,' he said. 'You're not going anywhere. You're not allowed to leave me.'

'But I am. You know I am. I heard the morepork, John-Cody. I heard him the past two nights and I heard him again just now. Three times he called my name.'

John-Cody stood in the lee of the house, the shadows deepest close to the walls. He stared at the darkened branches of the fuchsia and felt the tightening in his chest. Then he stepped across the short expanse of grass and bent to the hollow bole. Very carefully he lifted the earthenware pot that had rested there for a year and placed it inside the canvas bag he had slung over his shoulder. The walk to Pearl Harbour took him ten minutes, back the way he had come, past the office to the bend in the road and the quiet inlet where he had fished years ago. It was where Southland Tours kept the boats that they used to ferry people across the lake. He walked quickly, the pack hanging from his shoulder, one hand against the cold stone of the jar to steady it.

'Don't forget what you promised me.' She whispered it to him, her lips close to his ear.

'I won't.' John-Cody stared at the lake as the first slivers of gold began to beat a path across the surface. The sun was rising behind them, the sky clear now: it would be a perfect spring morning.

'Tell me. Tell me what you're going to do.'

He looked at her then, his voice breaking as he tried to get the words out. 'You want to be burned and your ashes placed in the bole of the fuchsia.'

'For one year only, counting from today, not when

you burn me.' Again she gripped his face and he could feel the urgency in her fingers. 'I want to watch over you for one year. You're going to need me. I can see that.' She paused then, eyes half-closing. Again he thought he was losing her, but her eyelids fluttered and she looked evenly at him once more. 'But after that you free me, you understand? Free me, John-Cody Gibbs, then forget all about me because I won't remember you.' Her words were harsh, features stiff and taut. 'I'll be gone for ever, tasting the breath of eternity.'

Mahina rested her head against him; then, loosening her grip round his neck, she took his hand in hers and pressed back the fingers so that his palm was flattened and he felt something cold and smooth against his skin. Glancing down, he saw it was the tangi-wai, the sliver of pounamu greenstone she had kept with her since childhood. She looked across the opaque surface of the lake and smiled. The sun ran in gold streaks on the water and the summits of the Cathedrals were brilliant against the sky.

'It's going to be a beautiful day,' she whispered.

And she was gone. He felt the breath go out of her: her limbs limp against him, head sagging to settle on his chest. Next to him the gum tree was naked and silent. The water lapped at his feet and Sierra, who had been gambolling among the stones, stopped where she was and looked over.

He had carried her body back to the house and then telephoned Jonah and her father, Kobi, who still lived up in Naseby. Kobi had bought what had been the old general store, no more than a warehouse by then, and built himself a single room inside it, roof and fireplace and all. Jonah was working in Omakau and said he would go and collect him. He had been against Mahina's cremation, which was in keeping with her father's Eastern European origins rather than the Waitaha traditions of their mother. He had come round, however, when John-Cody told him why she had wished it, and it was afterwards that he had requested to crew on the boat. Jonah had a skipper's ticket gained when he worked for Ned Pole, driving crayfish boats in and around the sounds. But he'd given up working for Pole when Mahina fell ill.

Tom drove the Z boat standing up and John-Cody sat and listened to the murmur of conversation from the diggers occupying the seats behind him. Halfway across the lake he got up and watched the sun lighting up the valley. Looking back again, he saw that Tom was watching him.

'How you going, mate?'

John-Cody managed to raise a smile. 'I've had better days.'

'I reckon.' Tom looked at the canvas pack. 'Everything set?'

John-Cody nodded.

'Are you going to live on the boat after?'

'I don't know. I'll see how I feel.'

'I hope you've got her shipshape. You know how she loved that boat.'

John-Cody smiled then and took tobacco from his pocket. 'She looks as sweet as, Tom.'

'Good on you.' Tom patted his shoulder and turned back to the windscreen where the bow wave lifted spray to smatter the glass.

The crossing took forty-five minutes before they docked at the power station wharf at West Arm. It was still only eight o'clock and John-Cody was glad he had made the early start. The sandflies were not out in force yet and he had left his bottle of repellent back on the boat. The wharf was quiet at this time of day, the first of the parties of tourists not yet in the national park. The green-roofed information centre was dwarfed by the mountains that rose between Lake Manapouri and the sea fiords. Trees clung to their flanks and choked the valleys: silver beech interspersed with red and mountain beech, marble-leaf, wineberry higher up on the pass, and at the shoreline kahikatea and rimu. Mahina had called this place the last garden of Tane, god of the forest and birds.

They disembarked and Tom pointed out the driver of one of the company twin cabs who was going over the hill to the exit site of the second tunnel, where millions of gallons of water were being pumped into Deep Cove. John-Cody was able to hitch a ride. The driver was quiet, sensing his mood. John-Cody had seen him a couple of times during his year living on the boat. Alex, who ran the office, had kept in touch with John-Cody by the ship-to-shore radio and organized the few eco-tours he had undertaken. She had urged him to keep working even though, with Mahina's death, the boat had been paid off. She told him that Mahina would hate to think of him giving up on everything they had striven to build over the last ten years. There were currently twenty-two charter boats operating in the sounds of south-west New Zealand and theirs was the only one that took no fish from the sea.

The driver dropped him on the road above his wharf. They had had it only a year before Mahina died; the permit was probably the last that would be granted by the Department of Conservation. The *Korimako* was berthed alongside, brilliant white in the sunlight that beat down on the water. John-Cody could feel the sweat on his back and the sore patch on his shoulder where the strap of his pack was chafing.

He set the pack carefully on the bench seat that surrounded the table in the saloon, then sliding down the for'ard steps he ducked into the engine room and felt for the light switch. He went through his rigid routine of checks before he fired up the auxiliary. Now he had power for the generators and upstairs he could make some coffee. He stood a moment on the bridge, palms moist, before twisting the ignition key. The massive Gardner engine fired into life. He let her idle while he took off the for'ard and stern lines, then finally the spring, which he coiled before depositing it back on the wharf. Instinctively he hit the horn three times, put the gears astern and backed away from the wharf. Moments later he was chugging up Deep Cove with the wheelhouse doors slid open and a cup of coffee at his elbow.

Jonah had driven Mahina's father down from Naseby after John-Cody phoned them. It took six hours and when they got there John-Cody had already arranged things with the undertaker from Te Anau. He had wanted to come and take her body away immediately, but John-Cody reminded him that Waitaha sensibilities were to be respected and they must wait till Jonah and his father had seen her.

Jonah was a wide-shouldered man who looked entirely Polynesian, though the reality was that the Maori had intermarried with Europeans for generations now. There were no full bloods remaining and few, if any, half bloods. Jonah and Mahina had probably been quarter blood, their mother half-blood Waitaha when she married Kobi, who had landed from Hungary. He was a small stooping man and he looked wizened as he stood at the foot of the bed gazing at the face of his daughter.

'That's exactly how her mother looked,' he said softly. 'Same thing took her. Almost the same age.' He shook his head and tears broke at the corners of his liquid blue eyes.

Jonah laid a massive hand on his shoulder. His hair was long and black and untied today; normally he liked to wear it in a ponytail. 'I still don't think she should be burnt,' he said. 'Waitaha people aren't burnt.'

'No, but pakeha sometimes are.' His father looked stiffly at him. 'She's half Hungarian, Jonah. It's what she wanted.' He turned to John-Cody. 'Show me the tree.'

They stepped to the window and John-Cody pointed to the pink-barked fuchsia just the other side of the glass. A hanging bird table dangled from one of its lower limbs and a fantail pecked at the apple he had placed there yesterday evening.

'For a year?'

John-Cody looked back at him and nodded.

'That's good.' Kobi turned back to his daughter once more and brushed her hair with his fingertips. John-Cody moved to the dressing table where a sealed envelope with Kobi's name on it rested at the base of the mirror. He handed it to the old man.

'She wanted you to have this.'

Kobi looked at the pale blue envelope, nodded and slipped it into his jacket pocket.

John-Cody put the *Korimako* on autopilot and went below to turn on the deck hose. He pulled on his wet-weather gear then sprayed the deck down, conscious of the build-up of rust every time he raised the anchor. They had bought the *Korimako* on a wing and a prayer; the name was the Maori translation for bellbird, which seemed fitting given their garden and the fuchsia and the chorus that greeted them most mornings. She was a buck-eye ketch almost nineteen metres long, her twin masts both the same height with no booms; steel-hulled and steel-decked with no wooden boards to rot, and she weighed seventy tonnes. John-Cody had flown to Australia, bought the best fully commissioned charter boat he could locate and sailed her back with Tom Blanch and Jonah crewing for him. It was Tom who had really taught John-Cody the ways of the sea after he landed in 1974. He had spied the South Island from the deck of a Hawaiian trawler, his third vessel since he had sailed from Bellingham.

He steamed up Deep Cove now, glancing to port and the entrance of Hall's Arm, which had been one of Mahina's special places: there they could turn the engines off and listen to nothing but the sounds of the fiord. Ahead was the Malaspina Reach, named in honour of Alessandro Malaspina, an Italian who commanded a Spanish expedition in 1793. John-Cody had learned it all from Mahina and it flooded back now as he took her ashes out to sea, the *Korimako* cutting a perfect line through the calm dark water. As he approached Espinosa Point a dolphin breached on the port bow and John-Cody smiled: they always came visiting when Mahina was on the boat, as if they knew she was there, as if they could communicate with her in some strange and wonderful way. She always said they were far more intelligent than humans, that long ago they had learned that life on land had a sell-by date and to survive they had to migrate to the sea. Vividly he remembered sitting on the dive platform with her as they paddled their feet in the freezing water while the pod played beneath them. Mahina told him that if God ever wanted to communicate something to man again he wouldn't use a human being. No-one would believe another human, but they might a whale or a dolphin.

He walked to the bowsprit as First Arm opened on the port side with Bradshaw and Thompson Sound to starboard. The dolphins had been in Bradshaw the last couple of times he had seen them. He didn't always see them; there were occasions when the guests that chartered the boat were disappointed, but never when Mahina was on board.

Quasimodo breached right under the bowsprit before settling on the bow wave to surf. There were ten or twelve dolphins now, all grouped together riding the wave with whistles and clicks, and John-Cody wondered if somehow they knew. Was this their parting shot, the funeral cortege on the bows? He went back into the wheelhouse and flicked the boat into neutral. No bow wave now, nothing to keep them there. He wandered for'ard again and lit a cigarette. The wind was getting up and clouds massed over the Tasman. The wind cut the Gut north of Bauza and whistled through the spreaders. The dolphins were still gathered under the bow, rolling over one another, playing, caressing, diving and calling out. All at once Quasimodo lifted his head out of the water spy-hopping like a bowhead whale, and John-Cody felt the hairs lift on the back of his neck.

'Can you feel her, Quasi? Do you know where she's at?'

Quasimodo dived again, showing the lump in his back between the dorsal fin and his tail; he came up again and blew gold in the morning sunlight.

John-Cody engaged the gears and eased the revs higher, Seymour Island on the starboard quarter now and beyond it Espinosa Point and Yuvali Beach where he had first spoken to Mahina. The pain in his chest almost suffocated him. She had been his love from the day they met to the day she died. Sudden instant love, like two souls meeting right there by the deer trap on Yuvali Beach.

He was twenty-four and had been living in Manapouri for two years, working with Tom on a crayfish boat in the sound and trapping deer for the farms. John-Cody's sense of adventure had almost made him join one of the helicopter crews where the really big money was, but after they went to three funerals in a week he decided terra firma or the deck of a boat under his feet were far better options.

He and Tom ran ten deer traps, worked out carefully in terms of design and location, and they took it in turn to check them. Tom kept the crayfish boat moored at Deep Cove and when all the pots were down they would go and see what they had caught.

71

Live deer were beginning to fetch good money then, though the government was still paying per hide and they shot as many as they could.

That particular day he had run the dinghy up onto Yuvali Beach and heard the deer trying to escape his trap. Tom was moored further out by Seymour, taking care of last night's crayfish catch. John-Cody had a rifle slung over his shoulder and he crunched his way up the beach to the trap. Inside was a beautiful hind, two or perhaps three years old. He stood and crooned softly, calming her till she remained still and he could think about netting her and getting her back to the boat. He would need Tom for that, but he had to get her nice and steady first.

'She's beautiful, isn't she?' The woman's voice came from nowhere and John-Cody whirled and saw nothing; the disembodied words hung in the atmosphere like mist. 'She's young. She'll breed well. I'm glad you didn't kill her.'

He looked round, seeing nothing until he noticed the little aluminium dinghy tied high up on the burn. When he turned again he saw her standing to the left of the trap, half hidden among the red-flowering rata. She wore shorts, though it was cold, and just a T-shirt so the swell of her breasts and the tightness of nipples showed through. Her face was dark and her eyes flashed as she crossed the sand barefoot, mud from the banks of the burn climbing above her ankles. Her hair was thick and long and pushed behind one ear, its blackness tinted with the natural henna of the Polynesian, iridescent with the sun behind her.

'You're John-Cody Gibbs the fisherman.'

She walked in a circle around him, and he couldn't

take his eyes off her. Her legs were smooth and brown and taut with muscle, her waist slim; she moved with the grace of a cat. She wandered right up to the trap and leaned on the fence, then made a cooing owl-like sound in the back of her throat. The hind dropped her head and her ears flattened and she took her first tentative steps towards the wire.

'They're so beautiful,' the girl said. 'It's a shame they are so destructive.'

'Who are you?' John-Cody recognized the dinghy tied up on the beach and he had seen the girl at Deep Cove once or twice.

'Mahina.'

'That's a beautiful name.'

'You think so? I'm not so sure.' She wandered down the beach where she paused before the water and gazed across Pendulo Reach at their boat. John-Cody could see Tom on deck sorting the crayfish into size and weight.

'Why d'you catch crayfish?' She looked over her shoulder at him.

'It's my job.'

'My father hunted crayfish before my mother died and my mother's father before him. With each generation of people the crayfish have got smaller.'

John-Cody stood up and thought of what Tom Blanch had told him when he first came here, how Tom as a boy had followed the trails of the kakapo, the flightless ground parrot. Now the only trails left were from deer. 'People have to eat,' he said quietly, walking down the beach to join her. 'Everybody needs food.'

She nodded. 'But we take more than we need. We take what can't be replaced.' She stood for a long moment, then glanced at him again and pointed to the mountains. 'Did you know that what goes on above the water is echoed exactly below it? Life, death and rebirth, John-Cody. When the forest dies, trees slip into the fiord to feed it. The slip above the water is reciprocated beneath it. Both the forest above and the coral below begin to regenerate at the same time. If not, there is no balance and without balance the world cannot function.

'You're from America,' she said. 'You might understand what I'm saying.'

He frowned. 'You mean people round here don't?'

'Not really. A few perhaps, but there are livings to be made and eyes go blind when that is the case. Ears have a habit of turning deaf.'

John-Cody raised one eyebrow. 'What exactly are you telling me?'

She stepped up close then, her feet sinking in the chill of the sand. She laid a warm palm against the flat of his chest and looked into his eyes. 'I'm telling you there is more to life than just catching crayfish.'

She had come to his house that night, the little crib he rented between Manapouri and Te Anau. Tom told him it used to be the Manapouri schoolhouse and had been moved onto a farmer's land where it had stood empty for ten years. He had lit a fire in the stove and cooked some feral deer steaks when he heard a truck pull up outside. Glancing out of the window he spied Mahina climbing from the driver's seat. She carried a bottle wrapped in crepe paper, was barefoot and wore the same shorts and top she'd been wearing when they spoke at Yuvali Beach.

John-Cody figured she was about eighteen. He

74

had seen her brother around, a great hulking Maori called Jonah. He was still only a kid though he liked to hang out with Ned Pole and the other chopper crews. They knew each other to nod to and John-Cody wondered what Jonah would think if he knew his big sister had invited herself for dinner.

He recalled that night vividly and with a fondness now as he steered the *Korimako* towards the Shelter Islands. He looked at his watch: late morning. He had dawdled out here knowing that he didn't want to let her go. He had thought that maybe this would be the end of it for him, that he could release her; let her go and get on with his life without her. For a year he had been a prisoner of this moment and now the moment was upon him he knew he would rather remain a prisoner than face the future without her. The emotion welled up in him and threatened to boil over, as if the real mourning would start now, as if the last twelve months had been nothing but preparation.

The Shelter Islands were ahead and the dolphins lagged behind the boat, their escort duties over now. They would stay close to Bradshaw; rarely had he seen them beyond that point. West of the Shelter Islands the sky had darkened and cloud squeezed the horizon white to grey and black.

As the boat steamed beyond the islands he could see the Hare's Ears, twin rocks out to sea that kept boats away from Febrero Point. His whole body tingled, every sinew, every muscle, every sense as alive as he had ever felt it. He stood on the brink of something: he did not know what, but he was more alive in her death, more aware of the life around him

75

than he had ever been. The last time he had felt anything vaguely close to this was when he had stood on the Camas prairie, not yet twenty-one, looking down on the wreckage of the FBI agents' car.

He put the boat back on autopilot and looked at the pack, which still lay where he had left it on the seat by the saloon table. The Shelter Islands were beam on to port now and it was time. This is where she wanted her ashes scattered, between the Nee and the Shelters, where the Tasman Sea met the sound. Taking the earthenware pot he went out on deck and stood for a moment. The sun was showing her face again through a sucker hole in the cloud, though it was raining in Corset Cove only a hundred metres to port. He walked to the bowsprit and the memory of that first night together, just talking in front of his fire, was burnt into his mind. No touching, no kissing, nothing but the mingling of voices and thoughts. He recalled thinking how immense her knowledge of her country was, the land and the ocean and the way all things fitted together. He forgot she was barely eighteen, for she spoke with the wisdom of her ancestors. Her eyes were on fire and her skin shone in the glow from the stove. Their words mixed with a richness he had never felt before and she delved into the recesses of his soul without him even knowing she was doing it.

He stood now on the bowsprit and as he began to unscrew the lid of the urn the wind rattled the spreaders above his head. It caught the length of his hair, uncut in twenty-five years, and he saw her again in his mind's eye, sitting by the fire in the house they had built in Manapouri. She took the brush to his hair, stroke after stroke, night after night, year after year as gradually it faded to silver.

Back in the wheelhouse he rummaged among the tray of tools he kept behind the global positioning system till he found what he was looking for. On deck he stuffed the scissors in the back pocket of his jeans, then placing Mahina's urn under his shirt he climbed the jib mast to the spreaders thirty feet above the deck. He stood with one foot on each spreader, the hoop of the crow's nest at his back, and faced the Tasman Sea. Taking the scissors from his pocket, he grabbed his hair in one hand and cut it off at the shoulder. He heard the grating of the blades, felt the tugging against his scalp, and imagined the pull of the brush as she worked to make it shine. The clump of hair came away in his hand and he swivelled round so his back was to the mast. Again he worked the lid of the urn loose. The wind lifted and pressed him against the metal hoop. He felt the first spots of rain and the sheets rattled left and right. He took the open urn and lifted the mass of silver strands, holding them both above his head. In a cloud of greyed white the wind took the ashes and the wind took his hair: together they flew one last time before Mahina was lost to the sound.

THREE

Libby and Bree flew into Christchurch at the beginning of November, the plane landing at midnight roughly twenty-four hours after they left Heathrow. Bree was exhausted, walking through the arrivals lounge like a ghost, rings of darkness dragging at the skin of her eyes. Her face was white, her backpack, magazines and Walkman dangling in hands that trailed at her sides.

A two-hour stopover in Singapore had broken up the journey and Libby, leper-like, had gone into the smoking room for a cigarette. Bree had sat on a plastic seat watching the news on television, her face like thunder.

When Libby had asked her what she felt about the move, she said the only thing she knew about New Zealand was that the Kiwis called English people Poms.

'If they call me that at school, Mum, I'm never going to forgive you.' She had said it with vitriol on her lip and the same darkness in her eyes that Libby recognized in her own from time to time. She could have told Bree the truth then, let her know just how dire their financial situation had become, but she didn't. Financial worry wasn't Bree's problem and if she did tell her there was every possibility that word would get back to her parents, which was the last thing Libby wanted.

So she kept quiet, but she did have serious misgivings. She was sure Bree could handle school: school was school and kids were kids wherever you were in the world. But she would be away quite a lot; much of her research would have to be done a good distance from where they were staying in Manapouri. Quite how she would swing the child care without completely messing up her daughter's head she did not know.

She smoked a cigarette behind the glass panel and felt distinctly unclean. Bree watched her out of dark eyes and when Libby came out again she moved one seat down.

'Have you any idea how ridiculous you look? Watching you is like being at the zoo.'

Libby said nothing.

'I mean, hello. It's so embarrassing. There's my mother chugging on a fag behind a glass wall in an airport.'

Libby compressed her lips. Bree made a face: Libby laughed and Bree looked at her for a moment and then she laughed too. 'I hate you,' she said.

'I hate you too.'

'Good. Then we're equal.'

'Equal.'

'Good.'

'Right.'

'Why did we have to come?'

'Because I needed the job.'

'Yeah, right.'

'What's that supposed to mean?'

'You had a job in France. You had two jobs. How many jobs do you need?'

'Bree . . .' Libby sighed, hesitated a moment then said: 'They were part-time jobs and even added together they didn't pay enough to keep us.'

Bree stared at her then and Libby exhaled heavily through her nostrils. 'I wasn't going to tell you, but I guess you're owed some sort of explanation for yet another move. I didn't want to move again, darling, not after you were settled in France, but money was so tight I didn't have enough to pay the rent. If I hadn't got the job in New Zealand we wouldn't have had anywhere to live.'

Bree frowned at her. 'What about Vimereux?'

'The landlord was about to throw us out. The rent was too high, darling. I just didn't earn enough to cover it and get us everything else we needed. I couldn't allow him to evict us. We'd have been homeless. I couldn't let that happen. So you see, I had to take this job: it was the only one on offer that paid enough to keep us.'

Bree looked unimpressed. 'I don't believe you. You wanted it because it's proper research.'

'Of course I wanted it. It's in my field. Who wouldn't want it? But that doesn't change the fact that I couldn't afford for us to stay in France.' Libby sat forward and took Bree's hand. 'Do you think I like hauling you round the world like this? D'you think I want you to be constantly starting new schools, having to try and make new friends? Bree, it's the last thing I want. But what I earn has to be enough to keep us together. I have to go where the work is.'

Bree looked at her for a moment longer then got up and walked away. Libby watched her wandering among the shops, looking at trinkets and seeing nothing. She felt for her, having to deal with so much change all the time. She wished she hadn't had to tell her how it really was, but perhaps in a way it was better. This was a new start for both of them, a new country with new possibilities: there would be many difficulties along the way and they had better be in it together.

The morning after they arrived it was raining: they had to be up at 5 a.m. to catch the shuttle bus that would drive them across country to Manapouri in the far south-west. It rained much of the way there and the driver told them, almost gleefully, that they had just experienced the worst spring floods ever. The River Clutha had burst its banks and most of the roads had been closed. Bree sat in silence and sulked; summer was supposed to be on its way yet everything looked cold and damp and miserable.

They arrived late in the afternoon. It was almost five o'clock when the bus driver pulled into the village and turned into a quiet residential street.

'There you go,' he said and opened his door. 'I'll just get your bags and you're set.'

Bree and Libby sat where they were for a moment, looking at the low cabin-style house on their left. The roof was green and made of corrugated iron as so many of them seemed to be. Two short drives, one at either end of the house, were split by a multitude of shrubs and trees so that half the building was hidden: it gave the impression of being set snugly back from the road, though in reality the distance was no more than twenty feet. An old Toyota pick-up truck was parked under the lean-to in the drive and Bree could see a red telephone box standing beside it. All at once she smiled and Libby breathed a sigh of relief.

The rain had stopped halfway between Queenstown and Manapouri and the sun came peeping through clouds to cast rainbows over the hills. The driver had been something of a tour guide, pointing out mountains and rivers to them as they passed. They saw for themselves where the Clutha had burst its banks; fields and low-lying areas were swamped, the water reaching almost halfway up the tree trunks. He told them it was the worst flooding the South Island had suffered in its history. But the rain had stopped now and the grey of the sky had been replaced with patches of brilliance.

'Aotearoa,' Libby said, pointing at the sky. 'The land of the long white cloud.'

'I know.' Bree was still staring at the front of the house. 'I read about it.'

'Let's see if anyone's in.'

Leaving their cases where they were, Libby led the way down the path: bird tables hung from the trees and seed had been freshly scattered on the lawn. The sun was behind them now and high, warming their backs through their clothing. Libby knocked on the front door. 'I suppose our bit is next door.' She pointed to the right where a second porch overlooked the path running across the front of the house. A box of logs was stacked neatly to one side.

There was no reply. Libby knocked again but still received no answer.

'Great,' Bree said. 'We come all this way and

there's no-one here. What're we going to do now?'

'I'm going to think for a minute, if you'll let me.' Libby looked at her then, one hand fisted on her hip. She tried the door and found it wasn't locked. They peeked inside: one large room divided into kitchen and living area, two chairs and a settee, the walls vertically panelled in wood, ornaments littering the stone mantelpiece. A wood-burning stove was set on a raised fireplace in the near corner and a box of kindling stood next to it. The place smelled musty, as if no-one had lived there for a while.

'I booked through Fiordland Ecology Holidays,' Libby said. 'Let's try and find the office.'

'How can we carry the bags?'

'We'll leave them here.'

Between them they shifted the bags into the carport and Bree made a closer inspection of the telephone box, which was old, the paint chipped, but the phone itself was still there. There was a fridge and a chest freezer, and a bag of seed – looking as if mice had been ransacking it – hung from a hook in the ceiling.

They walked the few yards to the main road then turned left and a little further on the lake came into view. Libby stopped and stared across the vast expanse of water. Mountains thrust at the sky in the distance, their tips a swirl of white cloud which hung mist-like and unmoving. A boat moved leisurely across the surface of the lake heading for a promontory of rocks, which jutted from the southern shore.

Bree came alongside her and stood for a moment. A sense of peace descended; both of them could feel it. They could hear no sound save the rustle of wind in the trees and the faint hum of the boat on the lake: no cars, no voices, only birdsong rising behind them. Libby took Bree's hand. 'Come on,' she said. 'There's only a couple of streets in this town, we'll find the office.'

Turning onto Waiau Street Bree spotted the office, painted green and standing in a little wetland where cabbage trees were sprouting. They crossed the wooden bridge to the porch and Bree stopped to watch silvereyes feeding on scraps of bread thrown down for them. She had never seen the little birds before but had bought a booklet in Christchurch and recognized them from their picture, small and blue-backed with their eyes marked in silver.

Libby opened the sliding door and they stepped into a large room with a counter on one side and partitioned at the back. A couch was set under the window and a TV and video stood opposite. The door to an inner office was open behind the counter and she could hear somebody talking on the phone. Bree stood at the window and watched a group of young people sitting at an outside table next door, at Possum Lodge, the local backpackers' hostel. One boy in his late teens saw her watching and waved. Bree went red and came away from the window. She sat on the couch and then a dog poked its head round the side of the counter and looked thoughtfully at her. Brindle coloured, it seemed to have the head of an Alsatian. For a moment they looked at each other, then the dog yawned and wandered over. Bree beamed as she rested her chin on her knee.

Libby was at the counter. A woman in her forties sat at a computer screen in the smaller office beyond it, talking on the phone. She swivelled round: she had shortish hair clipped at the ears with pins, and very blue eyes. She smiled and lifted a finger to indicate a minute. Libby leaned on the counter and watched Bree and the dog playing together by the couch. The woman put down the phone and came through.

'G'day,' she said. 'Can I help you?'

'I hope so. I'm Dr Bass and this is my daughter Bree. We've rented the place up the road but there's no-one at home.'

The woman's face fell. 'Ah,' she said. 'I'm sorry. I thought that was all organized.'

'You mean it's not?'

'Don't worry.' The woman smiled. 'I'm Alex. I spoke to you on the telephone. Look, have a seat, let me make you some coffee and I'll call John-Cody on the radio. It's been a difficult day, I'm afraid, and things have run away with themselves.'

Libby bit her lip, trying hard to be accommodating. She was going to have to work with these people for at least two years. 'The floods,' she said.

'Among other things, yes.' Alex went behind the partition and put the kettle on. She came back and saw the look on Bree's face, the dog still lying at her feet.

'I see you've met Sierra, Bree. She's part Australian sheepdog and part wild fox. She came over from Sydney when we got the boat.'

'Boat?' Bree looked puzzled.

'The *Korimako*.' Alex sat down next to her and fondled Sierra's ears. 'You know what, Sierra hasn't had a run today. How would you fancy taking her down to the beach for me?'

Bree's eyes widened. 'I'd love to. Will she come with me?'

'Of course.'

'Do I need a leash?'

'No. Just tell her what you want her to do and she'll do it. John-Cody trained her and she does pretty much what she's asked.'

'Who is John-Cody?'

'John-Cody Gibbs: he's the boss. This is his business. He's on the boat right now in Doubtful Sound.' Leaning back on the couch Alex pointed to the map on the ceiling. 'You see that thin stretch of water the other side of the mountains? That's Doubtful Sound: it goes all the way to the sea.'

Bree was on her feet. 'Come on, Sierra,' she said. The dog got up and padded down the steps with her and crossed the little bridge over the patch of wetland. At the kerb Bree stopped and Sierra sat and then the two of them crossed to the grass and the dirt track leading down to the lake. Libby leaned in the doorway with her arms folded.

'That's the most contented I've seen her since I told her we were coming.' She smiled at Alex. 'Can I step out here and smoke?'

'Of course: I'd join you only I quit.' Alex looked longingly at the pack of Camels Libby took from her bag. 'I'll see if I can get hold of the boss.'

John-Cody steamed gently back into Deep Cove and watched the fishermen from Ned Pole's mini fleet tying their boats together. A couple of the crew were handing boxes of crayfish from one deck to the other and laying them on the communal wharf. Pole had six boats in all and four of them were tied up there: John-Cody had seen another, the *Brigand*, by the Nee Islands late in the day.

After he had scattered Mahina's ashes he trawled First Arm looking for the dolphins, but he found no trace of them. His sense of loss was more acute than ever. There was a weakness in his limbs and his eyes burned. He was doing his level best to let Mahina go – but how could he let her go when there was such hopelessness in his chest? He fingered the ends of his hair where he had cut it and steered using the wheel, not the pilot, something he rarely did these days; but right then he needed the feel of wood under his hands.

The VHF radio crackled where it was housed on the dashboard.

'*Korimako, Korimako, Korimako*: this is *Kori*-base. Do you copy, boss?'

He picked up the transmitter. 'Loud and clear, Alex.'

'Listen, I have Dr Bass here in the office with me.'

'Who is Dr Bass?'

'The scientist from England, the one who'll be studying the pod in Dusky Sound. The research programme – remember?'

'Oh, shit.' John-Cody passed a hand across his brow. 'That's not today surely?'

'It is today. She's right here and due to move into the homestay. What shall I do?'

That was the one bit of preparation Alex had asked him to do, her way of getting him off the boat, prompting him into some kind of action. For a full year he had stagnated, given up on himself and the business. Let everything go to pot. She had told him about the homestay rental and asked him to arrange a cleaner. He had clearly forgotten.

'Alex, nothing's ready. I never got it organized.'

Silence.

'Did you get that, Alex? Over.'

'Loud and clear: are you coming back over the hill?'

John-Cody thought about it. The boat had been his home for a year. He glanced around him at the bridge and saloon, steps for'ard and aft, galley on the starboard side.

'I guess I better, huh.'

'I think it would be a good idea. Look, I'll call Lynda and see if she can clean. And I'll get them booked into the Motor Inn for tonight.'

'OK.' John-Cody thought for a moment. 'She's got a daughter, right?'

'Yes.'

'The homestay'll be too cramped, Alex. Besides, I can't go back. They can have my side of the house. Get Lynda to clean my side and shift the stuff I haven't already moved down to the green shed. Tell her I'll pay her double if she can do it tonight. And Alex' – he paused for a moment – 'tell her to be careful with Mahina's clothes. They're in boxes in the wardrobe.'

'OK. Look, I'll wait here in the office till you get back. Over and out.'

John-Cody put the handset down and brought the boat round in an arc to berth on the port side. Two of Pole's men looked up from their work. John-Cody ignored them: already the Southland Tours catamaran was tying up on the big wharf. They would be loading the bus and he needed a ride over the pass. He berthed the *Korimako* in one fluid movement, for'ard at the dock then wheel to starboard and hard astern, neutral and she glided in on the port side with barely a bump against the tyres. Outside he put on the for'ard spring to keep her where she was and switched off the engines.

Quickly he made the checks, closed the doors and tied off to stern and bow. He was at the top of the black metal steps as the Southland Tours bus came up from their wharf. Jim Brierly was driving and John-Cody flagged him down. The passenger doors opened with a hiss and Brierly, a heavy-set man from Te Anau, squinted at him.

'G'day, Gib.'

'I need a ride, Jim.'

'We're full, mate.'

'I can stand.'

Brierly smiled. 'Go on then. I shouldn't, but seeing as it's you.'

John-Cody climbed the steps and stood with his back to the windscreen, looking at the faces of the tourists who stared back at him.

Brierly drove the bus across the mountain pass. He gave no commentary on the return trip; the passengers had been out for five or so hours and were weary. He pushed the microphone away from his mouth and looked at John-Cody. 'So how you going? I've not seen anyone on your boat for a while.'

'I haven't felt much like clients, Jim.'

Brierly looked at him again. 'You cut your hair. I knew there was something different about you. God, I never thought I'd see the day. It's still bloody long but it's a start, I reckon.'

John-Cody raised a grin and fingered the frayed ends at his shoulders. 'Does it look bad?'

'Awful.'

They passed Pole's men on the wharf by the hostel, their truck loaded with crayfish boxes.

'Looks like they had a good day: Old Ned'll be pleased. From what I hear he needs the money.' Brierly looked round again as they started up the hill. 'Is he still after your wharf?'

John-Cody nodded. 'And the boat. He's not getting either.'

'You two still don't get on then, eh.' Brierly shook his head. 'Pole's all right, Gibby. He's just trying to make a living, same as the rest of us.'

'Like the gold mine in Australia.'

Brierly made a face. 'Fair play to him, mate. He had a go. That's all anybody can ask.'

'I heard he stretched himself too thin. It's why this Dusky deal is so important.'

'Possibly. People gossip, Gib. Pole's a big man, there's those that'd like to see him take a fall.' He looked keenly at John-Cody then. 'Same as there's those who wanted to see you take one.'

John-Cody nodded.

'The funny thing is, mate,' Brierly went on, 'you and Pole are alike in lots of ways.'

John-Cody thinned his eyes.

'You both know the bush, the water, better than just about anyone. You're both decent blokes. It's a pity you don't get along.'

'We stand on different sides of the fence, Jim.'

Brierly nodded, working the steering wheel through his hands. 'I suppose that business with Eli didn't help.'

John-Cody stared at the floor and he heard the crashing of waves on the bow, the flapping of the jib on the luff spar.

'I'm sorry, mate.' Brierly looked at him, red-faced. 'I shouldn't have brought that up.'

Libby had heard what Alex said on the radio, heard the response through the static and her heart sank. What with all the stress she had been through with Bree, this was the last thing she needed. Alex came over and sat down next to her on the couch.

'I'm so sorry,' she said. 'You must think we're awful.'

Libby tried to smile.

'I should never have left it to him, not today anyway.'

'Why? What's today?'

Alex bit her lip. 'He buried his wife today, his common law wife anyway.'

'Oh my God. I'm sorry.'

'Don't be. He scattered her ashes on the sound. She died a year ago. It was a promise he made to her and he fulfilled it today.' She smiled and patted Libby on the thigh. 'So you see, nothing is ready for you. But this is Manapouri and we're nothing if not resourceful. Tonight I'll get you booked into the motel and the house will be ready tomorrow. There is some good news: John-Cody told me to prepare the big half of the house, his half, for you. There are two bedrooms and you'll be much more comfortable.'

'That's very kind. Thank you.'

'No worries.' Alex smiled and collected her car keys from the counter. 'You fetch Bree and I'll get your bags. See you back here in five minutes.'

Libby wandered down to the beach, where she stood in the shelter of the last line of trees watching her daughter playing with the dog at the edge of the lake. The ragged heads of mountains reflected in the water like glass, so still now after the rain. The beach was a mixture of shingle and bigger stones, some boulder size further along the shore. Bree had not seen her; she was busy throwing sticks for Sierra who dived into the water, swam for all she was worth and then came paddling back, a weed-soaked twig between her jaws. Each time she dropped it at Bree's feet without being prompted. Bree looked up, saw her mother and waved. Libby felt her heart lift for the first time since she had made her decision to come here.

Alex drove them to the motel and pointed out her house as they passed. It faced the lake across the main road, which led to Te Anau. It was hardly what Libby would call a main road: they'd seen fewer than a handful of cars in the couple of hours they had been there. Alex's house was large and set back from the road, a massive dormer window cut into the attic. Libby strained her neck to look as they drove past.

'That must be one hell of a view,' she said.

Alex smiled at her in the rear-view mirror. 'It's why I bought the house. That attic window wasn't there. I had it put in because I knew the view would be spectacular. I wasn't concerned with the house.'

They pulled up outside reception. Libby climbed out and between them they unloaded the bags. Libby noticed there was a restaurant and something called the Beehive Bar attached to the motel. They would get something to eat and drink at least.

The room was nothing fancy but clean and serviceable. The breeze-block walls were painted yellow and flower-patterned curtains hung at the window but the view over the lake was partly obscured by trees that Alex told them had recently been planted along the shore. It was why she had bought a house set at the back of her section, which was raised up on the hill. People who had built lower down had had their view spoiled and apparently they were up in arms about it.

'That's the difficulty with this part of the world,' she said. 'It's always a fine balance between development and conservation.'

'I think it's the same all over nowadays.'

'I'm sure it is. It's always more acute, though, when a place depends so much on tourism.'

Alex left them alone then, suggesting they come to the office whenever they were ready in the morning. Everything would be sorted by then. Bree said goodbye to Sierra who didn't seem to want to go. Alex told her she could walk her any time she liked.

'So what do you think?' her mother asked when Alex had gone. 'Still the back of beyond?'

Bree made a face. 'I like the lake, and I can't wait to explore the garden. Did you see it? It looks huge.'

'I didn't get a proper look but I will tomorrow.'

'One thing is bothering me, Mum.' Bree sat down on the bed, hands under her thighs.

'What's that, darling?'

'Who's going to look after me when you're in Dusky Sound?'

John-Cody rode across the lake with Southland Tours and walked the short distance to the office. Alex was still there when he went in. 'I'm sorry,' he said. 'I completely forgot. Did you get them settled?'

'Manapouri Motor Inn, and I've also arranged for Lynda to do the cleaning as you asked.'

'Great.' He slumped down on the couch and Alex brought him some freshly brewed coffee: she stared at his unkempt hair, her brow furrowed.

'When did you cut that?'

'This afternoon.'

Alex sat down, hands clasped in her lap. 'A year to the day: I'm sorry, I should have been more thoughtful. I'd never have booked those people in if I'd thought about it properly.'

John-Cody patted her hand. 'Don't worry about it, Alex. You told me the date ages ago. I should have thought about it too. Was she very fed up?'

'No, she was pleased about you giving them your half of the house. That was good of you. Bree's a sweet wee girl and she's going to need her own space. I wonder who's going to look after her while the mother's in Dusky?'

'There's always someone needing dollars. Her mother will work it out.'

'She's a bright child. Very English: it'll be interesting to see how she fits in at school.'

John-Cody stood up. 'I figure I better get down to the pub and apologize personally.' He blew out his cheeks. 'Thanks, Alex. I don't know what I'd have done without you this past year.'

'More work maybe.'

He screwed up his face. 'You think?'

'I don't know, but talking of which . . .' She crooked her index finger at him and led the way to the inner office, where she indicated the board on the wall. John-Cody stared at the dates, locations and numbers.

'Charters?'

'We're coming into the season. What're you going to do – sit on your butt all summer?'

He stared at the bookings, the numbers of guests and the costs. He had run barely a handful of charters since Mahina died and they had been the few scientific studies they were committed to. The idea of tourists on the boat suddenly appalled him.

'I'm not sure I can do it any more, Alex.'

'Then sell to Ned Pole.'

John-Cody stared wide-eyed at her.

'*He*'s trying to make a living.' She shook her head at him. 'Boss, you're the most knowledgeable man in Fiordland, but everything you know you learned from Mahina. You can't let her down now she's dead.'

'What about crew?' His lips were dry and cracked.

'Jonah, of course.'

'Of course.' Again he looked at the dates. 'Next week.'

'Dusky and Preservation Inlet: it's as good a time to start up again as any. I've had new leaflets printed and they're working. Our web site is buzzing; most of it's referred business from previous clients. Between the two of you, you created a network of people who actually give a damn. You can't stop now.' She laughed then. 'Besides, this is the first season where we'll make a profit. It'd be a real shame to pass up that opportunity.'

John-Cody rubbed his chin with a palm. 'Does that mean you're here for the duration?'

'I'm here just as long as you want me. I'll never have Mahina's system, but I did spend twenty years in business. I think I can handle things. You just drive the boat, eh? Leave the rest to me.'

John-Cody was trembling; he was not at all sure he could go on. Right now he felt weak, vulnerable, lost. 'We'll talk about it,' he said. 'Can you lock up?'

'Don't I always?'

'Thanks.'

He was at the door when she called him back. 'Where are you sleeping tonight?'

He looked at the couch. 'There, I guess.'

'And tomorrow? I'm not having you sleeping in my office every night.'

'I'll probably go back over the hill.'

'If you do you'll have to come back to organize the stores for next week's charter.'

John-Cody rolled his eyes skywards. 'You'll be the death of me, Alex.'

'Somehow I don't think so.'

Libby and Bree ate dinner in the restaurant. They ordered steak and chips and served themselves from the salad bar. The restaurant was busy, but they got a table in the window and watched the sun setting over the Hunter Mountains. Next door, the bar was pretty raucous. Libby had to go through to get herself a drink when she could not catch the barman's eye from the restaurant side and she picked her way between the assortment of farmers and tunnel diggers in mucky jeans and gumboots. They smiled and winked and exchanged glances. Libby had been through it a hundred times before, though southern man, from what she'd seen so far, was way out there on the edge of things. She bought a beer and as she turned she saw a particularly tall man wearing an ankle-length stockman's coat watching her from where he stood by the pool table. He wore an Akubra cowboy hat high on his head, and his tanned face was gnarled like old wood. He lifted his pint glass. Libby nodded to him, thought no more about it and went back to the restaurant.

No sooner had she sat down than the man appeared in the doorway, spied them and came over. He stood for a moment at their table. Libby looked up at him and he smiled. He was very tall, well over six feet and slim, and he wore square-toed cowboy boots that made him look like something out of the old west. She noticed a scimitar-shaped scar at his left eye.

'You must be Dr Bass, the scientist.' His accent was Australian, friendly but harsher than those of the New Zealanders she had spoken to.

'That's right.' She shook his hand when he offered it.

'Nehemiah Pole.' He smiled again and winked at Bree. 'My mates call me Ned.' He sat in a vacant chair without being invited and rested his elbows on the table. 'And what's your name, little lady?'

Bree went red, looked at her mother and swallowed a mouthful of chips. 'Bree,' she said quietly.

Libby laid her fork down and looked sideways at Pole: she could smell the wax in his coat, thick in her throat like linseed.

'What can I do for you, Mr Pole?'

'Oh, I'm just saying hello. I see Alex dropped you here instead of Gib's place.' He twisted his mouth down at the corners. 'I figure the homestay's not ready yet, eh? Gib's lost the plot lately, poor bloke. Not his fault of course, but there you go.' He sat back. 'I came over because I reckon you're going to need a boat while you're here.'

'You knew I was coming then?'

'Everyone knew you were coming, Dr Bass. DoC put a moratorium on marine mammal viewing permits while you carry out your research.'

'In Dusky Sound?'

'In any of the sounds. Nobody can get a permit while you're here.'

Libby pursed her lips and nodded. 'That makes sense.'

'Not if you're running a tour boat,' he said rue-fully. 'But that's another story. I thought I'd let you know I can lease you a boat if you want something to get you around. I reckon you'll be basing yourself at the Supper Cove hut, up at the head of the sound there.'

'To tell you the truth I've not thought about it. I've got other things to figure out first.'

'Like school, eh?' Pole smiled across the table, showing white teeth. 'You'll be just fine, Bree. They're a good bunch of kids in Te Anau.' He looked at Libby again and fished in his pocket for a card. 'Anyway, give me a call when you want the boat. I can get you a tow to Dusky if you need it.'

Libby took the card. 'Thanks but I think I've already got that bit organized.'

'With Gibbs? You be careful—' He broke off. 'Ignore me, I shouldn't be saying that.'

'Saying what exactly?'

Pole stood up. 'Oh, it's nothing.' He turned to go, then paused and smiled again only this time his eyes were cold. 'Ask him why the *Kori*'s got a roller-reefing jib.' He tipped his hat, then sauntered across the restaurant once more.

Bree wrinkled her nose at her mother. 'What's a roller-reefing jib?'

'A jib is a sail, darling. Apart from that I couldn't tell you.'

John-Cody walked into the Beehive and nodded to a couple of farmers he knew. AJ, the ginger-headed barman, was serving and he poured him a pint of beer.

'Have you got that scientist next door?' John-Cody asked.

'He most certainly has.'

John-Cody recognized Pole's voice from behind him. He had seen him leaning over a pool cue when he walked in. Slowly he turned and looked up at him. A good three inches taller, Pole at fifty-two was still at his fighting weight: the big man in the Te Anau basin. During nine years of shooting deer from helicopters he had gained the reputation of being invincible. When sons and husbands and brothers were dropping in such numbers that Te Anau was dubbed 'Widow City', Pole was shooting deer, making big bucks and surviving. Twice he was in a chopper when it had to auto-rotate because the engine gave out and twice he walked away from the wreck. He lost four pilots and two fellow shooters but each time he had survived. People began to think he bore a charmed life. Mahina thought it much more likely that he had a pact with the devil. As far as John-Cody knew, Pole had been brought up in Cairns, Australia. He was a veteran of the Australian Special Air Service and particularly proud of his Vietnam War record.

'Listen, mate. I heard you had a bad day and I feel

for you,' Pole said quietly. 'But you could give a place a bad name. Nobody's more sorry about Mahina than I am, but you can't go letting people down. This is a tourist town, word gets around and people get tarred with the same brush. You either do it properly or make way for somebody else.'

John-Cody looked him in the eye, wrinkled pockets of flesh redder than the tan of his face. 'You know what, Ned? I don't need a lecture from you.'

'I reckon not. But somebody's got to say something. You're lucky that woman's as accommodating as she is.'

John-Cody held his gaze. 'I'm here now.'

'Yep, you are.' Pole took a black cigar from his pocket. 'But for how much longer? Your heart's not in it, Gib. You know it's not. Get out while the going's good. You know our offer stands.'

John-Cody took tobacco from his pouch and rolled a cigarette. He always felt awkward in Pole's presence. After what had happened between them, the fact that Pole had never openly blamed him when so many others did made it harder to dislike the man. If he analysed it objectively he didn't dislike him. Pole was all right as a human being, though there had always been a sense of testiness between them, even before the accident: just rivalry perhaps, two personalities each as strong as the other but on different sides of the game.

Pole lit his cigarette for him and snapped out the match. 'Think on, mate, eh.'

'I'm not going to sell you my boat or the wharf. You know I'm not, Ned. Not now, not ever.'

Pole leaned on one of the tall tables. 'Never say never, mate. You don't know how things can change. Besides, you'll see sense in the end. You're getting in the way of people's jobs. Progress, Gib, progress.'

'Is that what you call it?'

'It's our livelihood, mate: tourism. You and me and everyone else round here. Think on that. The offer's a fair one, and you know we're good for the money.' He chinked glasses and went back to the pool table.

John-Cody could see a woman and a girl he didn't recognize eating dessert at a window table in the restaurant. Beyond them the sun was down, the lake gloomy and laced with shadows. He'd let them finish before he went over to apologize. Pole was right, he should have been here or at least he shouldn't have forgotten, but he had had his head up his butt for a year now and today was the worst of all. He smoked the cigarette and his hand trembled slightly.

He studied his guests through the hatch. The woman faced him: he couldn't place her age, late twenties maybe. She was very attractive, jet black hair, dark eyes and a dark tan to her skin. She wore a T-shirt and jeans and from this angle she looked trim and fit. Her daughter was sitting with her back to him so he could not see her face, but she was skinny with blond hair. Must take after the father, he thought. He crushed out his cigarette and went through.

Libby saw him coming, a tallish man trimly built with a battered face and grey eyes. His hair hung to his shoulders and it looked as though it had been cut with an open razor. He wore a denim shirt rolled back at the cuffs, jeans and lace-up boots. She couldn't take her eyes off his haircut. He stopped at their table and smiled, eyes bunched and twinkling in the lamplight.

'Dr Bass?'

Libby nodded.

'John-Cody Gibbs: I am so sorry.'

Libby moved back in her chair to make room for him. John-Cody sat down and looked at Bree. 'You must be Bree. It's very nice to meet you.'

Bree smiled at him. 'I met your dog. She's lovely.'

'So Alex told me. Apparently she's pining for you already.' Bree's face fell and he laughed. 'Don't worry, I told Sierra she'd see you tomorrow.' He winked at Libby then looked back at Bree. 'Now tell me something,' he said, leaning on his elbows. 'How did you get such a pretty name?'

Bree went a little red and she sat on her hands, looking down at her plate.

'It's actually Breezy,' Libby said for her.

Bree looked up. 'That's what I was christened.'

'You weren't actually christened, Bree.'

'Well, it's what's written on my birth certificate then.' Bree smiled at John-Cody again. 'It's because I breezed into life.'

'Is that so?' John-Cody glanced at Libby.

'Thirty-three minutes from first contraction to birth,' Libby told him. 'It was the easiest half hour of my life.'

John-Cody laughed and folded his arms across his chest. 'Look,' he said, 'I'm paying for the motel tonight. I've already spoken to the owners and they'll bill me. So don't worry about it.'

'You didn't have to do that.'

'My pleasure, I'm the one that screwed up.' He smiled and got up. 'Anyway, I'll leave you in peace. Any time you like, tomorrow the place will be ready and yours is the first door as you look at it.'

102

'Can I explore the garden?' Bree asked him.

'Bree, you can make it your own.'

'It looks fantastic.'

'It's pretty wild. I've not done a whole lot to it just lately.'

'Where will you be living?' Bree asked him. 'In the bit that we were meant to have?'

John-Cody lifted his eyebrows. 'I live on the boat pretty much these days. I'll show you some time.' He looked at Libby then. 'Anything you want to talk about – I'll be around tomorrow.'

'Thank you: and it's very kind of you to give us your half of the house.' She smiled at him and shook hands. He touched an index finger to his temple then pointed it at Bree. 'Take it easy, Breezy.'

They both watched him go then looked across the table at each other. 'What a terrible haircut,' Libby said.

'Yes, but he was very nice. Men never know how to cut their hair properly, Mum. You know that.'

Libby laughed.

'The other man was all right, too,' Bree went on. 'What a name though: imagine calling someone *Nehemiah*.'

'Yes,' Libby said. 'It's almost as bad as calling them Breezy.'

FOUR

Ned Pole left the bar and climbed into his twin-cab Mitsubishi. He sat for a moment, watching the shadows spread across the lake and thinking about the scientist and her daughter. He had spoken at length with both the council and the Department of Conservation when her appointment was published in the newspapers. His backers had got wind of it and had been on the phone right away, demanding to know how it would affect their plans. His wife was in the US at the time and he told them not to worry, that it was nothing he couldn't handle. He had appeased them for a while, but they had reminded him of what he already knew: he needed this deal much more than they did. They could go elsewhere and do something similar; he had his Australian debts to pay off before he was made bankrupt. They reminded him that John-Cody Gibbs had been the last submitter in opposition and what they didn't need now was another one.

He started the engine and revved it for a moment, before grinding in first gear and pulling out onto the road for Te Anau. Tom Blanch drove by in his beaten-up Triumph and Pole nodded to him. Why couldn't Gibbs have just stayed fishing with Blanch instead of getting off on the environmental kick?

He drove slowly home. There was much on his mind tonight. The fishing boats were doing all right and his one tour boat was attracting customers although he did not have a marine mammal viewing permit. Even without one he still approached the seals and dolphins. A couple of times Gibbs had witnessed him doing so, but he seemed less inclined to have a go about it than he used to be. Mahina's death had changed things for him.

Mahina's death had changed everything and yet Pole didn't feel the sense of freedom he'd thought that he would. She haunted the recesses of his mind as she'd always done. He looked at the crucifix dangling from the rear-view mirror and rebuked himself all over again. She had been beautiful though and he had coveted her like he coveted no other. He thought of his first marriage: the birth of his son and his wife's attitude after. For a long moment the world rolled by unseen and he drove with one hand on the wheel, his mind lost in long and distant shadows.

He snapped out of the reverie and again considered his position. He wanted the *Korimako* and her wharf so he could get people into the floating lodges by sea. If he could procure those two things then his application for Dusky would be pretty much complete.

He turned off the main road just south of Te Anau and nosed up the winding drive that led to his fifteen-acre spread. Jane was in the States and would not be home till the weekend, which pleased him in one way, but it also gave him a lot of time to kick his heels and think. She had left him with pretty much the same ultimatum as his backers and she had more of a point. Thinking of her brought on thoughts of his father and he shook those thoughts away.

Parking the car, he walked towards the house, pausing as Barrio whinnied at him from the top paddock. Pole stood at the fence for a moment and watched him tossing his great black head and pawing the ground into furrows. Barrio had been Eli's horse, a present from Ned on his twenty-first birthday. He saw Eli's face in his mind and closed his eyes tightly. Jane had never known him: they had met and married some time after his death. He looked again at Barrio, a stallion in his prime and barely ridden in five long years.

The house smelled of tanned leather: Jane complained about it, but Pole told her that was the man she had met and married. That was the man her American friends were so keen on. He'd had a gun in his hand since he was five years old, when his father took him pig hunting for the first time in the hills west of Cairns. Pole recalled the sheer delight on the old man's face when he shot that first pig and dipped his hands in blood as he gutted and cleaned the carcass. He was a good shot, the best: a sniper in Vietnam, ensuring a certain amount of safety for the unit he was attached to. When he moved to New Zealand, primarily for the deer hunting, it was not long before every helicopter crew in the Te Anau basin was vying for his services.

Upstairs in his office he ran a grizzled palm over his rifle collection and squinted at some of his deer-head trophies; he looked at his King James Bible and the photograph of Eli, which he always kept side by side. Maybe tomorrow he would ride Barrio.

* * *

Libby phoned the office the following morning and ten minutes later John-Cody arrived in the pick-up truck they had seen parked in the drive. Sierra was in the back and she jumped down as soon as she saw Bree sitting by the roadside waiting. Bree made a tremendous fuss of her and John-Cody lowered the tailgate of the truck then went to help Libby with the luggage. The morning was clear and crisp and bees hovered over the heads of purple flowers; spring in Southland with the sun high above the stillness of the lake. The Cathedrals were climbing silver spires and the only cloud, puffed cumulus, clustered far in the west. Libby thought John-Cody looked drawn and tired as he lifted their bags into the back of the truck: his face was lined, a little red about the eyes as if sleep had evaded him most of the night.

He parked under the carport and Bree asked him about the phone box. He told her that it used to stand at the corner of Home and View Street and when they sited the new one down by the shop he brought it home for posterity. At the door he laid their cases down and fished the keys from his pocket. Libby noticed his hands were trembling slightly as he fitted the key in the lock.

The house smelled of Mahina: it hit him as he set foot over the threshold. He should have come here alone first, rather than just phoning the cleaner to make sure everything was ready. The stillness in the room was the same stillness he had experienced a year ago when the morepork called and Mahina joined her ancestors. The wooden walls seemed dark and cold and the whole place had a hollow feel about it. All the furniture was there, together with the pictures, except for those of him and Mahina which he had asked Lynda to put in a sealed cardboard box and leave in his guitar shed. The bookshelves still stood against the far side of the kitchen counter, which split the living room in two. The door to the bathroom beyond the kitchen was open and he could smell bleach and soap. It was empty and yet in the same moment it was as if Mahina still dwelt here.

Libby moved behind him and took in the contours of the room properly for the first time. It had a wonderful atmosphere, and she knew they could live here: there was a cosy cabin feel that Bree would love, a warmth and a sense of peace. The fireplace was stacked with fresh wood, the mantelpiece covered with shells and trinkets and bits of stone; the pictures that dominated it were of the sea and creatures of the sea. She could smell the essence of the house, the happiness that had lived here.

'This is lovely,' she said.

'I'm glad you like it.' John-Cody looked at Bree. 'There's a single bed in this room.'

He pushed open the door immediately to the right and Bree gazed on a sun-filled room with a wide bed and a red duvet covering it, bookshelves and cupboards and a massive photograph of a Californian otter dominating the bedhead. John-Cody closed his fingers over the tangi-wai stone in his pocket.

'Look, I'll leave you guys to it,' he said. 'If you need to go to Te Anau feel free to take the Ute. She's a bit ropy but she works. There should be fruit juice and coffee, milk and stuff in the fridge.' He smiled at Libby. 'I'll be down at the office if you need me.'

He left them then and walked stiffly across the road,

tension in his back and shoulders. That had been harder than he'd thought. Logic had told him to let them have his half of the house, as he doubted he would ever set foot inside it again. But standing there in the doorway with memories of that final night flooding back and the scent of her everywhere: suddenly the presence of strangers had been an invasion. Perhaps he should have just put them next door after all.

No, Mahina would not have liked that. She would have approved of his action: a young girl like Bree needed far more than just a bunk bed against a wall for a bedroom. He walked down to the office. All at once the sky was clouding above the mountains, rainy weather rolling in from the Tasman.

Alex was on the phone and John-Cody plugged the kettle in for coffee and waved through the window to Jean Grady as she walked up the road. Two fishermen drove by in the direction of Pearl Harbour and he stood on the porch smoking a cigarette and watching the white-headed waves scuff the surface of the lake. Alex had put food out and the birds were gathered on the porch and between the flax and cabbage trees in the self-styled wetlands.

He thought about the charter Alex had organized for the following week. Eight guests. Could he do it? It had been a long time. Perhaps he could. Alex was right: Mahina would never forgive him if he just quit now. He thought about the mood of the guests after each trip was over, the camaraderie that was engendered after four or five days on a small boat. He thought about how some people changed after they had been up the Camelot River or listened to the sound of silence in Hall's Arm, with either sun or rain beating down from above. He thought of Commander Peak, where he could put the *Korimako* within a few feet of a thousand-foot waterfall, which pounded the fiord so hard the spray littered the deck.

Alex moved next to him. 'Two people have cancelled for next week.'

John-Cody was almost relieved. 'So that's just six. Hardly worth doing.'

Alex laughed, folded her arms and looked at him with a glint in her eye. 'Boss, if you're not going to run any more tours we might as well pack up and go home. What would you do then? Go back to fishing? Tom drives the Z boats now. You wouldn't have a partner. We've got half a million dollars' worth of boat in Deep Cove. You might as well sell it to Ned Pole and his backers.'

'No,' John-Cody snapped at her. 'No way: not the boat or the wharf. I'm not selling him anything.' He blew on his coffee. 'And I'm not going to roll over and lie down over Dusky Sound either.'

'Fine. Then we run the charters or let the *Korimako* rust.' Alex flared her nostrils at him. 'You have to stop feeling sorry for yourself, boss. You had over twenty wonderful years with the best woman I've ever known. She was beautiful, intelligent and passionate. She loved you more than any man deserves to be loved. She's gone now, but you had the best time with her. Treasure it. Don't tarnish it now that it's over.' She pushed herself upright. 'Most people don't get to taste that kind of emotion for a single day, never mind twenty years.'

John-Cody smarted, colour prickling his cheeks. He watched her back as she went through to the inner office and then heard her begin to tap at

110

the computer keyboard. He followed her and looked at the itinerary: seven days in Dusky Sound and Preservation Inlet. 'OK,' he said. 'What do I need from Te Anau?'

Bree unpacked her clothes, setting them neatly in her drawers with Sierra at her feet. She was enjoying this much more than she'd thought she would and much more than she was telling her mother. The cabin was like something from *Little House on the Prairie* and Sierra trotted at her heels like a young puppy. The lake, the beach and that white-barked tree were wonderful, and she couldn't wait to get her stuff unpacked so she could explore the garden. Her mother had the back bedroom, which had two swing doors like a saloon in a western movie. The window was massive and looked out on a pink-barked fuchsia tree that peeled perpetually. John-Cody had told her it did that to keep the moss from killing it.

Her mother was still unpacking and Bree called through that she had finished and was going outside. It was still warm but the sky was clouding over and it looked as though it was going to rain again. She didn't mind so much now they were no longer travelling. She made her way round the front of the house, where John-Cody had a little table set between two fixed wooden chairs just out of the rainfall area under the eaves. Next door jutted out a little bit further and the eaves were hung with wind chimes and bird tables. The front garden was a mass of shrubs and plants and all kinds of trees. She made her way under the carport to the back garden. A woodpile covered with pale blue tarpaulin was set on a raised section of grass to the left and Bree noticed the axe sticking up out of the chopping block. There was no such thing as central heating down here, only the open fire. She wondered what that would be like in the winter.

John-Cody had told them it didn't snow much, but it could get bitterly cold. The back garden dropped away from the house, studded with trees and little hedges and flax plants. She made out a pond and a greenhouse and at least two sheds. There was a bench table and chairs like you might see at a picnic area in a park and she trailed her index finger over the wood. Sierra walked alongside her, tongue lolling and dribbling gobs of saliva. Something caught her attention, a rabbit perhaps, and she darted off into a copse of trees which separated the garden from the main road. Bree wandered between tree and shrub and listened to the birdsong above her head, strange calls that she didn't recognize and some that she did: she had seen thrushes and blackbirds and sparrows here, along with the silvereye and tui. The pigeons were huge and green-breasted and much more attractive than those in England or France.

Sierra barked. Bree looked round and saw John-Cody coming down the little slope to the pond. 'What you doing, Breezy? Exploring?'

'Yes. It's a huge garden and so different everywhere. It must have taken ages to get it this way.'

'Twenty-two years, near as makes no difference.' He smiled. 'Sweet as, though, isn't it?'

'Oh yeah, it's brilliant.'

'Have you seen the hut?'

Bree shook her head, then followed him between two giant ferns and past the compost heap. He led her beyond another woodpile and the caravan, broken down and battered now, standing against the fence to next door. He pointed to a green hut with sliding glass doors, a concrete porch and a corrugated plastic roof. 'Have a look.'

Bree opened the sliding door and saw a room with a bed and a desk and its own bathroom. Pictures of dolphins bedecked the walls and there were little ornaments on the table; two smaller windows dominated the far wall.

'More bed and breakfast room?' she asked, looking back.

'Yes. But I don't rent it any more.' He swept back his hair. 'You can come and go as you please. Make it your den if you like.'

'Are you sure? Oh wow. Wait till I tell Mum.'

'Tell Mum what?' Libby appeared between the ferns and stood there in shorts and T-shirt, a woollen cardigan round her shoulders.

'Look, Mum.' Bree showed her the hut. 'John-Cody said I could use it as my den. It's got a shower and toilet and everything.'

Libby took a closer look and then she glanced at John-Cody, who was sitting on a tree stump rolling a cigarette. 'Thank you,' she said.

Her eyes told him there was more in that thanks than he realized, but he didn't know why. He wondered what sort of problems Libby had encountered in coming here. She seemed far too qualified for the work that DoC and the university were offering: normally people who were working for their doctorates did this sort of thing, not those who had them already.

He licked the paper down on his cigarette and stuck it in the corner of his mouth. All at once a thought struck him. 'When do you need to get Bree into school?' he asked.

Bree looked at her mother and her face fell. Clouds again on her horizon when they had been banished by the magic of the garden.

'As soon as I can, I guess,' Libby said. 'She's missed a lot already.'

'Not that much, Mum.' Bree looked at John-Cody then. 'We came out during half-term so I haven't missed that much.'

'Why d'you ask?' Libby said.

'Well, I was just thinking: the bulk of your research is going to be in Dusky Sound. I've got a seven-day trip to Dusky and Preservation Inlet this weekend. We had two guests drop out this morning. Why don't you and Bree take their places?' He smiled at Bree. 'Give you a bit of a holiday before starting a new school.' He looked back at Libby again. 'And it would let you see the lie of the land from my boat. Dusky's a big place, Libby: three hundred and sixty islands.'

'That sounds fantastic, but what about the cost?' Libby sat down on the wooden-backed chair on the porch. She took her last Camel from a packet and snapped open her lighter.

'It won't cost you much. Alex has already bought all the food. There's just a ninety-dollar charge to cross the lake two ways. I use the Southland Tours boats: it's easier than running a small one of my own.' He lifted his hands. 'That's it, though. You could give me a hand now if you like: come down to Te Anau and pick up the stores with me. I could do with the help and I can show you around at the same time.'

They drove into Te Anau, the three of them hunched together on the big bench seat of the pick-up or Ute as John-Cody called it. He drove with one hand on the wheel, a Native American bracelet of bead and bone at his wrist. Sierra rode in the back, standing with her head above the cab, barking at the few cars they passed.

The drive was north, twenty kilometres with farm-land on the right and scrub and the Wairau River on their left. They could not see it from the road, but John-Cody promised to take them down on the way back. Libby rode with her arm out the passenger window and Bree in between the two of them. John-Cody could smell Libby's scent across the breadth of the cab and it occurred to him that no woman had been in here since Mahina. She used to ride pressed as close to him as she could get without interfering with the driving. He smiled at the memory: pain in his breast but suddenly it was fondness rather than mourning. It had been like that this past year: some-times the pain was so bad all he wanted to do was kill himself and at other times something would prick his consciousness with a fondness that made him laugh out loud.

They came to the Supply Bay turn and he slowed, thought for a moment then swung left onto the dirt track. Libby frowned at him.

'Supply Bay,' he told her. 'It's where the barge will ship your boat across the lake. I might as well show you where it's at while we're passing.'

What boat? Libby thought. I haven't got a boat yet. She thought of Nehemiah Pole and his offer of some kind of launch for her research. She would cross that bridge when she came to it. The first thing to do was to get Bree settled and into school.

Libby had not dared to hope that things would go this well. Since their chat at Singapore airport Bree had been easier, as if she accepted that the move was not actually selfishness on her mother's part, but a matter of survival. School could be awkward though: less so for Bree than for other children perhaps because she was used to changes, but nonetheless nerve-racking for both of them. Bree had to deal with new classmates, the fact that she was English and that her mother would be in Dusky Sound for long periods at a time. Libby had to find someone suitable to look after her and deal with the sense of loss she always experienced when the two of them were parted. It was another bridge she would cross when she got to it. Notwithstanding her worries about Bree, she was excited about the work, and right now John-Cody's offer of a boat trip was just what the doctor ordered. Bree had been really up for it and it would give them quality time together before reality set in.

Libby glanced sideways at John-Cody as they bumped and lurched over the gravelled track that wound down to the lake. He was watching the road and his face looked old yet handsome in a grizzled sort of way. His hair did nothing to enhance the overall image, mind you, and she wondered why it had been cut so badly. He seemed to take care with the rest of him. Apart from the ragged edges, his hair was grey and wavy and thick and his features were tanned like oiled leather, lined in deep furrows about the eyes and mouth. His nose was strong and his chin square and dimpled. He must have felt her glance because he looked at her suddenly, not smiling. She looked away, feeling the burning sensation in her own cheeks, amazed at herself for staring so openly.

John-Cody worked the wheel through his hands and stopped the truck on a concrete wharf with two flat barges moored against it. The wind had picked up now and the clouds were low and purple, smothering the Hunter Mountains to the south. They could see the village across the lake and John-Cody pointed to the barges.

'When we get you a launch sorted out we'll load it on my trailer. The electricity company will take it across the lake and we'll drive over the hill to Deep Cove, then if you like I can give you a tow to Dusky in the *Korimako*.'

'That would be brilliant, thank you.'

'That other man said he'd be able to rent Mum a boat,' Bree said.

'What other man?' John-Cody looked down at her.

'Nehemiah Pole.'

'You met him, did you?'

Libby nodded. 'In the restaurant just before you arrived.'

'He's got some good boats.' John-Cody was gazing through the windscreen, scattered now with raindrops.

'He told us to ask you about your boat,' Bree said suddenly.

'Bree.' Libby clicked her tongue.

John-Cody looked round. 'It's OK. What about my boat?'

'I don't remember exactly,' Bree said. 'Something about reefing.'

117

'Roller reefing,' Libby said. 'The jib or something.'

John-Cody started the engine. The waves were suddenly fuller in his mind, white against the black of the rocks as they steered west of the Hare's Ears, and Eli was out on deck. 'Roller reefing means the sail is self-furling.'

Libby was watching him, leaning against the window which was closed now against rain that drifted off the lake. She felt awkward all at once. John-Cody's eyes bunched at the corners as if too much sun was in them.

'Ned's referring to an accident at sea.' He put the truck in gear. 'A jib hank got caught in the forestay. One of my crew went overboard while trying to straighten it out.' He gunned the truck up the hill. 'His name was Elijah Pole: Nehemiah's son.'

They were silent then, a fractured space between them as they drove down the road to Te Anau. Bree felt suddenly very sad: she touched John-Cody on the arm where he held the wheel. 'I'm sorry,' she said.

'Hey.' John-Cody smiled. 'Forget about it. Accidents happen at sea. A lot of time has passed since then. People blamed me at the time but then they were bound to.'

'But it wasn't your fault,' Bree said. 'You said it was an accident.'

'I was the skipper, Bree. Technically it was my responsibility.'

'And Ned Pole blamed you,' Libby said.

John-Cody sighed. 'He's hardly my biggest fan, and I guess he blamed me, yes. But he kept quiet about it. Or at least he didn't say anything to my face. Other folk did, but not Nehemiah. I've always wondered why.'

They drove on and he pointed across the fields to their right. 'Manapouri airport,' he said.

They saw a dirt road leading beyond a five-bar gate that was locked with a chain. What looked like a prefab building stood at the head of the track and a windsock beyond that.

'Bigger than Heathrow,' Libby said with a laugh.

John-Cody laughed too. 'Mount Cook fly in from Queenstown when the weather permits it.' He gestured beyond the airport. 'There's a wonderful place just the other side called Kepler Mire, an intricate series of marshlands that's a protected area now. Amazing from the air. If you go up in the float-plane you'll be able to see it, a network of silver lines like mercury in the earth.' He looked at Libby again. 'I don't know what your budget's like but a float-plane is the quickest way in and out of Dusky. Once you've got your boat down there I guess you'll want to leave it at Supper Cove.'

They were coming into Te Anau now and John-Cody pointed to a wooden building between some conifer trees on their left: it was the local Department of Conservation office. They swung left on Lake Front Drive and headed past various motels and a backpackers' hostel: John-Cody showed them the underwater trout aquarium and told Bree it would cost her a dollar to visit, roughly 30p. On the left Lake Te Anau was mottled with whitened dots of spray where the rain bounced hard now, slapping off the water like concrete. They saw a floatplane moored alongside a wooden wharf and a scenic flight helicopter tied down against the wind. Nobody was flying today and one of the pilots waved to John-Cody as they drove past.

John-Cody fumbled in his shirt pocket for the list that Alex had given him and Bree flattened it so he could look. 'Shopping and laundry,' he said. 'Sounds familiar.'

'Do you run lots of tours?' Libby asked as they parked in front of the supermarket.

John-Cody thought about that. The season had been chock-a-block when Mahina was alive: trips running into each other with barely a day in between to restock the stores and clean the boat. 'Not so many these days,' he said, and opened the driver's door.

The supermarket manager was ready for them, a small man with a deep suntan and white hair combed over a bald spot.

'G'day, Gib,' he said. 'Alex phoned ahead so all you have to do is load it in the truck.'

'You'll bill us?'

'Of course.' The manager smiled at Libby and John-Cody introduced them and told him what she was going to do.

'That's interesting,' the manager said. 'The fishermen have known about the pod in Dusky for years. It's a pity it has to take someone with letters after their name to verify it.'

Libby laughed. 'Not for me, it's not.'

'I'm sorry, I didn't mean to sound . . .'

'Don't worry, I'm not offended. I know what you meant.'

She looked at the revolving cigarette dispenser above the checkout. 'You don't sell Camel Regulars, do you?'

'I'm afraid not.'

'You should give up, Mum,' Bree said, her mouth turned down at the corners.

120

Libby bought a pack of cigarettes and stuffed them in the pocket of her shorts. Then she helped Bree and John-Cody load the boxes into the back of the truck.

'There's no grog on the boat,' he told her, 'at least none provided. There's an off licence over the road if you want any.'

'What's grog?' Bree asked.

'Alcohol.' Libby shook her head. 'I'll be all right. I might pick up some wine tomorrow.'

They climbed back in the truck and drove to the fruit and vegetable shop on Milford Road, then turned into the industrial estate road and stopped outside the meat wholesalers. Libby and Bree waited in the truck while John-Cody picked up the fresh meat order and stowed it carefully in the cool boxes. After that it was Fiordland Laundry for the bedding they would need for the bunks. John-Cody got back behind the wheel and blew out his cheeks. 'Well, I don't know about you, but I fancy a flat white in the Olive Tree.'

'Flat white?' Libby squinted at him.

'Coffee.'

'That's a great idea. But could you show me the high school first?'

He smiled. 'Sure, it's on the way back.'

Bree watched carefully as they drove back down the main street and turned onto Howden Street. The school was a series of grey and green buildings on the right-hand side of the road. Children in grey and green uniforms were milling about on the forecourt and playing fields. John-Cody pulled over and switched off the engine.

'Do you want to go in? I know the headmaster

pretty well. Mahina used to teach an ecology class from time to time.'

Bree looked at him then. 'Was Mahina your wife?'

'Yes. After a fashion anyway: we lived together for twenty-two years.'

'She's dead now, isn't she?'

'Bree.' Libby went very red, but John-Cody lifted a palm.

'It's OK. Yes, she's dead, Bree. She died just over a year ago.' He looked beyond her at Libby. 'Do you want to go in?'

'Now's as good a time as any, I suppose.'

John-Cody opened the driver's door and Bree slid across the seat on his side. They walked up the concourse and Bree felt every eye upon her. She had been through this many times before, other people's scrutiny, and yet she always had the same sense of dread in her stomach. Involuntarily almost, she reached for her mother's hand.

John-Cody knew everyone, or at least that's how it seemed. Most of the kids yelled out to him and they called him Gib or Gibby as if he were an old friend. The teachers they met en route to the principal's office called him Gib, although some of the women used John-Cody and Libby could see concern in their eyes. She realized then the kind of position this man must have had in the community.

She had noticed it in the supermarket and the vegetable wholesalers, and the women at the laundry had all looked slightly gooey-eyed at him. Was it his loss that moved them or something more maybe? She had never seen so many people taking such an interest. It's a small town, she told herself. He's been here for years. He's a fixture, that's all.

The principal was a small man named Peters. He had grey hair neatly combed back from his face and a thin moustache sprawled the length of his top lip. He looked across his desk at them as John-Cody made the introductions.

'I'll meet you outside,' he said. 'See you around, Mike.'

'Good as. Take care, Gib, and give my best to Jonah.'

'I'll do that.'

Bree watched Peters as he sat down again, fisted his hands under his chin and looked at her. 'Well, Breezy, is it?' He lifted one eyebrow.

'We call her Bree,' Libby told him.

'Bree then. What's your favourite subject?'

'I haven't got one.' Bree shifted forward in her seat. 'I like science, I suppose. I must take after my mum in something.' She glanced at her mother then back at him again. Clear-eyed, she spoke with confidence. 'I like all subjects.'

'Bree's been to school in quite a few countries,' Libby explained. 'I don't know if that's a good or bad thing really. My job takes me around the world a lot.'

'Can you speak any languages?' Peters asked Bree.

'French and Spanish fluently.'

'Really?' He sat back and drummed his fingers on the desk. 'Well, there's not much call for either of those here, although we are a tourist town. We do teach Japanese, though.'

Bree's eyebrows shot up. 'Wow. That sounds great.'

'What about sport?'

Bree shrugged.

Libby explained that she had never been that sport-minded. Peters looked at her then.

'This is New Zealand, Dr Bass. Everyone's sport-minded.' He turned to Bree again. 'The girls play the same sports as the boys, and that includes rugby. You'll be expected to join in.'

Bree didn't say anything, trying to keep the fear from her face. She hated games, had always done so: the only thing she had been vaguely good at was lacrosse and they only played that in the school at Vimereux. The thought of being flattened in the mud with a dozen girls climbing on top of her was appalling. Libby sensed her reaction and quickly intervened. She explained that they had the trip to Dusky Sound to make and then Bree would begin lessons.

Peters looked less than impressed. 'The half-term holiday is over, Dr Bass. She really should be in school.'

'Yes, I know that, Mr Peters.' Libby looked evenly at him. 'But my research is going to keep me in Dusky Sound a lot and Bree needs to know where I am. Her life's been turned upside down just lately and it's important she has a bit of a break before she starts again.'

'Even so, it's not good to miss lessons. The curriculum waits for no-one.'

'Bree's a bright girl, Mr Peters. She arrived in France not knowing the language and a year later she was fluent and in the top three of her class.' Libby got up and held out her hand. 'We'll see you after we get back.'

'All right.' He shook her hand. 'If you're going to be away a lot, though, we'll need to know details of Bree's child care.'

Outside, John-Cody was waiting for them in the truck and he leaned over and opened the passenger door. 'Everything OK?'

Bree made a face at him. 'They're going to make me play rugby.'

'No worries: you'll be wearing an All Black jersey in no time.'

They had coffee in a little restaurant at the back of a small parade of shops, and were joined by a wild-eyed Maori with long black hair tied at the neck. John-Cody introduced him as Jonah, Mahina's younger brother, and told them Jonah would be cooking on the boat.

'So you better eat it,' Jonah said, thinning his eyes at Bree. 'Or I might just eat you. You look like you'd make a good feed.'

Bree looked terrified and Jonah laughed out loud. John-Cody rested his chin in his palm and looked at Libby. 'As you can see, Jonah has no children of his own.'

'I'm sorry,' Jonah said to Bree. 'I don't mean anything. Ignore me.'

'I will.'

'Good on you.' He looked at Libby then. 'Forgive me,' he said. 'It's just that the old man here has been perched on that boat for so long I never thought we'd leave Deep Cove again. I'm excited, that's all.'

John-Cody looked at him. 'I'm glad you're here,' he said. 'I need a hand to load the stores.'

They drove back to Manapouri and dropped Libby and Bree off at the house, then John-Cody and Jonah took the truck down to Pearl Harbour and transferred the stores to the boat that would ferry them across the lake in the morning.

'That Libby looks like one sweet wahine, Gib,' Jonah commented as they loaded the last of the boxes.

John-Cody leaned on the rail and looked across the inlet where evergreen trees shrouded the far bank. 'You think so? I can't say I've noticed.'

Back at the house Libby made some phone calls and Bree went into the garden. She took her paper and envelopes down to the hut and lay on the bed. She could hear the leaves being blown about on the roof above her head.

Dear Dad,

Well, we've arrived in Manapouri and it's not as bad as I thought it was going to be. We've met this really cool guy called John-Cody Gibbs. I think you'd like him: he's old and his haircut is awful, far too long, but he's really nice. Sort of quiet and friendly and cool. He's got a boat called the Korimako. *I've got a new room. The house is a bungalow so there are no stairs or anything. Mum's busy, but we're all going on the boat tomorrow to a place called Dusky Sound. I've told you about that before. It's where Mum's going to study dolphins. There's a lot of us going down there tomorrow for a week. I hope I don't get seasick. I'm sure I won't.*

Anyway there's this great dog called Sierra. She's here with me now. I think she likes me. I don't think John-Cody's taken a lot of notice of her lately so she hangs out with me. He can't have because he's been living on his boat and Alex told me that dogs aren't allowed in the

*national park without a special permit. Alex is
cool, she lives by the lake and has this huge
window in her attic. She says I can go round any
time and look at the view. Maybe I will.*

*I've been to my new school but I'm not start-
ing till we get back from Dusky Sound. You
know what a sound is, don't you. Of course you
do. Anyway the school seems OK. I'm going to
learn Japanese and there's a bus so Mum won't
have to take me. I still don't know who's going
to look after me while she's working. At least I'll
have Sierra. She's been staying with Alex, but
John-Cody says she can stay here tonight. This is
her house after all. By the way, I'm writing this
in the hut. That's what it is, a hut, but it's got a
bed and a shower and toilet. John-Cody says I
can use it for a den. He's a really cool guy
actually. Anyway, they play rugby at school, even
the girls. I'm useless at games except lacrosse
and I'm terrified of playing rugby. It's really bad
news, but at least I've got a week on the boat
before I have to think about it. We should see
dolphins and seals and maybe even whales. I'll
write again when I get back.*

Love always, Bree

FIVE

The letter from the bank was what Pole had expected, no more, no less: they wanted their money back and they wanted it soon. Folding it away, he climbed the stairs to his study and stood in the window, looking out across Lake Te Anau. Jane had redesigned this window for him. She was good at things like that, making the most of the house he had built after his first wife took off to Australia with Eli when the boy was nine years old. As soon as he hit eighteen, though, Eli was back in New Zealand, working first with his father then with Gibbs of all people. Pole glanced at his smiling face in the photo on the desk, and wished his son had remained in Australia. To this day his mother blamed him for Eli's death.

Barrio stood in the field and snorted up at him as if he could smell his presence, and Pole went out to the barn where the horse tack was hanging. He led the horse, saddled and jangling his bit, out of the field and walked him in a circle. Jet black and big-boned, he stood over eighteen hands in height; his mane was long and uncut and it flew as he tossed his head in the wind. Pole stepped into the left stirrup and Barrio walked on so he had to hop on one leg before hoisting himself up.

No sooner was he in the saddle than he felt the beast tense to spring away, but Pole had been riding almost as long as he had been walking and he checked Barrio's zeal. He made him walk backwards then sideways, then in a small circle to show him who was in charge. Then he settled into a rising trot towards the road. A grass verge bordered the tarmac virtually all the way to Manapouri, and as they turned right Pole squeezed the horse into a canter.

Now he was in the dust-blown hills of the Northern Territory, riding out after pigs with his father, just a few days before he went to Vietnam. He had been in the army for three years when the war blew up and his father was telling him how to look after himself in the jungle. 'You're a big man, son. Make sure they know it. Don't stand for any nonsense and trust the Lord to guide you.'

He would never forget his father, tall and thin and very upright. His chin jutted at the world and he took the ribbing from his mates about his Sunday churchgoing with a calm assurance, as if he knew things that they did not. He was teetotal and never smoked, but he hunted and fished and was a mean fast bowler for the local cricket team. Pole had watched him take five wickets in two consecutive overs one Saturday afternoon. Expectation surrounded him like an aura. Ned was his only son and he never let him forget it. Stand up straight, boy, and look this world in the eye, was his attitude. Your real reward is in heaven, but God isn't going to thank you for wasting your time down here.

129

Remember the parable of the talents. Get things done, Nehemiah: be somebody I can be proud of.

Pole galloped along the road to Manapouri, feeling Barrio's immense power with every loping stride. He rode low in the saddle, preferring the longer stirrup used by the stockmen rather than the English version. He knew the parable of the talents by heart. Matthew 25: *For the kingdom of heaven is as a man travelling into a far country, who called his own servants, and delivered unto them his goods. And unto one he gave five talents, to another two, and to another one . . . Then he that had received the five talents went and traded with the same, and made them other five talents . . .* He rode on, his father's face in his mind and those words ringing in his head.

Tom Blanch pulled over in his Triumph and Pole reined Barrio in.

'G'day, Ned. That's some kind of horse you got there.' Tom leaned one arm out of the window, his white hair standing up from his forehead, lips hidden in the thickness of his beard.

'I reckon: that old brumby I bought for my son, remember.'

Tom looked beyond Pole to the Murchison Mountains, part of the Southern Alps that straddled the west coast of the South Island.

'How long has it been now?'

'Five years.' Pole let Barrio's head drop and dismounted. From his shirt pocket he took a black cigar and offered it to Tom, who shook his head.

'I'm trying to give it up, mate.' Tom watched him light the cigar, saw the hunted look in his eyes. 'How's business?'

Pole exhaled stiffly. 'Business would be a bloody

'sight better if Gib would withdraw his submission.'

'On Dusky Sound?' Blanch smiled. 'He's not going to do that, Ned.'

Pole looked back at him. 'I don't mind telling you, Tom, I need that activity permit. I mean I really need it. There's so much riding on this deal . . .'

'You know what,' Tom said, 'when you first put that idea forward I never thought you'd get this far. You had the whole bloody town against you.'

'I did to start with, mate.' Pole flicked ash with his third finger and looked at the end of his cigar. 'But people saw sense in the end. This venture's going to bring in a lot of jobs, Tom. People round here need jobs.'

Blanch made a face. 'I hear you, mate, but I hear Gib too. I don't agree with all he says or does but he's my oldest friend.'

Pole half-smiled at him. 'It's a pity he didn't stick to the crayfish boats with you.'

'I reckon.' Blanch lifted his eyebrows. 'He met Mahina though, didn't he?'

Pole nodded, eyes sharp, suddenly looking through him. 'Bewitching, wasn't she?'

'That's one way of putting it.' Tom started his engine. 'I've got to get along, mate.'

Pole touched the brim of his hat, crushed his cigar under his heel and swung back into the saddle.

Libby and Bree walked down to the boat for the lake crossing, and Libby stopped to buy wine in the dairy. Bree had been there already yesterday afternoon, posting the letter to her father in America. The woman who ran the shop had told Bree her name was Mrs Grady and Bree watched her stamp the envelope with a return address before slipping it into the bag for the postman to collect.

Half an hour later they were steaming across the lake and Libby went on deck, where Jonah and John-Cody were sitting. She took the pack of cigarettes she had bought from her pocket and broke the filter off one. Jonah lit it for her, his eyes full of his smile.

'You look pleased with yourself,' she said.

'I'm going over the hill, Libby. My sister's boat: it's been a long time, and the way he's been behaving' – he jerked a thumb at John-Cody – 'I was beginning to think I'd never get back.'

Libby sucked on the cigarette and the wind took the smoke and she watched the waves kick up in their wake. Mahina: a woman she'd heard mentioned many times in the two days they had been here; a personality she had not known, yet in a strange way could feel. She thought of these two men with their differing memories and affections; the comment from the principal yesterday morning; even Nehemiah Pole's remarks in the pub. Mahina was everywhere and nowhere and she seemed to dominate this small town in a way Libby had never come across.

She could not spend time thinking about that, however. Dusky Sound and her research beckoned and she was grateful to John-Cody for this opportunity of a guided tour. He was looking across the lake, back the way they had come: they could see the water tower and Alex's window from here. He drew on his cigarette, clipped it and put the butt in his shirt pocket. As he turned, their gaze met and he came over and leaned on the rail.

'You OK?'

'Fine, thank you.'

'Listen, there's no couples on the boat so you go aft and take the cabin next to mine. It's got a double bed and a door so you can get some privacy. The chart table is right outside and you might want to use it to work.'

'That sounds good. Thank you. But what about a berth for Bree?'

'Don't worry about Bree. I'll put her in the freezer bunk.'

Libby lifted her eyebrows.

'Trust me. She'll love it.'

It started to rain before they reached West Arm. The clouds that had hovered over the mountains all night began to bleed and a fine mist of drizzle peppered the surface of the lake. Libby felt the moisture on her face and her jacket was spattered with droplets. She went back inside and found Bree chatting away to a small man in his early thirties with a little stubble on his chin. His name was Carlos. His mother Anna sat with them and smiled as Libby poured herself some coffee. She told Libby that although she was Spanish she had married an Englishman and now lived in a house in a forest fifty miles from Brussels.

Carlos's first language was French, and it was noticeable in his accent. He was delighted to find a twelve-year-old in New Zealand who could chatter away to him in his native tongue. Libby sipped coffee and listened, picking up bits and pieces and marvelling at how fluent Bree was. John-Cody was up by the wheel, leaning with his back to the wind-screen, one booted foot crossed over the other at the

133

ankle. He was talking to the skipper, but his eyes caught Libby's. He smiled and she could feel the warmth across the cabin space between them.

At West Arm Jonah trotted up the gangplank and came back with a massive metal luggage trolley. He, John-Cody and Carlos shifted the bags and the boxes of stores onto it then Jonah hauled it back up the gangplank one-handed. They boarded the bus with the day-trippers and the driver pulled away from the wharf. Libby sat with Bree and listened to the commentary as they travelled the twenty-two kilometres across the Southern Alps. The rain was falling more heavily now and Bree stared wide-eyed as the driver explained that West Arm had some one hundred and fifty inches of rain every year as opposed to the fifty or so in Manapouri and Te Anau. Her eyes grew wider still when he informed them that over three hundred inches fell in Deep Cove.

'That's twenty-five feet.' Bree gawped at her mother.

John-Cody leaned over the back of the seat in front of them. 'Above the waterline Fiordland's a rainforest, Bree,' he said. 'Warm air comes east off the Tasman Sea. It hits the mountains and rises, then it meets with colder air higher up and it rains. It's a constant cycle.' He cocked his head to one side. 'Convection. You must have done it in science.'

Bree nodded.

'It's accentuated here because of the climate and the height of the mountains.'

Bree was staring at him. 'Do you teach people that on your boat?'

John-Cody laughed. 'I don't teach them so much,

Bree. I talk to them, tell them about Fiordland, then if they want to they can learn for themselves.'

'How do you know it all?'

He thought for a moment and then arched his brows. 'Mahina taught me, I guess.'

'She must have been very clever.'

'She was.'

'Have you got a picture of her?'

His eyes narrowed.

'I have.' Jonah shifted in his seat and fished a battered leather wallet from his pocket. He took out a small photograph, glanced at it briefly and passed it over the back of the seat. Bree took the photo and Libby looked on as she studied it: a very attractive Polynesian woman with dark skin and henna-tinted hair.

'She's beautiful.'

Jonah nodded. 'She was the best sister a man could ever have.'

'Was she older or younger than you?'

'Older. And much wiser.' Jonah was speaking freely, fondly. John-Cody was silent once more, facing the front. Libby stared at the back of his head. 'Mahina knew more about this place than anyone I've ever met,' Jonah said with pride, 'even people twice her age. She was the only person I've known who could hear the Tuheru.'

'Tuheru?' Libby asked.

Jonah looked over the seat at her then. His eyes were large and deep brown, set back in his skull. 'The dimly seen people,' he said softly. 'They live in the mountains and their voices travel in the mist. Most people can't see them, very few can hear them, but they're out there. People from long ago.'

135

'Fairies,' John-Cody said.

'Aha!' Jonah rolled his eyes. 'So *you* say. They're real all right. Mahina could see them.'

The bus driver dropped them on the road above the wharf and Libby glimpsed the deck of a boat, white between the trees. John-Cody asked them to form a chain on the steps and hand the boxes and bags down. It was raining harder now and a chill had crept into the air. Bree went on deck with John-Cody and Jonah, but the others were told to remain above until the gear was loaded and they had the engines and heater running.

Jonah went below to start the auxiliary and light the diesel stove at the foot of the for'ard steps. Ten minutes later, the gear loaded and everyone aboard, he untied the boat from the wharf and they were in the channel with a gentle wash spreading out from the stern. John-Cody had stripped off his wet-weather gear and boots, which he left by the port door. He went through a safety check with the passengers then allotted them each a bunk. Libby dumped her bag on the floor of the double-berthed cabin at the stern, glancing briefly at the skipper's cabin next to it. They were the same, only his had a curtain as a door to enable him to react quickly should circumstances demand it.

The chart table was set just below the aft steps, which led up to the saloon, galley and bridge all in one large squared space. The boat was wood-panelled and carpeted, with a shower and toilet aft and another up for'ard. Bree had the freezer bunk, a double bed set above the twin freezers and the only one with a porthole at eye level. She was absolutely delighted and crawled on all fours

136

to gaze at the mountains rising above the water.

The sun was seeping through a blue space in the clouds as Libby joined John-Cody on deck: he was hosing it down to clear the grime that had collected from the boxes. 'The sun's coming out,' Libby said.

He grinned at her. 'Sucker hole, that's all. The rain's set in for the day.'

Libby walked to the bowsprit and leaned against the rail. She could smell the change in the atmosphere, a moist sweetness coming off the hardwood trees that completely covered the mountains. Everywhere she looked was green, with just a hint of red now and again where southern rata was flowering. Clouds clung in low wisps like smoke, some as low as eye level, and the tops of most of the mountains were totally obscured. The diesel rumbled under her feet, vibrating slightly through the steel deck, and yet she could still hear water falling. The rivers had been swollen as they came over the pass, very high against the stanchions of one or two of the bridges. Water was falling now, cascading down the sides of the mountains where the alpine rivers were boiling.

As they left Deep Cove John-Cody came alongside her and she could smell him, his woollen sweater dampened by the drizzle. His bib-and-braces waterproofs reached to his chest and his sleeves were pushed up to reveal tanned forearms, the Indian bracelet dangling at his wrist. He pointed to the left. 'Hall's Arm,' he said, 'a beautifully peaceful place. See that water falling?' She could not miss it: the whole of the cliff face at the entrance to the narrows was one massed curtain. 'Commander Peak,' he told her. 'There's no natural waterfall there. That's all due to the rain.'

The surface of the fiord was all at once white with rain, the drops falling so hard now that they bounced back and cast everything the colour of mist. Libby clasped her hands together. 'I see I'm going to get wet over the next couple of years.'

John-Cody laughed softly. 'Oh yes, Lib. You're going to get very wet.'

Jonah called from the wheelhouse that coffee was ready and they went back inside. John-Cody took his cup and stowed it in a space behind the radar screen. A black woollen fisherman's cap lay over the gimbal-mounted compass. The front windows were misted and Libby could see that, in addition to the glass, they were covered with perspex.

'Why the reinforcement?' she asked, cupping a coffee mug in her hands.

'Sub-Antarctic weather.' John-Cody pulled a face. 'The waves down there can be serious. I'd hate to lose my front windows.'

'How often do you go?'

'Two or three times a year. DoC charter the boat to weigh sea lion pups.'

'There are sea lions down there?'

'On the Auckland Islands there are. Hooker sea lions, endemic to this part of the world.' He sipped coffee. 'We've got fur seals here in Doubtful and a bunch of them down at Dusky. You'll see a lot of them if you're going to identify the dolphin pod.'

'There definitely is a resident pod?'

'Definitely. I've been working these fiords for years now. They're as resident as the ones we've got up here, it's just that nobody has proved it technically.'

'Until now.' Libby paused for a moment, glancing

up the channel as they passed Elizabeth Island on their starboard side. 'What about noise pollution from boats?'

'You mean as regards the dolphins?'

She nodded.

'Who knows? If you want my opinion, it's damaging. I don't know how damaging. At the moment there're only a handful of tourist boats working up here. Twenty-two in the whole of Fiordland.'

'All with marine mammal viewing permits?'

He snorted. 'Some of them haven't even got permits to take people out on the water. Libby, don't let DoC's moratorium fool you. Most of the skippers keep to the rules, but there's always some that don't. There's a few up here who just go their own way completely. Ned Pole's got plans for Dusky Sound that could be absolutely devastating.'

Libby rested against the back of the seat that was set round the table behind her. Jonah had the lid off the middle and Bree was helping him stow food in the dry store.

'What d'you mean?' Libby looked at John-Cody in profile.

'Pole's the front man for an American hotel chain. They've put forward an application to place floating hotels, lodges they call them, in Dusky and Breaksea Sounds.'

Libby looked sideways at him. 'You mean permanent placements?'

He nodded. 'They want two in Dusky and one initially in Breaksea, followed by two more. They'll berth five hundred people in each. Apparently the company's bought some decommissioned cruise liners.'

139

'You're joking.'

'I wish I was.'

'Surely DoC will oppose it?'

'They have so far, but it's not within their jurisdiction.'

'Fiordland's a national park. How can it not be their jurisdiction?'

John-Cody poured more coffee. 'Fiordland is but the fiords themselves are not. They *were* in the national park,' he explained, 'but the park boundaries were redefined in 1978. The Tasman Sea had been the western boundary, but then it became the mean high-water mark. DoC's jurisdiction ends where the water begins. That means the regional council is the only arbiter of what goes on in the water and it's they who have to decide whether to grant permits or not.'

'But you can oppose them, surely?'

'Oh yes. And we do.' He looked beyond her for a moment. 'Pole has managed to get most of the original submitters on his side, but I've fought him all the way and I'll go on fighting him. If hotels are allowed in the fiords it'll just be the tip of the iceberg.'

'What are submitters?'

He explained to her that when somebody applied for a water activity permit various potentially interested parties were always notified. They 'submitted' written opposition or assent. 'Mahina and I are always notified when something affects the fiords.' He broke off then. 'Or rather we were. It's just me now.'

He moved to the wheel, a sudden weariness about him as if the words themselves fatigued him. Libby

140

watched as he stared through the windscreen. 'You loved her very much, didn't you?'

He spoke without looking round. 'Yes,' he said. 'I did.'

They steamed up the sound, Libby in the prow with Bree by her side. John-Cody was in the stern repairing one of the shackles that held the dinghy on the transom. Jonah was busy fixing lunch in the galley. They passed Ferguson Island and the entrance to Crooked Arm and all around them mountains clad in garments of green climbed as far as grey swirling cloud. They were approaching the Malaspina Reach now and the marine reserve known as the Gut. Beyond that was the Tasman Sea.

Libby had set up her laptop on the chart table so she could begin to make some notes, disturbed by what John-Cody had told her. Floating hotels meant a lot more people and therefore boats and that could have a detrimental effect on any population of bottlenose dolphins. She had studied the chart for Dusky Sound as well as one that detailed the whole of the south-west coast, and she felt she was beginning to get her bearings.

On deck again, Bree suddenly shouted and pointed. Libby looked where she gestured and saw plumes of condensation punching vertically into the air. 'Go and tell John-Cody,' she said. 'The others will want to see.'

Bree ran astern and moments later John-Cody stood next to Libby. 'Dolphins on the port bow,' she told him. He looked and saw a group of them, moving close to land in the deep-water troughs off Rogers Point: sleek grey backs arching with dorsal

141

fins skyward then disappearing below the surface, arching again and disappearing.

'They're hunting,' John-Cody said.

'Yes.'

'I think that's as close as we'll get.'

'You don't want to get closer?'

'They look busy to me. Don't you think?'

'I'd say so, yes.'

'Then let's not disturb them. They know we're here. They'll come and see us if they want to.' He moved back astern and told the other guests where they could find binoculars if they fancied a closer look. The weather was going to break badly, a storm had been forecast for later in the day and he wanted to be out of the Tasman before it hit.

At the Shelter Islands the wind rasped in the forestays and waves scudded into foam-coloured horses that chewed black rocks and lathered the kelp till it looked like soaped rags in the water. Libby gazed ahead and saw the swell beyond the Nee Islands and wondered if Bree would survive the journey without being sick. There was a definite roll under her feet now and she looked round to see her daughter lilting slightly as she made her way from the port quarter past the bridge to the lockers in front of the windows. Jonah had stowed vegetables in the one on the far left and Libby had seen the hose for a dive compressor protruding from another. She counted ten compressed air bottles in the rack and wondered how much dive gear John-Cody had on board. If she saw dolphins in Dusky Sound she wanted to get underwater.

The swell really began to take hold as they left the shelter of the fiord and headed for the Hare's Ears.

Beyond that they were in the Tasman and had four hours of sailing to the head of Breaksea Sound.

'Will we go in at Breaksea?' Libby asked him.

John-Cody made a face. 'Depends on the weather. Normally I like to sail straight for Dusky and moor in Luncheon Cove. I come back through the Acheron Passage and Breaksea. How's Bree with seasickness?'

Libby shrugged. 'To tell you the truth, I don't know.'

He nodded. 'Well, there's paper sacks on her bunk if she needs them.'

'Thank you for that, by the way.'

He squinted at her.

'The freezer bunk: she loves the little window.'

'Porthole.'

'Porthole. Right. She can see out when she's lying in her bunk.'

'That's why I gave it to her. When we hit the real swell she'll be able to see underwater too.'

They sailed south on the Tasman with the wind to starboard and Libby stood on deck gazing at the coast of New Zealand, where jagged black rocks rose from boiling surf into cliffs of grey granite. Gulls cried above the seals that watched their departure from the headlands of the Nee Islands, the beach-master bulls with their snouts in the air so they could see all the way round. Bree was on the bridge with John-Cody, Jonah at the saloon table. The other guests – Carlos and his mother, two Canadians and two elderly ladies from Christchurch – were in the glasshouse, watching the waves thundering at the stern.

Libby stared at the rugged coastline. The rain still hung in the air, though it was finer here with more

143

breaks in the cloud. She thought about the challenges lying ahead. So much had fallen into place, the house was great and John-Cody had given them carte blanche to change it around as much as they liked. School for Bree would be the next hurdle, but her daughter was adaptable if nothing else, and apart from the prospect of the rugby scrum she should be able to cope.

For herself there was the initial dolphin identification process in Dusky Sound: she would need to get the boat organized and liaise with the Department of Conservation and Steve Watson in Dunedin. She had her own equipment but it would need to be modified if she was going to film the dolphins underwater from the boat. John-Cody had told her that somebody had developed a helmet-mounted camera that operated below the surface and she should be able to take advantage of a similar system. She had a lot of computer equipment and DoC would provide a mini generator so she could use it at the Supper Cove hut, which would be closed to other visitors for the duration of her stay. That would give her some privacy at least; the last thing she needed was a group of trampers turning up when she had been on the water all day.

The wind was whipping the waves into frenzy now and they came cascading over the bows with every trough the *Korimako* plunged into. The sea washed over the steel deck and Libby stepped back inside the wheelhouse. She stripped off her wet gear and John-Cody took it down to the engine room to dry. The diesel heater was pumping into the for'ard cabin below and Libby went backwards down the steps and sat down on the library bunk. The bookshelves were lined with works on New Zealand and Fiordland in particular, though she also saw books on whales and dolphins and a couple on the Sub-Antarctic islands. She flicked through one and listened to Jonah and Bree up top, making pizza dough.

'Tell me about the Tuheru, Jonah,' Bree was saying. 'You really think they're real?'

'The Dimly Seen?' Jonah's voice was an octave lower than usual. 'Of course they are. But no-one ever sees them so no-one knows what they're like.'

'You said Mahina saw them.'

'She did, but she told little. You see, Bree, they only show themselves to people they can trust. They knew they could trust Mahina because she was so much like them. She lived half her life in the bush.'

'So you don't know anything about them?'

When Jonah replied his voice was deeper still. 'I know this much, they're nothing like the Maeroero.'

'The what?'

'Maeroero: savage hairy people with long bony fingers like witches who hated human beings. Bree, they were terrifying. They *are* terrifying and they like nothing better than a good feed of men, women or children. They catch you by spearing you with their jagged fingernails and then they eat you raw. At night they come down from the high places and kidnap men and women, carry them off and eat them. No-one they take is ever seen again.

'The homes of the old people were Tapu,' he went on. 'That means sacred. The Maeroero thought nothing of Tapu and they desecrated the homes of the people who came in the great canoes from Hawaiki. The Tuheru could be dangerous but the

145

Maeroero were monsters. If you walk in the bush when we get to Preservation Inlet – beware.'

'Don't you frighten my daughter, Jonah,' Libby called.

His dark shaggy head appeared at the top of the steps and he leered at her. 'Never mind her, Libby. You just watch yourself when you're alone at Supper Cove.'

John-Cody poked his head out of the for'ard bunkroom. 'Jonah, quit scaring the guests and cook lunch.'

Jonah bent lower so he could see him. 'Aye, sir, Cap'n, sir.' He made a mock salute and Bree laughed. John-Cody shook out the duvet cover he was holding and smiled at Libby.

The sea was rough, a swell rising to four metres and the wind at thirty knots. The four-metre swell could be uncomfortable for some people; one of the women from Christchurch was already popping seasickness tablets.

Jonah made sandwiches – it was too rough to do any serious cooking – and passed plates through the aft windows of the galley to the glasshouse. Libby sat with Bree and John-Cody at the table and every now and then he would get up and check the way-points he had fed into the global positioning system. The dotted rhumb-line traced their path between each waypoint and he made sure that they did not stray more than half a nautical mile either side of the line. Bree asked him why he was not steering by the wooden-spoked wheel and he explained about the automatic pilot. Libby watched him and noted how attentive he was. Every time the boat lurched or moved differently or the engine note altered a

146

fraction he was up and watchful: as if the *Korimako* were part of him, an extension of his being.

Jonah sang songs in Maori and tried to teach Bree, and then Bree said she was tired and climbed into the freezer bunk and drew the curtains. There she lay on her side and watched as the water crashed over the porthole. Sometimes she saw the grey of the sky and at other times the dark green of the ocean. She looked for fish, but couldn't see any.

The weather was turning really bad now and at five thirty John-Cody made everyone be quiet while he sat with a pen and notepaper listening to the forecast on the VHF radio mounted on the dashboard. When it was over he turned the volume down and looked at Jonah. 'We'll go in at Breaksea,' he said. 'It's blowing sou'west and over forty knots. We'll not make any headway.'

By six o'clock they were running between Breaksea Island and Oliver Point and Bree was kneeling on the dining-table bench looking out of the galley window at the seals perched on the rocks. She had been ecstatic earlier when Jonah spotted a whale blowing, west of Dagg Sound. Everyone crowded onto the windward quarter and Carlos said it must be a southern right or a humpback. Libby smiled and told him it wasn't a southern right because it had a dorsal fin, but it wasn't a humpback either. She took a pair of binoculars from John-Cody and immediately recognized it as a minke. John-Cody looked himself and was impressed. It was a minke all right, and a big one at that.

'You know your stuff,' he told her.

'I ought to. I've been studying cetaceans for the better part of my life.'

They steamed due south now, out of the worst of the sea and sheltered by the heights of Resolution Island on the windward beam. They were running the Acheron Passage with the light gradually fading and Libby and Bree were on deck, watching the mountains that formed the eastern wall pass at seven and a half knots. The judder of the engine sent shivers through the deck, and the jib, which John-Cody had hoisted at sea, was now furled again on the forestay. Jonah was cooking and the smells that drifted from the galley made Libby's mouth water. All they had eaten since breakfast were the sandwiches.

John-Cody came up from astern with another bottle of rainwater. There was plenty of fresh water in the tanks, but for cold drinks there was nothing like the rain gathered in the barrel lashed against the stern rail. He diluted some juice and passed a glass to Bree. He told Libby that often the dolphins could be found at the entrance to Wet Jacket Arm, which they were passing now on the leeward side. Together they crossed the deck and leaned on the rail and Libby took a cigarette from her pocket. John-Cody lit it for her and they scanned the darkened waters of the fiord for signs of dolphins blowing. They saw nothing though and Jonah called them in for dinner. John-Cody had the pilot on and had slowed the revs to a crawl as he ate his meal, glancing at the green outline on the radar screen every now and again.

'Man, it's good to be back on the boat,' Jonah said, as he sat down with his plate of food. 'It's been too long, Gib. Far too long.'

John-Cody was smiling, looking more at ease than at any time Libby had seen him.

'You're right, it's good and I'm not as rusty as I thought I'd be.'

'It all comes back to you, eh? Like you'd never been away.'

John-Cody sipped water and winked at Bree, who was stuffing food into her mouth and gabbling away to her mother at the same time. Libby just sat and listened and relaxed.

They anchored much later in Cascade Cove at the south-western end of Dusky Sound. It was fully dark now and John-Cody had navigated with the radar and the shadows of the mountains that rose up on all sides. They'd felt the breath of the storm as they steamed up the Bowen Channel, waves licking the bows as they had done at sea. They had listened to opinions on the weather criss-crossing the airwaves between various fishing boats on the VHF. During the day it was scanning channels all the time, but now John-Cody switched to channel 11 for the night. Bree stood at the wheel and listened to the gossip between various friendly skippers and laughed to herself at some of the jokes.

Later, though, as the storm reached its zenith the tone became more serious: one of the vessels was having some engine trouble and John-Cody silenced everyone while he listened. For an hour he sat there, half expecting to answer a Mayday call, but the skipper got her running smoothly enough to seek shelter and he relaxed.

'The angry sea, eh?' Carlos ventured.

John-Cody looked round at him. 'The sea isn't angry, Carlos. Or cruel or any other adjective people like to attach to it. The sea doesn't give a damn. It just responds to the wind.'

149

Entering Cascade Cove, Bree was already in bed and Libby was sitting opposite her on the library bunk. 'This is so cool,' Bree said, sitting up and peering again through the porthole. 'I love this bunk: it's so cosy and I can see out and hear the water against the side and everything.'

Libby smiled. 'It is kind of neat, isn't it? Last week we were in France and here we are on a boat at the bottom of the world.'

'And it's such a great boat.' Bree looked at her then. 'I'm glad you brought me, Mum.'

Libby got up and went over to her. 'Are you? Really? You're not fed up about yet more change in your life?'

Bree made a face. 'I'm not looking forward to school, but I understand now. I'm glad you told me.'

'What, you mean about the money and everything?'

Bree nodded. 'It'll be all right here, though. I mean we'll have enough to pay John-Cody the rent and everything, won't we?'

Libby smoothed her daughter's brow. 'Yes. We'll have enough. Don't worry, darling, everything will be just fine, I promise you.'

The sound of the anchor chain running out rattled through the hull and speech was suddenly impossible. It went on for some time and Libby and Bree looked at each other, Bree with her hands to her ears and her nose wrinkled. Then they felt the slight movement as John-Cody let the boat go astern then swing till they were at the widest point in the cove. There were twenty-seven metres of water under them and the anchor bit and dragged a little. John-Cody told Jonah to put the claw on the chain. It would chatter and wake him if they dragged too far in the night.

Cascade Cove was out of the main channel, around the point from Pickersgill Harbour where Captain Cook had moored the *Resolution* and set up his observation post. John-Cody told them how Cook had made spruce beer from the rimu tree and tea from the manuka while he refitted his ship. The first European house ever built in New Zealand had stood in Luncheon Cove, and later a sealing gang led by William Leith had built a ship there. John-Cody told them that after a visit to Pickersgill Harbour in the morning, he would show them inner Luncheon Cove and if they were lucky they could snorkel with seals.

Bree drifted towards sleep, wrapped in her duvet and watching the bright light of a star way up in the sky. John-Cody came down to get some of the now dry wet gear from the engine room and saw her gazing through the porthole. The sky was clear now, the wind having died and the clouds thinned to a milky mist, like curtains of lace on the stars. 'Is that Venus up there?' Bree asked him.

'No, it's Sirius. The brightest star in the sky.' He rested his elbows on the edge of her bunk. 'Mahina called it Takura, the winter star. Takura is a woman who brings the winter. On cold nights she shines extra brightly to warn of coming frosts.'

Bree looked at him and frowned. 'But I thought it's supposed to be summer.'

'It is. She just likes to remind us she's there and that one day she'll be back.' He patted her hand where it lay outside the covers. 'Did you have a good day today?'

151

'The best.'

'Good on you.' He winked at her and switched out the engine-room light.

Later Libby lay in her bunk feeling the slight swell and listening to the water slapping the hull with a sound like a half-empty barrel. It sloshed and rolled and she was rocked gently to sleep. Before she dropped off, John-Cody made a final check of the boat, in darkness. She had left the door to her cabin open to avoid condensation and she saw him in silhouette as he climbed the steps, his head framed against the pale sky through the for'ard windows. He rummaged quietly around – everyone else had turned in – then he slid down the steps again and she heard him settle in his bunk. His light was out and his breathing came evenly through the space between their cabins. The bunk was comfortable and warm and Libby could smell the smells of the boat, hear the little metallic creaks from the hull and the wind now and again in the spreaders: she sank deeper into the mattress and sleep came very quickly.

The following morning they weighed anchor and John-Cody flaked the chain, hoisting it into loops with a boat-hook as it rolled back into the locker so that it didn't get tangled up and jam when they tried to let it out again.

They steamed to Pickersgill Harbour and Captain Cook's astronomy point and Jonah and John-Cody let the dinghy down from the transom. Everyone but Jonah climbed into the dinghy and John-Cody steered it across to the wooden walkway that marked the landing point. Libby and Bree wore waterproofs and gumboots. John-Cody told them that gumboots or bare feet were a prerequisite in the bush. It rained most days of the year, no matter that the sun could be shining and the sky clear when they transferred from boat to shore.

The forest was a tangle of beech trees, scrub and rata, with supplejack and hard and soft tree ferns climbing everywhere, particularly where the deer had not been in any numbers. John-Cody held the boat steady while they landed, then tied off to a branch and clambered ashore. Libby stood and watched while he made his way over the slippery patches of rock, being careful not to step on the ridges but only the valleys between: that way his footing was sure and he didn't end up floating in the fiord.

Bree ran her hand over the bark of one tree that was so thick with lichen it felt like damp fur. The forest was dim and it dripped water. Fallen leaves underfoot were moist and mushy and everywhere you looked the woodland was tangled and primeval. John-Cody crouched next to a supplejack vine and bent it right over.

'Bree,' he said, 'this is supplejack. See how bendy it is? The Maori used it for basket making.' He spoke to the others then. 'Somebody once told me that this place with its hardwood forests and tangle of secondary growth was the last garden of Tane, god of the forest and the birds. If Tane's garden isn't looked after properly, then the forest will wither and the world will be plunged back into the darkness before Rangi and Papa were separated.' He explained the creation myth to them and told them about the forest and the wildlife that lived there. Bree watched him, drinking in his words. He spoke

153

in a low voice with hints of his Louisiana birth still rubbing the edges of his accent.

'There are other great gardens in Aotearoa,' John-Cody went on, as they made their way through the tangled bush towards Lake Forster, 'but I think this is the most special, the most unspoilt.' He led them along a barely discernible path with crown fern growing either side of it and twisted tree roots lifting from the rotting vegetation.

'The secondary growth trees grow on the lower levels between the hardwoods,' he said. 'Kamahi, fuchsia, wineberry. Most of the hardwood is silver beech and every few years the trees cast their seeds to ensure continued growth.' He half-smiled. 'The mice and rats have a field day.' He stopped again and gathered up a crown fern in his hand, squeezing the body of the plant and letting go. 'We need to ensure we look after the forest, to be certain the regeneration goes on, and that we don't interfere so much that we destroy what's here. So far we've managed to avoid that, but the introduction of deer and possum has done a hell of a lot of damage. Neither of them are native and they eat secondary growth trees.'

Back at the dinghy he told them how the land lived and died and lived again. He pointed across the bay to Long Island where a great bare patch of rock was exposed like a livid scar on the mountain.

'Tree avalanches,' he said. 'They happen all the time here. The growth becomes too much, too heavy, and then gravity takes over and there's a slippage just like snow in the Alps. The vegetation peels off the rock and ends up in the water, where tannin from the soil and foliage gives it that tea colour you can see.'

He pointed to the fresh-water layer where the surface was sepia-coloured in places and darker brown in others. 'The nutrients feed the world under the water – fish, plant life, etc. The fiords hold all kinds of wildlife: there are coral trees down there that are thousands of years old.

'When the bare rock is exposed on the mountainside, the process of regeneration begins. It's gradual: mosses and lichen form the first layers, and down in the estuarine places, toi toi and jointed spear grass grow. The wound begins to heal and slowly the land repairs itself. The birds and animals help.' He looked at Bree again. 'Bellbirds, Bree, are pollinators. Did you know that?'

Bree shook her head.

'Next time you're in the garden, watch one eating an apple. They lick out the flesh with really long tongues. That's how they pollinate plants, moving from one to another with pollen on their beaks and tongues. It's all part of a very delicate ecosystem: life, death and rebirth makes Fiordland what it is, a regenerating rainforest.'

They crossed the sound after lunch, weaving their way through the many islands where fur seals watched from the rocks and swam among the kelp. John-Cody steered with the wheel now, watching both sides of the boat through the open doors and keeping the bridge clear. He guided the *Korimako* into Luncheon Cove where the forest looked so primordial, so old and unspoiled, that Libby would not have been surprised to see dinosaurs wandering through the bush.

The trees came right to the lip of the cove, which was circular and flat with rain sheeting in icy blasts across the surface of the water. It proved to be only a short shower though, before the sun came out and was reflected in the new and sudden stillness. Some of the tannin-stained rocks looked almost pink as the sun bounced over them and the water was tinted green and yellow in places where it was shallower. John-Cody dropped the anchor then walked on deck and gazed across the cove to a mound of rocks on the northern lip. Libby followed his eyes and saw movement.

Picking up binoculars, she saw a group of fur seal pups watching them with interest, their eyes black and round like saucers.

'This is where the first house I told you about was built,' John-Cody said, 'where the sealers had their station. Nobody knows the numbers of fur seals before they came, but it's estimated that as many as two and a half million skins were taken. Captain Cook didn't take seals for commercial purposes, but he was here in 1773 and was the first European to use them as a resource. Blubber for oil, skins to mend rigging and meat for eating, of course.' He laid his hand on Bree's shoulder. 'Now there's something like ten thousand seals in Fiordland and nobody hunts any of them.' He looked down at her. 'How would you like to swim with the pups?'

He fished 7mm wetsuits out of the dive locker, found one that would fit Bree and Libby took her below decks to change. Libby had a drysuit with her for her research; the fiords were cold even in summer and she didn't fancy hours underwater without one. For all the time Bree had spent with her mother in various parts of the world, she had never worn a wetsuit before and she had never used a snorkel.

Dressed and ready, they went back on deck and John-Cody fixed Bree up with a pair of dive boots and a mask and snorkel. Carlos was going to swim with her and he was waiting in the dinghy. Libby joined them and John-Cody steered away from the *Korimako*, giving the rocks a wide berth. He eased off the throttle and they sat on the water, idling and watching as a young adolescent bull lifted his snout from the large rocks in the middle of the pile. 'He might try to spoil things,' John-Cody muttered, 'but we'll give it a shot.'

Carlos eased over the side and floated off on his belly. No need for fins; the suits were so buoyant the fins would have done nothing but slap the surface and scare off the pups. Bree sat on one side of the boat and watched as two pups slipped off the rocks, escaping the watchful eye of the bull, and swam towards Carlos.

John-Cody helped Bree into the water and she held on to the rope that he twisted round his fist. She gasped as the cold hit her, her breathing suddenly rushed. It steadied, though, and she trod water for a moment or two.

'Remember, Bree, you can't sink. That suit will keep you afloat better than a life jacket. So relax.' His voice was gentle and soft and Libby sat with one hand fisted to her mouth, watching her daughter's eyes focused on his through the mask. She was pumping air up and down the snorkel though her face was still out of the water.

'Listen to your body,' John-Cody was saying, 'feel what it's saying to you. Just relax and go with it. Listen to your breathing. You can't sink. If you want to have a break then just roll on your back and crab

157

your hands and feet. Let go: look at the sky. It's beautiful from that angle. Remember, you can't sink.' He showed her how to clear her mask then she rolled over, put her face in the water, tried to breathe and lifted her head again, spluttering.

'It's OK, Bree,' he said. 'Just relax. You can do it. Gently put your face in the water. Do it little by little. Ease your face under and hold on to the boat.'

Bree did as he told her and she breathed, jagged little gasps at first then slower and deeper. 'That's it,' he said. 'Gently does it. Good. You're doing just fine.'

She lifted her face again, spat out the snorkel and beamed at her mother.

'Now listen,' John-Cody said. 'We'll be right here. Stick close to Carlos and if you don't want the pups swimming up to your face just hold your hands out in front of you. They'll come that far and no further. OK?'

Bree nodded, put her snorkel back in her mouth and let go the rope. She rolled on her belly and paddled her way over to where Carlos was surrounded by seal pups. John-Cody sat back and nodded. 'She's a natural,' he said, watching her.

'You're the natural.' Libby smiled. 'A natural-born teacher.'

He laughed. 'I'd last five minutes in a classroom.'

'Who said anything about classrooms? That was brilliant, John-Cody. Bree's got great confidence in her academic ability but not much else. She's never had a mask anywhere near her face and look at her, swimming with seals in New Zealand.'

'We'll just keep an eye on that bull.' John-Cody was standing up in the boat once more, watching the beach-master on his promontory. 'Bree's a good kid,' he said, 'plucky and very bright. She'll do all right.'

The rain came sheeting down again and Libby lifted the hood on her waterproofs. John-Cody stood with his hair getting wetter, monitoring the bull every time he went into the water.

Bree was squealing, pups coming at her from all sides with wide black eyes and whiskers twitching, so graceful underwater, almost as if they were flying. Libby looked to the tree line and heard the high-pitched screech of a weka. Last night John-Cody had told them the difference between a weka and a kiwi, which a lot of people mixed up. The weka started each cry from roughly the same note, whereas the pitch of the kiwi kept rising. She thought about being here with the Tuheru and Maeroero, having the wild people for company in the dead of night. Jonah and his stories: never mind scaring Bree, she was the one who would be sleeping alone in the bush.

'This is a wonderfully atmospheric place,' she said, as John-Cody sat down again.

'I think so.'

'When did you first come here?'

'1974. I was on a fishing boat. We landed a catch at Bluff Cove.'

'From the US?'

'Hawaii.'

'Like the Maori.'

'Excuse me?'

'Landing from Hawaii.'

He smiled. 'I guess. I never thought of it that way.' He watched the bull again as he hauled himself out of the water, then turned to Libby once more.

159

'Waitaha, Jonah's tribe: they were the first Polynesians to colonize the South Island. Mahina and Jonah were half Waitaha and half Hungarian. Mahina looked full-blood Maori to me though.'

'Like Jonah?'

'Just like Jonah, only with a henna tint in her hair. You saw her picture yesterday.'

They sat in silence, watching Bree and Carlos slapping about in the shallows. John-Cody looked beyond them and all at once he was aware of Mahina's presence, in the rain and in the mist that had settled like woodsmoke over the massed ranks of beech trees crowding the edge of the water.

SIX

Bree was cold but full of it when she came out of the water, shivering in her wetsuit. John-Cody held the dinghy steady against the dive platform while she clambered out and climbed the steps to the deck of the *Korimako*. Libby helped her up and Jonah was waiting on deck with a kettle full of warm water. Libby held the neck of Bree's suit open while Jonah poured the warm water inside. Bree squealed with delight as the warmth dribbled down her back and into the legs of the suit.

She and Carlos took hot showers while they got under way: John-Cody had promised to show Libby the Supper Cove hut, which meant steaming the length of the sound before turning round and heading for Preservation Inlet. Jonah was busy with food, so Libby flaked the chain and signalled to John-Cody in the wheelhouse when the anchor showed at the waterline. Back on the bridge, she thanked him.

'That was wonderful for Bree, John-Cody. I don't think I've ever seen her quite so excited.'

'My pleasure.' He stood at the wheel, guiding the boat out of the confines of Luncheon Cove and back to the Many Islands. He had considered leaving Supper Cove till the way back, but decided that once they were finished at Preservation Inlet he would sail straight up the coast to Doubtful. The weather outlook was pretty good for the next few days, so he hoped they would make the passage without incident.

As he steered between the Many Islands he heard the whine of a floatplane overhead. He went on deck and shaded his eyes where the sun was trying to break through. He picked up the plane flying in from the east, following the line of Cook Channel; it arced above them, dipping low, and then made a series of circles. He bunched his eyes, aware of the direction of the wind on his face and wondering if they would land.

Libby moved next to him, her scent in his nostrils. He glanced at her as the floatplane made a pass right above the boat and a face pressed against the passenger window.

'Do you know them?'

John-Cody nodded grimly. 'Nehemiah Pole.' He pointed to Heron Island. 'That's one of his proposed sites.'

Libby watched as the floatplane circled once more then headed north-east. 'They mean business then.'

'Oh, definitely. There's millions of dollars involved.' John-Cody squatted on the corner of the vegetable locker. 'Pole's married to an American lawyer, Lib. She's a tough woman and she's got access to a large clientele in the United States, rich folks, the hunting and fishing fraternity. With her contacts and Pole's reputation down here, they're offering the ultimate wilderness experience in one of the last unspoilt places on earth.' He shook his head. 'It sounds great in the brochure, but if it happens they're going to change that wilderness experience for ever.'

'Five floating hotels,' Libby said.

John-Cody nodded.

'That's not so many. Dusky's a big place.'

He frowned at her. 'It's only the beginning though, isn't it? Think how many people will be watching the outcome of this application. If Pole gets his surface water activity permit then a whole stack of other people will be slapping in applications, Southland Tours at the head of the queue.' He got up from the locker. 'Dusky, Breaksea, Bradshaw, Thompson, Doubtful – the list goes on and on, Libby. We give one inch here and they'll take every mile of fiord they can get.'

Libby watched him go back into the wheelhouse, the wind on her face now, rain again in the air. Bree was sitting at the saloon table, hair still wet and hanging to her shoulders, drawing a picture of the seals she had been swimming with. John-Cody picked up the radio and called Alex at base to check in. Everything was fine and he hung up the handset, leaned back against the wood of the bench and folded his arms. Libby was in the prow, her elbows on the pulpit rail looking down at the cut glass of the water.

Supper Cove was situated on the banks of the estuary at the very head of the sound, which comprised two arms. Shark Cove was to the south, slimmer and narrower than Supper Cove, which was wide and flat-bottomed and heavily silted close to the shore. Rimu grew on the edge of the beech forest, thick and tightly woven, penetrated only by deer trails and twin footpaths that led north to West Arm and south to Lake Hauroko. The hut itself was set on the northern bank of the cove, visible from both the water and the air. John-Cody took Libby across in the dinghy and they picked their way up the shingle beach to the first line of trees. Inside, the hut was spacious, with an open fireplace in one wall and dry logs laid out in readiness for a fire. A notice confirming Libby's usage was pasted on the door and on the table, which pleased her. She should not be receiving any unwelcome visitors. Maori bunks that could sleep three or four were fastened to one wall with a smaller single bunk against the other. There was a pot-bellied stove and a water pump, its source one of the many streams that gushed out from the bush.

John-Cody looked at the stove, checking the chimney pipe for any sign of leakage, then he stood up and dusted his hands on his jeans. 'This'll be just fine,' he said. 'How long do you plan to be here?'

'No more than a week at a time: I still haven't worked out who is going to look after Bree.' She shook her head. 'The last thing I want to do is leave her when we've only just got here.'

John-Cody could see the concern etched in her eyes. 'You want somebody she knows at least, somebody she likes.' His eyes brightened then. 'You ought to ask Alex. She and Bree hit it off. Her place is big and she rattles around in there all by herself.'

Libby looked up at him. 'You think she might do it?'

He shrugged. 'I don't know. But it can't hurt to ask.'

Outside Libby heard a weka shriek and she started.

'You'll hear a lot of them at night,' John-Cody told her. 'And kiwi. There's brown kiwi down here.'

Libby moved to the door and gazed at the density of the bush, tangled and massed against the water like a wall of green darkness. 'Along with the Maeroero no doubt,' she said.

They sailed for Preservation Inlet with the afternoon waning and darkness gathering in the west. John-Cody stood at the wheel and Jonah served an early dinner. They sailed with the wind from the north, down the West Cape towards Cape Providence and Chalky Inlet. Libby sat at the chart table and made some notes on what she had learned in Dusky, remarking on the fact that she had seen neither hide nor hair of any dolphins. The sea to the east was flat and grey with nothing to mark their distance from the land: clouds, thick and choked, lay against the horizon. Yet one look to leeward and the western cliffs rose black and treacherous all the way south. The *Korimako* pitched and rolled as three currents clashed beyond Cape Providence where the Tasman met the wash from Chalky Inlet and the Foveaux Strait.

They moored that night in Useless Bay. The wind had moved nor'west and would be coming from the south in the morning. A gale had whipped the Tasman into a frenzy of broken waves, which chewed at the sound beyond Kisbee Bay. John-Cody listened to the forecast on Bluff Radio: the squall would blow itself out during the night and the sun would be shining tomorrow.

Libby woke early with light streaming through her porthole. She heard movement in the galley and looked at her watch. Six thirty: the other guests would still be sleeping. She got up and slipped a sweatshirt over the long T-shirt she sometimes wore as a nightdress and climbed the wooden steps to the saloon. John-Cody was stirring sugar into a mug of coffee: there was no sign of Jonah, the only sounds the creaks and little groans the *Korimako* made continually. Libby smiled at John-Cody and he indicated coffee with a swirl of his finger. She nodded, bent to the for'ard steps and peeked down to where Bree lay sound asleep in the freezer bunk. She crouched for a few moments, just watching the peace on her daughter's face, a peace she had not seen in a good couple of years. Maybe all that had gone wrong in France was actually a blessing for them; Bree looked as happy here as Libby had ever seen her. She felt John-Cody move behind her and he handed her a steaming mug of coffee.

'Let's go on deck,' he said quietly. 'We won't disturb anyone out there.'

Taking a bottle of washing-up liquid from under the sink, he spread some of it on the door runners and slid the starboard one back. 'Keeps them smooth,' he whispered and they stepped out on deck.

Libby wore no shoes and the steel deck was surprisingly warm against the soles of her feet. John-Cody wore a T-shirt and jeans and he stood with one hand across his chest and looked the length of the bay. The water was flat and still, only the faintest ripple visible, not a breath of wind and already there was heat in the sun.

Libby sipped coffee. 'Have you got anything particular planned today?'

'Bush walks.' He pointed south-west. 'The

166

lighthouse at Puysegur Point gives you great views of the straits and halfway back is Sealers Beach, wild and wonderful in this weather.' He stood and sipped coffee. Libby looked at his hair, silver and hanging to his shoulders where the ends were uneven and frayed. She'd had a great desire to do something about those broken ends from the moment she clapped eyes on him. Her own hair was loose today; when she was working she wore it in a French plait. She leaned on the rail next to him and breathed in the silence, aware of the smell of salt in the air, a dryness to it coming in off the Tasman. A mollymawk glided low over the entrance to Useless Bay before banking back in the wind ten feet above the waves.

'That guy's a long way from home,' John-Cody said quietly. 'White cap: they breed on the Auckland Islands. That's nearly five hundred kilometres south of here. Mahina . . .' His voice was trapped in his throat. 'Mahina loved it down there. She used to crew for me, cook for the Department of Conservation teams that were measuring the giant herbs, the daisies and lilies that grow on Adams Island.' He looked round at her. 'The Aucklands are an amazing place, Libby. The plants have a very short growing season so they grow faster and flatter than their cousins do up here. The rata forest is incredible. The seeds look like little threads and they ride on the back of the wind from here to the Sub-Antarctic.'

He rested against the rail with his back to the water, and in his mind's eye he saw the flat calm of Carnley Harbour to the north of Adams Island. Beyond the shores lay the tangled forests of rata: umbellata, the ironwood that had grown and massed

167

and interwoven without interruption for nine thousand years. He recalled the first time that he and Mahina had been ashore: the bellbird's wonderful song rising to crescendo then dying in their ears. The moss underfoot so soft, they had taken off their boots and buried their toes deep in the carpet-like texture; above their heads the canopy of tangled branches formed a natural cavern, which was strangely hushed and quiet. Not much further on, their way was blocked. As the forest climbed higher it shrank to knee height, the incessant drag of the wind beating any perpendicular growth into flattened sideways submission.

He looked at Libby once more. 'That mollymawk is really a small albatross. It breeds on the cliffs of Adams Island facing into the wind with no land between it and the Antarctic.' He broke off and the expression in his eyes darkened; when he spoke again his voice was much softer. 'I've sailed that southern coastline only once and I don't want to do it again. It's the most desolate, most lonely place I think I've ever been. It's lonely right in the soul. I've sailed with people on board, but there's a silence that seems to get right inside everyone.' He shook his head. 'I can't explain what I mean exactly. I guess it's something to do with the history. In 1864 the *Grafton* was wrecked in Carnley Harbour. Five crew got ashore and their captain, a man called Musgrave, kept a diary for the twenty months they had to survive before they were finally rescued.' He pushed himself away from the rail. '*I have been round both capes and I have crossed the western ocean many times, but never have I experienced – or read – or heard of anything in the shape of storms to equal this place.*'

John-Cody took tobacco from his pocket. 'Mahina made me read those words before I sailed the first time.' He smiled fondly then at the memory. 'It is one hell of a place, Libby. Believe me.'

Libby moistened her lips with her tongue. 'Southern right whales breed there, don't they?'

'In winter they do. I've seen them from May till November. I was part of a crew that tried to film a cow giving birth once, but we couldn't get the footage.' He sighed. 'That would have been a first. The trouble was it was night, and the underwater lights attracted great shoals of krill. We couldn't see a thing.'

Bree came on deck then, rubbing her eyes. 'Is breakfast ready yet?' she said.

They moved the *Korimako* to Kisbee Bay and dropped anchor again. Libby could see an old white boathouse on the shore. John-Cody took them across in the dinghy and moored on the beach. Bree wandered up to the boathouse, which had a cabin attached to it, an old bed with no mattress in the middle of the floor and a stove with fresh wood lying beside it. Rats scampered into the corners, making her shudder, and as she came out she saw her mother looking at the headstones in the tiny graveyard.

Libby stared at the six names and then turned again, the wind on her face from the sea. 'I wonder what it must have been like to live down here,' she murmured.

John-Cody lifted his shoulders. 'They were miners. A guy called Johnston discovered gold in 1868. At one point there was a settlement of two thousand people. They built a lighthouse on Puysegur Point.'

He pointed to the gravestones. 'They're all that's left of the colony.'

Libby looked back at the headstones, four men and two women. For a moment she wondered who they had been, what their lives were like. She looked across the bay where the sun bounced all the colours of light off the surface of the water and the *Korimako* lay at anchor, a perfect white against the bottle green of the islands. Nothing much had changed here. She stood where they would have stood and saw the same landscape they would have seen all those years ago.

As if he could guess her thoughts, John-Cody laid a hand on her shoulder. 'It has changed,' he said. 'It's no longer the virgin land that it was, the mining saw to that. The slaughter of seals, the introduction of deer and stoat and possum.' He cracked a wide smile. 'But it is still beautiful.'

They walked in the gradually rising heat though the trail was soggy underfoot. John-Cody wore no shoes or socks and Libby decided to do likewise, wearing just cut-off jean shorts and a T-shirt. She loved walking barefoot, the feel of the land between her toes a delight.

John-Cody had watched her as she climbed down to the dive platform and for half a second he was reminded of Mahina. That's how she would have been, in shorts and no shoes so she could feel the forest against her skin. The realization had been startling and he was quiet as he steered the little boat to the beach.

Now he moved ahead with Carlos and his mother, the other two guests who had joined them on the walk. Libby trailed behind them with her arm round

Bree's shoulders and they climbed the old gold-miners' trail with the land falling away on their right and the sea green and blue and spittle among the rocks. John-Cody led them up the hill and into the bush where the trees grew closer, the trail still discernible. They walked for maybe an hour, passing the marker for Sealers Beach, then the trail opened onto a cliff top and Libby spied the white walls of the lighthouse on Puysegur Point. The wind blew hard here and a few clouds had lifted to spoil the sky.

When they got to the point they looked down on a staircase of jagged black rocks falling hundreds of feet to where the sea thrashed the land. Libby stood in the weight of the wind and listened to the sound of water breaking hard, then sucking back with a hiss before rising to beat the rocks once again. John-Cody came alongside her.

'Now you see why they needed to build a light-house. Get caught on those and it's all over.' He turned to Bree. 'Can you hear that sound? That sucking and hissing and silence before the crash of the waves again?' He squatted next to her and pointed out the whitecaps close to the shore. 'Water on rock: that's the worst sound a seaman can ever hear. It sends a shiver right through your heart.' He glanced at Libby. 'This is New Zealand's Cape Horn. The wind blows ten knots harder here than any-where along the coast.'

He led the way back. Carlos told them his mother was tired and they would go back to the dinghy and wait. Sealers Beach was another half-hour walk and she was not up to it. Bree said she would go back with them because she was not up to it either. That left Libby, who wanted to see the beach

171

where tea-coloured fresh water ran out to the sea.

She followed John-Cody, the trail steeper and lined with tangled secondary growth, twigs and sticks poking at her bare feet. The vegetation dripped water that mingled with her sweat and by the time they reached the top of the slope she was soaking. The banks of the slope were damp and muddy and brown water ran over their feet in rivulets. Libby stopped a little way behind John-Cody and looked down through the canopy of trees to a square of deserted beach where a twin-armed river of tannin-stained water spread across the sand. On three sides the bush crept like a hairline and Libby could hear the breaking of waves on rock. John-Cody paused in front of her.

'Something, isn't it?' He looked back at her then as she stood above him: shorts cut to the top of naked thighs, legs brown and slender, the lines defined with muscle. Her skin ran with mud and water and again, for a moment, he saw Mahina. Yuvali Beach when she was just eighteen and dressed as Libby was now.

He suddenly realized he was staring; realized Libby was looking back at him and the breath caught in his chest. Colour scarred his cheeks and he looked away and down and turned to the trail once more. Libby looked after him: she had felt the intensity of his gaze, the way his eyes for a moment had feasted on her and as she watched him move off she was aware of a fluttering sensation in her belly.

The sand was firm underfoot, cool against her soles. She wandered to the twin rivers where shallow water ran between massive turret-like boulders some thirty feet in height that broke up the path to the sea. The water was icy and she gasped at the sudden contrast, goose pimples breaking the flesh of her legs. John-Cody perched on a rock and rolled a cigarette, his own feet in the water.

'Could be the Bahamas, eh?'

She smiled and waded through the water to him. 'This is fresh, right?' She pointed between her toes.

'Uh-huh.'

'So I can drink it?'

'You can.'

She squatted in front of him and as she bent to cup her hands for a drink he glimpsed the tops of her breasts. Her chest was smooth and flat, the clavicle pronounced and her breasts swollen and milky, white compared to the rest of her. Libby cupped the water to her mouth again and again and John-Cody held his cigarette and stared. The last time he had been here was with Mahina and for a moment he felt as though he had betrayed her. Memory was all he had now: she was gone, lost, and with every day that passed she would fade and fade. Which was what she wanted, what she had told him would happen when they sat together that last night on her thinking stone with the gum tree silent beside them.

He stood up, drawing smoke into his lungs and exhaling in one breath. She was fading now, right there on Sealers Beach. But he didn't want her to fade: he didn't want to forget her or her to forget him. He imagined her now in the silence of the bush with the Tuheru, delighting in the other world where the garden of Tane was undiminished and colour and form and variety cast the trees he saw here into shapeless grey and brown.

'John-Cody?'

He looked round sharply and saw Libby standing

173

close to him, hands behind her back, looking up into the closed silence of his features.

'You were miles away.'

He clipped his cigarette and put the butt in his pocket, then he led her to the boulders and showed her the caves and the slippery ridges of flat rock that looked like the work of glaciers. Far in the south the weather was changing. He turned his face to the wind, gazed back at the sea and his hair blew round his head.

'It's blowing nor'west,' he said. 'It'll turn sou'west later, ten knots slower. Look for lightning on the horizon around teatime. It happens that way down here when a nor'wester turns from the south.'

SEVEN

The following Monday Libby woke Bree early for school. She sat up, rubbed her eyes and looked at the crisp new uniform they had bought in Invercargill.

'D'you want cereal or porridge?' Libby asked her.

'Porridge, please.' Bree yawned and stretched and then wondered at her choice, suddenly aware of the stones gathered in the pit of her stomach. Today reality dawned after the magic of life on the *Korimako*: she had yet another new school to get used to.

Libby left her to get dressed and went into the kitchenette, switched on a ring on the stove and fetched milk from the fridge. Bree had had porridge on the *Korimako* every morning for a week, cooked by John-Cody who always took over in the galley at breakfast time. She came out of her bedroom still wearing her pyjamas with a towel draped over one shoulder, hair tousled, her eyes still puffy with sleep. She went through the little laundry space to the bathroom beyond the kitchenette. Libby poured porridge oats into the pan of boiling milk, aware of the knots in her own stomach: she would take Bree in this morning, give her some moral support on her first day.

John-Cody had told Libby she could use the truck. Once Bree was settled she needed to go and see Ned Pole about the motor launch he had offered to rent her. John-Cody didn't seem to like the idea of her renting from Pole, and had spent a lot of time on the phone when they got back from Preservation Inlet. But he couldn't find any other boats available and in the end he had muttered something about Pole's boats being as good as any. Libby wondered at him, sharing his concern about what might happen in Dusky Sound, but at the same time she understood that people had to make a living. It was the age-old question of balance, economics versus ecology. Somewhere there had to be a happy medium. John-Cody didn't like Ned Pole and Pole didn't like him: that was evident from the conversations she'd had with both of them. She considered their history and what was between them now and it occurred to her that the Te Anau basin was a very small place indeed.

She also thought that, given the situation with her research, there was every possibility that she too would find herself opposing the big man; but he had offered her a boat in the full knowledge of why she needed one, and he was the only supplier at present.

John-Cody had brought them back from Preservation Inlet via the Acheron Passage because another squall had blown up in the west. But she had seen no dolphins in Dusky Sound. John-Cody seemed a little perturbed himself, telling her that in windy weather they were often located at the entrance to Wet Jacket Arm, but there was no sign of

176

them there even. They had steamed north to Breaksea and back out to the ocean for the four-hour sail to Doubtful Sound without catching so much as a glimpse of them. Libby was itching to get back, set something up at the Supper Cove hut and trawl the arms of the sound on her own. Perhaps in a smaller, less intrusive vessel she would have more chance of sighting the pod.

Sighting them was one thing: photographing and identifying them was another completely. Then there was the question of sex, whether a dominant female governed the pod. There was a hell of a lot of work to be done before she could begin to think about the levels of communication between them and the possible effect of the territorial changes that more tourism would bring.

Bree came out of the shower and went back to her bedroom, taking a bowl of porridge with her. She was very quiet and Libby really felt for her: first-day nerves for the umpteenth time in her life. She had left the tap dripping and Libby turned it off. As she did so she heard John-Cody's electric shaver through the wall. She paused long enough to listen for a few seconds, and found herself imagining him standing in front of the mirror. The two bathrooms backed on to each other and that was the weakest point in the walls. She wondered if he could hear the fall of their shower.

In the kitchen she poured herself some tea and stood at the back window, looking over the garden to drink it. She heard the clatter of possum claws on the corrugated iron roof and wondered if she would ever catch sight of one. According to John-Cody, there were millions of the creatures eating their way through the forests every night, but the only ones she had seen were flattened on the road between Manapouri and Te Anau. She looked at the pink bark of the fuchsia and the hanging bird table where a fantail was cleaning its feathers. Bree talked about bellbirds, and Jonah had told them that when Mahina was dying she had lain between the fuchsia and the red beech so she could listen to them. But Libby had not heard a single note, let alone seen one, since they had been here.

Bree came out of the bedroom with the half-eaten porridge sticking to the side of the bowl. She looked neat in the summer uniform of open-necked blouse and sensible black shoes.

'Are you OK, darling?'

Bree shrugged and looked at her watch. 'Let's just go, shall we?'

'You'll be early.'

'I'd rather be early than late.'

Libby climbed behind the wheel of the old Toyota and started the engine. Bree got in next to her, new school bag on her knees, socks rolled down to her ankles. The sun was over the lake, though Leaning Peak was swathed in cloud as they turned onto Cathedral Drive. They passed Alex walking to the office from her house and she waved and mouthed good luck to Bree. Sierra was in the back of the truck and she barked at Alex as she barked at everyone they passed, and Alex rolled her eyes to the sky.

It took twenty minutes to drive to the school and Bree said virtually nothing all the way there. She gazed to the left, watching the lake roll out of sight, taking in the signs to Supply Bay and Rainbow Reach and the Kepler Track. Farmlands spread away

178

beyond the airport on the right, and various vehicles were rumbling towards Manapouri. Halfway to Te Anau, Libby slowed as a pale-feathered Australian harrier swooped low over the cab and, talons extended, settled on the corpse of a road-killed possum lying on the grass verge.

'He's old,' Bree muttered, looking through the window.

Libby squinted at her. 'How do you know?'

'The feathers: they get paler as the bird gets older. That one's very old.'

'Where did you learn that?'

Bree shrugged. 'John-Cody told me.'

Libby turned into Howden Street where other parents were dropping off their children. She pulled over outside the school and reached for her daughter's hand. Bree squeezed and Libby touched her cheek with the backs of her fingers.

'Do you want me to come in with you, darling?'

Bree pursed her lips then slowly shook her head. 'I'll go by myself.' She looked sideways at her mother. 'I may have to play rugby in the winter, Mum. I'd better be able to walk in by myself.'

'OK.' Libby leaned over to kiss her but Bree shied away, self-conscious already under the gaze of the children gathered in the concourse.

'You know where to go?' Libby asked her.

Bree was half out of the truck now. She nodded and closed the door. Libby watched her walk into school, dragging her feet ever so slightly, then she noticed that various other mothers were there, some of them watching. They were not watching Bree, however, but looking at her sitting in John-Cody's truck.

179

Bree walked past a group of girls a year or two older than she was and none of them said anything. They just stared at her and she looked straight ahead, pushed open the swing door and walked the length of the corridor to the secretary's office. The principal had told them that the school comprised forms one to seven and she would be in form two.

A girl her age was waiting outside the door to the secretary's office. She looked up as Bree came in. 'Are you Breezy?' she asked.

'I prefer Bree.'

'Sounds like cheese.' The girl shrugged. 'I'm Angela Brownlow, head girl in our year.' She was pretty with curling blond hair and the beginnings of a suntan. Her sleeves were rolled up to her elbows and she looked older than her years. 'Anyway, you're in my class. Mrs Billingshurst asked me to look out for you.'

'Who's Mrs Billingshurst?'

'Our form tutor, silly. Didn't Mr Peters tell you that?'

Bree just smiled.

'Come on,' Angela said. 'I'll take you to registration.'

Libby looked for Ned Pole's house on the road back to Manapouri. She had left the instructions John-Cody had given her back at the house and she drove up and down the main road until she discovered the shallow turning and the long hedged drive. It opened onto a gravel turning circle with a log-cabin-style house, built on two levels with paddocks running up the hills to the tree line. She could just glimpse patches of the lake below the Murchison Mountains.

Pole stood on the balcony and looked down at her as she got out of the truck.

'G'day,' he called. 'I just made some coffee.'

Libby shaded her eyes from the sun and looked up at him, silhouetted in a long lean shadow against the sky.

'Come on up.' He pointed to the door directly in front of her. 'Door's open.'

Libby went into the house, not sure about going upstairs until she realized it was built upside down with the bedrooms on the ground floor. She knew virtually nothing about Pole but could sense the touch of his wife in the soft furnishings, wall colourings and the general air of good order. The stairs led onto a wide landing with the open-plan kitchen leading off it. Pole stood at a work surface with his back to her and she sniffed the aroma of freshly ground coffee. He turned and smiled and for the first time she thought he was quite attractive. He was lean and straight-backed, probably a few years older than John-Cody.

'How you going?'

'Good, thank you.'

'Get your little girl into school, did you?'

Libby nodded. 'It's her first day.'

Pole passed her a cup of coffee. 'She'll be all right. Sugar?'

'No, thank you.'

He led the way into a study where deer heads and racks of antlers adorned the walls. Libby sipped her coffee and stepped beyond the desk to the balcony. The sun warmed her face. Pole lit a black cigar and flicked ash with his third finger.

Libby looked back at the deer on the walls, noting

their dull eyes and dry black nostrils. 'Do you shoot a lot of deer, Mr Pole?'

'Ned, please. Only my bank manager calls me Mr Pole.' He looked beyond her then, to the paddock where a huge black stallion was trotting the line of the fence. 'I used to shoot a lot of deer. I still hunt but no longer commercially.'

'I heard you were a good shot. You used to work on the helicopters.'

Pole squinted at her. 'Gib told you that, did he?'

'Yes.' Libby looked at the photograph of the young man on Pole's desk. 'He also told me why the *Korimako* has a roller-reefing jib.'

Pole leaned on the balcony rail and spoke without looking at her. 'You asked him then?'

'Yes.'

'What did he say exactly?'

'He said the previous jib had hanks and your son died trying to untangle one from the forestay.'

Pole squinted at her, then looked again at the stallion.

'Is that him on your desk?'

'That's him.'

'A good-looking man.'

'He was.'

'John-Cody said it was an accident.'

Pole pursed his lips.

'He said you didn't blame him, even though other people did.'

Pole flicked ash again. 'I've worked on boats, Dr Bass.'

'It must have been terrible for you.'

He nodded to the stallion. 'Barrio there was Eli's.

182

I bought him for his twenty-first birthday. He only rode him once.'

'I'm sorry.'

'So am I.' He looked at her then. 'Libby,' he said. 'Is that short for Elizabeth?'

'Liberty.'

He smiled. 'I like that. Means freedom, eh?'

She nodded.

'I like that.'

Libby felt a little uncomfortable. Pole seemed distant, preoccupied. She moved the conversation on. 'You told me you could supply me with a boat, a launch of some kind, something I can leave at Supper Cove.'

He nodded. 'I can give you a tow too if you want.'

'That's not necessary.'

'Going with Gib then, are you?'

'He offered ages ago. Before I even got here.'

'Fair go: the *Kori*'s a good boat.'

'He told me you wanted to buy her.'

'I do, her and the wharf.'

'So you could take people to Dusky by sea?'

Pole nodded, flicked ash and stuck the cigar between his teeth. 'DoC won't allow any more wharfs in Deep Cove. It's the ideal place to ferry people from if they don't want to fly.'

Libby put her coffee cup down on the rail. 'You know if I think there is a dolphin pod down there I'm bound to oppose your plans.'

'Yes, I know that. But my plans won't interfere with any dolphins.' He cracked a smile then, only not with his eyes.

'They might if you're landing planes on the water and running high-speed boats, not to mention diesel engines from floating hotels. John-Cody told me where you plan to site them. I've looked at the chart and the sound generated could reverberate through the whole fiord. Nobody's ever created an acoustic model of Dusky Sound, Mr Pole. We don't know what the implications might be.'

'What about the implications of all those new jobs going begging? New Zealand's economy is hardly booming right now.'

Libby shrugged. 'I'm a scientist, Mr Pole. The economy isn't my problem.'

Pole finished his coffee and smiled at her again. 'I tell you what,' he said. 'Let's talk about your boat instead.'

'Are you sure you still want to help me?'

'I'm not helping you. I'm a businessman, Liberty. If I don't lease you a vessel, somebody else will. Feelings don't come into it.'

They went down to the yard again and he led the way behind the house to a large barn-style garage. Libby saw an eighteen-foot motor launch with a canvas hood over the wheel area. It was sitting on a steel trailer. She walked round it, taking in the lines. It was in good condition and the engine was an outboard Evinrude. She had used similar boats before and instinctively she knew it would more than suit her purpose.

'It looks very good,' she said. 'Can I afford it?'

'I don't know. Why don't you tell me?'

Bree had two lessons, maths and information technology, and then there was a fifteen-minute break and the whole school descended on the playground. Some of the girls threw a volleyball around, others a rugby ball. The boys had a cricket pitch set up on the playing field in double quick time. Bree had sat next to a girl they called 'Biscuit' during the lessons, but she had not said much and struck Bree as a little bit timid. Now she stood alone by the netball posts and watched everyone watching her with the extra-special scrutiny reserved for a new student. Three girls from her class were sitting on a low wall with a tousle-headed girl in the middle. Her skirt was hiked up her thighs and her small breasts pressed against the material of her blouse as she pulled her shoulders back. Jessica Lowden: Bree had already singled her out as potential trouble. There was generally one to watch in every class and she had experienced a few over the years, some worse than others. This one had a tough and confident face and what appeared to be the respect or fear of most of her classmates. As Bree watched, the three of them slipped off the wall and sauntered across the playground, eyes on her, eyes all over her, greedy, intimidating. Bree felt her heart begin to beat that little bit faster.

'What kind of a name is Bree?' Jessica faced her, back to the netball post. 'We were told it was Breezy.'

'It is. I just shorten it to Bree.'

'Sounds like cheese,' one of the others said. 'Smelly French cheese: Cheesy Breezy.' They laughed then and Jessica turned up her nose. 'Smells like cheese, too: definitely smelly cheese.'

Bree folded her arms, then unfolded them again. Jessica's stare was full and unnerving and she had that hardness about her mouth that a person couldn't reason with.

'Not only smelly and cheesy, but a Pom to go with it.'

Bree moved to get past her, but Jessica stood in her way. Bree looked at her, then beyond her to where she saw a dark-haired boy watching from the cricket pitch with his hands fisted on his hips. She recognized him from their class.

Jessica sniffed the air again and coughed. 'Ugh, you stink.' She coughed again and the three of them descended into fits of laughter.

Bree walked across the playground to where Biscuit was standing, sipping from a paper cup of water. She might be timid and say nothing, but right at that moment she was Bree's only point of refuge.

'Are you OK?' Biscuit said when Bree got to her.

'Fine. I'm just fine.'

Libby drove home, having agreed terms with Pole. It had been a strange meeting but, as he had pointed out, business was business. She knew they were going to be on opposite sides of the fence, but he seemed a decent enough man. She told John-Cody about it when she got back to the house.

'He's all right,' he said. 'People like him: he's a big man down here, still got a hell of a reputation. Not just here either, all over the South Island. His wife's not stupid. I'm not saying it's why she married him, but he's central to any plans of the kind the Americans are looking at. He's what they call marketable, I guess. I've seen some of the promotional stuff they're going to use in the States and it's all about Ned.' He made a face. 'I take a different standpoint to him and I don't agree with some of his business methods, but it's not personal.' He shrugged. 'Me and Tom have different ideas too, but he's still my friend.'

'Tom?'

'Tom Blanch: you haven't met him yet, my old skipper. He'll fix us up with the barge at Supply Bay.'

John-Cody said he would go over to Pole's place himself and hook the trailer up to his Ute so they could tow the boat down to the barge, but he would sort out the lake crossing with Tom first. Tom lived only ten minutes' walk away and John-Cody set off with Ned Pole on his mind. He didn't care about going to his house to get the boat and in a way that surprised him. But then he had surprised himself already lately, effectively moving into the homestay when they got back from Preservation Inlet. The trip had eased his soul somewhat: he felt he was no longer failing Mahina by sitting on the *Korimako* day after day wondering whether to end it all.

When they had got back across the lake at the weekend he'd had no idea what his intentions were, beyond going for a last meal in the pub with the guests as usual. Afterwards he just went to the homestay and climbed into bed. That had been a weird moment, listening to Libby next door in the bathroom that he and Mahina had shared for twenty years. They had showered together under the same fall of water that he could hear falling on Libby now. He imagined her at Sealers Beach, in her shorts and barefoot with mud climbing the skin of her legs. His mouth dried and his tongue grew thick and he was appalled at himself: it was only a year since Mahina had died and another woman could do that to him.

He had tossed and turned all night, contemplated going back to the boat first thing in the morning, but he didn't. When he got up he cut the grass, which always took an age because he did it so infrequently

187

and there was a lot of it. Then he mooched about the garden, shovelling compost and putting food out for the birds, inspecting the trees that had been partially felled by the electricity company on the section next door. He had checked his possum traps but they were empty. Then he cleaned the old hunting rifle Tom had given him for his twenty-third birthday; he hadn't used it in years. When he and Mahina had got into the ecology charter business, hunting seemed incongruous, even though the deer were not native and the damage they did was devastating. He still ate feral venison whenever he could get it and he always told hunters when he came across fresh spoor in the bush, but he had not shot one himself for a long time.

Bree had helped him with the bird tables, told him again how much she had enjoyed the trip and thanked him for teaching her to snorkel. He showed her the frogs in the pond that she could hear croaking at night and she helped him with the grass clippings. He had glimpsed Libby watching them through the window and it gave him a start, seeing her dark hair in the half-light cast by the sun's reflection.

He had watched them driving to school this morning; he'd meant to come out in time to wish Bree all the best but they had gone earlier than he'd expected. So he just went to the office, bumping into Alex along the way. He had opened his file on the national park boundaries: he had written to one of the newly elected Green Party members of parliament and he was waiting for a phone call. He was sure that somehow the change in boundaries from the Tasman to the mean high-water mark was a mistake that could still be rectified. If that was the case, the likes of Nehemiah Pole could whistle for their floating lodges. In the meantime, though, he wasn't going to hold his breath and he owed it to himself, and particularly to Mahina, to fight the application all the way to a full hearing.

When Pole had first put in his plans a year or so ago, there had been many submitters against him, but one by one they seemed to have dropped out. Five of the other charter companies who operated in Doubtful Sound had opposed him initially, as well as the Department of Conservation. Southland Tours had not put in a submission, which was understandable given that they were one of the largest operators in the area. They ran buses into Milford every day and boats on day trips from there, and they had two large overnighters and a similar operation running in Deep Cove. If Pole and his backers got their way that would open up all kinds of opportunities for them. John-Cody could see a day when the wilderness he fought to protect would be lost for the next generation. He had been pondering these thoughts when Libby came back from Ned Pole's place and told him about the boat.

Tom Blanch was in his garden when John-Cody got there, sweating under a polythene tent that stood fifteen feet high and eighty feet long. Beneath it were the twin upturned hulls of the catamaran he was building. Tom was fifty-seven years old and knew more about the seas round the South Island than any man alive. He had been John-Cody's mentor and friend for twenty-five years. The cat was a project he had undertaken four years previously and already the hulls were shaped and set with bulkheads and the masts lay in the garden, perfectly tooled from the North Island kauri timber that shipbuilders loved so much. He looked up from where he was standing on a section of hull, embraced by a scaffolding platform he had fashioned himself.

'G'day, Gib. How you going?'

'Good, thanks, mate. See you're still at it.'

'Got to be. That's if I want to launch her next year.'

John-Cody ran a palm along the smooth flank of the hull.

'Heard you took a tour out last week. That was about time.'

'You think so?'

'It's been a year, Gib. A man's got to go back to work some time.'

John-Cody sat down on a workbench and took out his tobacco. 'It was hard, Tom.'

'But good though, eh?'

John-Cody nodded. 'Yes, I'd be lying if I said it wasn't good. Good to be out there again.'

Tom looked at him then and laid down his sander. 'I know we don't agree on everything that goes on in the fiords, Gib. But you do a good job. The *Korimako* is the only boat that really stands for something.' He shrugged. 'Me, I like crayfish, but what you're doing is important. I'd hate to see you give up on what you and Mahina created.'

John-Cody stuck his cigarette paper against his lip. 'I appreciate that, Tom. Especially coming from an old fisherman like you.'

Tom looked darkly at him. 'Less of the old, I can still cut it when I have to.'

John-Cody laughed. 'You keep telling yourself

190

that. Hey, listen. Can you arrange for the barge to take Libby's boat across the water?'

'That the new scientist I've not met yet?'

John-Cody nodded.

'I heard she was young and pretty.'

'I hadn't really noticed.'

'Jean Grady's been spreading the word. Apparently you gave up your half of the house for her.'

'She's got a daughter, Tom. It wasn't a difficult decision.'

Tom nodded. 'I reckon. But it's the kind of situation that makes tongues wag in a small town, mate, especially women's tongues.'

John-Cody shrugged. 'So let them wag if gossip makes them happy. It makes no difference to me.'

'What's the daughter like?'

'Bree. She's a nice kid. In fact it's her first day at school today. I hope she gets on OK.'

'Te Anau can be a tough town, Gibby.'

'She's bright and I reckon she can be tough when she has to.'

'Then she'll be just fine.' Tom looked enviously at his friend's cigarette. 'Where'd you get the boat for the scientist?'

John-Cody snorted. 'Nehemiah Pole.'

He drove over on his own to hook up the boat for Libby. She was busy in the office, making phone calls to Dunedin and talking to Alex about the possibility of her looking after Bree when she was in Dusky Sound. He drove slowly, one hand on the wheel, an arm out of the window, and watched a pair of harriers performing their courtship ritual, two black shadows against the blue of the sky. Pole was in the paddock when he got there, exercising Barrio on a lunge rope. He looked round when he heard the truck, tipped back his hat and took a rag from the back pocket of his jeans.

John-Cody parked and got out, grinding the butt of his cigarette into the stones. He leaned on the open door and the wind plucked at the roots of his hair. Pole watched him for a moment then unclipped Barrio's lunge rope. The stallion bucked and kicked and sprang away up the hillside. John-Cody watched Pole as he made his way to the fence with his long, slightly bow-legged lope.

'You're pretty good with that thing,' he said.

Pole looked at the rope, then back at Barrio. 'Eli's horse, Gib.'

'I know it.'

Pole climbed the fence and dropped beside him. He looked at the battered Ute and raised one eyebrow. 'You reckon that old wreck'll cover it?'

John-Cody smiled.

'It would've been just as easy for me to give her a tow.'

'I'm here now.'

Pole looked at him then, as if sizing him up. He took a cigar from his shirt pocket.

'You want some grog?'

John-Cody shook his head.

'Coffee then?'

'No, thank you. Let's just hook up the boat and I'll get out of here.'

Pole moved his shoulders. 'Suit yourself. Back your Ute up to the barn.'

John-Cody backed up and climbed out again. Pole

was standing on the trailer and he told him to come back a little more so he could get the cap on the ball joint. John-Cody got behind the wheel again and they manoeuvred the trailer and truck till the coupling was settled. He killed the engine and hooked up the lights himself while Pole leaned against the hull of the boat and watched him.

'Pretty woman, Gib.'

'Who is?'

'Dr Liberty Bass.'

'You think?'

'Don't you?'

John-Cody straightened. 'I never thought about it.'

Pole pushed himself away from the boat. 'Very attractive.'

'I hadn't really noticed.'

'No life after Mahina, eh?'

John-Cody tensed, the muscles knotting up in his arms.

'She was a good woman, Gib, no doubt about that. Very good woman. But life goes on, you know. There's other fish in the sea.'

John-Cody wiped sweat from his eyes. 'You know what, Ned? You have no idea what you're talking about.'

Pole looked evenly back at him and folded his arms across his chest. 'No idea at all, nobody has but you, huh?'

John-Cody looked sideways at him. 'What's that supposed to mean?'

'She's dead, Gib. Life goes on, that's all.'

'That's not what you just said.'

Pole's stare was chill and cold. He looked at the

193

ground between his feet, and drew his lips back over his teeth. He was about to say something when a car pulled into the drive and the moment was broken. He stepped past John-Cody and looked through the open doors of the barn.

'There's Jane back,' he said. 'I guess she must've flown in from Queenstown.' He glanced at John-Cody. 'Are you finished here?'

John-Cody nodded and got behind the wheel of his truck. He eased the boat and trailer into the drive. Jane Pole emerged from her car and went to join her husband. She wore a two-piece suit, and her grey hair was pulled back from her high cheekbones and thin-lipped mouth. They looked coldly at each other as John-Cody passed. When he was gone she turned to her husband.

'What's he doing with that boat?'

Pole smiled at her. 'I rented it to the scientist who's staying in Dusky Sound. I thought some good PR wouldn't hurt our application.'

His wife stared at him. 'My God,' she said, 'you're actually thinking for once. Pity you didn't do that before you mortgaged our home for a gold mine without any gold.'

Pole flared his nostrils, cheeks white at the bones. 'Don't start, Jane.'

She stepped away from him, then paused and turned back. 'I won't. You just make sure you pull this off, Nehemiah. Our backers are still keen. Mercifully your reputation is as a hunter, not a businessman, or we wouldn't see them for dust.' She turned and walked into the house.

For a long moment Pole watched the space left behind her, in his head his father's face and his father's voice and five gold talents rattling on a table.

John-Cody drove the boat to Supply Bay where he had arranged to meet Libby and Tom. His heart was troubled and he sucked hard on a cigarette, Pole's eyes and Pole's words burning into his mind. What did he mean back there? Nothing, Gib, he told himself. He meant nothing. He's trying to wind you up, unnerve you: he's playing mind games is all.

Libby had asked Alex to pick up Bree from the bus stop, as they would not be back from Deep Cove in time. She told her she thought Bree would come straight to the office anyway, so she could see Sierra, but it might be best to go and meet her. She felt really bad about not being there on her first day, but she needed to get the boat to Deep Cove as soon as possible and a barge was making the crossing that afternoon. It was the age-old dilemma, trying to juggle her work with finding time for Bree. She thought about it for a long while, though, wondering if she might ask John-Cody to take the boat over the hill by himself. But she couldn't do that, she hardly knew him and he was doing her a favour as it was.

She hitched a lift with Tom Blanch and liked him immediately. He was a gentle-looking soul with a twinkle in his eye and an easy smile emanating from somewhere deep in his beard.

John-Cody was at Supply Bay before them, the boat hooked to his truck; he was under the canopy checking the VHF radio when they pulled up.

'You two finally met then,' he said. 'No need for me to make introductions.' The breeze blew his hair about his face and he took a tie from his shirt pocket and drew it into a knot at the back of his head.

'We're old friends, Gib.' Tom put an arm round Libby's shoulders and squeezed. 'Looks like a good boat.'

'It's all right.' John-Cody stood upright. 'There's no single side band, but the VHF should pick up Bluff Radio from Dusky.'

Tom nodded. 'Mine always did.'

'That's what I thought.' John-Cody looked down at Libby. 'I guess you're all set.'

At West Arm they unloaded and John-Cody rechecked the tow bar then hauled the launch over the Wilmot Pass. It started to rain pretty hard and by the time they passed Helena Falls they were in full flow. At Deep Cove he swung the truck round and backed the trailer right into the water. Libby helped uncouple the bows then he showed her how to pump the fuel and start the engine. She had back-up tanks of petrol and it had been agreed she could store more at Supper Cove.

Once the boat was in the water Libby backed her out and round, then chugged beyond the line of cray-fish vessels that belonged to Pole. John-Cody drove the truck to his wharf and parked by the side of the road. He went down to the *Korimako* and climbed aboard as Libby drew the launch up to the dive platform. The boat secured, she swung herself over the rail, to where John-Cody stood looking beyond her. He pointed over her shoulder.

'Wave dancers,' he said.

She turned and saw half a dozen dolphins blowing against the far wall of Deep Cove. The rain fell as slanted grey drizzle and their blowholes pumped jets of steam into the cooling atmosphere.

'They don't often get this far up the sound,' John-Cody said.

They watched for a while and Libby was a little irritated. Twice now she had seen the dolphins of Doubtful Sound but she hadn't glimpsed so much as a dorsal fin in Dusky. John-Cody suggested coffee and they went inside. He disappeared below and the deck vibrated as he fired up the auxiliary engine. Libby filled the jug from the tap, then selecting a tape she switched the cassette recorder on. John-Cody lit the diesel stove and when he came up the steps Libby was in the galley spooning coffee into the cafetière.

'You like it strong, don't you?' she said.

'Strong as.' He went on deck and hosed down the for'ard section.

Libby waited for the kettle to boil, singing along to the tape and watching him through the wheel-house windows. She liked the fluidity of his movements: he seemed so much at ease with himself, even when he was just holding the hose. He looked more at home on the *Korimako* than he did on dry land: the boat moved as part of him, it felt like him, smelt like him. They had the same sense of quiet, a similar kind of assurance. He looked up, caught her eye through the blurred glass then bent to his task once again. Libby poured the coffee and took his out on deck. Across the far side of Deep Cove the dolphins were moving systematically along the wall; she could see the arch of their backs, the rise and fall of dorsal fins. John-Cody poked the nozzle of the hose through the scuppers and took the coffee from her. Libby was watching the pod: it had turned now and the dolphins were making their way back to the entrance of Deep Cove. She glanced down at the launch bobbing at the back of the boat. '*Wave Dancer*,' she read.

'That's what I call them.'

Libby shook her head. 'No, I mean my call sign when I'm in Dusky. I'll answer to *Wave Dancer*.'

Bree didn't have a good first day. At lunchtime Jessica Lowden and her cronies wouldn't leave her alone and pretty soon the new nickname had worked its way round the playground. During the afternoon she just got her head down and studied hard. The tutors told her they would be making an early assessment of her abilities and she found the work they placed before her pretty easy. Others in the class clearly didn't and that disturbed her even more. It would not be the first time that 'Boff' had been added to the other nicknames she acquired. By the time four o'clock came round she was weary of it all and her horizon looked grey again all at once.

She was not sure where to get the bus and had to ask her tutor, who took her outside and showed her. Jessica was hanging round and for a moment Bree thought she would be getting on, but mercifully she didn't. Bree kept away from her till the bus pulled up then she settled into a seat by the window, while Jessica and her friends made faces at her from their perch on the low wall. Bree ignored them, let the air escape from her chest and closed her eyes. She just wanted to see her mother. It had been bad, as bad as she had thought: no, worse.

She felt someone sit down in the seat next to her

and looking up she saw the dark-haired boy who had watched from the cricket pitch when Jessica first taunted her. She looked beyond him to the seats across the aisle and they were empty: she realized then that he had deliberately sat with her and she shrank against the window, waiting for more barbed comments.

But he looked at her and smiled, then looked beyond her to the window and stared at Jessica and her friends. They stared back for a moment then moved off the wall and swaggered down the street.

'How you going, Bree?' the boy said to her. 'How was your first day?'

'It was OK.'

'She didn't give you too much lip?' He pointed to Jessica's departing back.

'No.'

'Good on you.' He took a can of Coke from his bag and ripped off the ring pull. He drank deeply, wiped his mouth and offered it to her. She took a sip and handed it back to him.

'Thanks.'

'No worries. Are you living in Manapouri?'

She nodded. 'Next door to John-Cody Gibbs.'

'I know Gib.' The boy smiled again and Bree looked at his face in profile, strong and tanned, red at the cheekbones: he must be nearly thirteen because he had soft dark down forming along his jaw and hairs beginning to grow on his arms. He smelled sweaty, but not in a bad way. 'I'm Hunter Caldwell,' he said. 'I live out at Blackmount so we'll be on the same bus.'

That was all he said. For the rest of the journey they sat in silence, but when the bus stopped outside the office Hunter moved out of the way and told her he would see her tomorrow. Bree nodded and got off and then the bus pulled away from the stop. She stood in the spitting rain and watched for a moment then felt Sierra at the back of her legs. Looking round, she saw Alex coming towards her.

'How was your day?' Alex asked.

'All right.' Bree looked for her mother but couldn't see her, and dropping to one knee she fondled Sierra's ears. 'Where's Mum?'

'She's at Deep Cove, Bree. She had to get a boat across the pass. Don't worry, she'll be back in a while.'

Bree nodded, dropping her gaze. The one day she really needed her mother, the first day at a new school: didn't she think about that? Bree looked at the ground and tears built against her eyes. But she forced them down: she would not let Alex see her cry.

Alex watched her, head to one side, and sensed her mood. 'Would you like to take Sierra down to the beach?'

Bree got up without looking at Alex and called the dog to heel. They crossed the road and started down the track to where the rain was chipping at the surface of the lake. Sierra raced off into the trees to sniff for rabbits. Bree wandered between the trees and stopped just at the edge of the shingle. A solitary boat was crossing the lake, the hull painted red. She thought about her mother and being here in New Zealand. She thought about France and the friends she had left behind: she thought about Isabelle and Sylvie and how it probably would have been better if her mother had just married Pierre after all. She reflected on her day at school, kicking at a stone half buried in the mud at her feet, and then she burst into tears.

Sierra heard her and looked up from where she was dragging at a boulder in the shallows. Bree stood under the tree and wept, feeling very small against the mountains. Why were some people so horrible? She would never forgive her mother for naming her Breezy: what on earth was she thinking of?

Sitting on the white stone by the eucalyptus tree, she ignored the drizzle and took a pen and paper from her school bag: she would tell her father all that had happened. She asked him why he had let her mother take her away from him, why he hadn't stepped in when she wanted to call her such a stupid name. She took her time, watching a pair of scaups skating across the water while Sierra went after the biggest stones. When she was finished she walked up to the shop and asked Mrs Grady to post the letter.

EIGHT

'*Wave Dancer?*' Bree wrinkled her nose at her mother as they stood waiting for the bus.

'Yes, I needed a call sign so when I'm in Dusky you can get me on the radio. John-Cody will show you how to work it. We can talk every day and you can tell me all about school and your day, and it'll be just like I'm with you.'

Bree looked unconvinced.

Libby smiled and took her hand. 'Look, I'm really sorry it has to be like this, darling. But there is no other way. The longest time I'll spend down there is a week. Then I'll get the floatplane back and be home in no time. If there's an emergency or you really need me then the plane will come and get me. It only takes about half an hour by air so there's nothing to worry about.'

'OK.' Bree tightened her grip on her mother's hand, suddenly a little frightened. Everything was still so new and difficult at school. The first week was over and nothing had improved: now her mum was off to Dusky Sound and would not be back till the floatplane picked her up next week. That meant

Bree would have not only the second week at her new school but the coming weekend without her. She forced down tears, reminding herself that she had been here many times before: not that it made it any easier. She had told her mother nothing of what was going on with Jessica and her gang, the nicknames, the jibes, the bullying at break time.

'Are you going to be OK?' Libby asked. 'Alex has agreed to sleep over at our place, as you know, rather than uproot you to hers. John-Cody should be around at the weekend and I'll be home next week. You'll have Sierra and you can talk to me on the ship-to-shore as often as you like.'

The bus was rumbling towards them along the main road and Bree bit her lip. She didn't want to get on with tears in her eyes or a red face or anything: she would be a teenager next year and crying would be really stupid. Letting go of her mother's hand, she shouldered her bag and stepped closer to the kerb.

Libby bent for a kiss and Bree offered a quick cheek then moved away and held her hand out for the bus. Libby took the hint. Bree got on without looking back and Libby stood there for a long moment, fighting tears of her own; when she turned she saw John-Cody standing at the corner with a mug of coffee in his hand. She pursed her lips and walked back, arms folded and looking at the ground.

'Tough one, eh,' he said quietly. 'She'll be all right. Sierra'll look after her. I've never seen a more devoted dog in my life.'

'Alex'll be cool, won't she, John-Cody?' Libby looked up at him, a little choking sound in her voice.

Instinctively he slipped an arm about her shoulders. 'Of course she will. Alex is more than capable. Last night she told me she was really looking forward to it.'

'And she doesn't mind sleeping over at our place? She's only just had her window put in.'

'That's no problem. She'll have her window for ever.'

'It's only till I can get something more permanent sorted out.' Libby pushed stiff fingers through her hair. 'God, I hate this. I feel as though I'm abandoning her.'

John-Cody held her away from him and she could smell the sweetness of coffee on his breath. 'Don't worry, Lib. You're a single mother who works. You're doing it for Bree, keeping body and soul together. Bree will be just fine. Now, get your gear ready. If we're going to make Supper Cove tonight we have to hit the road.'

John-Cody had told Jonah he didn't need him for the trip to Dusky. Libby could help him where he needed it on the way down the coast and he was more than capable of sailing the *Korimako* back on his own. He was due in Doubtful for a two-day tour the day after tomorrow anyway, and Jonah had dashed up to Naseby to visit his father while he had the chance. John-Cody half wished he could have gone with him; he hadn't seen Kobi in months and was mindful of how frail the old man was becoming.

They cast off from the wharf at Deep Cove, Libby washing down the deck as John-Cody steered the *Korimako* past Elizabeth Island. He flicked on the autopilot and messed about in the engine room, popping his head up from the for'ard steps every now and again to check their position. Libby stood at the port door, keeping an eye on the pilot: she leaned where John-Cody leaned and studied the water ahead of them. She checked the temperature gauge, making sure it didn't exceed forty degrees, and watched the compass shift in the alcohol-mounted gimbal. She put water on to boil then went astern to check on the *Wave Dancer*. The little boat bobbed along behind the dive platform, surfing the wash kicked up by the propeller.

Back in the wheelhouse she made coffee and put music on and studied the gauges some more. The radar and GPS were both switched off but she was determined to watch John-Cody if he entered any waypoints when they cleared the Hare's Ears.

He didn't. They had the daylight with them: the radar showed the massed cliffs of the west coast as green blobs on the screen and he knew this part of the world like the back of his hand. Libby stood against the starboard door with him across the bridge as the *Korimako* wallowed from side to side, bows punching into a wind that howled from the south-west.

'Have you ever seen dolphins south of Dusky?' Libby asked him.

He nodded.

'Where?'

'About twenty ks north of Port Ross.'

'Where's that?'

'The Auckland Islands.'

'What species?'

'Bottlenose. I've seen them a few times in roughly the same place, north of the Sub-Antarctic fishery management area.'

'How many?'

'Fifty, sixty maybe.'

'How many times have you seen them?'

'Every time I go down.'

'That's a long way south.'

'Tell me about it.'

'What about in Port Ross itself?'

'Never.'

'So you don't think they could be resident down there?'

'Do you?'

Libby shrugged. 'I don't know. The pod in Doubtful are way south of where bottlenose should be. They generally prefer tropical shallow water.'

John-Cody nodded. 'Don't you just love the way nature thumbs its nose at our ideas of what is and what's not what it should be? Mahina used to love that.' He caught himself thinking about her again, the times they had been on this boat together.

Libby sensed the sudden melancholy. 'Talk about her if it helps,' she told him. 'I don't mind.'

John-Cody sat down at the table then and studied the inside of his coffee cup.

He told Libby what had happened, how the cancer was everywhere in no time, tunnelling inside her body. He told her of his promise, how she wanted her ashes placed in the fuchsia tree for a year; then he sat for a moment with his hands clasped together. Libby watched him, one arm hugged to her waist.

'I've never heard bellbirds in that fuchsia tree,' she said.

He looked up at her. 'Neither have I. Not since she died.'

Both of them were quiet for a moment then Libby said: 'Do you believe in an afterlife?'

He shrugged. 'I don't know. Mahina did. She told me she was going to taste the breath of eternity.' He touched his hair, rubbing the frayed ends between his fingers. 'She used to spend hours brushing my hair. It was really long then.' And he saw her again in his mind's eye, naked by the fire after making love for hours: him cross-legged, the glow from the flames red and bronze and gold on his skin. He could feel the warmth of Mahina as she knelt behind him and took the brush to his hair. He closed his eyes and felt the lump lodge in his throat. He stood up suddenly. 'Anyway she's gone now.' He looked down at Libby. 'Have you ever been in love, Lib? I mean really truly in love: so much so you can't get through the day without speaking to that person at least three or four times, telling them how much you love them, how they dominate your every waking thought. Have you ever had anyone feel like that about you?'

Libby shook her head. 'No. I'm sad to say I haven't.'

'It's all consuming. It takes you over completely. I met Mahina by my deer trap on Yuvali Beach when I was twenty-four years old. She came to my crib that night and we talked till dawn. I never spent a night away from her after that unless I was at sea. Then I called her on the ship-to-shore two or three times a day and I didn't care who was listening.' Again he touched his hair. 'I cut this off when I scattered her ashes.'

He went out on deck and she watched him work his way astern, where he unzipped the flap on the glasshouse and smoked a cigarette. Libby stayed by the wheel, watching the dials, and thought about all

207

that he had told her. She realized then, perhaps for the first time, the full extent of his loss.

They made Dusky Sound early that evening: the daylight was bright till almost nine o'clock and John-Cody guided the *Korimako* in at Breaksea and down the Acheron Passage. Only a couple of hours' steaming and they would be in the Supper Cove estuary where Libby could unload her gear. She had masses of it, including a diesel-driven generator to run her hydra-phone lines and computers. She'd asked John-Cody what were the chances of some-body stealing or vandalizing the stuff when she was back in Manapouri. She could bring her laptop out with her, but not much else on a floatplane. He doubted anything would happen and told her that a couple of fishermen friends of his lived on an old barge that was permanently moored off Cooper Island; he'd ask them to keep an eye on things for her.

'When you dive, make sure you put a flag up on your boat,' he told her, and indicated the blue flag he had furled on the starboard sheet. 'Anything blue will do. Run it up your aerial mast where it can be seen. No boat will pass within two hundred metres of you at more than five knots if you have the dive flag up. The other thing you must do is put a call out to any other boat you can raise and tell them what you're doing. Give them the time and how long you'll be down. They can call you up at a fixed time later and if you don't answer they can raise the alarm.'

'Not that it'll do me any good if I'm stuck underwater.'

He made a face. 'It's a precaution, Libby. The

sounds can be weird places to dive, especially on your own. Spooky even, sometimes.'

'I can do spooky. What about sharks?'

He shrugged. 'We get mako and white pointer out here. Keep away from the seals.' He smiled then. 'Don't worry, I've dived here for twenty years and the only shark I ever saw was swimming away from me. You won't have any bother.'

'Anyway,' Libby said, 'I won't be diving for a while. I've not clapped eyes on a single dolphin so far.'

'You'll see them all right.'

'You're sure?'

'They live here.' He grinned wickedly at her. 'We just need a scientist to tell us that.'

They dropped anchor in Supper Cove, Libby watching the chain run out while John-Cody eased the boat astern. The Department of Conservation hut was off to port, still visible in the gathering gloom. Libby stood on deck, gazed across oil-coloured water and was suddenly filled with trepidation. The estuary was flat and silted, rimu and kahikatea on the shoreline, beech trees crowding the banked earth higher up. Already she could hear weka shrieking.

The Hilda Burn ran into the cove near the hut and John-Cody told Libby that was where the DoC workers had rigged up the pump so she would have plenty of fresh water. The Seaforth River fed the estuary from the mountains and if she had to she could follow it and walk to West Arm. There was another hut en route and there was always someone at the power station if she hit any kind of trouble. Libby looked at him and nodded.

'You're not going back tonight, though, are you?'

He shook his head. 'No, we're moored for the night now. I'll help you set up your gear and check your boat in the morning, but then I have to leave. I've got to meet the next party of guests in Deep Cove.'

'So you're not going back to Manapouri?'

'Not till the weekend, I'm not.'

'Will you do me a favour when you get back?'

'Of course.'

'Will you keep an eye on Bree for me? This is going to be really hard on her and she's had to put up with so much already.'

'Love to.' He smiled then and his eyes were grey and gentle. 'And don't worry, she'll be just fine. If she really misses you badly I'll fly her in on a float-plane.'

Libby cooked dinner and John-Cody brought an acoustic guitar from his cabin and picked at the strings. There was still a bottle of white wine in the fridge locker and Libby shifted the lid and rummaged among the milk and butter tubs to get it. She poured them each a glass and sipped hers while she listened to him playing.

'I don't recognize those songs,' she said when he laid aside the guitar.

'They're my own.'

'You wrote those? You're good.'

He made a face. 'Not as good as I could have been, or should have been for that matter. I was playing the clubs on Bourbon Street when I was fifteen. Sometimes I used to skip school so I could busk in Jackson Square.'

'New Orleans.'

210

He nodded.

'I've never been there.'

'I used to spend most of my time in the French Quarter, where the musicians hang out. That was before I got my draft notice.'

She frowned.

'Vietnam, Libby: I'm that age, forty-eight almost. My buddies and me got our papers all at the same time.' His eyes dimmed then and for a moment he was back on Bourbon Street.

The Stiff Cody Band had just finished their final set at Big Daddy's bar and was gathered upstairs drinking beer.

John-Cody sat in the strange silence with percussion still ringing in his ears and stared at the piece of official paper they had all received that morning. It called him to take a physical examination so he could go and fight in South East Asia.

The French Quarter was muted, even for one o'clock in the morning. A major storm had blown in from the gulf and the mud-coloured waters of the Mississippi crashed against the underside of the west shore bridge. Decatur Street was empty, as were Chartres and Royal all the way up to Bourbon. The strippers downstairs had earned hardly any money and the band had finished early.

John-Cody read the letter for the tenth time, laid it down and shook a Lucky Strike from the crumpled pack in his pocket. His Fender lay across his knees and he looked at the polished frets and bit his lip.

'I don't even know where Vietnam is.' Dewey, the drummer, stared through the half-darkness at him. John-Cody was listening to the flapping of a shutter across the street as the wind howled in the narrow spaces between the buildings.

'You got a map?'

Dewey shook his head. 'What if I get killed?'

'You won't get killed.' Jimmy Tibbins sipped froth off a can of beer. 'The army'll train you, stupid.'

'So what?' Dewey gawped at him. 'Marines still get killed. Don't tell me you haven't seen the body bags on TV.'

'Wars kill people, that's what they do.' John-Cody looked beyond his friends to where the drape lifted in the draught from the window. 'My dad told me that's how it was in Korea and how it was in World War II and all the other wars there's ever been. He said wars are good for nothing except killing lots of people. Thinning the population, he called it. Good for that and no more.'

'We've only got to last one year,' Tibbins said. 'I could do that.'

'Could you?' John-Cody drew on his cigarette. 'Maybe, maybe not: maybe the first time you're dropped into the jungle some VC pops up and puts a bullet in your head.'

He stopped talking and Libby looked at him, from where she leaned on the surface in the galley. The wine bottle was still half full and she poured him some more and he picked up the guitar once again.

'What was it like out there?'

John-Cody concentrated on his finger picking. 'I don't know. I didn't go.'

They transferred all her equipment to the hut first thing in the morning then John-Cody loosed the

212

Wave Dancer from its stern line and Libby watched him from the wheel. The anchor was up on the *Korimako* and she backed the launch away, rocking in the wake as he hit the revs and the ketch hove to starboard. He came out of the wheelhouse and waved as the boat steamed full ahead for the channel. Libby waved back, aware of a sense of loneliness creeping up on her, and then his voice came over the speaker on the radio.

'*Wave Dancer*, this is the *Korimako*, do you copy, Lib?'

She picked up the handset. 'Copy that loud and clear, John-Cody. Over.'

'OK. You're all set. Keep in regular contact with any boats in the sound. Let them know who and where you are.'

'Will do. I'll call the office when Bree gets home from school.'

'OK. Avoid five thirty: that's weather forecast time. And after seven it's fisherman's radio.'

'Before five thirty then, or between six and seven.'

'OK. Good luck, Libby. Yell out if you need anything. I'll speak to the floatplane pilot, make sure he's set to come and get you next week. Over and out.'

The radio went dead and Libby twisted the tuning button so she could listen to the static for a moment, then pressed the scanner and left it. The silence lifted around her, sitting there alone in the boat as the *Korimako*'s engines faded away, and she felt very small against the primeval bush that smothered the height of the mountains.

Gradually the wash died away and the launch sat steady in the estuary. Libby took a cigarette from her pocket, suddenly in need of something to calm the jangling in her nerves. Around her the bush was hazy with low cloud; it hung in wisps of damp mist curled as if from a fire above the soaking vegetation. She thought of Bree, left to her own devices in a new school, and her heart went out to her. She thought of Alex who had agreed to watch her and she hoped they would be all right, the two of them. She realized then that this was the first time she had ever taken a job that separated her from her daughter.

Work, Liberty, she told herself. We need the money, remember. That's what you're here for. She revved the engine and spun the wheel and headed for the shore and the department's hut.

Inside she gathered her cameras and her portable hydra-phone with the long extension cable and loaded them into the boat. Then she changed into a drysuit and hefted a tank of compressed air down to the shore. She had obtained a mini compressor from the dive shop in Invercargill and, using the generator for power, she could fill her bottles at will. She had plenty of fuel and she placed fins, snorkel, mask and harness in the boat. She ate a handful of biscuits and brewed a thermos of coffee, then she steered the *Wave Dancer* out into the channel.

She chugged along at a few knots, gazing at mountains that climbed in green and brown with a hint of scarlet now and again. John-Cody had told her the land was shallower here, the fiords not so sharp or high as further north. But the cloud drifted low and cast the hills in shadow; the water was black and she had a tremendous sense of her aloneness, the insignificance of her existence in this vast wilderness that had evolved into the rocks and trees and falling vegetation she saw now. She was suddenly struck by a sense of awe and it occurred to her that she was seeing the place through John-Cody's eyes.

Cruising west into the channel she watched the water for signs of dolphins blowing, but saw nothing. An hour passed; another, and then finally she heard a noise that thrilled her. She closed her eyes to listen. *Powf, powf, powf* – harshly expelled air, small explosions of sound one after the other, then two together, no symmetry to any of it. She opened her eyes and saw half a dozen fountains of condensation off to her right. The dolphins of Dusky Sound were making their way towards her.

Bree sat at her desk and felt the damp paper pellet hit her in the back of the neck. She stiffened but did not flinch, did not look round. Jessica sat behind her with Sally Tait, shirts open at the neck, green skirts hoisted above naked thighs. Bree kept her head bent to her textbook and concentrated. It had started the previous lesson, when Jessica had made sure that she and Sally sat directly behind her.

Yesterday had been all right. Bree had got through the day without thinking about her mother too much, but when she got off the bus she had gone straight to the office and called the *Korimako* on the ship-to-shore. She had walked Sierra on Fraser's Beach and sat on the big white stone, trying to skim pebbles. Before they went home, Alex had taken Bree to her house to collect some night things and Bree had stood in front of the huge pane of glass which framed the lake and Cathedral Peaks like a picture. Later, Alex had made pasta and told her all about working with John-Cody and Mahina before

215

Mahina died, and the battles they had had trying to maintain the wilderness in Fiordland.

This morning Bree got the bus and Hunter smiled at her and she sat down two seats in front of him and everything had been fine. That was until maths.

'Hey, Pom. Hey, Pommie.' It was no more than a whisper, but Bree heard Jessica's voice from behind her.

'She only answers to Cheesy.' Sally this time, and then the two of them giggling.

Bree shuddered involuntarily. The tutor looked up from his desk and scanned the room through tortoiseshell glasses. The students were supposed to be silent, concentrating on writing the essay. Bree had her books arrayed in front of her and was checking the notes she had made for homework last night.

'Hey, Cheesy, what flavour are you?'

The tutor looked up again. 'Whoever is whispering can kindly refrain,' he said. 'These are supposed to be examination conditions.'

Moments later Bree felt another damp pellet, this time on her shoulder, and she shifted in her seat. Next to her Biscuit was buried in her book, tongue poking between thin lips as she concentrated.

Bree wanted to challenge Jessica, but she couldn't. She looked out of the window and then across the classroom and straight into Hunter's eyes. It was as if he'd looked up deliberately to seek her out and now he smiled and as he did she felt a sense of warmth in her veins. A third pellet hit her and this time she did not move.

'No sense, no feeling,' came the whisper from behind her.

*   *   *

The dolphins were heading straight for the boat, moving in unison through Nine Fathom Passage to the south of Cooper Island. Libby saw dorsal fins break the surface and she eased back on the throttle and reached instinctively for her camera. She focused and snapped the dorsal fins as the dolphins moved. Good shots: each fin would be different, would show variations of colour, markings, little nicks in the flesh. It was the first step towards identification; sexing them would come later when she got the underwater video set up.

She counted ten dorsal fins in all, and the dolphins circled the boat but did not approach too closely. She eased the throttle forward again and headed away from them, hoping the bow wave would attract them. She could snap them up close and, if they rolled, sex them. They didn't come, though, and she slowed again, arced in the channel and tailed them at fifty metres. They were chasing fish, hunting high in the head of the sound. They moved into Shark Cove and Libby was reminded of Pole's plans for floating hotels. She imagined high-speed boats, floatplanes coming in and helicopter pads. Jet skis maybe in summer.

She eased the *Wave Dancer* into a clump of silver beech trees that jutted out from the bush, branches growing up at right angles from the tangled trunks, in search of sunlight. She strapped on her tank, fixed fins and mask and entered the time on the dive computer strapped to her wrist. She called her position over the radio and was answered by a crayfish boat at the head of the sound. She did as John-Cody had told her, letting the boat know how long she would be down. Then she ran the dive flag up the aerial mast, stepped over the side of the boat and was engulfed in sudden darkness.

The water was cold, even through the drysuit: cold and very dark. Initially it was unnerving. She could see nothing, and very slowly she sank into the gloom. The fresh-water layer was ten feet thick here, though sometimes it was as much as thirty after particularly heavy rains, and it was stained brown by tannin seeping from fallen vegetation. Slowly she descended, bubbles rising from the demand valve in her mouth. She cleared her mask and gradually the blackness gave way to a yellow oily layer and then she was in salt water and visibility returned. Yet it was still pretty dark and she could feel the chill against her face as she moved in a slow circle to get her bearings.

She checked her depth then finned towards the walls of the fiord that dropped away sharply. Further into the middle the depth plummeted to three hundred feet and it was as great as a thousand in some places. Nothing grew here, no plant life: the rocks were bare and grey, brown in places and black among the shadows. Black coral clung to the wall, white in the gloom where the live coral grew round the black skeleton. Purple-coloured snake stars, resident cleaners who stripped away the waste and allowed the arms of the coral to grow, wrapped themselves round its stems. Libby's underwater camera hung from its tape and she moved along the wall, looking down into the darkness.

And then she heard the clicks as they scanned her, echolocating; and a smile leaked water into the sides of her mouth. Turning with a gentle sweep of her arms she still could not see them, but the clicks

218

buzzed and rattled as sonic pulses bounced off her, forming three-dimensional images in the heads of the dozen bottlenose hunters that grew up out of the shadows. She lifted her camera and photographed them as they approached her.

The pod swam close, phosphorescent in the sunlight that broke through the layer of fresh water. One of them – white on the belly with nicks at both the top and base of its dorsal fin – came very near. It slowed and its eye met hers, then it wheeled in for another look. Libby held out her hand and the dolphin dipped away with a thrust of powerful flukes; she was rocked back in the wake, but picked out the genital slits and felt a rush of excitement. The first member of the pod was identified and sexed in the same moment: Libby estimated him to be eight or nine feet long and she knew she would recognize that dorsal fin again.

She snapped the others as best she could, then the pod disappeared into the gloom and she was left alone with the silence of Fiordland underwater. Checking her dive gauge she rose slowly to the surface and came up some distance from the boat. She rolled on her back and, looking up at the grey of the sky, she saw a floatplane descending between the clouds.

Back in the boat she peeled off her harness and tank and started the engine. She had a name in her head: the first resident of Dusky Sound would be logged as Old Nick. She couldn't wait to tell Bree.

She followed the pod along Cook Channel where the dozen from Shark Cove were greeted by whistling, leaping dolphins coming in the other direction. Libby followed them between the islands and figured they were heading for the Acheron Passage.

As she came out beyond East Point she saw the floatplane riding the waves in the deep water and a tall man standing on one of the floats. She eased the boat closer and recognized the height and build of Nehemiah Pole. The radio crackled from the speaker on the dashboard in front of her.

'*Wave Dancer*, *Wave Dancer*, this is the floatplane Indigo 99. Do you copy?'

Libby lifted the handset. 'This is the *Wave Dancer*, reading you loud and clear. Over.'

'If you're looking for dolphins they're heading up the Acheron Passage.'

Libby paused for a moment. 'Thank you,' she said. 'I've seen them.'

It was Pole's voice. She could see now that he had a walkie-talkie in his hand.

'Is everything OK?' he asked. 'Anything we can do for you?'

Libby held the handset but did not respond immediately: she was watching the pilot keeping the nose of the plane turned into the wind. 'Thank you, Mr Pole,' she said. 'There's nothing I need right now. *Wave Dancer* out.' She eased open the throttle and headed for the Acheron Passage.

Pole stood and watched her go, the water lapping over his boots. He gripped the wing strut with the door open then swung up into the seat alongside the pilot.

'So that's Liberty Bass,' his wife said from the seat behind him. 'She looks young and pretty.'

Pole squinted over his shoulder at her.

'Is she going to be trouble?'

Pole didn't miss the intonation in her voice and he stared after Libby's boat. 'I don't know. Depends on what she can prove, I suppose.'

'Well, she can't prove that noise affects dolphins.' Jane Pole stared at the back of the pilot's head. 'Not in the time that she has anyway.'

Pole looked back at her again. 'What if she proves the existence of the pod?'

'That they're resident?' His wife arched her eyebrows. 'She won't do that either: not definitively. Not in time.' She touched the pilot on the shoulder and he eased the plane into the wind, increasing the strain on the engine. Jane looked back at her husband. 'I think we can deal with Liberty Bass,' she said. 'John-Cody Gibbs is our real problem. The proverbial thorn in the side: a thorn that needs to be dug out before infection sets in.' She pursed her mouth, puckering thin red lips into a twisted line. 'What I didn't tell you, Nehemiah, is that though they're keen, our friends in the States are becoming rather irritated. If something isn't done about Gibbs soon they might just look elsewhere.'

Pole's face lost its colour.

'Yes, my darling,' she said. 'And with what you've done to our property that leaves us high and dry. Actually it leaves *you* high and dry. I've got a good law practice back in the States, maybe it's time I paid more attention to it.'

Pole was silent for a moment, silent and embarrassed in front of the pilot. This was humiliation. He was the big man, the personality chosen to head up this deal, the one who had credibility with the hunters and fishermen the company were proposing to fly in. Yet Jane could cut him dead with a word. He stared through the windscreen, grinding his teeth. He felt her hand on his shoulder.

'Don't fret just yet, dear,' she said. 'In my considerable experience every man has some skeletons in his cupboard. The company wants to know what's buried in John-Cody's.'

Bree wrote another letter to her father, pad of paper hunched up on her knee as she rode home on the bus. She had an envelope in her bag and would post it as soon as she got off. She was seated on her own, oblivious to Hunter a few seats behind.

Dear Dad
  Bad day at black rock. I mean really bad day. Wish you were here. Mum's in Dusky Sound hunting dolphins and Alex is looking after me. I told you about Alex. She's really nice, but it's not the same. School is worse than I thought. I told you about this girl who thinks she's clever. She's calling me a Pom, Dad, the one thing I didn't want to happen. They all call me Cheesy but she's really nasty about it. You know, Bree and Cheese, Smelly and stuff like that. Jessica, that's the bad one, is picking on me in class. Everyone's scared of her so they all avoid me. I haven't got any friends. It's horrible with Mum away. There's no-one to tell. What could she do anyway? Wish you were here, we could sit on this cool rock by the lake and talk about it. You'd know how to handle it. I know you would. Lessons are all right, but break time is horrible. Jessica and her friends come looking for me and there's nothing

I can do about it. The girl I sit next to leaves me on my own because she doesn't want to get picked on. It only happens to me because I'm new. Why do I always have to be the new girl? I don't want to be new. Being new makes you stand out and I just want to blend in with everyone else. How long is it going to be before they accept me? I was doing really well in France, but now I could just cry. Sorry if this upsets you, it's not meant to.

Love from Bree

NINE

November became December and pretty soon it was Christmas: Bree broke up from school still the new girl, still isolated and ridiculed by Jessica Lowden and her cronies. She told no-one, bore her secret in silence and was just thankful when the term ended. No sooner was Christmas over, though, than they were into the new year and she had to face it all again. The world was tarnished, the beauty of Fiordland, the garden, walks with Sierra along the shores of Lake Manapouri all spoiled. School dominated her thoughts, stalking her like a silent ominous spectre, and the southern summer sunshine was dappled with spots of grey.

Libby had set up a series of hydra-phones in Dusky Sound. She spent weeks sitting in her boat attempting to identify the dolphin pod, and so far she had seventeen dorsal fin markings in her collection of photographs. The hydra-phones were situated in various underwater locations throughout the fiord, and linked to her laptop and the computer program she was running. Her days were spent alone on the boat with only the blowing of the dolphins and the crackle of static for company. She spent a lot of time diving, slowly getting used to the darkness and the silent chill of the water.

She had procured a surface-mounted underwater camera and now she was able visually to monitor the activity underwater while she was driving the boat. In the beginning finding the dolphins each day had been the difficult part, but that was no longer a problem; she was already an accepted part of the sound and the pod generally came visiting when she was out in the boat. The play or mating time was the best. She had learned from the reports of previous researchers that the females of Doubtful Sound gave birth annually and in summer, because they lived so far south. Dolphins were far from monogamous; they mated or made love all year round for re-creation and social cohesion. Libby would observe them with the underwater camera, the male under-neath, flipper to flipper, penis erect and easing his body against the female, their beaks together in a kiss.

She trawled the arms of Dusky Sound in the *Wave Dancer* and watched the high-frequency pulses appear as lines on her computer screen as the pod hunted and played and mated. Occasionally she saw the patterns alter as fishing boats moved past her and she thought of the floating hotel scheme, what John-Cody had said about jet skis and speedboats. Jet skis would be less of a problem for the dolphins as they were jet-driven with no propeller vibration. She knew there hadn't been any systematic research anywhere in the world regarding the effect of float-planes on cetacean behaviour. She was sure of one

225

thing, however: bottlenose dolphins were territorial and they would try to adapt; they would put up with a hell of a lot of disturbance before they were forced from their home. Finding a new home would inevitably mean crossing the path of another resident pod and that would involve a fight.

She heard them now as clicks through her headset. The spectrograph was moving, shadowy black lines on the screen, which rested on the little stand she had rigged up. Gently she eased the throttle forward and headed up the Acheron Passage. The day was bright with plenty of sucker holes in the cloud for the sun to peek through and Libby wore a sweatshirt and shorts and a pair of deck shoes. She kept close to the starboard wall where circular wisps of cloud wrapped round the silver beech trees that covered the rock like fur. Limbs stretched here and there, jagged and moss-bound, poking horizontally out from the rock to twist their fingertips skyward.

She saw the dolphins surface on the port bow and eased back on the throttle. Picking up binoculars, she counted fifteen animals moving slowly north and she could tell by the symmetry of their movement that they were hunting. She considered the importance of her research. It was an opportunity to lay down some hard facts as to the effect of man-made noise on a resident population of dolphins. To get any definitive information would take a hell of a lot longer than two years though. There was so much to consider: the nature of the fiord itself, relatively deep water in an enclosed space; the walls of rock would reverberate with any noise, making the consequences much harder to predict. Not only that, but there were all the islands, over three

226

hundred and sixty solid structures that lifted in great water-bound stalks from the silted bottom of the glacial trough.

There were also the different types of boats, the helicopters and the floating hotels themselves. Pole planned to use decommissioned cruise ships with their own generators. They would emit low-frequency sound, which could well interfere with the communication of the pod. The dolphins echo-located and communicated with one another at two very different frequencies: who knew which would be affected the most? They might not be able to talk to each other any more. They might not be able to hunt.

Libby looked at the tannin stain in the water and thought about how you could measure the impact. She couldn't do it alone, there was far too much work involved. Every arm of the fiord was contoured differently, the fingerprint of each rock formation totally unique. They would have to be seismically mapped and then the maths done, taking into account the density of the fresh-water layer on the surface, which altered depending on tides and the amount of rainfall.

She had been here a couple of months already and had identified only seventeen animals, and that was without sexing them all. The surface-mounted camera helped as she could often see the dorsal fin and genital slits at the same time: females were easier to sex if they were nursing because their lactation grooves would be swollen.

Libby moved closer to the hunters now and they swung in an arc towards the boat. One breached and she recognized Old Nick. He was a mature male and very big and whenever she had seen him he seemed to have a senior role in the pod. Was he the patriarch or could there be a dominant female? Most pods she had observed over the years were matriarchal. Old Nick was busy, though; he hustled and cajoled the smaller animals he swam with and breached higher than most.

Breaching was difficult to quantify in terms of behaviour, even after all the years of research on captive animals. She recalled asking her father when she was a child just why the dolphins leaped out of the water like they did. He had indicated that it might be because they were showing off to a prospective partner, but it was probably also for fun.

Libby watched Nick breach again then roll on his back and swim with his flippers out of the water. He dived and came up close to the boat, clearly showing his identification marks, and he whistled at her then dived once more and she saw him surface and blow and lead the pod further up the passage. A second dolphin joined him and Libby stood up in the boat, eyes sharp all at once: a smaller animal with a stubby flat-fluked tail. Something about him intrigued her and gently she increased the revs and followed the pod towards Wet Jacket Arm. The smaller dolphin breached again and Libby watched through binoculars. He was deformed: the tail looked disjointed as if it had been amputated and then sewn back at a shorter angle. The dolphin was almost a hunchback.

'My God, Quasimodo.' Libby spoke his name aloud then picked up the radio.

'*Korimako, Korimako, Korimako*; this is the *Wave Dancer*. Do you copy, John-Cody?' She released the

228

handset, caught a bite of static and then his voice came over the airwaves.

'Loud and clear, *Wave Dancer*: what can I do for you?'

'Listen, when was the last time you saw Quasimodo?'

'I haven't seen him for ages. Why?'

The dolphin leaped again and Libby felt the thrill rush through her. 'Because he's right here now, I'm watching him breach, halfway up the Acheron Passage.'

For a moment all she heard was static and then John-Cody spoke again.

'That's a first, Lib. I've never seen him in Dusky before.'

'Has anybody?'

'Not that I know of. What do you reckon – he's got visitation rights?'

'Possibly. But maybe it's the same pod. Maybe they split their time between Doubtful and Dusky.'

'No.' John-Cody sounded very sure. 'There's been too many occasions when I've seen them in large numbers here and down there on the same day. There are definitely two pods.'

Libby thought for a moment. 'There's always the coalition theory.'

'The what?'

'It's something we considered when I was working on the European dolphin watch project. Five or six males moving between pods to ensure that the gene pool is deep and fertile. It stops one pod from becoming overly inbred.'

John-Cody laughed suddenly. 'You might have a point there, Lib. Quasimodo always swims with his willie out. You think he's some kind of inter-sound stud or something?'

Libby laughed and the sound reverberated back at her. 'I'll bear it in mind for my thesis.'

John-Cody hung up the handset and looked round at Jonah who was busy in the galley preparing pasties for lunch. 'You hear that, Jonah? Quasi's in Dusky Sound.'

Jonah nodded. 'You know what else I heard?'

'What's that?' John-Cody leaned against the open port door of the wheelhouse feeling the warmth of the sun on his bare legs.

'The first joke you cracked since Mahina died.'

John-Cody thought about that and was quiet for a moment, gazing through the galley window at the estuarine green of Shoal Cove.

She came to his crib that first night and they talked up the dawn when he was due back in Doubtful with Tom. Together they had taken the Southland Tours boat across Lake Manapouri and sat on deck with the sun on their backs as it rode the saddle of the Takitimu Mountains. Neither of them had had any sleep, but Mahina seemed to be wearing her fatigue better than he was. The thought of hauling crayfish pots was appalling and he had decided he would appeal to Tom's generosity of spirit and suggest he trawl the deer traps for captured stock instead.

Mahina sat close to him, her shoulder against his upper arm so he could feel the warmth in her through the wind. The lake was flat and the shadows of islands and mountains scurried past in turn. Shafts of sunlight buried rainbows in the surface where the engines churned spray in their wake. John-Cody could smell the scent of the girl alongside him and was filled with the desire to take her hand in his and feel the warmth of her skin. Later he would call it intuition, her uncanny ability to perceive certain thoughts or actions, her knack of locating the dolphins of Doubtful Sound, having them swim alongside the boat and talk to her, whether or not there was a bow wave for them to surf. But at that moment she didn't look at him, just slipped her tiny brown hand under his where it lay on his thigh. She leaned her head on his shoulder and remained that way, John-Cody not daring to move, until they reached West Arm. That was before the power station was built and Tom kept a battered jeep so they could negotiate the pass.

They took the jeep that morning and Mahina sat next to him, her hand resting on his thigh all the way up the pass. Tom was waiting at Deep Cove; he clicked his tongue at the lack of punctuality, then he saw Mahina and a spark lit in his eye.

'G'day, young lady. How you going and how's your old man?'

'Just fine, Tom, Kobi's great.'

John-Cody stared at them both. 'You two know each other?'

'Course we bloody do.' Tom wagged his head at him. 'Kobi's been running a crayfish boat up the coast for years.'

'How come I don't know him?'

Tom shrugged. 'A bloke can't know everyone, Gib. Even a bloke like you.' He cocked his head to one side and looked again at Mahina. 'How'd you meet this joker anyway?'

231

'He was at Yuvali Burn.'

'There's a hind in the trap there,' John-Cody put in. 'I told you yesterday. We need to get her aboard the boat today.'

'Yeah?' Tom scratched the hairs on his forearm. 'You better get the other traps checked as well then. You want to take the dinghy?'

'We can take mine,' Mahina said.

'OK. I'll meet you off Seymour Island later.' Tom winked at Mahina then went below deck and the two of them stepped into her dinghy.

They checked the traps one by one: deer could survive in them for weeks, as they were placed strategically on trails where plenty of secondary vegetation was growing. If for some reason John-Cody or Tom didn't check the traps for a while it didn't matter. John-Cody had seen deer use their foreleg to push a small tree into a bend just so they could eat the juicier leaves higher up the trunk.

They got to the Camelot River estuary at the head of Gaer Arm, where John-Cody had built a circular wire trap beyond a copse of kahikatea. Supplejack grew in dark vines from the floor and southern rata flowered red. Easter orchids clustered in vast numbers and when they bloomed they filled the air with a sweetness you could scent across the whole of Doubtful Sound.

The day was hotter than the previous one and no clouds blocked the sun from the trees. John-Cody paused to listen to a helicopter in the distance, then walked barefoot up the little beach and into the cool of the trees with Mahina at his side. A large male tui watched them from the branch of a silver beech, his white breast feathers curled like bells on his chest.

232

Two mating scaup scampered in slapping footsteps across the flattened water of the estuary, before taking to the air with a screech. John-Cody stood for a moment, aware of the crash of the waterfall fifty yards into the bush, splintered by the sound of birdsong. He could recognize a few of them now, having been here a couple of years. Tom had taught him to pick them out, and he had also been harried and hassled from above when he stepped too close to a nesting karearea or falcon; they were known to dive-bomb people who strayed too far from the path.

Mahina told him that the amount of birdsong one heard was indicative of the health of the forest. Stoats attacked birds, eating their eggs and their young and sometimes the adults too if hunger was driving them hard. Not only stoats; possums ate the eggs and over the years the bird population had steadily declined. The flightless takahe, discovered high in the Murchison Mountains back in 1948, was now found only in the alpine grassland zones. The trail-finding kakapo of old was restricted to the handful of conservation areas where it had been systematically reintroduced.

Mahina moved ahead of him, picking her way silently through the tangled Camelot bush: she was small and lithe and as quiet as her Waitaha ancestors. She knew where the trap was. She knew where all John-Cody's traps were, having watched him for over six months. He had never known she was there. No-one ever knew she was there, fading as she did into the mystery of the forest where she was hidden by Tane Mahuta. She heard the Tuheru talking about John-Cody, watching him from inside the trunks of trees or etched into rocks. They let him be, content to observe how he moved, how he hunted, the respect he paid to their garden when he was shooting deer, the particular reverence with which he treated any fallen animal. His presence was acceptable to them. It was acceptable to her.

She turned now as the sound of falling water grew louder, and looked into the sea-grey of his eyes. She held out a hand for him and he took it and his flesh was warm against hers. She worked tiny fingers over the calluses at the base of his fingers, hard mounds of yellowed skin where hours of work on fishing boats had taken their toll. She had noted the indentation marks from a year with the scallop knife off Hawaii. He had told her everything last night; she witnessed the pain standing like a livid scar in his face, the light of fear in the deepest part of his eyes. She had not said it to him then, but the peace she sensed in him echoed the peace of Waitaha, her ancestors from Hawaiki: they, unlike any other ocean traveller who strode the shores of Aotearoa, had never taken up arms.

She held his hand as they approached the deer trap and before John-Cody could see it he heard the deer move. He slowed and glanced at Mahina and then he eased aside the stems of supplejack and gazed through the tangled foliage. He glimpsed the tan colour of her hide, greying to buff at throat and tail.

'Wapiti,' he whispered.

They stood together and watched the animal for a while, John-Cody trying to work out exactly how they would get her and the red deer hind at Yuvali Burn onto Tom's boat. If there were any more in the other traps he would have to leave them till later, because two live deer were enough for the small

234

crayfish vessel. Two breeding age females: he was looking at three thousand dollars.

The sun beat on their heads through the treetops and John-Cody could feel the sweat in his hairline. It rained most days in Fiordland, but when it was hot it was blistering. He stood there, perspiring, with the sound of falling water in his ears and then Mahina lifted her hands to his face, cupped his cheeks and tilted his head to meet hers. He kissed her and closed his eyes and felt his heart in his chest and a sudden quivering in his limbs. Lips against lips, slightly apart, breathing each other in, he took her in his arms and held her, aware of her warmth, the slight damp of her skin under his fingers. Her arms were bare, just the singlet and shorts of yesterday. He drew her closer to him, eyes closed and strands of wild hair against his cheek. She led him further into the bush and the sound of the water grew louder and he could see it now, cascading in broken ribbons of white over the sudden sharpness of the cliff, like in a wound of black rock against the bottle green of the forest. The water tumbled into a shallow pool, before forming a stream or burn that ran to the Camelot estuary. Mahina stood in the shallows now, feet lost in silted vegetation, and she pulled her singlet over her head.

John-Cody remained where he was, stunned by the suddenness of the movement. She stood holding the garment in one hand, the ends trailing in water that coursed around her feet. Her breasts were small and high and the flesh was mottled with goose pimples at the aureole of the nipple. She closed her eyes and tilted back her head and the spray from the waterfall licked her face like gossamer. She stepped back and the fine mist became a shower, which threaded her skin and ran in slivers off her neck and shoulders. She stepped closer still to the waterfall and then gazing into his eyes she unsnapped the button of her shorts. For a moment longer she stood, shorts unfastened, the waistband billowing to the sides so the shadows below her navel were visible. John-Cody worked the air from his throat in a long swallow. Mahina turned her back on him, eased her shorts over her hips and stepped out of them.

She stood naked, the perfect line of her back narrowed to her waist and buttocks that shivered and clenched with the sudden chill of the water. Legs slim and dark, the muscles pronounced against the skin, arced into nothing where her feet were lost in the shallows. Still she did not face him, didn't look back: it was as if she was alone with the forest and the silent ghosts of her ancestors. John-Cody remained where he was, his own feet rooted in the forest floor, the lump rising again in his throat. His stomach was a wreath of tangled knots, his palms moist, and he was aware of the sudden ache in his loins as desire rose hot from his belly.

Then Mahina turned so their eyes met again and she stepped back under the water and her hair was plastered to her shoulders. The water shimmered off her skin like a curtain, flattening her breasts and tightening the nipples so they jutted taut and youthful and hard. His eyes roved the flat of her stomach where the water ran like oil and rushed between her legs where the mass of curling hair spread flat and wet and jet black.

She held out a hand to beckon him. John-Cody

peeled his own T-shirt over his head and he could smell the scent of Easter orchids, heady all at once in his nostrils. The bush came alive with the very tingling in his being: he gazed on Mahina's nakedness and she gazed on his and the desire deep within him. He could smell the cast beech seed and the moss, the lichen that hugged tree trunks and covered bare rock like body hair. He sensed the scurry of insects and the flutter of tiny wings and, beneath it all, the very stillness of the forest.

If the water was cold he didn't notice. His eyes were on Mahina as she tipped her head back into the falling torrent then reached for him and he pressed himself against her.

They made love standing up with the water chilling them, John-Cody rooted among the stones and Mahina climbing him till her head was close to his and her legs wrapped about him like twin constricting serpents. They moved to the bank and the carpet of fallen vegetation and made love again while the captured wapiti doe looked on from beyond the wire. Afterwards they lay on their backs, the sun on their skin warm and weary-making through the canopy of trees. The falling water seemed to still in their ears: Mahina half lifted her head and looked at him.

'Can you hear them, John-Cody?'

'Who?'

'You're pakeha.' She lay down again, her palm on his breast. 'How could you possibly hear them?'

John-Cody eased damp hair behind her ear. 'Hear who?'

'Listen.' She placed the line of her index finger against his lips to hush him and he listened, but all he could hear was the water and the slight breeze that luffed like a sail in the treetops.

'If you listen you can hear their voices.' Her face was solemn now and John-Cody listened hard: he heard the dull chimes of a male bellbird calling for its mate, but no more.

'They can hear you.' She sat up and looked into the green. 'Don't you know they watch you when you think you're alone in the bush? I've seen them watching you. Perhaps they led me to you.'

Now he sat up. 'What are you talking about?' He cupped her cheek in his palm. 'What're you saying, Mahina?'

She kissed his fingers. 'I think you're the man of peace who came to the people of peace in the last garden of Tane.'

'I don't know what you're talking about. Who are *they*?'

And then she smiled and her smile he would remember to his dying day. She entwined her fingers in his and drew him close again. 'The Tuheru, of course, the Dimly Seen of the mountains.'

They sailed back down Gaer Arm and John-Cody saw a couple of Pole's crayfish boats beyond the reef in Precipice Cove. A long time ago Jonah had worked for Pole and some members of the crew were still his drinking pals. He came alongside John-Cody where he watched from the port doorway.

'The fishing's not been good. Not for a while now.'

John-Cody squinted at him. 'I wondered why so many of his boats were tied up.'

'Some of the crew have been laid off.' Jonah shrugged. 'Whatever he does it never seems to work out. That gold mine in Victoria, I don't know what he was thinking about. Probably started to believe his own publicity. You know he mortgaged his house? From what I hear, if the Dusky deal doesn't go ahead he'll lose it.'

John-Cody made a face. 'That'll please his wife.' It disturbed him though: it made the fight for Dusky Sound all the more desperate.

The sky had been cloudless this morning, but now it was gradually choking with thunderheads. The boat was full, fourteen guests, and John-Cody was glad the rain had been only a light summer drizzle so far, enough to get the waterfalls going so they could see the sound in all its glory. But they could also see the tops of the mountains. He watched the guests now, milling about on deck, taking in the primordial, almost surreal atmosphere of Fiordland. They would spend the last night at the head of Hall's Arm, where the entrance to the narrows was reflected with a glass-like stillness and the water could be the sky and sky could be the water.

He realized he felt calmer than he had for a long time: when he woke in the mornings at the homestay the emptiness was still there but it no longer chewed at him like a canker. He could hear Libby and Bree moving about next door, and sometimes if one or other of them raised their voice he would hear them talking.

Bree was forever in the garden and she did her homework at the desk in the hut with the sliding door open. John-Cody had rigged up a CD player for her and the garden beat time to Steps or B'Witched or one of the other bands he had never heard of. He had even picked up his twelve-string guitar, which

239

for so long had gathered moths in the other hut. He had plugged in his portable amp and finger-picked some New Orleans blues, or some of the songs he had composed during his time in McCall.

Jonah had noticed the difference in him and so had Tom and so had the women in Manapouri. They still fussed over him in the shop and when he picked up stores in Te Anau, but there was nothing like the level of concern in their eyes that there had been.

They steamed back down Bradshaw Sound and one of the female guests screeched as a dolphin leaped right in front of the bows. 'Your boat, Jonah.' John-Cody stepped on deck. 'Keep her as she goes. I'll get the wetsuits ready.'

Libby watched the sun disappear beyond the horizon and a half-darkness descended on Supper Cove. She had lit a small fire on the beach close to a good sitting stone and was warming a pot of coffee. Tom Blanch had given her the old tin pot and she set it now in the embers. She liked Tom, could see the years of wisdom in his eyes and the fatherly approach he had to John-Cody. They had had one brief conversation, where he told her it was good for the old sea dog to have them living next door. It stopped him disappearing up his own arse, as Tom liked to put it.

Libby had her laptop open on her knees, the twin battery pack giving her at least six hours, and she was studying some of the data and photographs she had scanned into the system. Seventeen dolphins positively identified, their specific markings gleaned from hundreds of pictures. She had given them all a letter/number combination for ID, but also names like Old Nick, Fantail and Droopy. Sighting Quasimodo today had been a real rush: for a long time she had favoured the idea of interbreeding between various pods, and now she had fresh evidence. If some males roved in a bachelor pack to ensure the strength of the gene pool, this would have sound practical results, though whether it arose from instinct or intellect, nobody knew. The definition of intelligence was a relative term anyway: many people believed that the dolphin brain was more highly developed than that of man. Their system of communication was one of the most advanced on the planet, dolphins and other toothed whales being the only marine mammals who were known to echolocate. They emitted recycled air as sound pulses then drew it back as a series of vibrations received through the lower jaw. Each tooth vibrated in a perfectly unique way that enabled the animals to identify what they were looking at, how far away and in what direction it was, and whether they wanted to eat it or not. The closest land relative they had in terms of echolocation was the bat.

And bats flew now, beyond the hut, dodging the line of the forest where the blackness was accentuated by the density of vegetation. John-Cody had told her there were two surviving species of peka peka, as the Maori called them, and both were endemic to the area. She looked over her shoulder and heard the flutter of leathery wings, grey against the lighter grey of the shadows that dominated the hillside. Somewhere far off a morepork called and she thought of the conversation she had had with John-Cody back in November.

Bree was asleep and they were smoking cigarettes

under the eaves of the house. He had told her about the night Mahina died, how she told him the owl called her name and she knew then it was time to go. His voice had cracked a little but his eyes were clear and Libby had been filled with an overwhelming sense of his love for her. At that moment her concerns about Bree, her research and the implications of Ned Pole's plans for Dusky Sound were banished and she wondered what it would feel like to be loved in the way that John-Cody had loved Mahina. She had watched him sitting in the stillness, his own special quietness enveloping him like a cloud.

Libby stoked the flames now as the night grew behind the hut and she thought about Mahina, the impact she had had on John-Cody's life and the lives of her brother and her father Kobi, whom Libby had still to meet. She imagined Mahina trawling the sounds in her dinghy, knowing every inch of water and forest as if it were part of her being. Libby knew very little about the spiritual traditions of the Maori but she saw Mahina as a gentle Waitaha guardian, a link with the past and the myth of the forest god, the earth and the sky. Libby had never met Mahina, never seen her save in the picture Jonah had shown them, yet she felt she knew her.

John-Cody had actually spoken little about her, his privacy intense, but on the few occasions he had elaborated, sometimes when Jonah brought up her name with the fond recollection of a sibling, Libby had gleaned some insight into who she must have been. Jonah described her as being in this world yet not of it.

The wind moved in the trees and Libby shivered:

again the morepork called and she wondered what she would do if he called a third time and she recognized her name. She shook her head and prodded the fire, took a cigarette from her pack and lit it from the embers: the flames lit up the beach and she thought she saw something move at the edge of the trees. She started, aware all at once of her heartbeat. This was not the first time she had felt like this, as if in some way she was being watched. The sounds were silent, almost spooky places when you were alone, especially at night. On more than one occasion when she had been in the boat, intent on the dolphins, she would glance up and swear a figure was watching her from just beyond the tree line. She would look harder, see the outline of a shadow, but when she turned the boat and went closer she saw nothing.

The darkness between herself and the hut looked all at once forbidding. Water slapped rock somewhere along the shore and the wind called like whispered voices among the trees. She took the coffee pot and made her way back to the lighted windows, trying not to see Jonah's face or hear the seriousness of his words when he talked of Tuheru and Maeroero.

TEN

Jane Pole was on the telephone in her husband's study. She wore a green suit and rested a long-nailed hand against the polished wood of the desk. Pole watched her through the open doors to the balcony, his back to the rail and January sun. Barrio whinnied and stamped in the paddock below, but Pole was intent on his wife's conversation with their backers in the United States.

'We know he came to New Zealand in 1974,' Jane was saying. 'He landed at Bluff Cove, Invercargill, and seems to have jumped ship. He was working on a trawler from Hawaii called the *Beachcomber* and then he hooked up with a Kiwi skipper called Blanch. They worked together fishing and trapping deer for a while then Gibbs met a Maori girl called Mahina Pavaro and they lived together for twenty-some years.'

'Two,' Pole said very deliberately.

'What was that?' His wife placed her hand over the mouthpiece.

'Twenty-two years.'

She turned her attention back to the phone.

'The point is they were never legally married.'

Pole watched her, the cool and calculating expression pasted on thin, almost hawkish features. His eyes narrowed to slits as he looked through her and the years rolled back and he saw Mahina again in the bush. That was just after she got together with Gibbs and he hated him for it. Pole was thirty years old then, with two years' Vietnam service under his belt. He had fought in denser jungle than any man he knew and had survived not only the enemy but snakes and spiders and punji-stake mantraps. He could shoot a running stag from the skis of any chopper at any speed and was making more money than anyone in the Te Anau basin. He was in demand from all the big outfits and could virtually name his price. He spent most of his life in the bush and was as soundless as a hunting cat.

He was kneeling in deep cover by the carcass of a young hind when a rustle in the bush disturbed him. He saw movement between the dripping trees ahead and his gaze deepened as he realized he was looking at a young Maori woman picking her way through the undergrowth. His throat tightened as he saw she was naked.

'Ned!'

He started and looked at his wife. She had put the phone down and he hadn't noticed, so lost had he been in reverie.

'Sorry. What did they say?'

'They're worried about the hearing. They're pushing, Ned. We need to do something about Gibbs before then. If we don't they think we'll lose.'

Pole bit his lip, still not fully concentrating. 'No date's been set for the hearing.'

'That's not the point.' She looked at him, head slanted slightly. 'Are you sure your heart's still in this? If you go soft on me now, you can kiss it all goodbye. Not just this deal but the lot.' She stepped away from the desk, arms folded across her chest. 'If we lose this property I'll be back in the US faster than you can spit.'

Pole stared at her. 'Of course my heart's still in it. As you're so keen to remind me – it's all I've got.' He drew himself up and stood square, shoulders back, looking down at her. 'And as for going soft, you might think you're tough, Jane, but you'd last five minutes out there.' He pointed to the mountains against the horizon.

Jane tipped back her head and laughed. 'Oh Ned, give me a break, please. I wouldn't be stupid enough to be out there in the first place.' She walked over to him and laid a hand on his chest. 'Darling, I know you're good in the bush. Why do you think I married you?' She tapped him on the temple. 'Not for your brains surely. It's a good job you can hunt and that you look so good, because businessman of the year you are not.'

Pole flinched. He saw his father's face in his mind's eye. *Be someone I can be proud of.*

'You should thank your lucky stars you've got me,' Jane went on. 'If I weren't around you'd be living in a tent by now. Stick to your rifles, Nehemiah. It's what you were bred for.'

Pole stood where he was, the tips of his cheekbones white. Jane ran her hand up and down the hard muscles of his stomach, lingering at his belt.

'What're they going to do?' he asked her.

'Arrange for a private investigator to look into

246

Gibbs's background, Hawaii, the States, etc., see if he can't drag up something we can use. We can do our bit from this end too, or rather you can.' She looked at him then. 'Can't we use the accident in some way?'

The tone of her voice was brusque and matter-of-fact. Pole winced beneath it.

'Gibbs was the skipper,' Jane went on. 'It was his fault, his responsibility.'

Pole stared at her. 'It was five years ago.'

'So what? Your son still died.'

Pole stepped around her. 'There was an inquiry, Jane. He was exonerated.'

'And you just accepted that?' She stared at him now, brow furrowed. 'You of all people, the big man of Te Anau.'

Pole looked beyond her, through the open window to the paddock where Barrio stamped and snorted, running up and down the fence as if he scented a mare in season.

Jane looked at him from under shadowed eyelids. 'It may have been five years ago, but inquiries get reopened. Especially when somebody died. There must be something we can use.'

Pole had no answer for her. He went outside and crossed the yard to the paddock, the shadow of his father haunting him, the shadow of Eli's ghost stalking the recesses of his mind: grandfather and grandson, the knowledge between them of how he had failed them both. He paused at the fence, rested a booted foot on the bottom rail and sought a cigar from his top pocket. On days like today he hated Jane with a vengeance, but for all the ice water in her veins he knew she was right: they had to use everything to win this, particularly now the Bass woman was ensconced in Dusky Sound with her camera and her hydra-phones. He knew Gib and Mahina had never married and he suspected something else but couldn't prove it. Every time he had broached the subject Gib had carefully avoided it. Then Eli went to work for them, which put him in an intolerable position.

He would never forget that day when the telephone rang on his desk upstairs and the police told him that his son had been involved in an accident. The chill had started in his hair and worked its way to his toes. He knew the accident was bad and he knew it was on Gib's boat. He didn't know how bad until he crossed the lake to West Arm and saw the body bag on the dock. Mahina was there but she didn't come forward when Gibbs approached him. Pole had looked beyond Gibbs and his gaze met fully with hers for the first time in eighteen years. No words were spoken and both of them knew that with this between them now, none would ever need to be.

He clamped the cigar between his teeth and looked up to see Jane standing on the balcony with her jacket undone. He realized she was wearing nothing underneath and her hair was loose and long and she leaned so the jacket hung open and she looked at him with that slow darkness in her eyes. For a long moment they just stared at each other and then she turned and walked back into the house. Pole dropped his cigar in the dirt and ground it out. He strode indoors, unbuttoning his shirt as he went. The bedroom door was open and Jane lay back on the bed, completely naked. He dropped his shirt on the floor and unsnapped his belt buckle.

'When you talk to your man in the States,' he said, 'ask him to find out what outfit Gibbs was with in Vietnam.'

Bree got off the bus and looked through the window at Hunter. He waved, just one flap of his hand, but a thrill ran through her and she stood for a moment watching while the bus turned left for the Tuatapere road. They sat next to each other most days now both to and from school. Hunter probably had no idea what that meant to her, or if he did he certainly didn't show it. The bullying from Jessica and her cronies was getting steadily worse and Bree had no-one to confide in. She sat with Biscuit in most lessons but she was not what Bree would call a friend. She had always managed to find at least one special friend at school wherever her mother had sent her, even during the six months in the Baja California. In France she had been part of a trio that, when her grasp of the language grew strong enough, became a firm little friendship. So why was it so hard here? Maybe it was the fact that Jessica picked on her right from the start. She certainly had an influence over the form; all the girls were scared of her and she did just enough work to keep the tutors off her back.

All of which made Hunter's interest that much more important. None of his friends came in from Blackmount and the seat next to him was always vacant. He talked to Bree in his gentle Kiwi accent, his voice already starting to break; his eyes were deep brown, his skin tanned from the sun and he had ingrained dirt from his father's farm under his fingernails. Bree always sat with him in the mornings and he took the space next to her when they got back on the bus in the afternoon, all of which made life just about bearable. She hadn't told anyone about Hunter, in case in doing so she somehow broke the spell. He was the only reason she could face going to school.

School was different here from anywhere she had been before: it seemed to her that the one thing all New Zealand children had in common was sport and their love of it. They all seemed to be good at it, enthusiastic to the point of obsession, and she wondered why that was. She had talked to her mother about it, trying not to let her know that games was the one lesson where she felt weak and really vulnerable. It had soon become apparent that she was far and away the brightest in her class, even at Japanese, which she had started late. The tutors liked her, but her abilities set her apart and when games came round it gave the others an opportunity to get even.

Her mother said the country was like Australia and South Africa, young still and seeking its place in the world. Whereas England and the rest of Europe had found theirs through war and conquest over a thousand and more years, places like New Zealand were shaping their identity through sport. In a way it was a modern if benign form of war, country set against country, culture against culture on the field of play. None of that helped Bree, though, who was as bad at hockey and cricket as she knew she would be at rugby when the winter term came round.

She stood on the corner and watched the bus go, thinking about Hunter's eyes and how kind and gentle they were. He was big for his age, almost a head taller than his mates, none of whom seemed to poke fun when he got off the bus with Bree every morning. He was brilliant at sport: secretly Bree watched him on the cricket pitch when she was trying to play hockey. They had stuck her in goal, either to keep her out of the way or to take pot shots at her, she had not quite worked out which yet. Hunter could hit a cricket ball very hard and he looked really athletic when he ran up to bowl. Most people made fun of her name, which was ridiculous when she considered some of theirs, but Hunter called her by her initials, BB.

Bree turned back to the beach, gazing across the lake in the late afternoon sunshine. A pair of spur-winged plovers rose from among the black-trunked manuka in the wetlands. She thought about what John-Cody had told her: manuka was the tea tree and Captain Cook had made spruce beer from the rimu. There was manuka in the copse by the garden; often she would wander in there and sit on one of the stumps and smell the twigs with the rain on them. She loved that garden. Every day it seemed she learned something new, saw something she hadn't seen before, a new frog or a bird's nest. She had even glimpsed a possum high in the marbleleaf tree first thing one morning.

Lately she had taken to lying between the fuchsia and the red beech in the late afternoon with half an apple in her outstretched hand. She lay very still, so still that the male bellbird that sang from the lower branches overcame his fear and licked the apple as it sat in her hand. She watched out of half-closed eyes, hardly daring to breathe, as his snake-like tongue dug a tiny furrow in the flesh and she imagined him with nectar on his beak, moving from flower to flower, carrying the life of the forest.

John-Cody came walking up the road from Pearl Harbour. The guests were long gone and he had been sorting out a few things with Southland Tours. The sun was lower in the sky now and he could smell the change in the atmosphere: tomorrow would bring rain and a lot of it. He was thinking about Libby trawling up and down Dusky's various arms and the water turning white round the boat. He thought of yesterday's call, telling him that Quasimodo was in the sound. Was he just visiting or could he be part of a coalition between the two pods as she had suggested? He was looking forward to seeing her tomorrow night so he could discuss it with her.

Bree was approaching from the other direction, both of them converging on the office. She would be going to raise her mum on the radio before heading home with Alex. That had surprised him: he would not have put Alex down as a woman overflowing with maternal instinct, but she was brilliant with Bree and happily looked after her whenever Libby was working. At the weekends she had gone home for the odd night and John-Cody had kept an eye on Bree himself.

Bree saw him and waved. He waved back, then Sierra bounded out of the office, caught both their scents, looked left and right and raced up to Bree. She knelt down and flung her arms round the dog's neck. John-Cody shook his head: must be the quality of the welcome, he thought.

'Hey, Breezy. Take it easy,' he called.

She smiled at him, raised her hand and slapped his palm. 'Five high, Captain Bligh.'

It was their greeting grown up over the short time they had known each other, something else that kept her sane when her mother was down at Dusky.

'Good day?'

She shrugged. 'It was all right.'

'I spoke to your mum yesterday.'

'Did you?'

They walked up the steps and into the office. 'She saw Quasimodo in the Acheron Passage.'

Bree stared at him. 'You mean Quasimodo from Doubtful Sound?'

He nodded.

Bree had only ever seen the dolphin on video, but she knew all about him from her conversations with John-Cody. He had become something of a celebrity since he was first identified and named.

'What's he doing in Dusky?'

'We don't know. But your mum's got some theories.' John-Cody swept his hair from his eyes and smiled. 'Call her up on the radio.'

He left Bree to it, made a waggle-handed gesture at Alex and climbed into the cab of his truck.

Ned Pole's twin cab was parked out the back of the Motor Inn and John-Cody almost drove on, but he had been having a beer in that pub for most of his life and Pole wasn't going to stop him.

Pole's wife was with him and they were sitting at a table by the window overlooking the lake, a stack of papers between them. Pole saw him come in and his eyes sharpened considerably. John-Cody ignored them and ordered a glass of beer. He sat on one of the high stools and watched the six o'clock news, quietly rolling himself a smoke. Ned Pole moved alongside him, a shadow blocking the light from the window. He placed a half-empty pint on the counter and took the stool opposite. John-Cody saw that his wife was still at their table, though her attention was fixed on the papers. He looked back at Pole.

'Jane going to be around for a while, is she?'

Pole nodded. John-Cody could smell the beer on his breath.

'All the other submitters have come over to my side, Gib,' he said quietly. 'Why don't you do yourself a favour and just let it go? It's going to happen sooner or later, whether you object or not.'

John-Cody sighed heavily. 'Ned, give me a break, will you? We've had this conversation.'

Pole looked him in the eye. 'I've been instructed to offer you $120,000 Australian for the *Korimako* wharf.'

'That's generous, Ned. DoC must've turned you down for a new build.'

'$120,000 for the wharf and $650,000 for the *Korimako*: that's way more than she's worth.'

John-Cody took a long draught of his beer and weighed the glass in his hand.

'Why don't you call it an even $800,000?' he said.

Pole squinted at him. 'If that's what it takes.'

John-Cody laughed then. 'It's not what it takes. Not eight hundred: not a million or two million. The wharf's not for sale, Ned, neither is the boat. They never will be.'

Pole rocked back on the stool and felt in his pocket for a cigar. 'Gib, the people backing me won't take no for an answer. You understand what I mean?'

'Is that some sort of threat?'

'Take it how you want, mate. But believe me, I'm doing you a favour here.' Pole got up off the stool.

'You may not want to believe it, but I am. Take the money, Gib. Take the offer while it's there.'

'And if I don't?'

Pole stood for a moment and looked down at him. 'Some things aren't always what they seem, mate. Situations can change very quickly.'

Tom Blanch came in then. Pole touched his hat and turned away.

'What was that all about?' Tom sat down on the stool he had vacated. 'You two jokers not patched up your differences yet?'

'Ned was telling me how things aren't always what they seem.' John-Cody put out his cigarette. 'He offered me eight hundred thousand for the *Kori* and her wharf.'

Tom cocked a shaggy eyebrow. 'That's good money, Gib.'

'Australian, not New Zealand.'

'Even better.'

'That's what I thought.'

'So take it, why don't you?'

John-Cody smiled wryly. 'What do you want to drink, Tom?'

'Well, seeing as how you can afford to turn down such big bucks I'll take a shot of whisky and a big jug of Speights.'

When John-Cody came back with the drinks Jane Pole was watching him from her seat by the window. Something about the expression in her eyes unnerved him. Tom knocked the whisky back and splashed beer into glasses. Reaching down, he picked up a plastic shopping bag and laid it on the table. 'Got a little something for you, Gibby. Be a treat for that wee girl you got staying up at the house.'

John-Cody walked home and saw Bree putting seeds and fruit out for the birds in the front garden. Sierra was lying on the grass, her head cocked to one side watching Bree with the same faithfulness she had displayed since her arrival from England. An animal's reaction to a human being always interested John-Cody: they were no mugs and Sierra responded to Bree in a way she had not done with anyone else, except himself in the early days. Sierra must have smelled him because she got up, barked and trotted out to the road. John-Cody ruffled her ears and looked up to see Bree smiling at him. He could hear Alex in the house and he poked his head round the door and saw her nosing about in the fridge.

'Don't worry about it, Alex. Take the night off if you want. I'm home for a couple of days, I can look after Bree.'

'Can you?' Alex looked doubtfully at him. 'What are you going to eat?'

'You leave that to me.' John-Cody held up the plastic shopping bag that Tom had given him.

The house was still hard to enter, even with the two newcomers making it very much their home. On the occasions when he looked after Bree, John-Cody managed to sit by the fire in the evenings with Sierra at his feet until Bree went to sleep: then he would slip next door and Sierra would climb onto her bed and guard her throughout the night. He had not set foot in the bedroom since Mahina died.

'Are you going to cook, John-Cody?' Bree asked him.

'I am.' He selected an uncut loaf of bread and a

knife. 'Get me the butter from the fridge and some steak sauce if there is any.'

Bree squinted at him. 'Are we having steak?'

'We are.'

'What else?'

'Just steak and bread and butter: not just any steak, mind you. Tonight it's special, feral venison, cut thin and cooked on a manuka fire.'

He led the way into the garden and paused to listen to birdsong. 'Can you tell me what bird that is?'

'It's a male tui.'

'Good girl.' He listened again. 'And that?'

'Fantail.'

John-Cody glanced towards the trees by the bedroom window. 'We used to have a pair of bellbirds nesting in that fuchsia.'

'I know.' Bree looked up at him then, her head slightly to one side. 'They were Mahina's favourites, weren't they?'

John-Cody nodded. 'You know what though, I haven't heard one in that tree since she died.'

Bree frowned. 'Oh, they're there all right. The male takes apple from my hand.'

John-Cody wrinkled his brow.

'It's true,' she said. 'They're there. You just haven't heard them.'

They passed through the gap in the hedge and John-Cody scanned the fallen trunks on the patch of land that bordered the road. 'They wanted to clear these trees so they could build,' he said. 'I bought the land after Mahina died. One day I'll replant it.'

Bree sat down on a tree stump and John-Cody took out his tobacco and papers.

257

'So tell me,' he said, 'how do you like school?'

Bree didn't answer him right away. She was picking at a patch of dried earth with a stick. 'It's all right,' she said. 'They call me Cheesy Breezy though, or just Cheesy.'

John-Cody frowned. 'Who does?'

'Oh, some of the girls.'

'Are they bullying you?'

Bree shrugged. 'It's after the cheese. You know, Brie, the French cheese. It's stupid, not even spelt the same.'

'I think Bree's a lovely name.'

'It's typical of my mum.' Bree bit her lip. 'She does things on the spur of the moment and doesn't always think about what might happen afterwards.'

John-Cody rested his elbows on his knees. 'That's a grown-up thing to say.'

'Is it? I suppose I am quite grown up. I've had a different life to most people.'

'Have you?' He looked at her then. 'You know, I really don't know much about you, Bree.'

'Don't you? There's loads to tell. The things I've done in twelve years some people would never do in their whole lifetime.'

'What sort of things?' John-Cody snapped open his lighter.

Bree shrugged again. 'I've lived all over the place. I've been to school in lots of different countries, learned French and Spanish almost as well as I learned English. I've had my mum teaching me at home in Argentina. We lived on the coast at a place called Punta Norte and watched killer whales taking seals from the beach.'

'That must have been something.'

258

'It got boring after a while. Once you've seen it a few times you just feel sorry for the seals.'

John-Cody laughed then. 'I bet you do at that.' He drew on his cigarette and picked out a patch of fallen manuka. 'We'll use that wood over there,' he said, pointing. 'The sticks need to be fallen but still living so there's some moisture left in them. That way you get the real manuka smell when the meat's cooking.'

'Where did you get the meat? Did you shoot the deer?'

'No. Tom got it for me.'

John-Cody clipped the end of his cigarette and they set about gathering enough sticks for the fire. He asked her to run back to the house and get the hand axe for him so he could cut some bigger branches for when the fire got going. Bree skipped off and he watched her cross the lawn and smiled to himself, wondering what it would have been like to have children of his own. One of the first things Mahina had told him was that she couldn't have any because of a problem with her fallopian tubes.

They readied the fire, John-Cody taking a bunch of the thinnest sticks and laying them across one another in alternate racks till they were about five layers deep. He put his lighter to them, fanned the infant flames, sat back and watched them burn.

Bree stared wide-eyed. 'Just like that?'

'Just like that.'

'It's brilliant. I couldn't do that.'

'I'm sure you could with a little practice. I've had twenty-five years, remember.'

She nodded. 'Still, it's very clever. You're clever at stuff like that.'

'Thank you.' He looked at her then. 'I've never

heard you talk about your dad, Bree. Where does he live?'

She flushed a deep red and he immediately regretted his question. 'I'm sorry. I shouldn't be so nosy.'

Bree made a face. 'It's all right. I don't mind.' She stood up then and laid another set of sticks on the fire. 'Is this right?'

'Perfect.'

She crouched down, hitching her skirt higher over her knee and resting an arm on her thigh. 'That's another thing about my mother: she couldn't even tell me my own father's name. She didn't know it, so I don't know who he is.'

John-Cody was quiet after that. Bree sat on the tree stump, knees together, while he buried manuka spines in the soil and stood them over the fire with steaks impaled on the ends. He sipped from a bottle of beer and Bree drank fruit juice and both of them watched the spirals of smoke lift as they breathed the sweet scent of freshly burning manuka.

'It's lovely,' Bree said eventually. 'The smell.'

John-Cody nodded. 'So you never knew him at all then – your dad?'

She shook her head, puckering her lips as if a bad taste clung to the inside of her mouth. 'I think my mum went to a party and got drunk. Somehow she got pregnant. She was in a rush to get to Mexico to watch whales and she didn't even realize she was expecting me for the first three months.'

'She told you all this?' John-Cody lifted his eyebrows.

Bree nodded.

'That's honest at least.'

'Oh, Mum's always honest.'

260

John-Cody turned the steaks and Bree sat quietly beside him. Sierra was watching the meat drip juice onto the flames, where it hissed and sizzled in the embers. Bree sipped her drink and leaned forward to sniff at the drifting smoke. 'The food smells wonderful,' she said.

'It does, doesn't it? Old Tom taught me how to make a manuka fire, years ago when we trapped together in the bush.'

'You don't do that any more?'

He shook his head. 'I've not trapped or shot anything for years.' He told her then how Mahina had talked of the forest and the fruit of Papatuanuku the mother earth and how precious everything was. That every living being, be it plant or animal or person, was vital to the way the world lived in balance with itself and if that balance shifted then the long-term effects would be disastrous. He told her about Mahina's mother and her mother's parents and grandparents who traced their line back to the first Waitaha Polynesians who settled in the Te Anau basin: how they differed from the other Maori in that they were a people of peace, whose aim was peace in the world. He told her how the Waitaha had left other parts of Aotearoa because of war.

'Did they have white skins?' Bree asked him when he broke off. 'I read that they might have had white skins.'

'I don't know. Some Waitaha elders tell their history as leaving Hawaiki and travelling with a white-skinned, red-haired race for a time: they intermarried, so some of them would have been paler. It's maybe why the Waitaha-blooded people sometimes have red in their hair.'

261

'I suppose different tribes have different legends,' Bree said.

'I guess they do, yes.'

She looked at him then. 'Do you think you could ever love anyone else like you loved Mahina?'

John-Cody was quiet. He picked the steaks off the twigs and laid them on the bread he had cut in readiness. 'That's a hard question. I don't know is the real answer. Right now I don't think so, but I don't really know.'

Bree thought for a moment. 'It's good that you loved her so much. But maybe you need to let her go a little now.'

John-Cody looked at her clear blue eyes gazing back at him. He heard Mahina's voice in his head. *Free me, John-Cody Gibbs, then forget all about me because I won't remember you. I'll be gone for ever, tasting the breath of eternity.*

He sat by the lounge fire, listening to Bree getting ready for bed. Sierra lay at his feet and he had a book open on his lap. He was only flicking through it, not really looking at the pages. Darkness had fallen and with it the rain he had sensed in the atmosphere earlier. It rattled the corrugated iron of the roof now, and he knew it was set for the night. Bree came through in her nightdress and went to clean her teeth. He heard the water running and the sound of her spitting then she came to say goodnight.

'Are you going to read?' he asked her.

'No.' She shivered and knelt down in front of the open fire. 'I'm glad we cooked those steaks before the rain came.'

'The fire would have been a bit wet otherwise.'

They laughed and Bree picked up a log and settled it among the flames.

'Don't worry about what they call you at school, Bree,' he said gently. 'People can be very cruel.'

'It's because I'm new.' She lifted her shoulders. 'It's happened before. It's just never lasted this long, that's all.' She stood up and yawned. 'Thanks for cooking for me.'

John-Cody took her small hand in his. 'Thanks for eating it with me.'

She placed her other hand over the back of his and smiled. 'I hope I didn't upset you with what I said about Mahina.'

'Of course you didn't. We're honest, you and I.'

'Yeah.'

'Take it easy, Breezy.'

She leaned forward and kissed him on the cheek. 'Five high, Captain Bligh.'

John-Cody sat in the darkness as the fire drifted lower in the grate, then he yawned and stretched and stood up. The rain still hammered on the roof and from time to time Sierra would lift her head and sniff at the air. John-Cody ruffled her ears and looked out of the window into the gloom. He made a face and sat down again, leaning back so the recliner extended and he was able to lie almost flat. He stayed like that for a moment then got up and walked to the door of Libby's bedroom. His throat dried and he could feel his hands shaking. The door swung open and closed on itself behind him as he went in. He stood in the half-light that broke through the bare window and for a long moment he stared at the bed he had shared with Mahina. The bed she had lain in when she heard the morepork calling her name, the bed from where he had lifted her, where he had laid her again while he phoned Jonah and Kobi.

In the cupboard he found a spare blanket and went back to the fire. The embers were dying and he stoked them and threw on some more chunks of wood. He sat back in the chair again and wrapped himself in the blanket. Sierra was already on Bree's bed, having pushed open the door. Twisting round in the chair, John-Cody could see Bree's face, eyes closed and peaceful in the shadows that danced from the fire.

Eleven

Libby sat in her boat by the Passage Islands as the rain fell in curtains of grey, blending the surface of the fiord to white. She was watching her computer screen and finding it more and more difficult to separate ambient noise from that of the echolocating dolphins. She had been tracking the pod all morning, picking them up at Wet Jacket Arm. Old Nick was there, swimming round the others, moving up and down the ranks: Libby had watched him on the underwater camera and was feeling more and more convinced that he was the patriarch of the pod. She had noticed one older female though, who also seemed to have a special place in the pod, and she had called her Spray because she had dark spots like freckles running from her snout to her blowhole.

The rain rattled off the hood of her drysuit and formed puddles at her feet. Around her, Dusky was windswept and soaked and hanging with tendrils of cloud that dulled the mountains into slabs of drab vegetation. The boat shifted restlessly and she looked towards the sea, watching for darker water where the wind was up or the current was moving round.

Then she heard it in the distance, a high-revving engine, and she realized another boat was coming up the sound from behind her. Her engine was switched off, the dolphins still well within range, but now she could see the ambient noise changing on the computer screen and it altered again as the boat got closer and closer.

All at once Libby was excited: now she had control conditions, feeding dolphins in range and a high-speed propeller in the water. She watched the screen for activity, seeing how the approach of the boat made it more and more fuzzy, until she swivelled in her seat and felt the wake against the gunwales. She looked at the screen again, unable to distinguish the dolphin clicks from the interference. She could isolate the section later, take it to pieces and come up with a theory about the effects of the activity.

The approaching boat slowed; it was a launch not unlike her own but much more powerful, with four men on board and fishing rods stacked against the canvas roof. As it came closer the bow dipped and the driver spun it in a circle then accelerated once more. He came straight for Libby's boat then slowed right down again and chugged alongside. Libby saw Ned Pole smiling at her: three other men in wet gear were with him, none of whom she recognized. Then she saw the deer carcass, bloodied and soaked by the rain, laid out in the stern.

'Libby. How you going?' Pole touched the brim of his hat.

'Turn your engine off.'

'What?'

'Turn your engine off.'

266

Pole twisted the key in the dash and the engine shuddered, vibrated and then died away into stillness. Libby sat where she was and stared at her computer while the ambient noise subsided. She was looking for echolocation clicks but couldn't find any.

'What's the problem?' Pole was standing up in the bows.

Libby looked up at him. 'You are. Congratulations, Ned. You succeeded in chasing away the dolphins.'

'What dolphins?' It was one of the others: she recognized an American accent.

'Why were you steaming flat out up the sound like that?' Libby looked at Pole again. 'Showing off to your clients? You can't just blast up and down the sound. You know I'm conducting research here.'

Colour smudged Pole's face at the cheekbones. 'Look, I'm . . .'

'Forget it, the damage is done.' Libby indicated the laptop. 'You see this? I was monitoring the resident pod echolocating for food.' She tapped the screen with a stiff finger. 'They're not there any more.'

Pole had gathered himself now and shook his head. 'There is no resident pod in Dusky.'

'Oh, give me a break. Of course there is. You know there is. It's why I'm here, remember – to prove it.'

'Maybe, but until you do there isn't one. How long is it going to take you – two, three years?'

Libby stared at him. 'Oh, so that's how it is,' she said. 'At least I know now. I tell you what, Ned, I'd put my reputation on the line today if that's what it takes.'

Pole stared at her for a long moment, his face

scarlet now. The three clients looked uncomfortable, one of them sucking at a can of beer. Pole started the engine and put his boat astern, touching his hat as he went. 'Sorry if we disturbed you.' He spun round again and the wash rocked Libby's boat, then he headed back up the channel. In the distance Libby could hear the rotors of a chopper coming in to lift out the deer.

She sat down, blew out her cheeks and waited for her heart rate to settle before she looked once more at her computer. She didn't yet know if Pole had made the pod move on or not. She didn't know what pitch or frequency his engine was working on, but the dolphins were gone and something told her it was more than mere coincidence.

Nehemiah Pole steamed back up the sound, his clients silent around him. He slowed the launch down as they entered Cook Channel. His mind was working overtime. The scientist had guessed right, he was showing these guests the site for the first hotel. They were big-time hunters from one of the largest US gun clubs and he had been guiding them into the bush after deer. He showed them his favourite haunts. He told them tales of the old days, how the choppers took over the area: how he would leap from the skis with a net and wrestle the deer to the ground when it was more profitable to trap rather than shoot them. He tracked red deer into the bush, and they all bagged one. Up until just now they had been as happy as Larry and so was he. But that scientist could be much more trouble than he had first thought. He needed action and he needed it now, before DoC really got their claws into the council and forced some kind of moratorium.

The hunters sensed the change in his mood. Gone was the affable backwoods hunter; in his place a brooding businessman who could sense the best opportunity of his life beginning to slip away.

'You OK there, Ned?' one of them said to him. 'Looks like a great spot for a lodge.'

'What?' Pole glanced round at him. 'Oh yeah. I'm sorry I couldn't show you properly.'

'Going to happen though, is it?' The man with the beer leaned on the stern. 'I've got clients aplenty, Ned, but not if it's not going to happen.'

Pole shot him a stiff glance. 'It'll happen, mate. No worries.'

'I can count on that, can I? Print my literature?'

'You bet your life you can.' Pole lifted the satellite phone from where it lay under the dash and punched his wife's number at home.

'Jane, it's me. Has the company been in touch yet?'

'Not yet, no.'

Pole was quiet, biting his lip and thinking.

'Why, Ned? What's wrong?'

'Nothing. I just wanted to know, that's all.'

'Where are you?'

'Still in Dusky: we're flying a couple of deer out. I just bumped into that scientist and I think she might be more trouble than I first reckoned.'

For a moment his wife was silent. 'Don't worry about her, Ned, worry about Gibbs. She's one researcher. Even with the university behind her she's nothing, she can't prove the existence of anything in the time scale she's been given, certainly not whether dolphins are affected by noise. Gibbs is the thorn in our side. Get rid of him and we'll win.'

* * *

Libby was driven back to Supper Cove by the rain, which showed no sign of abating. The wind was lifting, coming in as a westerly, and the sea roughened into salted grey flakes out by the peninsula. She had trawled around for a bit longer and picked up the dolphins talking to one another between Five Fingers Peninsula and Parrot Island. She watched them for a while, thought about diving then decided to go back to base and cook something hot to eat.

She dried off in the hut and made some soup, which she sipped while separating the information created on the computer. The radio suddenly crackled and a voice came over the airways.

'*Wave Dancer*, *Wave Dancer*, this is the fishing boat *Huckleberry* on channel 66. Do you copy?'

Libby picked up the transmitter. '*Huckleberry*, this is Dr Bass. What can I do for you?'

'Greg Charles here, the skipper. Look, we're a fishing boat and we've just landed a hell of a catch in our nets.'

'What kind of a catch?'

'What I think is a bottlenose dolphin.'

Libby pulled on wet gear and gumboots and stepped out into the rain, which was sheeting harder than ever now and silting the estuary from the river. She untied the boat, started the engine then backed out into Supper Cove. She switched on the radio.

'*Huckleberry*, *Huckleberry*: this is *Wave Dancer*. Where exactly are you?'

'We're taking shelter in Cascade Cove,' the skipper came back. 'It's blowing a hooley out there. Wind's up to forty knots.'

'OK. I'll be there in half an hour.' Libby eased

the throttle higher and the wake lifted behind her.

The waters of the fiord slapped into the bows as she headed back down Cook Channel. The westerly was still blowing and the wind speed that the *Huckleberry* skipper had talked about was coming straight at her. No wonder they'd sought Cascade Cove as shelter; it was an all-weather mooring and they needed one in this. She had caught the weather forecast as she headed out and the wind was increasing to storm force and would not blow itself out until morning. She looked at her watch: nearly six now and the sky was black overhead though darkness would not officially fall till much later. She hit the scan button on the VHF and called the *Korimako* base.

'Is Bree with you, Alex?'

'No, Libby. She's not.'

Libby was disappointed. She had missed her daughter last night because of bad atmospherics and now she had got through, Bree wasn't there. 'Where is she?'

'In Te Anau with John-Cody: we've got a Doubtful trip over the weekend and she's gone to get stores with him.'

'Oh, OK. How is she, all right? I tried to get through last night but couldn't.' The radio crackled with static rain and Libby did not hear Alex reply. The wind was driving the rain right into her face now and the clouds licked so low about the mountains they almost formed part of the forest. For the first time since she had been out here, she thought about putting on her life jacket. She pressed the transmitter once more. 'Alex, tell Bree to try me later, if she can before fisherman's radio.' Libby

271

hoped Alex had heard her and hung the handset up. The fiord was dark and brooding now, mountain and water and no glimpse of the sky, just chipped and angry cloud. All at once she felt alone.

The wind died as she entered Cascade Cove and she was glad of it. She knew she was no great shakes at the wheel of a boat and this was as rough as she had seen it. She saw the *Huckleberry* through sheets of falling water, the deck lit up with the work lights as she came alongside to port. A crewman in yellow oilskins threw her a line. She tied off at the bow and climbed the ladder that overhung the gunwales. Her booted feet slipped on wet metal rungs and the crewman helped her up and over the side. She could see the dead dolphin, untangled from the nets now, beyond the twin and rusting winches set in the stern. The crewman nodded to the bridge where an older man stood in the doorway smoking a pipe. 'That's Glen, the skipper.' Libby made her way over and Glen stepped aside for her.

The boat was like the *Korimako* in that bridge and galley and saloon all occupied the same squared space. Libby could smell fried fish and saw the remains of their meal still clinging to plates that cluttered the table.

'DoC told us to report any dead dolphins to you,' the skipper explained.

'That's right. Thanks for doing it.' Libby stripped the hood from her head and shook loose her hair. 'What happened?'

The skipper shrugged. 'We were coming into the sound between the peninsula and Seal Islands. The storm blew in on a westerly and we thought we'd best lay up till the morning. I don't know where we got the dolphin, but I'd say fairly close to the mouth of the sound.'

'Can I look?'

He smiled at her, showing one missing tooth. 'That's what we called you for.'

She went out into the rain, the deck awash with water, translucent and shimmering in the bright glare of the lights. The dolphin was male, lying on his side with his beak slightly apart. Libby looked for distinguishing marks, fearing she might know him. The dorsal was not one she recognized though, and she dropped to one knee, pulling on rubber gloves and looking up and down his flanks. He was light grey in colour and his back was littered with dots like his smaller spotted cousins. He had several large bite marks in his flesh. The skipper stood alongside her. 'I reckon that was a white pointer or mako.'

'Have you measured the bite radius?'

He shook his head.

Libby took a tape measure from her pocket and did so. 'You're right,' she said. 'A mako or a small great white.' She glanced at the skipper. 'Close to the Seal Islands, you say?'

He made a face. 'Not close, but you know how it goes – where there's seals there's sharks.'

Libby set about working on her report. She measured the dolphin from snout to fluke and dorsal fin and she recorded the maximum girth. She photographed the dorsal and the flukes from both sides then she took a sample of blubber. Opening her knife she rested an elbow on her thigh. 'This is going to take me a while,' she said. 'Is that OK with you?'

'Whatever.' The skipper looked down at her then.

'Have you got good lights on your boat? You're going to need them later.'

Libby nodded and wiped the rain from her eyes with the back of her hand. 'I've got to pretty much disembowel this fellow. There's some plastic containers in my boat, do you think one of your lads could get them for me?'

'No worries.' The skipper sent someone to get the containers and Libby looked at the head of the dolphin. Carefully she cut into the gums of both jaws, taking out four teeth which she placed in separate zip-lock polythene bags. She went through the rest of the measurements she needed, then extracted the dolphin's stomach and liver and placed them in separate containers. When she finally stood up, the deck reeked of death and she stepped back from the carcass. Two crewmen, more used to it than she was, grinned as she turned away.

'Can we ditch him for you now?'

Libby nodded, gagged a little then fitted the lids on her containers. She went into the wheelhouse and accepted a cup of coffee from the skipper. She glanced at the dashboard and the single-side-band radio and a thought struck her. 'Can I use that?' she asked.

'Help yourself.'

'Thank you.' Libby put down the coffee cup and picked up the handset. John-Cody had a single-sideband in the house as well as the office and she called up the *Kori*-base, as the rain continued to batter the wheelhouse. Her boat would be waterlogged and she thought she would have to remove the plug and empty it before she ventured very far. She looked at her watch: nearly nine o'clock, she

274

shouldn't interfere too much with the fisherman's radio now. John-Cody answered and she was pleased to hear his voice.

'How you going?' he asked her.

'OK, I think.' She told him about the dead dolphin.

'It happens sometimes, Lib. Was it male or female?'

'Male. A young adult male.'

'How big?'

'Eight two from snout to fluke.'

'What kind of a shark?'

'I thought maybe a mako, but the skipper here thinks great white.'

'Either way big enough to kill a lone male dolphin. The crew has no idea what happened?'

Libby told him that it had been dragged up in their nets and they knew no more than that. She was about to tell him about Pole, then remembered it was an open line so she said simply, 'I had a visit from our mutual friend today: interesting graphics from the hydra-phone. Or at least I think there were. I've not had time to extrapolate the information fully yet.' She sighed then. 'Look, I'm tired and I want to see Bree. Can you get a floatplane to come for me tomorrow?'

'Sure.'

'Thanks. I'll wait at the hut. Tell the pilot to land as far into Supper Cove as the wind will allow because I still can't figure what effect the planes have on the pod. I tell you, John-Cody, two years is not enough: it's going to take at least two PhDs to create an acoustic model. Things change on a daily basis. Can I speak to Bree, please?'

Bree came on the line and Libby suddenly realized just how much she missed her.

'How are you, darling?' she asked.

'I'm OK, Mum. Is it raining there? There's a real storm here.'

'It's here too. I'm on a fishing boat at Cascade Cove.' Libby told her about the dolphin and Bree said she should be careful driving the boat back to the hut.

'When are you coming home?' she asked.

Libby brightened then. 'I've just told John-Cody. He's sending a plane tomorrow.'

'Oh great. I really miss you, Mum.'

Libby could hear the need in her voice and she had to force down a sob that lifted in her throat. 'I miss you too, darling. But I'll be there when you get home tomorrow. I've got to go now, the weather's foul and I've still to get back to the hut.'

'Be careful.'

'I will, don't worry. I love you, Bree.'

'Love you too, Mum.'

Libby hung up the handset, glad that John-Cody was with Bree on a wild night like this. She looked at the captain who cocked his head to one side. 'You know we've got spare bunks on board.'

She smiled. 'Thanks for the offer, but I've still got masses of work to do.'

The skipper watched her from the bridge while a crewman shone a torch down into her boat as she climbed aboard. The rainwater had not settled in the bottom as much as she had feared and she had no desire to fiddle with the bung in this weather. The crew handed the containers of stomach, teeth and liver down to her and she stowed them in the tiny locker, then started the engine.

'Go careful,' the skipper called and she nodded, switched on the powerful headlights and turned back up Cascade Cove.

The wind hit her up the stern as soon as she left the cove. The waves were swollen as if they were out at sea, and the water slapped the side of the fiord, sending phosphorescent spray up the walls before rolling back to create an alternative swell. It shuddered into the bows as she headed towards Supper Cove and shelter. Libby wanted to get home; the darkness was total now and the wind howled in her ears, plucking at her oilskins and working the hood down over her face. She sat at the wheel and steered into the darkness, mindful to keep mid-channel and well away from the cliffs. Distance was distorted in the dark and especially in weather as bad as this with a westerly blowing the storm right into the heart of the fiord. She piloted the boat carefully, forsaking her urgency for caution. She thought back to the time she had spent looking at the chart and tried to remember if there were any hidden rocks in Cook Channel.

There weren't and she made it through Nine Fathoms Passage unscathed. Ahead the sound ended in twin forks, with Supper Cove to the north. She gave the final island a wide berth and the estuary lay before her. The water was calm here, the heat taken out of the wind by the heights of Cooper Island. The *Wave Dancer*'s lights illuminated the cove and she eased well back on the revs as she approached the little jetty.

Back on dry land she wished she had left lamps burning in the hut. The building was darker than the shadowy bush that surrounded it and the patter of rain on tree and roof and water gave rise to all kinds of other inexplicable sounds. Libby was not one to be spooked easily, but this was as wild a night as she had seen and both the dead dolphin and Pole's appearance had disturbed her. The loneliness crept up on her as she made her way to the door. Inside she took off the wet-weather gear and the glow of the fire in the pot-bellied stove was very welcoming. Kneeling down, she opened the lid with the poker and fed more wood. Instantly it crackled and hissed and the sound was a pleasing distraction from the drumming of rain on the roof. Libby rocked back on her heels, watching the shadows cast along the walls. She took a cigarette from her pack and she sat there with it unlit, letting the warmth from the stove seep into her muscles. She was glad she had spoken to Bree and glad she had spoken to John-Cody. She'd call up in the morning if the atmospherics were better and find out when the plane was coming. She could synthesize the computer findings at home in comfort and with some company. With that in mind, she took her sleeping bag from the bunk and fell asleep by the fire, the sound of the rain rattling in her ears.

TWELVE

John-Cody was there to pick Libby up from Lake Te
Anau when the floatplane came in. She could see his
truck parked on Lake Front Drive as the pilot glided
gently down to the surface and landed with barely a
judder through the fuselage. The plane had been at
Supper Cove by nine thirty, when Libby was packed
and ready with the boat moored securely at the jetty.
John-Cody wore blue jeans and a sweatshirt and he
leaned on the bonnet of his truck waiting for her.
Libby was suddenly very pleased to see him and his
craggy face creased into a smile as she walked up the
gangplank. She carried her bag of dirty laundry and
her laptop slung over her shoulder. John-Cody lifted
the bag into the back of the truck and she climbed
into the passenger seat. 'You want to head straight
back or have a flat white in the Olive Tree?'

'Coffee sounds wonderful.' She smiled. 'It's good
to see you, John-Cody.'

'Good to see you too.' John-Cody pulled out from
the parking space.

'Thanks for looking after Bree.'

'I only did a couple of nights.'

'Yes, I know. But it was nice to know you were around last night, especially with that storm blowing.'

'That was a monster, wasn't it?' John-Cody peered through the windscreen at the sky where patches of blue were penetrating the cloud in places now. The wind was still in the air but much less fierce and the bulk of the rain had blown inland to batter Otago. They parked outside the small arcade of shops. John-Cody bought coffee and they sat by the fire in the corner.

'So how was Supper Cove this trip?' he asked her.

'Well, I told you about the dead dolphin. I've got the teeth and stuff back at the hut. I completely forgot to bring them out for analysis.'

'They'll keep.'

Libby stretched. 'It's lonely in there. I don't mind telling you, John-Cody, a girl gets stuck for company.'

He thought back over the past year in Doubtful Sound when he had lived on the *Korimako*, trawling the fiord by day and anchoring at night in Hall's Arm or Precipice Cove or out by the islands, with nothing but his memories and pain for company.

'I saw Pole,' Libby said. 'I tried to tell you last night, but I didn't know if the skipper of the *Huckleberry* was friends with him or not.'

John-Cody nodded. 'I understood where you were coming from.'

'He came racing up the channel when I was monitoring echolocation clicks.'

'Before I forget,' he interrupted her. 'Bree's having tea with Hunter Caldwell today.'

Libby wrinkled her brow. 'Who's Hunter Caldwell?'

He smiled then and sat back. 'He's a kid from her school. His parents farm up on Blackmount. I hope you don't mind, especially as you've only just got back.'

Libby shrugged. 'If it makes Bree happy, how can I mind?' She looked at him then. 'Does it make her happy?'

'Well, she was pretty up for the idea, put it like that. And she knew you were coming home today.'

Libby made a face. 'She sounded down when I talked to her last night. Have you noticed anything?'

'No, not especially.'

'I get so worried about her.'

John-Cody leaned across the table then and touched the back of her hand. 'Don't, Libby. She's fine. And she really wanted to go.'

'Are we talking a boyfriend or something?'

'I don't know. You'll have to ask her that.'

Libby sighed then. 'I do worry though, when I'm down in Dusky. Normally I used to be there when she came home from school. These days I hardly see her at all. I can't tell you how much I miss her.'

'She misses you too, but you know what, you're both all right. Bree's got Alex and I'm around some of the time. And now she seems to have Hunter Caldwell too. She's doing OK, Lib. Don't beat yourself up about it.'

She looked at him then, the softness in his eyes, the lines in his face, silver streaks running the length of his hair. She looked at his arms, taut with sinew and muscle, his scent reaching her across the table.

She finished telling him about Pole. 'I don't know what the outcome will be and anything I find won't be conclusive by any stretch of the imagination, but it is a start. The dolphins were hunting in range of the hydra-phone before Pole turned up and were gone as soon as he got there.'

'That could just be coincidence.'

'It could, yes. But my point is we don't know. We won't know without an in-depth study of the acoustics.'

'You're not going to get that in a hurry.'

'I know. I'm not going to prove definitively that the pod is resident either. If Pole gets his surface water activity permit it might be too late anyway.'

John-Cody blew out his cheeks. 'You know, you're the first person to show this level of concern in over a year.'

'Surely not?'

He nodded. 'When Pole's plans were first mooted a whole stack of people objected. But there's serious money behind this deal, Libby. Work is hard to find round here; there's not much in the winter and it's tough even in the season. It's a tourist town and the balance between economics and ecology is a precarious one.' He leaned forward. 'Pole singled out the submitters one by one and somehow he's won them over. The offers of work that have been bandied about don't bear thinking about. The only people who remained absolutely against the idea were Mahina and me.' John-Cody compressed his lips. 'DoC are against it in principle, but Pole's even got his supporters there.'

'Even though he operates without a marine mammal permit?'

John-Cody sighed. 'Technically none of us have them. They issued a few first time round, but we're still waiting for renewals. Pole's canny: he's had his application in for a long time. But DoC have got their moratorium in force and Pole could argue he's in exactly the same position as me.' He sipped coffee. 'Everything depends on the hearing at the regional council.'

He explained to her about the submission process, how unless the council themselves had serious reservations they merely acted as arbitrators. If the submitters' fears could be allayed by the party who sought the application, then invariably the permit was granted. If, however, the parties could not agree – as was the situation with Pole – then the case was heard in full council chamber, where lawyers could act on behalf of either party.

'And this will go to a full hearing?' Libby said.

John-Cody nodded. 'Pole's spent the year since Mahina died trying to smooth his path. He's done a pretty good job. I'm his last obstacle and he still thinks he can get by me.'

'He can't though, can he?'

'Not in a million years.'

They walked back to the truck and the sun was hot where it burst between the clouds. Crowds of tourists milled up and down the main street and a number of large tour buses were parked on Mokonui. Libby walked close beside John-Cody, delighting in his maleness, the ease she felt when she was with him. She could not quite put her finger on it but there was something about him that made her feel good about herself. She glanced at his face in profile, the lines about his jaw, the blue shadow where he had not shaved for a few days. They walked slowly and her elbow brushed his arm. The woman who ran one of the craft shops smiled at them and nodded to

John-Cody. Everyone knew him. It made her feel good to be with him. She recognized two mothers from the school talking together in front of the sporting goods shop and they looked sideways, gave each other a quick glance and looked away again.

Libby wound the window down and sat with her elbow resting on the sill while he backed out of the parking space and headed for the lakefront. He pulled over at the Southland Tours office to restack his brochures and did the same at the backpackers' hostel across the road from the floatplane building.

He dropped her outside the house then went down to the office where all was quiet. Alex told him that the weekend booking had been cancelled: the couple who had made the reservation had been involved in a car accident outside Queenstown. They were not critically injured but there was no way they would be able to make any kind of trip for a while. John-Cody rolled himself a cigarette, sitting on the porch, watching two canoeists on the lake. He had half promised Bree and Hunter that they could crew for him this weekend: the stores had been bought and the *Korimako*'s twin tanks were chock-full of diesel. Glancing over his shoulder, he watched Alex behind the counter, her face thin and grey, weariness in her eyes. 'How d'you fancy shutting up shop this weekend?' he asked her.

Alex cocked an eyebrow at him. 'It's the middle of the season.'

'So what?' He stood up. 'You look tired, Alex. Crook about the eyes. It's my fault. You work your backside off all year and then get landed with a twelve-year-old girl to look after.'

'Are you offering me a holiday, boss?'

'I'm offering you a weekend on the *Korimako* with Bree and Hunter. Libby too, if she wants to go.'

Alex looked sideways at him. 'You don't think she would?'

'I don't know. She's only just got back from Dusky.'

'She'll go.' Alex leaned her elbows on the counter. 'She'll jump at the chance of spending some time with you.'

John-Cody stared at her, feeling the colour leaking into his cheeks.

'It's true. She likes you, boss. She likes you a lot.'

'You're kidding me. How can you tell?'

'It's a girl thing. Don't look so surprised, lots of women find you attractive.'

John-Cody sat down on the couch and crossed his ankle on his knee. He stared at Alex, genuinely taken aback.

'Do you mean you really haven't noticed?'

He shook his head.

'You must be blind because everyone else has.'

He thought about it then, the two women in the street just now with the knowing looks, the Grady sisters clucking round him since Mahina died. He closed his eyes at the memory.

'It wouldn't bother her.'

He looked again at Alex.

'Mahina: it wouldn't bother her.' Alex came round from behind the counter and sat down next to him. 'Boss, if you don't mind me saying so you've been a different person since Libby and Bree showed up. You were a pain in the butt till then. I mean, everyone understood your loss, but you hid over the hill for a whole year. That's a long time. You were crummy company and you looked suicidal.'

John-Cody could feel pain building in his breast. He wanted her to stop talking like this and yet at the same time he wanted her to go on. Alex took his hand.

'You loved Mahina like nobody gets loved. The women in this town watched the way you loved her and despaired. I know what I'm talking about, boss. I'm one of them. Nobody gets loved that way any more, worshipped and cherished and treasured. She was the most precious thing in your life and everyone in the Te Anau basin knew it.'

A lump had formed in John-Cody's throat. 'When she died part of me died with her, Alex. All I wanted to do was die.' He sat up straighter. 'You know, I spent months on the *Korimako* just wanting to put on my dive gear, head out to the Gut and jump over. I wanted to swim down into the blackness and not come up.' He pursed his lips at the corners. 'Swim till my air ran out and be too deep to make it back to the surface.' He paused then. 'I couldn't, though, could I? I promised I'd scatter her ashes exactly a year after she died.'

Alex nodded, her hand resting lightly on his shoulder. 'That's partly why she asked you.'

He looked up at her.

'Mahina loved you, boss. But she had a sense of mortality and immortality that you'll never have. She knew it was time to go and she went with more dignity than anyone I can think of. She had a level of acceptance about things that most people never attain. She fought until the fight was over then she just accepted it for the reality it was and she died.'

Tears rolled on his cheeks now, without a sound. John-Cody hadn't heard anyone speak like this before, yet Alex's face was gentle and full of understanding.

'Mahina knew you might try and kill yourself, boss. That's partly why she said what she did. It's Maori tradition to watch over those who are left behind but rarely for as long as a year. The fuchsia and the bellbirds – of course she loved them: but I think she thought if you knew you had one final obligation to her you'd get through that year and maybe through it all.'

John-Cody drew breath. 'You know, I thought I was as low as I could get out there on the boat, but the real desolation hit me the moment I let her go.'

Alex nodded. 'For a while. But you had to come back here. You had to organize things for Libby and Bree. And you've done it. Heavens, you've even been back in the house.' She lifted her eyebrows. 'These past few nights with Bree.'

'Bree's a good girl. She's had a tough life.'

Alex beamed then. 'Look at you, getting involved with it all. You're moving on. I bet when you wake up each morning the ache isn't quite so bad.' Alex stood up then. 'Mahina told you to let her go, boss. Maybe you finally should.'

John-Cody drove to the nameless place, the track to Rainbow Reach halfway to Te Anau. He swung off the main road then pulled into a grassy space on the right, which overlooked the wetland loop that had once been part of the river. The cloud was pushed right back, like a cuticle at the edge of the sky, and the dome of the world burned powder blue above his head. He could feel the heat of summer through his clothes and a line of sweat gathered at his hairline. He leaned on the bonnet of the Ute and looked over the water at the island, green and black with manuka stands. The ground slipped away at his feet and he could see silver beech and cabbage trees and a tall thick-barked marbleleaf.

Three black swans glided on the surface of the water, the pair who had mated for life and the last of their offspring, not yet willing to seek a life of its own.

This was his place. He sat in the grass now and took out his tobacco. Mahina had her blue gum tree and favourite thinking stone, but the nameless place was his. He had called it that because it was not named on any map and the only people he had seen here were the occasional duck hunters in the season. Over the past couple of years even they seemed to have moved on.

He made himself a smoke and stuck it against his lip without lighting it. He thought about all that Alex had told him: he thought about Mahina and he thought about Libby. It was a weird thing: he had not consciously thought about her, other than the practicalities of getting her boat down to Dusky and helping out with Bree. He smiled when he thought of Bree. The night before last, after they had spoken to Libby on the radio, he had played guitar and she had sung along. He enjoyed her company; she was bright and she had her own opinions. He had thought a lot about Bree but not really about Libby.

He stared across the stillness and Mahina crowded his mind once again: her face, her eyes, the sound of her voice ringing inside his skull. But Alex was right, since he had come back here, faced things down and taken up some responsibility again, the pain was less acute. Maybe Mahina did fear what he might do when she died and made him promise accordingly. The one thing she knew he would do was keep a promise made to her.

He looked across the water and saw a pair of plovers circle one another. The Wairau was tumbling over itself to get to Lake Manapouri, high with the recent rain. He could hear the water rushing, sucking at muddy banks, breaking free earth rich in minerals and carrying them downstream. Perhaps there really was life after Mahina: he still had this place, the silent beauty that was Fiordland. He had a wharf at Deep Cove and he had the *Korimako*. Nobody could take those from him now: he and Mahina had insured their lives in relation to the debt of the business. With her death he no longer owed any money and the recent trips that Alex had organized had pretty much been profit. That was a first in his lifetime. Pole could covet the boat and the wharf all he liked because he would never get them.

He stood up feeling empowered all at once and was aware of a tingling sensation in his limbs. He felt strong, alive; vital suddenly to all that surrounded him. He was as much a part of this place as Mahina had been before him. All that she was she had imparted to him and now she was gone *he* was what stood between the land and people like Pole.

Libby was in the garden lying on a blanket reading a novel. She wore a bikini top and cut-off jeans and her skin was tanned. Her hair was long and thick and black, reaching halfway down her back, loose now and sprinkled with perspiration. John-Cody stood for a few moments in the shade of the carport just watching her. He stepped onto the lawn, discarding his shoes, and the grass felt lush and deep under his bare feet. Libby too was barefoot and she rolled on her back and shaded her eyes when she saw him.

'Can I make you a cup of tea?' he asked her.

'You certainly can. I'd love one.'

John-Cody looked up at the pigeon cooing softly in the topmost branches of the red beech. 'This weekend,' he said, 'I sort of half promised Bree that she and Hunter could crew for me on the boat.'

'That's fine with me,' Libby said.

'Except the trip's been cancelled.' John-Cody crouched on his haunches next to the blanket. 'So how would you fancy coming out for the weekend? I told Alex to shut up shop: we could get a ride across the lake with Tom when Bree finishes school. Come back Sunday night.'

'You don't have to do all that if the trip's been cancelled.'

'I want to.' He made an open-handed gesture. 'Would you like to come?'

'I'd love to.'

'I thought you might be sick of the fiords by now.'

Libby looked in his eyes and felt sudden warmth in her veins. 'I'm sick of being alone in them. I love the fiords, John-Cody. But they're much better with company.'

They sat in the garden drinking tea and appreciating the sunshine. Libby watched the way he sipped from his cup and the way he took his tobacco in one hand, rolling the loose strands against his palm before setting them in paper. The sound of a car on the road outside broke the moment: two doors

290

opened then footsteps crunched on the gravel drive. John-Cody looked up as Jonah's massive frame blocked the sun for a moment. Jonah smiled at him and winked at Libby, standing with his hands on his hips. 'I've brought someone to see you,' he said.

An old man shuffled from under the carport, stooped, head bent, leaning heavily on a stick. 'Kobi.' John-Cody jumped to his feet.

The old man looked at him and scowled, but the scowl became a grin. 'G'day, you old joker, I thought it was time I saw what you were doing down here.'

John-Cody gave the old man a hug and Kobi patted his back with the twisted knots of his hands, then John-Cody, supporting him by the arm, introduced Libby. Kobi took his cap off and smiled at her.

'So you're the scientist looking at Dusky Sound,' he said.

'Yes, I am.'

'How do you like it down there?'

'It's beautiful.'

Kobi nodded and Libby warmed to the old man immediately. He settled himself on the grass and John-Cody rolled him a cigarette, which he nipped between forefinger and thumb, letting smoke trail from his nostrils. John-Cody told Jonah about the trip at the weekend but he said he couldn't make it. John-Cody then turned his attention to Kobi.

'What about you, old fella? It's years since you went on the boat.'

'I'm too old.'

'Don't be daft. Of course you're not too old.'

'I'm too old, Gib.'

'Oh come on, Kobi.' Libby took his hand and it

was warm though the skin was weak and thin and broken with blue veins. 'You're not too old.'

'I can't get down the steps.'

'We'll help you.'

He winked at her then. 'Will you put me to bed as well?'

Libby laughed. 'Come on, come with us. It's only for the weekend.'

Kobi made a face then looked at John-Cody. 'What d'you reckon, Gib? You really think I'm up to it?'

'I wouldn't go climbing the spreaders but yes, of course you're up to it.'

'All right, I'll come.' He still held Libby's hand. 'On condition that you tell me all about what's happening in Dusky. I haven't been to Dusky Sound in years.'

Bree was delighted when they picked her up from the Caldwell farm that night. John-Cody arranged to get Hunter from the bus and head over the hill with the Z boat crew on Friday afternoon; he knew Tom could arrange a truck to haul them over the Wilmot Pass.

Bree was full of the farm and talked nineteen to the dozen, perched between them, as they trundled back to the lake with Sierra in the flatbed barking at every car they passed. John-Cody drove and listened, Libby interrupting her daughter every now and again to get a word from her about school. John-Cody glanced across the cab at Libby and as if for the first time he noticed her face, the deep black of her eyes, smooth high-boned cheeks and white flash of her smile. She was young and she was beautiful and for the second time since Mahina died he felt something stirring inside him.

That night he lay in bed in the homestay and could hear the pair of them chattering through the walls: his bathroom door was open and the sound echoed between theirs and his: water falling, Libby in the shower, calling to Bree for shampoo. He listened to the water coursing into the drains and for half a second he imagined her naked. His breath caught in his throat and he sat upright in bed, the sharp taste of betrayal on his tongue: for a long time he stared at his reflection, darkened as it was in the mirror.

They crossed the Lake of the Sorrowing Heart in brilliant sunshine the following afternoon: according to Tom, seated at the helm of the Z boat, the weather was set for the weekend. Even Deep Cove wouldn't see any rain. Tom had been as good as his word and a driver was waiting for them. Hunter and Bree sat in the flat bed of the truck with the luggage, while Alex, Libby and John-Cody occupied the rear cab. Kobi sat up front and looked as happy as John-Cody remembered seeing him.

On board the *Korimako* John-Cody took Hunter down to the engine room, went through the checks with him and told him it was his job to start the auxiliary in the morning. That meant no slouching in his bunk, which was across the gangway from Bree who got to the freezer berth before Alex. Kobi and Alex took for'ard berths, leaving Libby the double down aft next to the skipper. They untied and John-Cody hit the horn then let Bree back the *Korimako* out into Doubtful Sound.

They still had two hours before dark, so

John-Cody headed for Crooked Arm while Alex and Libby got busy making supper. John-Cody set the autopilot then went on deck with Hunter and Bree and pointed out every landmark between Deep Cove and the second arm of the sound.

Kobi sat on the vegetable locker with his coat buttoned and watched Hunter climb the mast to the spreaders thirty feet above the deck. He stood in the crow's nest like a lookout from the whaling days of Cuttle Cove back in the 1830s. Bree sat next to Kobi wearing her mother's sunglasses.

They ate dinner in the glasshouse with the plastic door rolled up and the sun beating on their heads as it slipped behind the heights from where the Lucky Burn cascaded. Bree and Hunter sat next to each other and giggled: Libby watched them and shook her head. John-Cody watched them all, watched the interaction between the two children, watched Libby and Alex and how well they got on. He listened to Kobi's stories of the old days of the fiords and for the first time in a while he felt happy.

Libby, Alex and the old man played cards at the saloon table while Hunter and Bree took showers. Bree came out with a towel wrapped round her and John-Cody swivelled on his plastic stool where he was poring over the chart table. Bree sidled next to him and leaned gleaming red elbows on his laminated charts. She picked up the blue radio booklet and asked him what EPIRBs were.

'Emergency position-indicating radio beacons or something like that.' John-Cody pointed astern. 'They're fixed to the transom next to the dinghy.'

'How do they work?'

'They start transmitting automatically if the boat

294

sinks.' He sat back and folded his arms. 'They detach themselves and give any rescuer the boat's last known position.'

Bree looked horrified. 'Have you ever used them?'

He shook his head. 'No boat I've been on has sunk.'

'How long have you been a sailor?'

'Oh, a long time. Since I was twenty.'

'Always here in New Zealand?'

'No, I started in a place called Bellingham in America, on a scallop dredger.' For a second he could see the darkened interior of that bar. He heard the first mate grumbling about the winch man going AWOL, and remembered how he had bitten the bullet and offered the man his services.

'Why didn't you stay in America?'

John-Cody looked through shadows of the past at her. 'I didn't like it very much.'

'Would you ever go back?'

He shook his head. 'No, Bree, I wouldn't. New Zealand's my home now.'

'Bree.' Libby's head appeared at the top of the steps. 'Bedtime. Let's move it along a bit, shall we?'

John-Cody looked up at her. 'Sorry, Mum,' he said. 'It's my fault.'

Libby wagged an admonitory finger at her daughter. 'No, it's not. It's hers. She's the proverbial chatterbox, especially around bedtime.'

They sat in the saloon and drank wine, listening to the whispered voices coming from the bunks below deck. Libby glanced at Alex and lifted an eyebrow. John-Cody rolled his glass between his hands and called out to Hunter. He told him not to forget what he had been told about the morning. 'I'll expect you on deck with the dawn, seaman. You got that?'

Hunter didn't reply, but the whispers subsided and Libby sighed with relief. 'Peace at last,' she said.

John-Cody sat across the table from her with Alex and Kobi in the middle. Kobi looked at Libby. 'So tell me about Dusky,' he said. 'Have you sorted out that dolphin pod yet?'

Libby smiled at him. 'No, Kobi, I haven't. So far I've identified just under twenty animals: I think they might be a patriarchal pod, with Old Nick as the leader.'

'You do?' John-Cody raised one eyebrow.

She nodded. 'I can't put my name to it yet, but so far that seems to be the case.'

Kobi sat with his hands together on the table. 'What about the hotels?'

Libby pursed her lips. 'I don't know. I think they'll get their permit before I can prove the pod is resident. They'll certainly get it before I can reach any conclusions on how engine noise might affect their behaviour.'

Kobi looked through her. 'So they'll build their hotels or whatever it is they're planning.'

'No.' John-Cody placed a palm over Kobi's knuckles. 'Not if I can help it. I'm going to fight them, Kobi. I am fighting them. It'll go to a full hearing and I'll get the best lawyers in the country if I have to.'

Kobi looked into the distance beyond him. 'Nehemiah Pole.'

John-Cody nodded. 'He's the front man but American business is backing him.'

'But he's the man on the ground.'

'Seems to be. I think they're attracted by his

296

reputation. Pole's a big draw, Kobi. He has a serious past.'

'He does at that,' Kobi said. 'I reckon he does at that.'

He went to bed and the others played a few hands of cards, talking in low voices, and then Alex yawned and stretched and John-Cody got up to let her get past and she went backwards down the steps to her berth.

Crooked Arm was silent, the heat lost from the day and a thin cool breeze bleeding through the netting clipped across the open doorway on the leeward side. John-Cody had rigged it up to keep the sandflies at bay. Libby sat back and yawned, then reached for the wine bottle and poured them another glass. John-Cody lifted his and inspected it and the silence grew between them. He could see a sky full of stars through the window and knew that tomorrow would be as good a day as today, Sunday too if they were lucky.

He looked at Libby who was deep in thought, arms folded under her breasts, leaning back in the seat. Her face was small and brown; eyes very dark, black almost in this light. She felt his gaze and smiled. 'I was miles away,' she said.

'Where exactly?'

'The Baja.'

'California – Sea of Cortez?'

Libby nodded and leaned forward. Her breasts moved under her shirt and he could tell she wasn't wearing a bra.

'I spent two years down there all in all. Bree was born there. Hell, she's got a Mexican passport.' She shook her head then. 'Typical me that is, I couldn't

297

even take enough time off work to cross the border and have her in the United States. That would have been much more useful to her in later life.' She wrinkled her mouth at the corners. 'You know, sometimes I don't think I've been much of a parent.'

John-Cody lifted a hand. 'I figure you do your best. I guess it's tough all round. Parenting is tough, not that I've ever been a parent.'

Libby glanced at him then. 'Mahina didn't want children?'

'She couldn't have them.'

'Oh, I'm sorry.'

'Don't be, Lib. We had a wonderful relationship, everything we could have dreamed of.'

Libby could hear the quiet passion in his voice, see it in his eyes and she felt inexplicably jealous. She considered the sound of her name on his tongue and realized she loved the way he shortened it. He sat back with both hands cupped round the wine glass before him on the table.

'I don't think you should be too hard on yourself as far as Bree is concerned. She seems happy enough.'

'Right now, maybe. Who wouldn't be in a place like this?' She smiled then. 'She gets on very well with Hunter.'

'She does.'

Libby sipped wine. 'Bree didn't want to come out here when I told her.'

'Children don't like change.'

'I really didn't have a choice this time, but I suppose I have dragged her round the world a bit. She's never been in one place for more than two years.'

'Variety.'

'Is that such a good thing at her age?'

'I don't know. But I guess most situations have advantages and disadvantages if you think about them.'

She looked at him. 'Did *you* want children?'

'I never really thought about it. Mahina couldn't have them, and I knew that from the beginning.' He gestured. 'I loved Mahina. That's all there was to it.'

'Did you marry her in a Maori ceremony?'

'I didn't marry her. We just lived together.' That sounded trite. It was not trite: he remembered taking her boat to the beach at Yuvali Burn, with the Malaspina Reach running out to sea before them. A wild and windy dawn, and as it grew light they had stood together on that beach, lashed by the rain, and made a vow to love each other till death.

'John-Cody?'

He looked up at Libby's enquiring face. 'We made a vow to each other. That was good enough. I've never been one for regular religion anyway.' He gestured to the open doorway. 'That's my church right there. Mahina's too.' He told her what they had done. 'We didn't need any witnesses. We figured Rangi and Papa knew what was what.'

Libby nodded. 'That's beautifully romantic.'

'You think so?'

'Yes.' She smiled at him. 'You're quite a romantic at heart, aren't you?'

John-Cody snorted. 'For an old sea dog maybe.'

'Do you know what Bree calls you?'

'Captain Bligh.'

'I didn't mean that, that's your thing. No, she calls you the quiet man of the sea.'

299

He laughed softly, deep in the back of his throat. 'I think I like that.'

They were still for a moment, a strong comfortable silence, then John-Cody stretched and said he was going outside for a smoke.

Libby stood up. 'I'll join you.'

They stood on the bows with barely a breath of wind coming up the sound. John-Cody had moored the *Korimako* in the sheltered bay where the Lucky Burn ran into the depths of the fiord. The sky was clustered with stars, millions of them, more than Libby had ever seen down here. She gazed up, her head back, neck long and straight, skin like smooth velvet in the half-darkness. 'I don't know any of those.'

John-Cody pointed south-east. 'There's the Southern Cross right there. You see it with the top down to the left.'

Libby followed his finger and stared, not seeing it at first and then she located it.

'The two bright stars down on the right are the pointers. You can find south from the Southern Cross if you have to.' He sat down on the dive locker and looked again. 'Above it you've got the Antlia constellation and Vela is to the right of that. Then there's – let's see – Carina and Volans, then Dorado right there.'

Libby sat down next to him. 'Did you learn all that by sailing?'

'Stellar navigation? No.' He pressed tobacco in his palm. 'Mahina taught me some, Tom Blanch too. Tom knows his stuff, or he did. He's not been to sea in the real sense of the word for a long time now though.'

'He just drives the Z boats.'

'Yeah. It's regular work and it gives him time to build that cat he's working on.'

'What's he going to do when he finishes it?'

'Sail round the world.'

'Will you go with him?'

John-Cody shook his head. 'No. I've got work to do here.'

'What you and Mahina started?'

He nodded. 'Try and protect what we have. This place is special. I want to keep it that way.' He looked sideways at her. 'People lose their hearts here, you know.'

Libby gazed up at the stars once again. 'I can see why,' she murmured.

In the morning Hunter was up early. John-Cody had been up for an hour, drinking coffee and talking to Kobi. The old man did not sleep well these days, rarely managing four hours before he was wide awake. Hunter looked across Crooked Arm, furrowed his brow and shielded his eyes from the sun. 'What's that?' he said and pointed. John-Cody looked where he looked, right across to the green wall of the fiord where spouts of spray were rising gold in the morning sun.

'Wave dancers,' he said.

'What?'

'Dolphins. Now you *can* start the engines.'

The dolphins were in a playful mood and rode the bow wave. Hunter and Bree pulled on wetsuits and John-Cody towed them behind the boat as they gripped the slats in the dive platform where the dolphins rose to greet them.

Later in the day he suggested that Libby might like to dive the Gut, the only marine reserve in Fiordland. She had left her drysuit at the Supper Cove hut and John-Cody rummaged in the dive locker for a suitable 7mm wetsuit. He checked the pressure on two bottles of air and sought his own harness and a spare one for Libby. She had her own snorkel, mask and fins, which she took everywhere with her. With the *Korimako* moored to the length of rope slung under the banks of Secretary Island, John-Cody went down aft to get changed. At the top of the steps he saw the door to Libby's cabin was clipped back and she stood with her back to him wearing only her knickers and pulling a T-shirt over her head. For a moment he gazed at the shape of her shoulders, the way her back narrowed so finely to her waist, the knots of her spine punching the skin as she bent forward. Her feet were small and her legs long and shapely. He rattled down the steps and she looked round at him and smiled.

'Need any help?' he asked her.

'I'll let you know in a minute.'

He ducked into his cabin, stripped to a T-shirt and his boxer shorts and then eased himself into the wetsuit. When he was done, Libby appeared beyond his curtain with her zipper needing fastening across the shoulders. Gently he lifted her hair out of the way and his fingertips brushed the cool flesh of her neck: he saw the tiniest black hairs at the nape and was aware of a weakness all at once in his limbs. Carefully he zipped her up and they went up on deck.

The children watched as he helped Libby on with her tank and checked the weight of her belt to make sure she was carrying enough to descend properly. He worked his own tank over his shoulders, fastened the clips across his chest and pulled the hood over his head.

'Hunter,' he said. 'There's a timer on the dashboard. Go and fetch it for me, will you?'

Hunter brought it back and John-Cody set it for forty minutes. He told Bree to run the dive flag up the shroud as soon as they were in the water. Then he clambered backwards down the ladder, squatted on the platform and fastened his fins. Libby was already in the water and cleaning her mask. 'You OK?' he asked her, and she tapped the top of her head with arced fingers before they descended together.

The fresh-water layer was only seven feet: they passed through the oily film of yellow where it met salt and then the world opened beneath them. Starfish clung to the walls just below the mixed layer, waiting for the fresh-water level to become even shallower so they could attack the mussel beds. Hydra coral, black and red, clung to the exposed cliff walls where the saltwater currents washed in from the sea and they could feed on the passing plankton.

They dived deep and John-Cody showed Libby coral trees hundreds of years old, protected here from the massive avalanches of vegetation above the surface. He pointed out beds of lamb shells that were older than the glacial fiords themselves and sea pens like quills waving in the current.

On the boat Hunter and Bree stood together in the stern and watched the bubbles rising. Bree stood close to him, aware of his breathing, the tanned skin of his forearms. Surreptitiously she glanced at his face in profile, the full redness of his lips, and she wondered what it would be like to kiss him. She had never kissed a boy before, had never wanted to. She realized then that she wanted to kiss Hunter and a squirming sensation gripped her stomach; she looked at the white metal of the deck between her feet.

'They're over there now,' Hunter interrupted her unconsciously and Bree followed the line of his finger to where the bubbles had drifted.

'How long have they been down?' she asked him.

'I don't know. I'll check.'

'It doesn't matter. Alex can keep an eye on the timer.' Bree didn't want him dashing to the wheel-house, didn't want the moment between them broken. Hunter looked round at her then and smiled. 'This is brilliant, isn't it?'

Bree gazed across at Marcaciones Point. 'The best,' she said. 'Just the very best.'

THIRTEEN

Nehemiah Pole was at home. Jane was back on the phone to the United States and he was listening intently, coiled at his desk with his elbows resting on the blotter. Jane's desk was at right angles to his so both of them could get the benefit of the view across the fields where the two bays and Barrio grazed the paddock. Jane was concentrating, chewing on the end of a pencil as she did when she was thinking hard. 'You're sure?' she said.

Pole felt the hairs lift on the back of his neck.

'Get the paperwork and fax it to me. *We*'ll take it from there.' She put the phone down and looked across at her husband. 'I think we just struck gold.'

Pole stared at her for a long moment then he stood up, fists clenched, and walked to the window. In his mind's eye he was at West Arm, Gibbs and Mahina together on the dock, an ambulance crew and the body of his son wrapped in plastic. He saw Mahina avoid his eye, saw himself gazing intently at her for the first time in years, as if with Eli's death some control had been wrested back.

Jane came alongside him. 'Assuming what we get

is good enough, it'll be up to you to do it.' She faced him, took him by his shoulders as if he were a child. 'The people in the States want to be distanced from any adverse publicity that might arise.'

Pole was quiet, gazing across the paddock.

'Ned?'

'What?'

'Did you hear what I said?'

He nodded.

She saw the clouds gathered in his eyes and she frowned. 'You contact the authorities right away, no messing about.'

'Why not speak to him first, tell him we know?'

'What on earth for?'

He shrugged. 'I don't know. Give him an option.'

'After the trouble he's caused us? Give me a break.' She looked at him then, puzzlement in her eyes. 'With what you went through in the bush I can't believe you said that.'

'Bush?' He was staring at her. 'What're you talking about – bush?'

'The jungle, of course: the army. What do you think I'm talking about?'

Pole stepped beyond her: he couldn't get the image out of his head, the body bag on the wharf and Mahina avoiding his eye. 'When will we know for sure?' he said.

'Just as soon as they get their hands on the prosecuting attorney's report.'

Bree went back to school on the Monday after the Easter holidays were over with thoughts of Hunter and Easter orchids in her head. She and her mother had accompanied John-Cody on the last Doubtful

Sound trip of the season and the whole of the Camelot estuary had been thick with the scent of the flower.

She saw Jessica Lowden squatting on the low wall of the school where the bus pulled up, and her heart sank. She recalled the same feeling when she went back after Christmas and she didn't know how she'd managed to get through the last term. Hunter wasn't on the bus this morning: Bree knew that he and his family had been up in the North Island for the holidays and he was returning to school a day later.

Jessica looked up as she got off the bus. 'Hey, Bree.'

Bree stopped, absolutely amazed. Jessica was smiling at her. She got up from the wall.

'Did you have a good holiday?'

Bree looked at her dumbly and nodded.

'Great. What did you do?'

'I went over the hill with Gib.'

'Did you? I've only been once. Not on the *Korimako*, you know, just for the afternoon with Southland Tours.'

They walked together into the school building, with Sally and Anna, Jessica's two cronies, behind them, equally as chatty. Bree saw Biscuit at the door to their classroom and she looked just as astonished.

'It must be weird for you,' Jessica prattled on, 'Easter and soon it'll be winter. In England it'll be summer now, won't it?'

'Spring. But not long till summer.' Bree laid her bag on her desk. Behind her Sally opened a packet of sweets and offered them to her. Bree took one rather gingerly as if she half expected Sally to snap the bag

307

shut on her hand. She looked up at Jessica who was suddenly looking sheepish.

'Look, we're sorry, OK? I mean about being nasty to you. It's just that you were new and your name was weird.' She shrugged her shoulders. 'Anyway, we're sorry.'

The tutor called them for the register then and Bree sat down, quite stunned by it all. For six months and more Jessica Lowden had made her life a misery. This was almost too good to be true. At break she sat on her own in the classroom and took her writing paper from her bag.

Dear Dad

You'll never guess what! Jessica Lowden's stopped bullying me. She's been doing it for half a year and we came back from the Easter holidays and she just stopped. She even said sorry. I nearly fell over. Brilliant isn't it because everything else here is so cool. I love John-Cody and he and Mum are getting on well. He was so depressed when we got here, but I talked to him about Mahina and I think he secretly fancies Mum. Mum is gorgeous. She's much younger than him but that doesn't matter, does it. I talk to him quite a lot.

She paused then and realized this was the first letter she had written for a while.

Sorry I haven't written for such a long time, I suppose I've just been busy.

Anyway, everything is cool especially now Jessica is being so nice. I don't even mind playing

rugby. I really like Hunter. Did I tell you about
him? We've been friends since I got here. I've
been to tea and he's come to tea. I haven't kissed
him yet, but I'm thirteen soon so I think that
will be the time. What do you think? I'll be a
teenager then. I'm not going to tell Mum, I'm
just going to do it or rather I mean I'm just
going to let him do it. That's a girl thing, Dad.
You wouldn't understand. Anyway, things are
really cool here now. I'll let you know when I've
kissed Hunter.

Lots of love, Bree

Jessica sat next to her in Japanese that afternoon.
Bree had picked the language up well and was one of
the best in the class. Jessica, on the other hand, was
not good and Bree hoped she wasn't sitting next to
her just to copy her work. The tutor raised an eyebrow; everyone in the school had been aware of the
enmity between the two of them, and this sudden
display of friendliness took them all by surprise.
During the lesson Jessica told her that she and her
friends were going down to Lake Te Anau after
school to look at the new boat Southland Tours was
putting on the water: Bree could go with them if she
wanted to. Bree thought about that. Her mother was
back in Dusky Sound and John-Cody was over the
hill starting winter preparations on the *Korimako*.
'You can come back to my house afterwards,'
Jessica went on. 'My mum will give you a lift home.'
Bree decided to phone Alex from Jessica's house.
Given what had happened in the past, she felt she
would be stupid to upset Jessica by turning down the
invitation.

After school she packed her bag and got her coat from the peg. Jessica, Sally and Anna were waiting outside for her and Jessica smiled when she came out.

'How you going?'

'Fine.'

Jessica pointed towards Matai Street. 'The new boat's moored by the sports domain.'

'Fine.' Bree walked by her side. 'What kind of a boat is it?'

'A catamaran, a new one.' Jessica's father was one of the skippers for Southland Tours, rotating between Milford Sound and Lake Manapouri. Bree had seen him sometimes at the helm of the boat they used when they went over to the *Korimako*.

They walked and told jokes and Jessica told Bree all about her family, her dad's job and her brothers and mother. She told her about living in Te Anau and asked her what living in England was like.

'It's fine except that when you're here people call you a Pom,' Bree said. 'I really hate being called a Pom.'

'Sorry about that: it's just a name. It doesn't mean anything.'

'I know,' Bree said. 'At least I do now.'

They walked the length of Bligh Street and Bree felt as contented as she had since arriving here. The letter to her father was in her bag, already stamped and ready to post at the shop when she got home to Manapouri. Getting things sorted out at school was the icing on the cake: she had Hunter, the house, John-Cody, the boat and Sierra. Life was suddenly pretty wonderful.

They came to the sports domain and Bree looked

310

across the stillness of Lake Te Anau. It was deceptive: from the town itself it looked quite small but in fact it was much bigger than Lake Manapouri, stretching many miles beyond Patience Bay to the north. 'Where's the boat?' she asked Jessica.

'It's not here yet. They're bringing it round in a little while.'

'Is your dad driving?'

Jessica nodded.

They walked across the domain towards the little harbour where the wealthy people kept their sailing boats. A red and silver twin cab was parked by the harbour and Bree could see a tall man working in the back. The sun was high but not very warm and she buttoned her coat a little more tightly. The lake shivered with ripples cast by the breeze skirting the town from the mountains. Jessica was quiet now, leading them very definitely towards the beach. She walked slightly in front of Bree with Sally and Anna behind them. The lake seemed very still again, the breeze dying. This part of it was much emptier than the section that fronted the town. Bree walked on, glancing now and again towards the red and silver truck.

Ned Pole thought about John-Cody Gibbs as he restacked the hay he had bought for the horses. He stood up in the flat bed of the truck and rubbed the small of his back; he was lean and fit and strong, but at fifty-two the first twinges of age were catching up with him. He pushed his hat to the crown of his head and saw four schoolgirls heading for the beach.

Jessica led the way down to the shingle, then bent for

311

a stone and skimmed it across the surface. Sally and Anna moved either side of Bree and dropped their bags on the ground: they too bent for stones.

'Let's see who can get it the furthest,' Anna said.

Bree put her bag down, knowing she was no good at skimming the flat stones but prepared to have a go. Jessica got three bounces with her first effort and Sally followed with two. Bree was about to try when she saw that Anna was poking around in her bag. She stopped and stood straight.

'Anna?'

Anna looked up. 'What?'

'What're you doing?'

'Looking for cheese.'

Bree felt the muscles cramp in her stomach. She looked at Jessica and saw her grinning wickedly, then Sally too. Anna was pulling the books out of her bag and tossing them to Jessica.

'Look at her, the boff. She thinks she's so perfect.'

'Cheesy Breezy: smelly Cheesy Breezy. Stupid name for a stupid stuck-up Pom.'

Bree felt the tears in her eyes. 'Can I have my books back, please?'

'*Can I have my books back, please?*' Jessica mimicked. 'Poor Cheesy: you really thought we'd be *your* friends. Friends of a boffy Pom like you. Here, let's see if the fish like cheese.' She threw Bree's English book into the lake.

'What's this?'

Bree looked round to see Anna holding the letter she had written to her father. She lunged for it but Anna stepped away and Sally pushed Bree, sending her sprawling on the stones.

* * *

Ned Pole swung himself down from his truck and heard a girl cry out from the beach. Looking over he saw one of them being shoved to the ground. Thinning his eyes he began to walk towards them.

Bree had cut her knee. She sat on the stones with blood oozing down her shin while Anna read her letter aloud and the others laughed and laughed.

'Us friends with you!' Jessica cackled at her and tossed another exercise book into the lake. 'You'll have to tell him you were lying, Cheesy.'

'Tell who exactly?' The voice was deep and male and rumbled at them from the pavement. Bree looked up at a tall figure partly silhouetted by the sun. He stalked down the beach and whipped the letter from Anna's hand.

'Mr Pole.' Jessica swallowed. 'We were just having a bit of fun.'

Pole stared at the two upturned books floating in the lake. 'Fun?' He looked as though he was going to spit. 'You call this fun?' He glanced at the graze on Bree's knee. 'Are you all right, young lady?'

Bree didn't answer him. He looked at the other girls, who were backing away from him now.

'I know you, Jessica Lowden,' Pole said. 'You get yourself home and wait there till I come round.'

Jessica paled.

'Yes, you be afraid. I know your dad, remember. I know him really well.' He took a pace towards her. 'You go home and wait. And tomorrow you'd better be nice to this English girl, you'd better be really nice.' He turned to the others. 'You too, you hear me? I know your parents and they know me. If you see me at your houses there'll only be one reason.'

313

He paused and looked again at Jessica. 'You're a bully, Jessica Lowden, and I don't like bullies.'

They turned tail and ran. Pole watched them go, Bree's letter in one hand and her bag in the other. He handed back the letter and bag then waded into the ice-cold lake to retrieve her books.

'I'm sorry,' he said as he handed them to her, water soaking him to the thighs. 'I think these are finished.'

Bree took the sodden books and as she did so the tears welled in her eyes and she sat down on the stones and cried and cried and cried. When she finally stopped Pole was crouched beside her in his soggy jeans, holding out a clean handkerchief. 'You're Bree, aren't you?' he said. 'Dr Bass's daughter.'

Bree nodded and snivelled and blew her nose in the handkerchief. She offered it back to him. 'You keep it,' he said. 'I've got plenty.' He looked at her then, resting his forearms on his thighs. 'Have they been giving you a hard time?'

She nodded.

'For how long?'

'Ever since I got here.'

'That must be tough.'

She nodded again.

'Have you told anybody?'

She shook her head.

'Not even your mum?'

'No.'

'No, I guess not. What about Gib? I've seen you around with him.'

She shook her head.

'You don't want to tell anyone?'

'No.'

314

'It'd be best if you did. They need to be stopped, Bree, before they go too far.'

'I don't want to tell anyone. My mum would only worry and there's nothing she can do about it unless she talks to the teachers.' She wiped her eyes on her sleeve and looked up at him. 'If she does that, it'll only get worse.'

'I hear you.' Pole stood up and his jeans made a squelching sound and he looked down at himself. Bree started to laugh and he started to laugh, then he held out his hand and she took it and it was big and warm and she wondered why neither her mother nor John-Cody seemed to like him.

'Look,' he said, 'I'll give you a lift home, drop you off so nobody knows what happened, OK? But I have to change first. We'll need to stop at my house.'

Bree stood in Pole's study watching Barrio cantering up and down the hill while Pole changed his clothes. He buckled fresh jeans in his bedroom then climbed the stairs and watched the thin, gawky twelve-year-old from across the landing. He watched her watching Barrio and all at once he saw Eli before his ex-wife took him back to Australia. He would have been about Bree's age when that happened, the last time Pole really remembered him as a child.

He came through and Bree turned and smiled. Pole stuffed his hands in his pockets and nodded towards the paddock. 'Beauty, isn't he?'

'Yes.'

'Can you ride?'

Bree shook her head. 'I do a little bit at Hunter's, but I don't really know how.'

'Hunter Caldwell: he's a good kid.'

Bree nodded.

'I could teach you if you want.'

She stared at him, eyes suddenly shining. Then they darkened again and Pole frowned.

'Not on Barrio, he's too big. Now Pinky – that's the littler of the two bays out there, the one with the pink tinge to her back legs – she's gentle.'

Bree's eyes followed where he pointed and looked at the smallest horse. She had a black mane and was narrow at the flank.

'You don't think your mum would like it, eh? Or Gib maybe.'

She looked between her feet.

'No worries: I understand. Think about it though. I'll teach you if you want.'

Bree looked at the picture on the desk. 'Who's that?'

Pole's eyes glazed. 'That's Eli, my son.'

Bree looked up at him then and she could see the same hurt in his eyes that she sometimes saw in John-Cody's. 'The one that died?'

'The only one I had.' Pole held out a hand. 'Come on, I'd best get you home. They'll be worrying about you.'

As they crossed the yard Barrio snorted and came down to greet them. Pole rested a booted foot on the lowest rail of the fence and mussed his mane with thick, callused fingers. 'Hey, big fella: say hello to Bree.'

Bree twisted her face up to Pole's then and saw the lines in the skin, like wrinkles in old leather beneath the blue of his eyes. 'I know what roller reefing is,' she said softly.

Pole looked down at her.

'I asked John-Cody. It's where the jib doesn't have hanks. There's a drum fixed to the luff spar with a retrieving line on it.'

Pole was staring at her, eyes glassy now.

'It means you can pull the jib in from the cockpit or just by the wheelhouse,' Bree went on. 'Nothing can get snagged. You don't have to go to the bowsprit.'

'That's right,' Pole whispered. 'You don't have to go to the bowsprit.' His eyes were flat slits and he saw Eli's white-fleshed face in death.

'How old was he?' Bree asked him.

'Twenty-one.' Pole nodded to Barrio. 'I bought this bloke for him. He only got to ride him one time.'

'Do you ride him?'

He nodded. 'Sometimes I do.'

'Are you good?'

'I don't know. Not bad.'

'John-Cody rides horses, doesn't he?'

Pole nodded. 'I think he used to.'

'Is he good?'

'Yeah. I reckon.' He looked at her then. 'If I taught you, you could get good.' He took her hand once more. 'Come on. You must be hungry.'

Bree sat by the fire in their side of the house, with just Sierra for company. Alex had been really busy in the office and had barely noticed that she hadn't phoned to say she would be late. She had glanced up and frowned when she saw Ned Pole drop Bree off further up the road, then turn his truck around and head back towards Te Anau. Bree had walked to the office and told Alex she had missed the bus. Alex was fielding phone calls for Possum Lodge next door so Bree took the opportunity of not having to explain any further and walked home with Sierra.

Now she sat by the fire, burning the letter she had written to her father. She held it by one corner till the flames caught then dropped it on the logs and took up her pen again. Gone was the contentment she had felt earlier; things were as bad as they had ever been, worse now because somebody knew and that was bound to make Jessica ten times worse. But she told her father everything, told him what had happened and how Pole had been there and how he had offered to teach her to ride. She told her dad how she would love to learn to ride but how could she ask her mother?

She got the bus in the morning without having spoken to either her mother or John-Cody on the radio the previous night. She had had a shower and gone to bed really early and fallen asleep straight away with the weight of Sierra on her feet. Now she stood on the corner with her bag still sandy on the inside, and waited till the bus came. Her face was stiff and cold this morning, there was a chill in the air and she knew she was close to tears.

Getting on the bus she saw Hunter and her heart lifted when he smiled and shifted in his seat to make room for her. Bree sat down, trembling a little, and he asked her how yesterday had been and told her how he hated missing the first day back at school: everybody else was over the sudden newness of it all and he still had to go through it. Bree told him it was all right and he would be fine. His mates had all asked her where he was, forgetting that he was visiting relatives in the North Island.

The bus pulled up outside the school and Bree saw

Jessica sitting as usual on the wall. Hunter glanced at her then moved into the aisle. As she stepped past him he took her hand and held it. Bree felt her heart leap against her ribcage.

'Are you OK, BB?'

'I'm fine.'

They got off the bus together and still he held her hand. She could feel the sweat building against her palm and she thought the moisture would make him let go for sure. Jessica had seen her and she and her friends got up from the wall. They looked at one another, then Jessica saw Bree's hand in Hunter's and she faltered. Blood flooded her cheeks and she stood with her mouth open. Hunter stepped past her, holding Bree's hand even more tightly than before.

'Catching flies, Jess?' he muttered. The colour burned deeper and Bree stalked past feeling as tall as Leaning Peak though her head barely reached Hunter's shoulder. They walked into the concourse area, up the path and into school. At the door to their classroom Hunter's mates were waiting for him. Still he held Bree's hand and let go only when they were inside the room itself. 'Let's get a Coke at break,' he said.

'That'd be great, Hunter.'

'See you later then.'

'Yeah. Later.'

Libby was attempting to calibrate information she had picked up from boats and floatplanes moving round Dusky Sound, when Alex called her on the radio. They talked for a moment and Libby asked her how Bree was and Alex told her she was fine, and that she had come home with Ned Pole.

'Pole.' Libby stared at the radio. 'Why?'

'Apparently she missed the bus. It was OK, Lib. He just gave her a lift.'

'Pole did?'

'Yes. I thought you'd like to know.'

'Was Bree OK?'

'She was fine, why?'

'No reason. I just don't think Pole's my greatest fan, that's all.'

'Well, he gave her a ride home.'

Libby hung up the transmitter and considered Alex's words, not really knowing what she thought or felt. She went outside and smoked a cigarette; felt a little dizzy and wished she could really want to quit. But what would she do when she was stressed, she asked herself.

She took her boat out and hunted for the dolphins. They didn't seem to be around today and she eased off the throttle at the bottom of the Acheron Passage, sitting wrapped up against the cold that blew in from the sea. The sound was a different place as winter approached: the trees were not deciduous but some of the beech was dying and this added a mottled brown to the green, somehow casting the vegetation more starkly against the mountains. Cloud hung lower and thinner like fingers of mist and the stillness of the water was flat and loose and reflected the ice grey of the sky. As she sat there deliberating she heard a floatplane heading in from the sea.

Shading her eyes, she looked for markings, recognized the plane and was filled with a sense of dread she did not understand. Perhaps it was the knowledge that Ned Pole had been alone in his truck with her daughter? Perhaps it was something else? Things were suddenly different and she could not fathom exactly why.

The plane circled then headed up the fiord and for a moment Libby thought it wasn't going to land, but it banked into the wind and slipped below the mountains to the north of Cooper Island.

The wind was due west and the pilot touched down and the wake slapped the hull of her boat. She sat and watched as the plane got very close, the engine idled and the passenger door swung open. Pole stepped onto a float with a rifle over one shoulder. Libby gazed at the windscreen but it was too dark to see who was with him.

'G'day,' he called, not smiling.

'Morning.' Libby looked back at him, unable to see his eyes under the rim of his hat. 'Alex told me you gave my daughter a lift home.'

He nodded.

'She missed the bus or something. Do you know why?'

Pole tilted his hat back and now she could see his eyes, blue and sharp like two shavings of ice. 'I reckon she was messing about with her mates and forgot the time.' He gripped the wing strut as a gust of wind carried the full length of the channel. 'I was heading for Manapouri anyway.'

'Well . . . thank you.'

'No worries.' Pole looked evenly at her. 'I'm not an ogre, Libby. Just a bloke trying to make a living.'

'I know. I have to fight you though.'

'I understand.' He paused. The wind lifted the back of his hat. 'You're not going to win, though. Jobs, that's what people want.'

'We'll see.'

Pole looked beyond her. 'Your daughter would like to learn to ride properly so she can help out at the Caldwell place.'

'She told you about Hunter?'

'Sort of: you know what kids are like.' Pole licked his lips. 'I'll teach her if you want. To ride, I mean. I bought a brumby for my boy but he never got to ride it.'

Libby felt her heart quicken. This was suddenly complicated. 'I don't know. I'll have to think about it.'

'Whatever. She's keen though.' Pole climbed back into the cockpit.

Libby went home at the weekend and spoke to Bree. They were sitting on the bed in the hut John-Cody had given her to use as a den; Bree was doing some homework and wasn't in the mood for heavy discussion.

'Everything's cool, Mum. Don't worry about it. He just gave me a lift, that's all. He was nice. I don't know why you've got such a big thing against him.'

'I don't have a big thing against him, darling. I'm in opposition, that's all.' She frowned. 'Why did you miss the bus?'

Bree flushed. 'Oh, I just did.'

'Bree?'

'It's cool, Mum. I just missed the bus.'

'Is everything all right at school?'

'Of course.' Bree got up and moved to the door, trying to think of something to say, to shift the subject before her tears betrayed her. 'Mr Pole said he'd teach me to ride.'

'I know. He told me.'

Bree turned then. 'You won't let him though, will you?' She said it sharply, an edge to her voice.

'Do you want him to teach you?'

'Yes. Then I can help Hunter and his dad at the weekend.'

Libby nodded, pursing her lips. 'OK,' she said stiffly, 'if you want to. I'll see what I can arrange.'

FOURTEEN

John-Cody drove Bree to Ned Pole's house and she felt a little awkward. He sensed it and ruffled her hair.

'Take it easy, Breezy. Everything's cool over here.'

'Are you sure?'

'Of course I am. It's good of Ned to teach you to ride.'

'Do you think my mum minds?'

'Not at all: she's pleased for you. You know she doesn't like having to spend so much time away from you. She's glad that you're getting to do things you want.'

'Are you sure?' Bree sighed. 'I'm not sure. You're both going to be fighting Mr Pole.'

'That doesn't have anything to do with this, Bree. It's got nothing to do with you.' John-Cody turned into Pole's driveway. 'You enjoy yourself. OK?'

'OK, captain. I will.'

He parked and switched the engine off and then Pole came out of the big barn, leading Pinky on a short rein. Bree looked through the windscreen, reached for John-Cody's hand and squeezed it.

'I'm nervous. Will you stay with me for the first bit?'

'Sure.' John-Cody got out of the truck and looked at Pole. Pole looked back at him for a moment and then he smiled at Bree.

'G'day, little lady, how you going?'

John-Cody pushed his hands into his pockets and wandered over. All at once this was more difficult than he had thought. Unlooked-for emotions lifted as he watched how Pole smiled so warmly at Bree and Bree ran her hands over the horse's neck as she bent her head, the bit and bridle jangling as she nuzzled. Bree laughed out loud. 'She's so cool. Can I ride her now?'

'Sure you can.' Pole looked at John-Cody. 'Are you sticking around?'

John-Cody was about to say something when Bree answered for him. 'It's OK, John-Cody, I'll be fine now.'

He stood there for a moment and he and Pole regarded each other and there was something a little smug about Pole's expression. 'Don't worry, Gib. She'll be just fine. I'll run her home when we're done.'

John-Cody left them then, drove back to the main road and swung right for Manapouri. He pulled off the road on the Rainbow Reach track and parked in the spot overlooking the nameless place. Bree with Ned Pole: and the two of them looking at each other across the yard like old sparring partners. He half closed his eyes and the horizon dulled to grey and the *Korimako*'s engine thundered in his ears. Eli was in the wheelhouse and they were almost at the Hare's Ears. John-Cody was below deck, fixing a leaking gate valve, and he could feel the full force of the swell against the hull.

The sea was much rougher than he had thought when they entered the Tasman from Breaksea Sound. But he had seen worse and it was only four hours' sailing to Doubtful and calm water again. They could have sat it out in Breaksea but the likelihood was they'd be sitting there for the next two days, as the weather was not about to change very much. Eli had been in rough seas many times before and John-Cody had thought nothing of it.

'Gib!' Eli's voice came from the bridge, then he appeared in the engine room doorway. 'I reckon we can get the jib up again.'

'Then hoist it, boy. Don't wait for me.'

Eli smiled his dark-eyed smile and gave a quick salute. John-Cody shook his head and grinned to himself. They had been running with the engine and the jib, but the jib had started to luff badly and he'd asked Eli to bring it down and tie it off on the bowsprit so they could hoist it again when they needed to. He turned his attention back to the leaky gate valve.

Raising the jib should have eased the roll a fraction, steadied the barrelling of the boat, but he didn't feel any difference under his feet and he knew he normally did. It didn't bother him at first, his ears thundered with the sound of the Gardner and the gate valve was being a bitch. It wasn't leaking badly but once he was on a job like this he kept on till it was fixed: you could not afford to leave anything on a boat. But the roll still didn't alter and after a few minutes it concerned him. Ducking his head out of the engine room he called out for Eli.

The boat pitched hard and he was knocked off his feet, grabbing the lip of the freezer bunk for support.

Eli must still be on deck. Securing the steel door to the engine room he went up the for'ard steps and swung round to face the bows. The jib was half up, luffing against the halyard, and there was no sign of Eli.

He yanked open the leeward door and gripping the rail for support he staggered up the deck.

'*Eli!*'

No answer. No sign of the boy.

'*Elijah!*'

Nothing save the wind, which howled through the sheets and slapped the furled canvas of the mizzen: nothing save the metallic rattle of the jib hanks on the halyard, the chink of metal on metal where a hook was snagged against the forestay. John-Cody stood rooted, the wind in his face, clothes soaked by spray as the waves crashed over the bows. The swell was almost five metres: he should never have let Eli do this alone.

'*Eli!*' He grabbed the twin rails of the pulpit where the jib had been tied off. He saw where the hank had snagged and he saw the flapping halyard line trailing through the rails into the foaming rush of the sea. No Eli. He turned around, scanned the empty deck and thought about going astern. Then he looked down again and Eli's white hand lifted against the hull of the boat. John-Cody felt the shiver rush through him: Eli was caught in the halyard.

Instinct took over and grabbing a boat-hook and lifebelt he leaned over the side, the sky scarred purple above him, weighted cloud bearing down on the pitching, tossing boat. Eli's face lifted from the waves, his hair washed over his skull, skin deathly white and eyes tightly closed. John-Cody tossed the belt over the side but Eli couldn't get to it. He was unconscious and snagged in the rope; coils of it had wrapped round his chest and kept him close to the boat. John-Cody reached down with the boat-hook and after a few attempts managed to secure a coil of rope. He hefted upwards, lifting Eli's face out of the water, then he tied the boat-hook to the rail.

Now he ran astern and attacked the shackles that held the dinghy to the transom. There was no way he could hoist Eli over the side by himself. The dinghy dropped with a slapping sound into the waves, and taking the bowline in his hand, John-Cody swung over the rail and jumped in. He had the outboard working with a yank on the cord and fought to spin the dinghy so it was not beam on to the waves. He headed round the leeward quarter to the bows.

Eli half floated, half sank, his face the chalked white of death that John-Cody had seen once before at sea. Still he grabbed him and despite the fury of the waves he managed to haul him into the dinghy.

When he touched his skin, when he prised his eyelids apart, he knew that no amount of heart massage would bring him back. Elijah Pole was dead.

He relived that moment now as he sat at the nameless place and thought about the strange feelings of jealousy he experienced knowing that Bree was riding horses with Ned Pole. He sucked on his cigarette, let the smoke go and was back on the boat with the wind in his hair and Eli lying dead at his feet. He knelt on deck over the boy's sodden and lifeless body and stared at the flesh of his face. The life was gone: the boy was gone. He didn't even look like Eli. Slowly, wearily he got to his feet and called the news in on the radio.

Mahina was waiting for him at Deep Cove along with the police and the coastguard. Everybody looked very small against the hillside and Deep Cove itself was as silent as the grave Eli would be placed in. John-Cody eased the boat alongside the wharf and threw the spring to Mahina. Across the pass at West Arm, Ned Pole was waiting.

Pole watched Bree ride Pinky in circles round the corral. She was doing well, using her knees and keeping her hands at the base of the horse's neck. Pole stood by the fence, talking to her in a low and gentle voice and commanding Pinky himself when Bree got mixed up.

'You're doing fine, Bree,' he told her. 'We'll have you herding sheep in no time.'

Bree beamed at him, delighted with herself. The horse felt good beneath her. She could feel Pinky's shoulder muscles, the great power in her back and legs: silently she squealed when Pinky responded properly to what she urged with her knees.

Pole watched her and saw his son. Not as the young man who drowned on the *Korimako* but the boy who had lived here before his mother took him home to Australia. He saw Eli and he saw himself in Cairns and his father leaning against the fence with a look of pride stretching the skin of his face.

'You're doing really well, Bree. You're a natural.'

'It hurts my knees to squeeze her,' Bree said. 'I'm not sure how much to do it.'

'Don't worry, you'll get used to it. More to the point, she'll get used to you.' Pole stepped away from the fence. 'Rising trot now, remember what I told you.'

* * *

329

John-Cody was in the office when Pole dropped Bree off and he came out onto the porch and nodded to him. Pole touched his hat and then he backed his truck around and headed for Te Anau. Bree bounded up the steps.

'Good?' John-Cody asked her.

'Brilliant.'

'You're not stiff then?'

She shook her head. 'Not in the slightest.'

He nodded. 'Are you going to go again?'

Bree looked up at him then. 'So long as you don't mind.'

'Why should I mind? Everything's cool. Take it easy, Breezy.'

She lifted a palm. 'Five high, Captain Bligh.'

He watched her cross the road and head for Fraser's Beach with Sierra at her heels, then he turned back to the office and found Alex looking at him.

'What?'

'Nothing.'

'Why are you looking at me like that?'

Alex smiled. 'No reason. Bree's a lovely girl, isn't she?'

'She certainly is.'

'She almost makes you wish you were a parent yourself.'

He turned once more and caught a glimpse of her disappearing into the trees. 'Yes,' he said. 'She does.'

Jane was back when Pole got home from Manapouri. Bree had helped him take off Pinky's saddle and brush the horse down and turn her out in the field. He saw Jane's car in the drive and as he

330

climbed out of his truck she appeared on the balcony, a sheet of paper flapping in her hand.

'When did this come, Nehemiah?'

Pole shaded his eyes with his hand. 'What?'

'This fax from America.'

'I don't know. I haven't been up there. What is it?'

Jane looked at the paper then back at him once more. 'Our little pot of gold.'

The beginning of May and winter was approaching fast. Libby had extracted various bands of sound from her computer recordings and established which were cetacean clicks, which were ambient noise and at what point the engines came in. She worked at the table under the window that faced the back garden and watched John-Cody down by the manuka grove, chopping firewood. He wore jeans and a T-shirt despite the cold and the muscles rippled his arms as he swung the axe, splitting the logs with one smooth blow. Now and again he laid the axe down and bent to the pile to stack the wood in the wheelbarrow. Sierra sat and watched him, tongue hanging out, till her attention was drawn by the movement of rabbit or possum.

Libby looked back at the computer screen, clicked the mouse and separated the sound waves still further, trying to figure whether Pole's arrival had sent the pod elsewhere. She knew she could not prove it: that would take years of research under controlled conditions and she needed an acoustic model of the sound first. That alone would take an eternity and all she had was a year and a half.

She found her mind drifting and her gaze wandering to the woodpile where John-Cody was

331

swinging the axe again. She wondered if he noticed her: the odd look had passed between them but she'd felt no vibes other than that. Normally she was pretty good around men, able to pick up any electricity fairly quickly. She caught herself thinking about John-Cody, snatching the odd glance here and there, but she had no idea what he was thinking or feeling. Mahina dominated his space like an unseen aura, and normally that alone would be enough to put another woman off. But it wasn't as if Mahina was clinging to him; rather it was as if he still needed to wrap himself in her memory.

And why not? Mahina had been dead for a year and a half now and John-Cody still loved her in a way that nobody had ever or probably *would* ever love Libby. She watched him as he loaded another stack of logs then turned with the barrow and made his way up the lawn. She watched him walking, arms taut as he pushed the barrow up the little hill. He didn't look at her; the sun was above his head and it probably reflected off the glass and made the window opaque. She turned again to her computer screen, but somehow couldn't concentrate. She was due back at Dusky tomorrow and for the first time she didn't want to go. Autumn was thinning and winter stalked the horizon and she had enjoyed the past week. Bree had been pleased to have her home when she got in from school and she had told her all about her weekend lesson with Pole. John-Cody had spent time with them in the evenings and they had played board games, talked and laughed a lot, the three of them.

Getting up from the desk, she went to the front door where John-Cody was stacking wood in the box for her. He looked up and smiled. 'It can only get colder, Lib. Dusky can be severe in winter, parts of Supper Cove get a film of ice over the water.'

'And the dolphins keep close to the sea.'

'Generally. But I've seen the Doubtful pod right up in Hall's Arm even in the middle of August.'

Libby nodded. 'Would you like a coffee break?'

He smiled and wiped the dust from his palms. 'That'd be great. Thank you.'

He sat outside on the little twin-seat and rolled a cigarette. The phone rang and Libby answered it then brought it outside and told him it was Alex.

John-Cody took the phone. 'G'day, Alex. What's up?'

'Ned Pole's just been in. He wants to see you.'

'Does he?'

'Well, what he actually said was you need to see him and you need to see him now.' She paused. 'It was weird, boss, there was something different about him.'

'What do you mean, different?'

'I don't know really. He was serious, I mean really serious. It gave me the shivers. He said he was going to sight in a new rifle and you'd know where he would be.'

John-Cody put the phone down and Libby brought him the coffee. He was silent, staring absently through the trees at the blue of the sky above the lake; birds moved in his line of vision and the clouds scurried towards the western arch. Something about Alex's tone unnerved him. He couldn't put his finger on why, but he felt a stone move in his gut.

Libby was watching him. 'Are you OK?'

He didn't answer right away.

'John-Cody?'

He picked up his coffee cup. 'I'm fine.' He drank deeply and set the cup down again. He had rolled a cigarette and now he stowed it in his pouch and stood up. 'I've got a couple of things to do, Libby. I'll be back a bit later.'

His shirt was draped over the bonnet of the truck and he pulled it over his head and stuffed the ends into his jeans. Then he got behind the wheel, told Sierra to stay with Libby and backed out into the road. He drove towards Te Anau and took the turning for Balloon Loop, which led him down towards the river. Halfway along the twisting dirt road he saw Pole's red and silver twin cab hunched to the side of the road. John-Cody slowed, grinding the gears on his old truck, and pulled up behind Pole's. He sat for a moment and rested moist palms on his thighs. He heard a sharp little report and knew Pole had a silencer on the gun he was sighting.

Pole lay on his belly and sighted the hunting rifle, using the wooden target set into the hillside at a distance of fifty yards. In the corner of his eye he saw Gibbs come into view and stop at the lip of the ravine. The unofficial rifle range was cut out of the trees, maybe seventy-five yards long and far enough away from anything and anyone to make it safe. Pole had been sighting his weapons here for twenty-five years. He sighted now on the little disc in the middle of the wooden target and reeled off three rounds in quick succession: they formed a tight ring but slightly high and to the left. Only a small adjustment was needed. It would wait, though.

He laid the rifle down, being careful not to get dirt in the barrel, and looked at John-Cody where he stood with his hands in his pockets, staring across the expanse of dirt between them. Pole screwed up his eyes: he saw Mahina for a fraction of a second and his breath caught in his throat; he saw his own son lying on the dock at West Arm. He saw himself, hands wrung out at his sides, every muscle tensed, his heart a wasteland of emotion.

He stood up and held the rifle loose in one hand, the leather strap dangling. John-Cody slid down the slope, dust rising from his boots, and Pole started towards him. John-Cody paused and flipped away his cigarette then walked over to the target. He was inspecting it when Pole came up to him.

'Nice shooting, Ned.' John-Cody spoke without looking round at him.

'You reckon?'

'A little high and to the left, but good grouping.'

John-Cody looked round now. Pole shouldered the rifle and felt in his shirt pocket for a cigar. John-Cody took out his battered brass Zippo. Pole took the lighter and inspected it.

'Did you get this in the military?'

John-Cody didn't reply. For a second the chill in the day was the chill on the Camas prairie as he looked down at the wreckage of the FBI agents' car. He sat down on a tree stump and took out his tobacco. 'What's on your mind, Ned?'

Pole sat next to him, his legs stretched long, boots crossed at the ankle. He smoked his black cigar and exhaled through his nostrils.

'This is a beautiful place. Don't you think?'

'Some of us want to keep it that way.'

Pole looked at him. 'We're not so different, you and I.'

'No?'

'Not really.'

'Then withdraw your application for Dusky Sound. If you and I aren't so different, do us all a favour and let things stay as they are.'

Pole laughed softly. 'Gib, you always were a romantic. You really think it matters whether I withdraw or not?'

'Of course it matters.'

'Then you're a bigger fool than I took you for.' Pole flicked ash from his cigar. 'If it isn't me then it'll be somebody else. Southland Tours were champing at the bit before I got my backing. Now they're only standing back to see how I get on. One way or another they'll be looking to do the same thing. Then it'll be the Yellow Boats and Wilson's Tours from Dunedin. We'll have companies from as far away as Hawke's Bay and the Bay of Plenty, even the Bay of Islands.' Pole sucked smoke. 'At least I'm a known quantity, Gib. I'm a local. I know the bush better than most. I know the sounds. If I do it strategically then I'll set the right tone and raise my own objections alongside you if anyone else wants a slice of the action.'

John-Cody looked at him, arms resting on his knees. 'Ned, it won't work. There is no bargaining position between us. There never was. Dusky Sound is sacred. There's too much activity in Doubtful already, I don't want the same to happen in Dusky.'

Pole nodded. 'But it's OK for you to operate.'

'I run an ecology tour.'

'It's still a boat on the water. According to Liberty

336

Bass the engine could be detrimental to the well-being of the dolphins.'

John-Cody looked at him. 'Yep, and as soon as she proves it I'll stop operating.'

Pole laughed then. 'You're lucky you can afford to. Mahina was well insured, I reckon.'

John-Cody smarted.

'Don't get jumpy with me.' Pole blew smoke. 'Most people round here are trying to just get by, you know. They've got debts and mortgages to think about.'

'And that includes you.'

Pole rubbed a palm across his jaw. 'Gib, I could show you bank statements that'd make your hair curl.' He looked sharply at him now. 'I've got nothing against you personally, though God knows I've got reason to.'

John-Cody was silent. 'I'm sorry about Eli. I'll always be sorry about Eli. It was my responsibility as skipper. But you know it wasn't my fault.'

Pole bit his lip. 'Elijah made the mistake, but he was inexperienced. It was swelling five metres, Gib. You should never have let him go on deck on his own.'

'If I was truly negligent that's how the inquiry would have found it. They didn't. You know. You were there.'

'You really wish you could believe that, don't you?' Pole stared into the black of the trees and saw his son's face in his mind. 'I could've been rougher on you, Gib. A lot of people said I should.'

'I know it.'

Pole worked his shoulders. 'I know the sea. I know what it's like out there when there are only two of you on board. Stuff needs to be done. A jib hank catching like that, it happens.' He chewed the end of his cigar. 'But maybe I should've been tougher on you. Eli was my only son, my child. I hadn't seen him since he was thirteen and as soon as I get him back he gets killed working an eco-tour for you.'

John-Cody looked sideways at him. 'Eli cared about the environment, Ned. He wouldn't like what you're planning for Dusky.'

'Now you're telling me about my own boy.'

John-Cody laid his tobacco pouch on his thigh. 'I'm telling you how I saw it. I'm telling you how it was when he worked for me.'

'If he hadn't worked for you he'd be alive today.'

John-Cody said nothing. Pole said nothing. They sat side by side as the sun slipped beyond westerly clouds and the day grew colder.

'Winter's coming.' Pole lifted the collar on his jacket. 'Season's almost over.' He smoothed leathery fingers over the butt of his rifle. 'I will put those lodges in Dusky Sound, Gib.'

'You *hope* you will, Ned. There's a hearing to get through. Remember?'

Pole was silent for a moment then he said: 'There won't be any hearing.'

'How do you figure that?'

'Because it's not going to get that far. You're the last submitter and you're going to withdraw your opposition.'

John-Cody laughed.

Pole's voice was quietly menacing now. 'You see, Gib, I've got the backing to buy your boat and your wharf and that's exactly what I plan to do.' He paused a moment. 'I told you once I'd be doing you a favour and believe me now when I tell you I am. When we start down there you can stay on as a skipper if you want to.'

John-Cody stood up.

'Sit down, Gib. I'm not finished yet.'

'I've got better things to do with my time.'

'I said, sit down.'

John-Cody sat. He didn't know why exactly but he sat down on the log again. Pole relit his cigar with the Zippo that he'd held on to throughout their conversation.

'How did it feel, Gib,' Pole said slowly, 'when you jumped that trawler in Bellingham? How did it feel to leave your mates to do what *you* were too scared to?'

John-Cody could feel the pulse thudding blood at his temple. Pole was not looking at him: instead he was staring across the open space of ground to the beech trees racked side by side against the river. 'We know all about you, Gib. We know why you left the US and what happened to you before you did. There are people over there that would be very interested in talking to you, even after twenty-five years. One of the Feds died in that car crash. Did you know that?'

John-Cody felt as though he had been punched. He sat where he was, the smoke from the cigar raw at the back of his throat.

'New Zealand immigration would be really interested in finding out about you too. You should've married Mahina properly, legally, instead of some half-arsed hippy whatever.' Pole stood up. 'Sorry to lay it so heavy on you, mate, but I need that project in Dusky Sound. I don't mind telling you my property is riding on it and Jane doesn't like the idea

339

of being homeless.' He paused. 'I told you I was doing you a favour. Right now nobody knows anything, but they will. I don't want to force you out of the country, but if you don't back off what choice do you give me?'

He started up the hill to his truck then he paused and looked back, tipping his hat higher on his head. 'There's one other thing I want to share with you,' he said. 'The reason I wasn't too hard on you over Eli.' He licked his lips. 'When I came down to the boat that day it was the first time in years that I could look Mahina in the eye.'

John-Cody was staring at him.

'You see, I had a little something going with her after you and she got together.'

'You're lying.'

'Am I? She liked walking in the bush with no clothes on, didn't she?'

John-Cody drove to the office and parked out the back. For a long time he sat in the cab and stared through the windscreen at the houses built on the hill behind Possum Lodge. It was unreal: Pole's face, Pole's words. He could feel himself trembling and he got out and sucked breath, but the day was still and stifling; the sunshine had gone and clouds gathered over the Kepler Mountains on the north shore of the lake. Again he was standing on the Camas prairie, ankle deep in fresh snow, looking down on the wrecked car and the two FBI agents, one of them dead now. He was back in New Orleans with the rain battering the building so hard the shutters slammed into brick. He saw the faces of his band, mouths agape, uncertain and certain and terrified all

340

in the same critical moment. Then he was on the highway, thumbing rides through St Charles Parish and up into Texas.

He could see Alex looking at him through the window. She was frowning heavily. John-Cody tramped along the porch and she met him in the doorway, a crust of bread in her hand for the birds. 'You look like you've seen one ghost too many.'

'I've seen Ned Pole,' he said quietly.

'And?'

He took a short breath. 'And nothing. Look, I'm going back over the hill, Alex. I've got stacks of work to do on the boat.'

Alex looked puzzled. 'OK.'

He turned to go.

'You mean now?'

'Yeah. There's a Z boat crossing in ten minutes. I'll catch myself a ride.'

'What about stores?'

'There's stuff in the freezer still. I'll manage.'

'When will you be back?'

John-Cody looked at her then, saw her and didn't see her. 'I don't know. You can get me on the radio.' He turned on his heel and walked towards Pearl Harbour, his shoulders stiff and square as if the weight of the sky was on him.

He walked uncertainly as if every step was his last. He passed the shop and Jean Grady called out a greeting, but he barely heard her and walked on, head down, aware of each crack in the pavement. He could smell the inlet as he turned the corner, slack green water beyond the tree line. The Z boat was at the jetty and Tom was performing his engine checks.

'You got room for me, partner?'

341

Tom looked up at him. 'Always, mate. You know that.'

John-Cody climbed on deck and lit a cigarette. Tom watched him through the glass and arched one eyebrow. He had seen that face a few times over the past year, but perhaps the darkness between his brows had not been so acute as it was right then.

John-Cody stayed on deck all the way across the lake, the wind and spots of rain driving in his hair. He wore only jeans and an overshirt and the wind had teeth as they passed South Arm but he did not notice, just sat rolling one cigarette after the other, his mind a mass of unanswered questions.

At West Arm he had to wait for a lift and half thought about walking the twenty-two kilometres, before Tom found him a driver. He rode in the passenger seat, saying nothing, thinking nothing, and barely muttered his thanks when he was dropped off at his wharf. The truck turned back for the tunnel and for a moment John-Cody stood above the trees with sandflies buzzing about his face. The rain had not started falling yet, but the clouds were bruised in purple and hung against the mountains, which seemed to murmur in the sudden discomfort of stillness. John-Cody stood and stared at the opaque surface of Deep Cove and for the first time the sound looked dark and malevolent.

He didn't know what to do. He realized it then: for the first time in his life he just didn't know what to do. He needed to talk to Mahina; more than anything he needed to do that. But he couldn't: she was dead, gone, lost to him, in the spirit world, the great Marae of her ancestors.

The *Korimako* felt alien as he stepped on deck and

slid open the wheelhouse door. This vessel had been a part of him, another limb almost, for over seven years, and yet she felt alien. She was lost, just as the wharf was lost and the cove and perhaps the whole of Fiordland as he and Mahina had known it. That last garden of Tane, overrun with tourists, the sound of silence battered by the whine of speedboats: fishermen and hunters racing the length and breadth of her arms. He sat on the skipper's stool in front of the radar screen and watched the rain race in myriad rivers on the perspex-covered windows.

How long he sat there he did not know, but then the radio interrupted the tenuous thread of his thoughts. '*Korimako, Korimako, Korimako*: this is *Kori*-base. Are you there, boss?'

For a moment he sat where he was. Alex came again, repeating the message, and then a third time before he got up and reached for the handset.

'Yes, Alex.'

'Oh, thank God, there was me thinking the Z boat sank or something. Are you OK?'

'I'm fine.'

'What the hell happened with Pole? He just drove by looking like he won the lotto.'

'Maybe he did.' John-Cody said it more to himself than to her. 'Look, everything's fine, Alex. I just need some time. Things have caught up with me. We've nothing booked in the short term, have we?'

'Nope. Our horizon is suddenly empty.'

'You're not kidding,' he muttered.

Alex went to the house and found Libby working. It was almost time for Bree to come home and Libby was just beginning to think about what to make for tea. 'Was John-Cody all right before he went out?' Alex asked her.

'He was fine. I haven't seen him since, mind you. Why?' Libby plugged the kettle in for tea.

'He went over the hill.'

'Deep Cove? He didn't say he was going.'

Alex shrugged. 'I think it was a snap decision. He came by the office just after lunch and I tell you I've never seen him look so grey and you know what – suddenly so old.' Alex sat down, her brow set in lines, chewing at her lower lip. 'He looked really old, Lib. Even when Mahina died he didn't look like he did today.'

'Alex.' Libby sat down in the chair beside her. 'You're frightening me.'

Alex blew out her cheeks. 'I'm frightening myself.' She looked round then. 'Something happened with Pole.'

'Is John-Cody on the boat now?'

'Yes. I spoke to him on the radio. He wants to be left alone.'

'Maybe Pole got his permit already. Maybe the submission doesn't matter.'

Alex shook her head. 'It doesn't work like that. This has to go to a hearing.'

Bree crashed through the door with Hunter in tow and thoughts of John-Cody were forgotten. 'Mum, can Hunter stay for tea?'

'Of course.'

'Great, and can we take him home afterwards?'

'Yes.' Libby looked at Alex. 'Where's the Ute?'

Alex held out the keys. She had driven it back from the office. Bree tossed her bag on the chair then led Hunter outside, hand in hand, with Sierra

344

leaping for attention. Alex and Libby stared at the departing backs of the children and then they looked at each other.

'Was that what I thought it was?' Libby said. 'They were holding hands, right?'

'It looked that way to me.'

Libby poured tea. 'My daughter with a boyfriend.' She set the teapot down with a jerk. 'Does that make me old, Alex?'

Libby dreamed about John-Cody and woke up in the middle of the night with his face against her mind. He was on the boat and watching the stars from the deck, his face half in shadow but great disturbance in his eyes. She sat up wide awake and questioned herself. Why should she dream that? She had never dreamed of him before. It must have been Alex coming round. She wondered again what might have happened with Pole.

She could see the ghost-like branches of the giant fuchsia tree weaving in the wind through the window. The night was not dark, the garden bathed in filtered light from the moon. She rubbed her eyes, knowing she was too awake to go back to sleep right away. The alarm clock told her it was two thirty and she got out of bed, covered her nakedness with a robe then flicked on the wall light in the lounge. Bree's door was closed. Libby made a cup of tea, conscious of the sound of Sierra snuffling, but aware that she wouldn't leave Bree's bed.

Libby sat in the big reclining chair with her feet tucked under her bottom. The room felt like her room, like she belonged here, which for her was strange. Long ago she had realized that such

345

womanly habits as home-making were not dominant needs for her; Bree was far better at keeping house than she was. Libby had always been pretty content to dump her gear somewhere near a sleeping bag and head out to sea in search of whales. That had all begun in childhood.

When she was still a little girl in Portsmouth, her brother told her one day that a gypsy was in town with a fin whale on the back of a lorry. Libby couldn't understand what he meant, feeling sure he'd said *thin* whale. How could a live animal which lived in water be transported around on the back of a lorry? The two of them spent their pocket money visiting the whale and Libby saw it was dead and stuffed and looked like plastic, all except its eye which peered back at her when she stared right into it. Ever since then, Libby had longed to see whales alive, swimming freely in the open sea. And if that meant living in some wild places, so be it.

She thought about John-Cody again and realized she was thinking about him a lot these days. When she was in Dusky she missed him. Partly that was the loneliness of her research and partly it was just him. She would see his face in her mind's eye; visualize his hands, strong hands, calloused at the base of the fingers from all the years at sea. She imagined him on the *Korimako*, quietly in command with nothing ever fazing him.

She got up and plucked a cigarette from the open pack on the mantelpiece and stepped outside. The moon was full above her head and the sky rang with starlight. She sat down at the little table and tried to recognize some of the constellations John-Cody had pointed out to her when they were in Crooked Arm.

She couldn't even pick out the Southern Cross though, which given the attention she had paid at the time should have been easy. Again she wondered what could have happened with Pole: John-Cody had been fine until that phone call, happily chopping wood, drinking coffee and then suddenly off over the hill.

Ned Pole lay on his back in the aftermath of love. His wife lay next to him, the bedclothes thrown off and the moonlight bathing their naked bodies. He stared at the ceiling, feeling the sweat drying on him. Jane drew her knees to her chest in the foetal position then rolled on her side and knelt up. Her hair hung to his chest, tickling the skin. She ran her hand over the hard muscles of his stomach and down into his groin.

'You should've got on to immigration.'

'No.'

'Why not?'

'Like I said, he needed an option. Everybody needs an option.'

'You're too soft.'

'You reckon?'

'I know.' Jane climbed off the bed and walked to the window. Pole watched her, naked in the moonlight, and Mahina invaded his head. He rolled on his side facing away, wondering why he had told Gibbs what he had. Jane spoke from behind him. 'We're almost there, Ned. Now is not the time to go soft.'

Pole ignored her, unable to shift Mahina's face from his mind. It was as if she was there in the room, haunting him.

'Ned?'

'I know what I'm doing.'

She snorted. 'There was a time when I might have believed you.' She paused then and Pole turned to face her again.

'Are you trying to tell me something?'

She looked back at him and her nipples puckered in the draught from the window. 'I'm telling you I did what you should have. Gibbs had his chance a long time ago.'

Pole stared at her through the darkness.

'Don't look at me that way. We're better off with him completely out of the picture.'

John-Cody spent a week on the *Korimako*, scrubbing the mini invasion of rust from the scuppers and the lid of the chain locker and the bottom of the wheelhouse doors. He cleaned the boat from top to bottom and didn't really know why. It was always cleaned after a trip, the beds remade and the heads scrubbed as they steamed back to Deep Cove on the last afternoon. Yet he needed to clean her; she was a part of him, and his mind was so blank he had to fill it with something. He tried not to think about what Pole had said. Pole and Mahina together: he tried not to believe it. He tried to keep the other part of the past where it was, in the darkest corners of his psyche, where after twenty-five years he had thought it would remain for ever. How could Pole have found out?

But he had a soldiering past, the Australian SAS: he must have retained good contacts, soldiers always did. Then there was his wife, the American lawyer, not to mention the massive business that backed them. That was all beside the point. Pole knew and there was nothing John-Cody could do about it. He stood on deck at Deep Cove, the mountain and the bush rising above the water in a primeval silence that still took his breath away. But he imagined hunters and fishermen piling down the steps to his boat, clambering all over the deck and dumping rods and rifles against the lockers. That or deportation. Was Pole serious? Of course he was. Perhaps he should get in touch with immigration himself before Pole did. But how could he do that? The outcome would be the same. Pole was right: there were people who would like to talk to him back in the United States. Perhaps he should just bide his time and see what happened. Maybe Pole didn't know as much as he hinted at. Maybe he was guessing and using his best guesses to bluff; some men could be spooked just by a good bluff.

Again he was back on that first highway out of New Orleans, guitar in its case, thumb hanging out for a ride. Texas and Arizona, New Mexico: his guitar playing earning his crust until the FBI caught up with him in McCall. He was too old to face all that again: there was too much water under the bridge. He looked across the cove where the land rose vertically and he heard weka calling their young; he trembled as the thought of swapping this for a prison cell tripped across his mind.

He didn't move the boat, just left her moored where she was, the only vessel in the fiords that didn't take any fish. He thought about all the fights he and Mahina had been through to keep this place as it was: the ongoing battles with people who were operating illegally, racing up to dolphins and seals without a marine mammal viewing permit; the bigger battles with people like Pole and others who had been before him, and the biggest battle of all about the boundaries of the park and why they suddenly shifted in 1978.

On the morning of the fifth day Libby called him on the radio. He was down in the engine room and didn't hear her at first, but the whistle and crackle of static rain through the speakers had a knack of working its way into his consciousness even if he was deep in the bowels of the boat. Something made him come out and he heard Libby's call sign. He climbed the for'ard steps and picked up the handset.

'G'day, Libby. Where are you?'

Libby heard his response and her heart lifted. A week had passed since she had spoken to him and she had taken the floatplane back to Dusky.

'Oke Island. I followed the pod up Wet Jacket Arm.'

'How's it going down there?'

'OK. I know I've said the opposite before, but the more time I spend with these guys the more I think the pod is matriarchal, not patriarchal after all.'

'You figure Spray's in charge then, not Old Nick?'

'I think he thinks he's in charge, but in reality she is.'

'That sounds familiar.'

Libby laughed. 'There's something else, John-Cody.'

'What?'

'I've identified four males that seem to be a bit detached from the pod, at least that's what my initial findings tell me.' She paused as a dolphin came right up to the boat and lifted his snout to whistle at her.

350

'I think there's cross-fertilization going on, a coalition.'

'You think that's why Quasimodo visits?' John-Cody asked her.

'No, Quasi's something of an enigma. When he's here he's very much part of the fraternization. He doesn't hang out with the four pals I mentioned just now.'

John-Cody was silent for a moment. 'It'll take years to figure out whether or not you're right, Libby.'

'I know. And we don't have years, do we?'

John-Cody was silent. 'Have you seen Ned Pole down there?'

'Not this week: all's been quiet this week.' Libby looked at the clouds drifting above Herrick Creek. 'What happened with Pole, John-Cody? You took off straight afterwards.'

Again she felt the weight of his pause. 'I didn't so much take off,' he said. 'I had things to do over here, Lib. The *Kori*'s a full-time occupation, if you don't keep on top of the rust it creeps up on you.'

'Alex said you just stormed off.'

'It wasn't like that. I just came over the hill. When are you back in Manapouri?'

'This afternoon. What about you?'

'There's no more charters planned. The weather's getting colder.' John-Cody paused for a moment. 'I might hang out here for a while. The *Kori*'s as much my home as anywhere these days.'

Again Libby was silent. 'Bree misses you,' she said. 'She likes talking to you.'

John-Cody held the handset and thought about that. He missed Bree too; over the last six months he

351

had become very attached to her, to the point of jealousy when she learned to ride with Ned Pole. He missed Libby as well, but he wanted to miss neither of them because there was no point if Pole carried out his threat. For a few fleeting seconds he wondered if he could actually sell Pole the boat, the wharf and everything.

'Are you still there, over?' Libby's voice came over the speaker.

He squeezed the transmit button. 'Yes, I'm still here.'

'The plane's coming around three,' Libby said. 'I've got to go to Invercargill to see DoC. Steve Watson's meeting me. I'm going to see what else the university can do about Pole's surface water activity permit. Help us out some maybe.' She hesitated then added, 'Come home if you can. Bree would like to see you.'

John-Cody came back a week later. He walked up from Pearl Harbour and could feel the winter in the air. Jean Grady was talking to Sonia Marsh, a single mother, outside the little shop: she had some mail for him.

'Have you been over the hill again?' Sonia asked him. 'We haven't seen you about.'

He nodded. 'Rust is eating the *Kori*'s deck, Sonia. I needed to get it fixed before the winter.'

'Oh, don't talk about winter. Winter's ages away yet.'

Jean came out with his mail. Absently he stood there and flicked through it: a couple of circulars, a letter from the council and then a brown envelope that made the hairs stand up on his arm. He hid it at the bottom of the pile; stood there a moment longer then walked up to the office. Alex was on the phone as usual and she waved to him.

All at once he needed privacy. A cold fist of fear had settled in his gut and he needed to be alone with it. He gestured to Alex, pointed towards Fraser's Beach then crossed the road and walked down the track into the trees. At the beach he hesitated, feet deep in shingle, the chilled waters of Lake Manapouri picking their way through the boulders.

He sat on Mahina's thinking stone and gazed at the silence of the blue gum tree: then carefully he slit the top of the envelope with his clasp knife. The immigration service was concerned about his status in New Zealand. It had come to their attention that he might have entered the country illegally back in the early 1970s. He stared at the page. An ocean-going trawler from Hawaii, Bluff Cove and Tom Blanch: they were right, it was illegal. He had no right to enter the country that way, no right to stay for a quarter of a century. He had never married Mahina, never attained any legal status. It had also come to their attention that the FBI might be interested in talking to him back in the United States. He held the letter loosely between forefinger and thumb: the wind tugged at it as wave tops crested on the lake and ran hard for the shore.

John-Cody heard someone shout his name and he looked up sharply, saw Sierra bounding over the rocks towards him and Bree waving from along the beach. He stood up and waved back, stuffing the letter into the pocket of his jeans, then crossed the shingle to meet her. The closer he got, the bigger her smile became. Sierra was ignoring him, in the water now trying to drag boulders out, as she loved to do.

'You're back,' Bree said, then hesitating for a moment she wrapped her arms about his waist. For a second John-Cody was taken aback, then hugging her seemed the most natural response in the world.

'I missed you, Captain Bligh.'

'Missed you too, Breezy.' He held on to her and looked across the lake and still she didn't let go. Her warmth flooded him. It was no good, though. He knew it was no good and he eased her away.

'So, how is school?' he asked her.

'It's OK.' She took his hand and they walked together back towards the eucalyptus tree. 'No worries.'

He laughed. 'Listen to you. *No worries*. We'll make a Kiwi of you yet.'

Bree kicked at a stone, her pigtails jiggling either side of her face.

'Your mum tells me you're getting on pretty well with Hunter.'

Bree kept her eyes downcast. 'He likes me a lot. I mean, it's almost as if he's my boyfriend.' She looked up at him, flushed scarlet then dropped her gaze.

'Almost?' John-Cody said gently.

'Well, you know.'

'Course I do.' He took her hand again and they walked to the gum tree and he paused and gazed, his memory sharp. Thoughts of the letter dried the inside of his mouth.

'Mahina's tree,' Bree said softly. 'Sometimes I sit on her stone. You know, when I'm down here with Sierra.'

'Do you?'

She nodded. 'It's a good thinking stone.'

'Do you do a lot of thinking, Bree?'

Again she nodded. 'I have done. Not so much now. I'm happier now than I was.'

They walked up the hill and John-Cody turned and looked back at the lake, still and silent as darkness began to fall. The Cathedral Peaks were spires on the far shore and the water looked chilled and frosted as the moon reflected on it. Bree was tugging his hand. 'Come on,' she said. 'It's time we went home.'

FIFTEEN

John-Cody lit the fire in the homestay and listened to Bree's music through the walls. Libby always asked her to turn it down, but she never did. He didn't mind: it was alive and vibrant and for the past few months had added to the vitality of his life. He squatted cross-legged on the floor and reread the letter from Dunedin. The immigration office wanted him to contact them as soon as possible and he was not sure what to do. A knock on the door made him look up and he folded the letter back into the envelope and opened the curtain. Libby smiled at him through the glass.

'Hi,' she said when he opened the door. 'Bree told me you were back.'

They stood there, awkward all at once. John-Cody was pleased to see her, but he didn't want to be. This was ending now. Everything was over, finished: he could feel it. 'I'm sorry,' he said. 'Come in.'

'If I'm not disturbing you?'

'No. I was just going to make some coffee.'

He stood back and let her in, and she warmed

herself in front of the fire. 'It's much colder now, isn't it?' she said.

'Bottom of the world.' John-Cody bent to the cupboard by the sink for the coffee pot. 'Summer's over, autumn's a blink then winter. It's the southern latitude.'

She sat on the arm of the chair. 'Have you seen the pod in Dusky in winter?'

'A few times. I did a lot of work on Cooper Island with a research team a couple of years ago. The pod was out and about then. That's when I first figured they were resident.'

'The most southerly pod in the world.'

He nodded.

'Unless of course there's dolphins in Port Ross?'

John-Cody poured boiling water onto the coffee grounds. 'I've never seen any.'

'But you have seen bottlenose not very far north of there. You told me.'

'Yes. About twenty kilometres.'

'So they could be resident in Port Ross?'

'It's possible but very unlikely.' He looked at her then, his head slightly to one side. 'You've always wanted to go down there, haven't you?'

'To the Auckland Islands – God, yes.' Libby smiled at him. 'There are southern right whales there in winter. You told me that yourself.'

He smiled. 'So the dolphins are really just an ulterior motive.'

'Of course not.' Libby folded her arms, her chin high. He saw the fire in her eyes. 'Imagine what the implications would be if there *was* a pod of bottlenose dolphins in Port Ross. It would be incredible. Their breeding habits would have to be totally unique.'

'Well, I guess anything is possible. All I'm saying is I've never seen a dolphin in Port Ross.'

They drank their coffee and she told him about her trip to Invercargill and the Department of Conservation. She had voiced her fears about Dusky Sound, but they had told her the research programme was restricted to two years for the time being. That was all the funding they and the university could come up with. Steve Watson met with her and she suggested an official submission to Southland Regional Council vis-à-vis Ned Pole, but Watson told her the university's position was already covered by DoC. That did nothing to allay any of her fears and she informed him that nobody knew what the long-term implications for a resident dolphin pod were. When she said they needed an acoustic model of the sound, he had looked at her and laughed. New Zealand putting tourism in Fiordland on hold for six years: that would be the day.

'So none of it's very hopeful,' Libby said finally, cupping her coffee mug in her hands.

John-Cody watched her face in the firelight, aware of the passion in her voice, the concern that lifted against her eyes.

'It's always the same story, the march of economic growth.' She stood up then and paced the floor. 'It was the same when I was with Greenpeace. It wasn't just about maintaining people's jobs. It was economic growth.' She clenched her fist. 'This planet can't sustain perpetual economic growth, John-Cody. And what's it all for anyway? Growth for what? More profit, more money, more material wealth and the evolution of man takes another step backwards.'

It was uncanny the way she reminded him of Mahina. This was their kind of conversation, deep into the night after they had made love and before they made love again. That was Mahina's release when the woes of the world became too much for her: she would bury herself in him, making love with the passion and fury of a lost race of beings.

Libby sat down again. 'I'm sorry,' she said. 'I'm just going off on one.' She looked at him. 'You never did tell me what happened with Pole, by the way.'

He made a face. 'Nothing that matters. The man gets under my skin, Libby. Seeing him like I did was a good excuse to go back over the hill.'

He sipped coffee, staring into the fire, the light from the flames reflecting the silver streaks in his hair. 'Bree told me she's getting on well at school,' he said.

Libby suddenly smiled. 'Hunter Caldwell.'

'That's what I hear. It's really neat. Bree's a great kid. So is Hunter. All the women love him.'

Libby sat down on the floor and drew her knees up, hugging them to her chest. She could smell him: the light had faded to nothing outside now and their faces were lit only by the fire. 'I could say the same for somebody else. All the girls love you, John-Cody. It's writ large in their eyes.'

He rolled a cigarette and twisted one end before putting it in his mouth. Libby took a stick from the fire and lit it for him. The sliding door to his bedroom was open and she could see the rumpled unmade bed and the window beyond with the spiked branches of the lancewood pressing the glass.

'People are pretty good round here, Libby. They're just concerned, that's all.'

'Yeah, right.' Libby laughed in the back of her throat. 'They may have been concerned initially, John-Cody, but women are women and you're about as good as a man gets in this part of the world.'

He squinted at her then. 'And that's a compliment? It sounds more like an indictment of the rest of them.'

'Who knows?' Libby made an open-handed gesture. 'I'm in no position to judge.' Silence. She looked up at him. He had pinched his cigarette between forefinger and thumb and was watching it burn down. 'It doesn't matter anyway, because no-one could ever replace Mahina. Could they?'

He looked in the fire, then lifted his eyes to her as if some form of explanation was required. 'She was more than my lover, Libby. Mahina was my whole life. She taught me everything I know about this place, every last detail. She taught me to see things in a way I'd never done before. Made me realize there was more to life than just making a living, just getting what you can. We used to talk into the night, sometimes all night. We took her boat into the sounds and we'd walk in the bush together, barefoot mostly, naked sometimes like people from a time long past.'

'Adam and Eve,' Libby murmured, 'in the last garden of Tane.'

John-Cody stared at the flames licking round a log. 'Can you sense that, when you're down there in Dusky?' He knelt beside her. 'When you're alone with the water and the forest and the clouds – can you not feel that, Libby? That sense of things beyond us, things that are hidden and lost but out there just the same.'

Libby laid her hand over his. 'John-Cody, some-times I think I can sense the Tuheru.'

He stared at her for a long moment and all at once she shivered. 'Supper Cove at night: just me and the hut creaking in the wind, rain on the roof and the mist gathered above the estuary. It hangs like a shroud down there; in the early morning the cloud is so low, so wispy you'd swear the forest was on fire.' She shook her head. 'Sometimes I think I'm mad, but I'm sure I've heard the dimly seen people whisper.'

He gazed across the fire at her. 'You believe they're there?'

'Fairy people!' Libby snorted. 'Of course not: there's no such thing.' She paused for a moment and stared at the fire. 'That doesn't stop me hearing them though.'

John-Cody put more wood on the fire, suddenly glad that Libby had come round and broken up his thoughts like she had. He considered the letter in his pocket and thought about telling her, but it was not her problem. He passed a hand through his hair, longer again now but with the ends broken still. Libby sat where she was, watching the movement in the fire, neither of them speaking. John-Cody clipped the end of his cigarette and laid the butt on the hearth. 'Is Bree in bed?' He could no longer hear music through the walls.

'She was getting ready. Sierra's with her.' Libby smiled. 'Sierra's been good for Bree, you know, really good.'

'Animals are like that sometimes. They sense things about certain people we've no inkling of.'

'Bree's had a tough time.' Libby bunched her lips. 'I've hauled her around like a rucksack pretty much all her life.'

361

John-Cody handed her fresh coffee. 'Yes and she's seen Mexico and the States, Africa and the Argentine. She can speak French and Spanish and is better at Japanese than classmates who've been studying it a year longer than she has.' He nodded. 'She's had a tough time all right.'

Libby looked up at him then and her eyes – dark in the darkness – softened. He looked at her, swallowed coffee and felt that strange yet suddenly familiar feeling well up in his breast. He couldn't quite discern what it was, but it was exciting and although it troubled him the pain was a good pain and he could deal with it. All part of the confusion of everything, he told himself as he rolled another cigarette. He was smoking more these last few days, ever since Pole got to him.

Libby stretched where she sat next to him. 'I guess I better get back next door.'

'Finish your coffee first.' Suddenly John-Cody didn't want to be alone. Alone meant thinking about a future that was closing in on him like the four walls of a cell. Libby watched him, saw the movement sharp at the edge of his eyes and wondered what was going on inside his head. He was pleasant always and softly spoken and he laughed, but she had no idea what went on in his mind: he gave nothing of himself away. He drew his cheeks in hard as he smoked as if he couldn't get enough into his lungs. There was desperation in the action. It unnerved her yet she didn't really know why. She finished her coffee, yawned and got up.

'Listen, thanks for the company.'

'Thank you.'

She stood a moment and he stared at the lines of

her face, hollows under the height of her cheekbones, eyes darkened into shadows by the firelight. He had no idea what she was thinking. He stood up and they faced each other, two feet between them, neither of them moving. Libby tucked her hair behind her ear.

'Anyway. I'd better get back.'

'Yes.' He stood, hands loose at his sides, sleeves pushed up. 'I'll see you tomorrow then.'

'Tomorrow.' Libby smiled and turned. 'Goodnight, John-Cody.'

'Night, Lib. Sleep well.'

'You too.'

He went to bed, listened to her in the shower and wondered.

He kept the letter from immigration in his pocket, transferring it when he changed clothes, as if he needed it with him but was impotent to act on it. He didn't know what to do: he didn't want to face it, the future and the past, inextricably linked. He half worked in the office, getting under Alex's feet until she suggested he might want to go back over the hill. He thought about that but knew he needed to do something about the letter, just couldn't figure out what. It was weird, as if all his decision-making powers had been stolen by Ned Pole's ruthlessness. He saw Pole down by the Z boat wharf at Pearl Harbour. He was in conversation with one of the skippers as John-Cody walked down to check on some lake crossings.

Pole saw him, said something to the skipper then climbed the steps and they met on the slope down to the main wharf. John-Cody looked him coldly in the eyes and Pole folded his arms across his chest. He stood tall, the brim of his hat pulled low, shoulders hunched into the weight of his stockman's coat.

'You didn't hang about, did you?' John-Cody said.

'You wouldn't have taken the offer anyway. You wouldn't sell the *Korimako* to me.'

'You're right. I wouldn't.'

'Then there was nothing to say, was there?'

They looked at each other.

John-Cody shouldered past him.

The immigration service sent him a follow-up letter two days later and he got in his truck and drove to Dunedin. He told Libby he was going to the city and she asked him to deliver some slides to the marine lab at Portobello.

He left Manapouri with the dawn and drove east, skirting the Takitimus to Mossburn and Lumsden, where he stopped at a dairy for coffee. Then he carried on through Balfour and Riversdale to Gore. Here he parked, had a cigarette and thought about what he would say to the immigration people when he got there. He wondered what sort of a case he could plead. Deep down he was filled with a sense of dread, a feeling that no matter what he thought or said or felt there was nothing he could do, because a past was a past and he'd been running from his for years.

Libby watched him leave. She heard him start the truck and opened the front door in her bathrobe and watched as he backed out without looking round and she stood there and listened till the truck was a rumble in the distance. The world seemed strangely quiet after that and she sat on the dew-covered wood of the chair, oblivious to the damp, listening while the birds woke up. John-Cody had changed: something had altered since that meeting with Pole. When they first met him he was quiet and subdued, but over time his spirits had lifted, as if the desire for life had been reawakened within him. But now he was back in his shell, closed down and removed from them once again. Bree had noticed it too: her conversations with him had been shorter, less frequent, and he no longer gave her his full attention.

Libby felt alone again in her research. Before, she had related every discovery she made about the identification and behaviour of the pod to John-Cody, but recently his interest had waned and she kept more of it to herself. That was fine, research was often a solitary business, but when she was at Supper Cove she found the fiord lonely and somehow desolate. Apart from perhaps Punta Norte, it was the most remote place she had ever worked in. Dusky was full of wonder, but so vast and empty of humanity it was hard to imagine floating hotels and speedboats and thousands and thousands of tourists.

The dolphins were completely at ease with her now and she had positively identified and sexed over thirty separate animals. But when she was cruising along in their wake, watching the images relayed to her by the underwater camera or observing the activity on her computer screen, she found herself thinking of other things, most notably John-Cody. She rebuked herself constantly over it: never had she thought so much about a man before. She wasn't sure what the feelings amounted to. Maybe it was just concern for someone who had become a friend? No, it was something more than that. She didn't do love affairs in the traditional sense: she was always too busy, had too much work, too many causes to fight. There was something about him, though, that got under the skin; she was aware of the same feelings in other women she saw in Te Anau and Manapouri. She was looked upon with a certain suspicion now, even jealousy perhaps, though heaven knew why. The man had an aura about him, barely discernible but enough to niggle away at you. The best of it was that he was completely unaware of it.

The starling occupying the nest in the silver beech tree popped her head out and echoed in the morning. Libby glanced up at the sound of the song: it ought to make her feel that all was well with the world, but somehow it didn't.

John-Cody found the immigration office in Dunedin and parked the truck. For a long time he sat as rain driving in from the coast beat on the windscreen, casting ropes of running water over the glass. He rolled a cigarette and smoked it with just a crack in the window and all kinds of thoughts coursed through his head. He could recall with absolute clarity the smell of Bluff Cove when the trawler unloaded her catch. He remembered sitting on the gunwales in his waterproofs, gloves stuffed in his pocket, watching while the coastguard searched the vessel for drugs. He recalled drinking a pint of Speights in the local bar, after the catch had been priced and a sale agreed. He recalled catching Tom Blanch's eye as he sat and chatted with the crew. They talked about fishing inshore along the coast, the deep-water fishery management areas off the Campbell Plateau and Solander Trough. He recalled again that first meeting with Mahina on Yuvali

Beach, the smell of moisture in the bush, the scent of the trapped hind, the mud and stones and tannin seeping into the sound.

Again he took the envelope from his pocket and scanned the contents of the two letters. He should have phoned them right away: that's what he should have done. But he was here now at least. He got out of the truck and his legs felt shaky. He amazed himself: forty-eight years old and the fear a new schoolkid experiences rolling like water loose in his gut. He dropped the butt of his cigarette and crushed it under his heel, then he looked up at the drab government building and went inside.

Three flights of stairs and he came into a hall, carpeted down the middle with polished boards on either side. At the far end was a reception desk at chest height and a woman behind it fielding telephone calls.

'Good afternoon,' she said with a smile. 'What can I do for you?'

'My name's John-Cody Gibbs and I'm here to see somebody about these.' He took both letters from his pocket and spread them flat before her. Quickly she scanned the contents.

'Do you have an appointment?'

'No. I just drove over from Manapouri.'

'You really should have made an appointment.'

'I'm here now.'

'OK,' she said. 'Just one moment, sir, I'll find somebody to help you.'

He took a seat in a plastic-backed chair and rested his ankle on his knee. He looked at the bottoms of his jeans, weathered and worn, and at the battered leather of his boots. He looked at his hands, musician's hands that had spent half their life at the wheel of a boat. He had grown up on the banks of the Mississippi River with tankers and all kinds of watercraft rolling in and out of New Orleans, but not once had he considered a career at the helm of one of them. It had been the blues and Bourbon Street and a recording contract in those days.

The glass-panelled door to his left swung open and interrupted his thoughts. A middle-aged man wearing a grey suit stepped out.

'Mr Gibbs?'

'Yes, sir.' John-Cody stood up. They looked at each other: maybe the same age, the immigration official red about the eyes, thread veins in his cheeks, dressed in a shirt and tie and neat white collar; and John-Cody who had cut his hair only once in twenty-five years.

'My name's Bridges. Would you like to come through, please.'

John-Cody followed him beyond the glass panels into a thin corridor that opened out into an office filled with young people at computers. Bridges led him between their desks to a partitioned office at the far end, which (when the door was closed) offered some semblance of privacy. He gestured to the seat facing the desk and took his own. John-Cody glanced at the picture of Bridges's wife and three children on the wall behind his head.

Bridges laid the two letters flat on the blotter. 'You decided to come straight here then.'

John-Cody made an open-handed gesture. 'I guess I should've phoned first, but . . .'

'That's OK.' Bridges licked his lips. 'You're here now.'

'Listen, the man who . . .'

Bridges interrupted him. 'Really, that's not important.' He took a file from the cabinet behind him and John-Cody was strangely appalled to see that it had his name typed on it. Bridges took a pair of glasses from his jacket pocket and put them on. He opened the file. 'You arrived in New Zealand illegally, Mr Gibbs. Is that the case or am I mistaken or misinformed somewhere?'

John-Cody shook his head. 'You're not mistaken. I jumped ship in 1974. A Hawaiian trawler called the *Beachcomber*.'

'Why didn't you apply for residency in the normal way?'

John-Cody made a face. 'I should've done. I just never got round to it. I hooked up with a couple of fishing boats and ended up in Fiordland. That was about the time the helicopter deer wars were on and there was money to be made hunting.' He went on to explain his life in New Zealand to Bridges, who listened patiently, his fingers clasped before him, elbows on the desk. John-Cody told him about crayfish gathering with Tom, and about the sounds and how they affected his life. He told him about Mahina and his life with her, a marriage in everything but name. He told him about the *Korimako* and her mission to educate people about the fiords, the flora and fauna. He told him about the boundary changes, the amount of fishing that went on, everything.

When he was finished he felt empty and realized it had all just poured out of him. Bridges had listened in perfect silence for almost an hour and John-Cody had unloaded on him. He told him he knew that Ned Pole was behind this: he told him why Pole had done it, about the Dusky Sound proposals, about Libby and her research. He even told him about Bree, though for the life of him he didn't know why.

When he was finally finished he sat back, feeling weak and weary and suddenly very old. He could see the expression on Bridges's face and it was as if he had pleaded with the executioner, not the jury.

'I understand what you've told me, Mr Gibbs. And I appreciate you coming here like this.' Bridges scratched his head. 'You've obviously led an exemplary life in New Zealand, quite literally by the sounds of it, and normally someone who has been here this long would be subject to a certain amount of sympathetic treatment.'

'But.' John-Cody interrupted him.

Bridges shuffled the papers in the file. 'This thing with the FBI: I've done some research and it appears you're still officially wanted in the United States. I'm afraid that leaves us no choice whatever.'

'Yes, but the circumstances surely . . .'

'Irrelevant technically: and much as an individual might dislike it, technicalities are what departments such as this work on, Mr Gibbs.' He sat forward then and his face was closed. 'I'm sorry, I'm afraid I have no choice but to serve you with a removal order.'

John-Cody lost his breath for a moment. He stared at Bridges. 'You mean deport me.'

'Yes.' Bridges moistened his lower lip. 'Well, sort of anyway: we'll ask you to leave voluntarily and believe me it's in your interest to do so. It'll be in writing, of course, and you have the right of appeal. Should you lose that appeal, however, you wouldn't be able to reapply to come here for at least

370

five years. Equally, if you disobey the order to leave voluntarily and we have to arrest you, you cannot reapply for five years.' Bridges paused. 'It's not for me to advise you on such matters, Mr Gibbs. But I have considerable experience and I don't think you stand much chance with an appeal. The FBI holds a warrant for your arrest. There's not much we can do but hand you back to them.'

John-Cody sat where he was. His hands rested like dead weights in his lap. He could feel sweat in his hair crawling like insects across his scalp.

'I'm sorry,' Bridges said. 'There's not much more to tell you except you'll have forty-two days to leave from the date of the order.'

SIXTEEN

Standing on the rain-lashed street, John-Cody felt like a dead man. It was over, finished: Ned Pole had won. He hoped against hope that Mahina was as good as her word and couldn't see any of this. He stood for a long time staring at his truck and not seeing it, the rain plastering his hair to his scalp. He was dead, or he might as well be. The core of his life had been ripped away; just when he had thought there might be some scraps left, somebody figured otherwise and anything he might have created after the death of Mahina was swept up like so much rubbish. He was standing by the driver's door of his truck, trying to think of what to do, when he recalled Libby asking him to take some papers to the marine studies centre in Portobello.

Like an automaton he got behind the wheel and drove out to the peninsula. He passed the envelope across the counter at reception and as he turned again his gaze settled on a photographic display on the wall. It showed a black-backed whale with no dorsal fin breaching high from the water: it was a southern right of the Auckland Islands.

* * *

Libby was sitting outside the house with Tom Blanch when John-Cody got back that evening. It was a four-hour drive from Dunedin and he did it without stopping. The road was clear and his mind calmer than it had been.

'How you going?' Tom called as he walked up the path.

'Hey, Tom.'

Libby smiled at him. 'Did everything go OK?'

'Fine.'

'You managed to get out to the peninsula?'

He nodded. 'Steve Watson wasn't around, but I delivered the stuff for you.'

'What were you doing in Dunedin?' Tom asked him.

'Just checking on a couple of things.'

Libby got up to make some coffee and John-Cody took the seat she had vacated and fished tobacco from his pocket. Tom looked out of the corner of his eye at him.

'What's the deal with Ned Pole, Gib? Libby tells me you've not been the same bloke since you two met at the range.'

John-Cody made a face. 'There's no deal, Tom: you know what Pole's like. He's determined to get those hotels in Dusky Sound. He was just reminding me of the fact, that's all.'

Tom squinted at him. 'And that's it?'

'That's it.'

'So why the long face? You were getting so much better.'

John-Cody flicked ash on the floor. 'It comes and goes, Tom. Some days are better than others.'

373

Libby brought the coffee pot and set it on the table between the two men. She went back inside and fetched the low stool from the bathroom. John-Cody watched the smooth backs of her hands as she poured coffee. He took his black with no sugar and warmed his palms on the cup. They sat in the quiet for a few minutes, the wind caressing the trees the only sound save the odd car on the road to Te Anau.

'So how's it going in Dusky, Libby?' Tom said.

'It's going as well as it can. Though not well enough. I'm pretty sure the pod is resident, but I don't have enough data to prove it officially yet.'

'Which Pole will use at the hearing.'

She nodded. 'Undoubtedly.'

John-Cody stared through the shadows that shrouded the trees. 'If you want to go to Port Ross I'll take you, Libby,' he said quietly.

Libby stared at him. 'What?'

'I said I'll take you to Port Ross if you want to go.' John-Cody looked at Tom. 'Remember those bottlenose dolphins we see every time we go down?'

'They're not in Port Ross. They're at least twenty ks north.'

'Libby wondered if they might be resident in the Aucklands.'

'I've never seen them there.'

'Neither have I, but that doesn't mean they're not.'

Tom frowned. 'That'd be right, I suppose, but I doubt you'll get dolphins living that far south.'

Libby glanced at him. 'Nobody ever thought they'd be resident as far south as Doubtful Sound, Tom.' She looked back at John-Cody. 'Why would you want to take me?'

He shrugged. 'We've not got any charters booked.

I haven't been down there for a while and if we do find dolphins it'll help your research.' He glanced at Tom. 'Anything that might hold up Pole is a good thing in my book.' He turned to Libby once more. 'Not only that, but the whales should be down for the season.'

Libby spoke to Tom then. 'Baleen whale communication is where I've been trying to break new ground, Tom. There's so little known. It's much easier with dolphins because we've had them in captivity for years. My father even trained them to fight in Vietnam.'

John-Cody stared at her then. 'He did what?'

She nodded. 'He was a marine biologist too, only he worked for NATO, with the Americans mostly. They wanted dolphins to take mines up the Mekong Delta.'

John-Cody got up and crushed out his cigarette. Collecting the coffee cups, he went inside and washed them carefully. Tom called his goodbyes then Libby came into the house and shut the door. The fire was burning low and John-Cody set logs in the embers, which caught and crackled immediately. He went out and fetched more from the box on the porch. Libby had poured herself a glass of whisky and waggled the bottle at him.

'Thanks.' John-Cody took a glass and sipped it, the liquor burning the back of his throat. Libby took the bottle and sat down on the floor by the fire. She motioned to the chair and John-Cody felt the tension ease out of him. He sat. She sipped her whisky staring at the flames and hugging her knees. Her hair was loose and hung long and black against her shoulders.

'Will you really take me to the Aucklands?'

'If you want to go.'

'There's very little chance the pod is resident there. No chance at all really.'

'I know.'

'So why do it?'

John-Cody shrugged. 'I've got a boat that's paid for. Most winters she just sits in Deep Cove, or gets hauled out of the water for painting down at Bluff. Why not go?'

'When can we leave?'

'Pretty much when you want. I'll have to sail round to Bluff anyway. That'll take a couple of days, then we need to get her ready for the Subs. Buy the stores etc.'

'I can't afford a charter on my own.'

'Who said anything about a charter? I'm offering to take you.' He finished his whisky. Part of him didn't want to leave her, but he knew he didn't want any more questions and if he stayed there would be lots more questions. He rubbed the heel of his palm in his eyes.

Libby looked up at him and sensed his pain. She had sensed it before, but this was somehow different. She was about to ask him when he stood up.

'I'm beat. I'll see you tomorrow. Are you going back to Dusky?'

'Not if we're heading south.'

'OK. I'll see you in the morning then.'

He stood under the eaves of his own porch and had a final smoke, one hand in his pocket gripping the teardrop stone that Mahina had given him a year and a half ago.

*   *   *

It took Libby three weeks to make the necessary arrangements. Nobody could land on the Auckland Islands without a permit from the Department of Conservation and even though she was already working for them she still had to jump through half a dozen hoops. She doubted that there would be any dolphins at Port Ross, but John-Cody was right, any fuel to the fire was useful, because she would still be a long way off proving residency in Dusky Sound by the time Ned Pole's hearing came round. Alex had been on the phone to Southland Regional Council about that, but as yet no date had been fixed. It was a fact now, though, that theirs was the only submission in opposition. Apart from the Department of Conservation, the others had all withdrawn after lucrative offers of sub-contracted work.

Libby had to find somebody to look after Bree, but if all else failed Alex said she would look after her, though she had been planning a trip to the North Island to see friends.

John-Cody worked on the *Korimako*, getting her ready for the trip round the coast to Bluff. Once there he would buy the stores, fuel up and fit the aluminium window shields to protect them against the Southern Ocean weather. Sorting through his charts, he noticed that the hand-held compass he kept in reserve wasn't working properly. There was a bubble in the alcohol and the needle was spinning wildly. He made a mental note to take it ashore and either fix or replace it. There was a large gimbal-mounted compass on the dashboard, but he had to have back-up for everything on this boat: he spent too much time in the Southern Ocean currents not to.

He crossed Lake Manapouri on the Z boat and when they landed he walked the short distance to Tom's house, where he found him waxing the starboard hull of his catamaran. Tom had an ocean-going skipper's ticket and John-Cody wanted him along on the trip.

'Do you really need me?' Tom asked him. 'You've got Jonah, and Libby can sail. It's not a commercial trip so the numbers don't matter.'

John-Cody leaned against the hull. 'No, it's not commercial. It's my own charter, Tom. The three of us could do it for sure. But the watches would be longer and if anything happened to me, I wouldn't trust Jonah to get Libby home.'

Tom licked his lips, hidden beneath the greyed mass of his beard. 'You sure you ought to be making a trip to the Subs right now? You really think you're up to it?'

John-Cody shrugged. 'Of course I'm up to it. To tell you the truth, Tom, I want something to do.' He smiled then. 'You know, when Mahina was alive we struggled for every cent. Now she's gone I've got a boat and a wharf and money sitting in the bank. I can get by on half a dozen good charters a year.' He paused. 'Besides, it'll take my mind off Pole.'

Tom nodded, pushing out his lips. 'That old buzzard's getting to you, isn't he?'

'Yes, Tom, he is. I've got a terrible feeling he's going to win this one.'

'Gibby, I learned something a long time ago and I think it's true, though it's taken me half my life to figure it out fully. A man can only really beat you if you let him. You understand what I'm saying?'

John-Cody looked him in the eye. 'I hear you,

378

Tom. You've been a good friend. Thank you.'

He walked back to the office and Jean Grady was hovering outside the shop. She looked troubled. 'I've got some mail for you, John-Cody.' She bent behind the counter and brought out a bundle of airmail envelopes tied with a rubber band. John-Cody stared at the first one, a name and address in America. It looked like Bree's handwriting.

'The little girl posted them,' Jean said. 'I always stamp foreign mail with a return address just in case it goes missing. All of these came back. I meant to give them to her earlier but there was only one, then all of these turned up at the same time.'

John-Cody counted seven separate letters. 'OK,' he said. 'I'll see that she gets them back.'

Jean handed him two letters of his own then and his heart sank as he recognized one from the immigration service. 'Is everything all right?' she asked him.

'Everything is fine.'

But he walked up the hill with his heart knotted in his chest. Alex had left for the day so he unlocked the office, closed the door and sat down on the couch. The map hung on the ceiling with one corner dangling. He had promised Alex he would fix it for her but had never got round to it. He turned the envelope over in his hands, listening to the wind that came off the lake. He laid the envelope on the table, took out his tobacco and made a cigarette. Then he laid that down and picked up the envelope again and this time he tore it open. Two terse lines informed him he had forty-two days to leave the country. The letter was dated almost a week ago.

He phoned Naseby to tell Jonah about the trip and

got Kobi instead. They talked for a few minutes and John-Cody was going to tell him to pass the message on and then he changed his mind. 'Look, Kobi, we've got a trip to the Subs planned. I'm going to drive up and get Jonah.'

The old man was quiet for a moment. 'Why do you want to do that? It's a long way, Gib. Jonah's got his Ute here anyway.'

'I know, but I fancy the drive. I haven't seen you for a while.'

'There's nowhere for you to sleep.'

'No worries, I'll stop over in Omakau, come by for Jonah and say hello. He and I can travel back the same day.'

'Whatever you want, Gib. It'd be good to see you.'

He put the phone down and went outside to smoke his cigarette. He thought about Kobi then, how distant and proud he had been when Mahina first introduced them, how protective he was over her: that had not lasted, though, and they grew to like each other quickly. He would never forget the pain in the old man's face when he looked down on his dead daughter. Jonah had stood beside him, holding his arm, supporting him. Kobi's face was white, deathly in itself almost: the etched markings of despair echoed John-Cody's and would remain imprinted that way for ever.

He deliberately waited till it was late before he headed back to the house: he had the stack of letters to give to Libby and he wanted to make sure Bree was in bed. Both lights were burning in the front windows which meant she was still up, so he went next door and made some coffee. There was no fire in the grate and the wood-panelled room was cold.

380

His bed was unmade and he sat on it and took off his boots, the pile of letters on the table in the other room. The kettle boiled but he left it and stepped into the shower.

The water was hot and fell fast against his skin. He stood with his head bowed, arms hanging at his sides, and thought about the days the immigration service had left him: only one month – so very sudden after twenty-five years.

Libby heard John-Cody come in as she washed the supper dishes. She heard the front door close and then the sliding sound of his bathroom door and a little later the rush of water and she knew he was naked under the shower. She bit her lip, aware of the little quiver in her belly and sweat at the top of her thighs. Bree came through and announced she was going to bed. Libby kissed her goodnight.

'You don't mind me going to the Sub-Antarctic?' she said.

Bree shook her head. 'Where will I stay – with Alex?'

'I suppose so. I haven't quite worked it out yet.'

'How long will you be gone?'

'A couple of weeks, I suppose. John-Cody says it depends on the weather.'

Bree nodded. 'OK, whatever: it's not like I haven't done it before.'

She went to bed and Sierra got up from the hearthrug and followed her. Libby tucked her in and switched off the light and as she came through once again John-Cody poked his head round the front door.

'You busy?'

'Not at all.' Libby was glad to see him. She always

was. His company was calming, good for her: she needed it. She got up to put the kettle on but he waved her back to her seat.

As he sat down she noticed the bundle of letters in his hand. 'What have you got there, a correspondence course?'

'I don't know.' He handed them to her and the lines deepened above Libby's brow. 'Jean gave them to me at the shop. It seems Bree posted them and they all came back again.'

Libby was staring at the first envelope, then the next and the next. They all read the same: *Michael Bass, 33 River Road, San Francisco*. They were marked 'address unknown'. For a long time she just looked at them, seven in all, turning them over in her hand.

'Is that her father?' John-Cody said. 'I don't mean to pry, but I couldn't help but notice the name.'

Libby didn't answer him: still she sat there, mouth half open. There was a sensation of cold inside her that numbed the feelings of guilt she lived with into insignificance: a sense of wrong, of things undone, badly mended and coming away at the seams.

'I'll leave you in peace.' John-Cody stood up, but Libby looked at him anxiously.

'No. Stay. Please.'

He sat down slowly. Libby put the letters on the floor and got up. Tiptoeing to Bree's door, she eased it ajar then listened for a moment. The sound of her breathing, measured and even, lifted from the bedclothes. Libby closed the door again then sought her bag where it lay on the counter. Finding a cigarette she broke the filter off and lit it with hands that trembled slightly. John-Cody sat where he was.

Libby stood for a moment with one hand fisted

382

against her hip. 'Bree doesn't know her father. She's never met him. She doesn't even know his name.'

She sat down heavily. 'I met him at a party in San Francisco. I got drunk. I probably did a little acid. I was doing a bit of that in those days. I never asked his name and when he was gone in the morning I didn't tell anyone we'd slept together. All I can remember is that he had blue eyes and blond hair, like Bree. She looks like him, I suppose, I don't remember exactly.' She lifted her shoulders and stared at the unopened letters. 'She's a great girl. She deserves more than this. Shit, anyone would deserve more than this.'

John-Cody listened to the choked little sounds in her voice. He sat forward and for a moment his own problems were forgotten. 'Are you going to open them?'

'They're Bree's. I can't do that, they're private.'

'That's true. But you can't give them back to her either.'

Libby looked across the space between them. 'You're right,' she said. 'Getting them back would be terrible for her.'

John-Cody cleared his throat. 'I'm not one for giving people advice, Libby, so ignore me if you want – but if I were you I'd open them.'

'You would?'

'Yes. You can't help her unless you know what the problem is.'

Libby's hand trembled. She picked up the topmost envelope and looked at the postmark. Mrs Grady had stacked them in the order they had been sent. She bit her lip, sucked on the cigarette and gazed at John-Cody. 'You think I should do this?'

'I've said what I think. You do what you think is best.'

Libby hesitated a moment longer then tore the first envelope open: she unfolded the single sheet of paper and Bree's neat handwriting seemed to rise off the page. Slowly she read the letter Bree had written on the plane coming from England. When she was finished, tears burned in her eyes.

'What does it say?' John-Cody asked gently.

Libby passed the letter to him and he read it carefully, then he read it again. He could hear Bree's voice: desolate, lonely and lost.

'She never talked to me.' Libby was chewing on her words. 'I always wondered why. I thought maybe she just got her head down and got on with it.' She stood up, paced to the fire, absently bent for a log and stood holding it for a moment. 'There's me thinking she was just fine and all the time she was telling her problems to her imaginary father.' She sobbed involuntarily and John-Cody got up, moved as if to hold her but stopped.

Libby controlled the sobs. 'Look at me, grizzling like a girl. I'm not the one who's been done to like this.' She sat down again. 'What was I thinking about? You can't bring up a child the way I have and expect everything to be hunky-dory. I've hauled her round the world so many times her head must be spinning. What on earth was I playing at?'

'You were thinking about work. Earning money for food and clothes and everything else a child needs.'

Libby was looking at him now, his face open yet grey and weary. 'I shouldn't be burdening you with this.'

384

'I know where the door is. I can leave if I want to.'
He hunched forward again. 'Listen, you did what
you did. What were you – nineteen? You brought
Bree up when you weren't much more
than a child yourself. She's a wonderful girl, Libby.
And that's a credit to you.' He got up and put more
wood on the fire, took his tobacco and rolled two
cigarettes. Libby pursed her lips and opened another
letter: it was dated just after Easter.

Dear Dad

*I wrote you a letter today but burnt it. I had
to. It was full of lies, not my lies, well not ones I
made up. Just lies. Things that I thought were
true but weren't. D'you know what I mean? This
is crappy writing, isn't it. I don't know what I
mean, never mind you. You see, there are these
three girls at school. I've told you about them
before. Jessica Lowden's the worst. I told you
they've been bullying me – well, it got really bad
today. It was the first day of term and Hunter
wasn't there which I hated. Things are so much
better when Hunter's there. Anyway, Jessica and
Sally and Anna were nice to me, which they've
never been. I couldn't believe it. Jessica sat next
to me in Japanese and after school we all went to
the beach at Lake Te Anau. Dad, I really
thought they were my friends and at break time I
wrote and told you. That was the letter I burnt.
They tricked me, Dad. They took me to the
beach, tripped me up and threw all my books in
the lake. It would have been much worse if Mr
Pole hadn't turned up. John-Cody and Mum
don't like him, but he's cool to me. He told them*

385

to leave me alone and then he took me home. He even waded into the lake to get my books. He was soaked when he came out. He's got this great house and land and horses and he said he'd teach me to ride. A terrible thing happened to him, Dad. His son Eli was killed on John-Cody's boat. I know what happened and it wasn't John-Cody's fault, but he still got killed. Mr Pole bought a horse for him and he only got to ride it once. I think that's why he wants to teach me. Mr Pole wants to put hotels in Dusky Sound, which is where Mum's doing her stuff. I think that's fine and Dusky Sound is huge. I don't think it would matter too much, do you? People have to go to work, don't they, and there's not much work down here.

Anyway they're still bullying me and school is awful except for Hunter. It's the worst I've had, Dad, the very worst. I can't tell Mum because there's nothing she could do about it and she'd only worry. Mr Pole was cool though, you should have seen Jessica's face when he told her he was going to see her father. Cool. Really cool.

It's been a bad day, but maybe things will get better now. Mr Pole told me he's going to make sure those girls leave me alone and I really want him to teach me to ride. I'm going to ask Mum. She won't be happy, but I'm going to ask her anyway. It'd be great to show Hunter how I can ride properly because he's so good. I hope John-Cody doesn't mind, though, he and Mr Pole don't like each other. John-Cody's so cool to me, Dad. I really love him. I hope he doesn't mind. He won't, will he?

*Anyway, I'm tired. Mum and John-Cody are
away and I want to go to bed.*
   Love you, I'll write again soon.
   Bree

Libby laid the letter down, her heart thumping.
She looked at the fire and then at John-Cody; she
passed him the letter. He read it in silence and the
two of them looked at each other, neither of them
speaking.

'I had no idea,' Libby whispered in the end. 'My
own daughter being bullied and I had no idea.'

'She's not the sort of girl to say anything, Lib.'

'Ned Pole of all people.' Libby shook her head.
'Nehemiah Pole. Good God, no wonder she wanted
him to teach her to ride.' She lifted her hands, palm
upwards. 'John-Cody, I know nothing about my
own daughter.'

'Yes, you do. But you're a parent, Libby. Bree's
nearly a teenager. Did you tell your parents everything when you were a teenager?'

Libby didn't answer him. She stared at the fire.
John-Cody slipped into silence and looked at the
letter again. Bree had worried that he might be
jealous. He *had* been jealous, taking her over to
Pole's house, leaving her there and seeing the delight
in her eyes when she came back. He and Pole were
both childless, him never having had the opportunity
and Pole having lost his only son on the *Korimako*.

Libby was watching him. 'Ned Pole knew my
daughter was being bullied when neither you nor I
did.'

'Well, much as I hate to say it, thank God
somebody did.'

387

They sat and smoked and drank whisky in silence and then Libby picked up the other envelopes and thumbed through them.

'Whatever it says in there, she's happier now.' John-Cody indicated the letters with his glass. 'That probably means the bullying is over. Ironically Pole is to thank for it.' His mouth twisted at the corners. 'Bree seems happy enough to me, Libby. She loves this house, the lake, Sierra. Hunter Caldwell's got a lot to do with it.'

'So have you. She confides in you, John-Cody.'

'You think so?'

'I've seen it. I've seen her around you. You're so gentle with her. She looks up to you, her quiet man of the sea. She's never had a male role model before. Pole might be teaching her to ride, but she looks up to you.' A thought struck her then and Libby sifted the pile of letters once more, inspecting the postmark on the outside of the envelopes. Apart from the Easter letter the last one had been posted at the end of January.

'What happened in January?' John-Cody said when she showed him.

Libby sipped whisky. 'I don't know. But it's about the time she started hanging out with you.'

Again silence, both of them considering the implications of what she was saying. John-Cody thought of his own letter from immigration and the little time remaining. He felt his breathing grow shallow and his face must have betrayed something because Libby suddenly frowned at him.

'Are you OK?'

'Yes, I'm fine. Frog in my throat, that's all.' He coughed and reached for his glass.

'Thank you,' Libby said when he set it down again. 'I mean, really thank you. You've had so much loss and yet you've been wonderful to us.' She looked round the room. 'You even gave up your home.' She paused. 'What's it like having us here?'

'It's good.'

'Are you sure?'

'Positive.'

'And Mahina, would she have been pleased?'

'She'd be delighted. No doubt she is delighted.'

Libby watched him for a while. 'You're lucky, you know,' she said.

He lifted his eyebrows.

'To have had somebody you loved so much for so long.'

'That's what Alex told me.'

'She's right. It's rare.' Libby put out her cigarette. 'Mahina was lucky. Very few women get loved like that in their lives.'

'Not you?'

She laughed a little bitterly. 'No chance. When have I had time to stop and think about love? I've hardly even thought about my daughter.'

She leafed through the letters on her lap. 'I don't know what I can do about these, except listen to Bree properly in future. I mean listen to the noises her heart makes. Hear her better. Take the time. Not get so caught up in myself.'

'That ought to work.' He stood up.

'You're not going, are you?'

He hesitated for a moment, awkward all at once in her presence. Then he sat down and she reached for more logs. The lights were dim and the flames cast

389

shadows that danced on the panelled wood of the walls.

'What are you going to do with them?' John-Cody pointed to the letters she had laid on the floor.

'I'll keep them and read them one by one, on the boat maybe as we head south.' Libby picked up the ones she had opened. 'I need to. I need to learn how she's really feeling.'

'Could you get in touch with her father?'

Libby arched her brows. 'After twelve years? I don't even know his name.'

'What about other people at the party?'

'I don't know. I was only the friend of a friend. I haven't seen the friend I went with since that night.' She shook her head at herself. 'Listen to me, what a great advert for motherhood. I was so drunk or stoned or both I dropped my knickers and didn't even ask his name.'

'Don't be so hard on yourself.' John-Cody said it with authority, not sympathy. 'Everyone can make a mistake. Do something they regret later.' He stared at her now. 'We do what we do. That's it. That's all there is. What we think at the time. You had a child and you got your qualifications and now look at you, possibly the greatest expert on whale communication in the world. Don't punish yourself. Guilt achieves nothing. It's a perfectly useless emotion.'

'You sound like you know what you're talking about.'

He looked at her then, darkness in his eyes. 'Believe me, I do.'

SEVENTEEN

John-Cody drove to Naseby in Central Otago. He was in no hurry, Kobi wasn't going anywhere: he spent most of his life in the room he had built in the general store and Jonah would be sleeping on a mat on the concrete floor. John-Cody would get as far as Alexandra or Omakau that evening and head out again in the morning. He drove to Mossburn and took the road for Queenstown and Lake Wakatipu. Libby was on his mind; he saw again the pain in her eyes, the guilt over Bree. She had sat there the other night thinking what a failure she was at motherhood whereas he could see only the success she had achieved in bringing up her daughter single-handed. There had been no compromises and perhaps in some ways Bree might have suffered from that: but in other ways she had benefited like few children before her. At twelve she had seen so much of the world, learned so much and was fluent in three languages. Many adults he knew would have killed for a childhood like that.

He drove with the letters from immigration in his pocket but quite why he needed to keep them that close to him he didn't know. He skirted Queenstown and crossed the river at Cromwell. The water at the Clyde dam was low and he was reminded just how close it had been to bursting back in November.

Now he was closing in on old haunts: he and Mahina had spent quite a bit of time up here in the early days of their relationship. Mahina was always looking out for her father and they would drive up from Manapouri half a dozen times a year. Central Otago was baking in the summer and freezing in the winter. It was high and the climate reminded him of Idaho where the snow could easily reach ten feet in February and the temperature into the hundreds in July.

He stayed that night in Omakau, had a couple of beers with an elderly English deer hunter he met in the bar and discussed old times in Fiordland. In the morning he left early and took a detour to St Bathans, where the cavalcade passed in summer. He pulled over by the blue lake and lit a cigarette. The morning was crisp and clear, a chill to the air but dry like the heat of summer. John-Cody leaned against the door of his truck and licked the paper on the cigarette he had made. The lake was still, glacial blue with twin wooden jetties on the northern shore. It beached at one end and in summer people flocked here from the neighbouring towns to swim and fish and picnic. He stared at the lake now: white-faced cliffs of sandstone sloped in varying degrees of gradient to lip the water, jagged in places and smooth in others, crowding the lake like a group of thirsty old men. He half-closed his eyes and recalled Mahina's smile, the laughter in her eyes as the two of them swam in the icy water, duck-diving and holding their breath for as long as they could before breaking the surface again. When nobody else was around they would swim naked, running to dive from the jetties then lying back on the volcanic sand to dry in the heat of the sun. English willow trees dominated the shoreline and when it got too hot they would take shelter under the many-fronded branches.

An Australian harrier called, breaking into his thoughts, and he shielded his eyes and saw it high above him, no more than a black dot in the sky. It glided on ruffled wings then turned and banked and turned again to settle among the willow branches. John-Cody clipped his cigarette and took out the three crumpled letters, which he read again, just to remind himself it was real. It was: the words were still there, still the same black letters typed on the white pages. His time here was over. Everything was finished and all he had now were the memories.

Back in the truck he drove the short distance to Naseby and found Kobi in the back yard of the store cutting wood. John-Cody pulled up and the old man laid down the hand axe and looked at him through the windscreen. The house *was* the general store, basically no more than a warehouse. The only way in was through the sliding door at the back, which led to a concrete floor where Kobi's unused car was kept; a separate door led to the single room he had built, roof and all, inside the warehouse itself. There was a bath but no hot water and Kobi washed in cold as he had done since his days at the mine beyond Danseys Pass. John-Cody got out of the truck and smiled at him. Kobi looked back and nodded slowly, a little moisture in the rheumy blue of his eyes.

'G'day, Kobi.'

'G'day, son.'

'How you going?'

'Good, thanks.' They shook hands and then John-Cody pulled the old fellow close and embraced him. He felt thin and small and frail and John-Cody was careful not to squeeze him too hard for fear of crushing the life in him. He held him at arm's length and looked in his eyes and saw the same familiar expression: Kobi often told him he had lived long enough to bury a wife and a daughter, too long in any man's language.

'Where's Jonah?'

'Gone to the dairy for lollies.'

John-Cody smiled. 'You want to brew me some coffee, old man?' He slipped his arm round Kobi's shoulders and led him towards the store. John-Cody carried in the wood and stoked up the pot-bellied stove whose cast-iron chimney reached to the home-made ceiling and up through the roof of the warehouse.

Kobi folded his arms and looked at him as they sat at the table. He was eighty-five and his neck hung in folds from his jaw; thread veins criss-crossed his cheeks and the end of his nose. His knuckles were stiff and enlarged with arthritis, fingernails long and yellow like the claws of an animal. His eyes were permanently moist, the pupil mixing with the white to form a filmy layer.

'So you're going to the Subs again,' he said quietly.

John-Cody nodded. He told him about Libby's passion for whales and the possibility of dolphins in Port Ross.

Kobi looked at him. 'There's no dolphins that far south.'

394

'Not resident, no. But that's not the point, Kobi. Libby wants to see the southern rights.'

Kobi nodded. 'She's not proved anything in Dusky then?'

'No.'

'Will she?'

'Probably not in time.'

Kobi was still. 'So you're going to the Subs. Jonah's going to crew for you?'

'Him and Tom Blanch.'

'Old Tom, eh? Sounds like a busy trip.'

'I need Tom, Kobi. If anything happened to me I'd need another ocean-going skipper.'

Kobi squinted at him then. 'And what's going to happen to you?'

'Nothing I can't handle.'

Kobi nodded slowly and scraped a roughened palm over his jaw. 'Are you over her yet?'

The question stung and John-Cody sat for a moment not answering. Kobi looked keenly at him. 'Well, are you?'

'I don't know. I think about her all the time.'

'So do I, but are you over her?'

'No.'

'I didn't think you were.' Kobi let go a stiff breath. 'You need to get over her, Gib. She'd be pissed off if she thought you weren't.'

'I know.'

'She had her mother's temper.' Kobi smiled with the fondness of memory. 'Waitaha. A people of peace, that's what they always told me, but boy what a temper.' He looked round then. 'You hear much from the joker Pole?'

'Now and again.'

'Hotels in Dusky Sound?' Kobi frowned heavily. 'Mahina would turn in her grave if she thought it would come to that.'

'I know it.'

'Isn't there anything anyone can do?'

John-Cody sighed. 'We can only wait for the hearing.' He got up. 'I'm going to take a walk, Kobi, see if I can find Jonah.'

'Try the pub.' Kobi looked keenly at him.

John-Cody nodded, turned for the door and turned back again. 'Kobi, did Mahina ever say anything to you about Pole?'

Kobi looked at him out of the corner of his eye. 'Say anything? No, she didn't. Why?'

'No reason.' John-Cody shook his head.

The problem of who would look after Bree while Libby was in the Sub-Antarctic was solved by Bree herself: two days before John-Cody and Jonah sailed for Bluff Cove on the first leg of the journey, Bree came home and announced that Hunter's parents had offered to have her for the three weeks or so they were likely to be gone. Libby phoned to confirm it with the Caldwells and they told her they would be delighted to have both Bree and Sierra. Libby put the phone down and looked at her daughter, who sat on a kitchen stool with the biggest smile on her face.

'See,' she said, 'I told you. They're cool about it. Hunter's parents are cool about most things.'

Libby nodded. 'So he's the one, is he? He's definitely your boyfriend.'

Bree cocked her head to one side. 'We're still just friends at the moment. I mean I haven't kissed him or anything. We hold hands all the time, though.'

'I know. I've seen you.' Libby sat down on the stool alongside her. 'You're sure you don't mind me going? I could stay. I mean I don't have to go. It was John-Cody's idea actually.'

'I know. He told me.' Bree took her mother's hand and squeezed it. 'Everything's cool, Mum. Everything's just fine. You go and find some whales or dolphins or whatever. I'll stay here and Hunter can coach me for the rugby season.'

Libby looked at her. 'You are joking.'

'No. I need coaching. I don't want loud-mouth Lowden on my case again.' She broke off. 'You don't know her, but take it from me I don't want her on my case.'

'Again? She was on your case before?'

'Yes.'

'But she's off it now?'

'Yes.'

'Completely?'

'Totally. Ever since I got off the bus with Hunter.'

'Hunter?'

'Yeah.' Bree's eyes shone. 'It was so cool, Mum. Jessica had been giving me a hard time, then one day Hunter just took my hand and held it all the way into class. She's left me alone ever since. Cool, isn't it?'

Libby hugged her. 'You bet it's cool. Tell me though next time, huh, if someone gets on your case. I'm your mum, remember.'

'OK.' Bree shrugged.

'I'm going to miss you,' Libby said.

Bree took an apple from the basket. 'Don't worry. It won't be any different to when you're in Dusky Sound. I can still talk to you on the radio.'

'The single-side-band, not the VHF.'

'Alex'll show me.'

Libby nodded. 'What're you going to do – get off the bus at the office and then get a lift to Hunter's?'

'I don't know yet. They don't have a radio at the sheep station. I'll have to talk to Alex. Don't worry, I'll sort it out, Mum.'

Libby laughed. 'I'll just wait for you to call then, shall I?'

John-Cody came in and dropped his bag on the floor. Jonah was already at Pearl Harbour, where a boat was waiting to take them across the lake. Bree told John-Cody about the offer from the Caldwells.

'Great,' he said. 'You should be just fine then.' He smiled, but there was a broken look in his eyes and Bree frowned: she went over to him, slipped her arms about his waist and hugged him.

'Look after my mum.'

'I will. Don't worry, we've got Jonah along and Tom. She's in very good hands.'

'No.' Bree held him at arm's length and looked into his eyes. 'I mean *you* look after her. I trust you, John-Cody.'

John-Cody laid a hand on her shoulder and squeezed, then lifted her right up and she threw her arms round his neck. He held her tight and closed his eyes and kissed her.

'Take it easy, Breezy.'

'Five high, Captain Bligh.'

John-Cody looked at Libby. 'I'll see you down at Bluff. Tom knows where the boat will be moored.'

'On Thursday.'

'Right.' Again he looked at Bree. 'Take care of Sierra for me.' He left then, hefting the bag over his shoulder. Bree stood in the open doorway and watched him go; she watched him walk as far as the corner, where he turned without looking back.

Nehemiah Pole was on one of his crayfish boats when the tourist bus dropped John-Cody and Jonah by the *Korimako*'s wharf. He stood on deck smoking a black cheroot with his skipper and mate behind him. Jonah nodded to him and went below to the engine room. John-Cody walked more slowly, savouring the sight of the sound, the height of Mt George, the clustered birdsong which burst all at once from the bush.

Pole watched him. 'I hear you're going south,' he called.

John-Cody nodded.

'Be careful down there.'

'You give a damn?'

Pole shrugged. 'For what it's worth – it wasn't me, Gib.'

'It was you, Ned.'

'Not in the way you think.'

Jonah was at the door of the wheelhouse wiping oil from his fingers with a rag. John-Cody ducked inside.

'What was that all about?' Jonah asked him.

'Untie us, Jonah.'

'Boss?'

'Get us under way.'

Jonah twisted the ignition key and the Gardner rumbled into life under their feet. Familiar vibration through bulkhead and steel deck: John-Cody knew every shudder, every variation in movement and sound. He watched Jonah cast off astern and then he let go the for'ard spring and they steamed into Deep Cove. He walked back on deck, went astern and leaned on the transom, watching as the black-framed jetty got smaller and smaller and smaller. On the crayfish boat Pole stood like a figurehead in the bows.

Libby waited for Tom to come by and pick her up in his twin cab. She had all her gear ready, computer equipment, hydra-phones and underwater cameras stowed in aluminium cases. Tom got out of the truck, looked at the pile and scratched his head.

'You planning on making a movie?' he muttered.

They took the scenic route to Invercargill via the Tuatapere road so they could drop Bree and Sierra at the Caldwells' farm. Bree gave her mother a big squeeze and pecked Tom on the cheek then raced off with Sierra to find Hunter. Libby talked through the radio contact details with the Caldwells then climbed back in the truck. Bree and Hunter came up the yard, riding one behind the other bareback on his pony; Hunter kicked the horse into a canter to flank their path to the road.

'Bree's a great kid, Libby,' Tom said as they drove south.

'She loves it here, Tom.'

'Course she does.' Tom gesticulated at the rolling empty countryside. 'Who would live anywhere else?'

Libby looked where he looked and nodded. 'You know what,' she said. 'I've never settled anywhere in my life. But I could settle here.'

They drove through the hills, up and over Blackmount and on towards Clifden and Tuatapere. They were in no hurry and Tom wanted to show her the coastal section between Te Waewae and Riverton before coming into Invercargill from the west.

'So tell me, Tom,' she asked him, 'what can I expect in the Southern Ocean?'

Tom didn't reply right away: he drove with one palm on the wheel and gazed ahead through the windscreen. 'That all depends. If we get a good window of weather we'll have an easy run down. If we don't, depending on how bad it is, Gib might hole up off Stewart Island for a while.'

'It can get that bad then?'

'Oh yeah: if it's blowing hard sou'west there's no point in putting to sea at all. You'll just sit there punching holes in big waves and getting nowhere fast. Best to wait till the wind drops or changes.'

'Will we sail?'

'Engine and sail, engine mostly. Sail helps with stability though.'

She nodded. 'And what are the Aucklands like?'

Tom sucked breath. 'Uninhabited and wild. You're down in the furious fifties, Lib, anything can happen. Gib knows more about that area than most so you'd best be asking him. All I know is there have been a lot of serious wrecks off those islands, mostly in the nineteenth century when ships were under sail. They used to get caught in the channels and smash onto the rocks.

'The western cliffs of the main island are treacherous. It can be the same around Port Ross; and the southern tip of Adams Island is the last land till you hit the big pack ice. The wind howls like you've never heard it before. It's incessant, like a pack of lost wolves, there when you fall asleep and there when you wake up.' He paused then and looked at her. 'Enderby Island is haunted. Me and Gib took an author down there one time. She wrote a book about the *Invercauld*, a boat that went down in a fury of a storm against the western cliffs. That was a terrible time: those that got ashore had the cliffs to deal with and they couldn't find any shelter.'

'When was this?'

'1864. Two ships went down in the same year. The first was the *Grafton*, skippered by a man called Musgrave.'

'John-Cody told me about him.'

Tom nodded. 'That crew were luckier than the *Invercauld*; they went aground in Carnley Harbour which is low and flat and separates the main island from Adams. Five men got ashore, Musgrave, a Frenchman and three crewmen. The third of January they were wrecked and they weren't rescued till 22 August the following year. Twenty months on the islands.' He paused and screwed up his face. '*I strive by occupying my hands as much as possible to dispel these sad feelings, but it is utterly impossible and melancholy is getting hold of me.* Musgrave wrote that in his diary.'

Libby felt a shiver at the nape of her neck. 'But he was saved.'

Tom nodded, his face thin and grey. 'He was, but the *Invercauld* wasn't so lucky. They went down on 14 May. Nineteen made it ashore, but when they were rescued just over a year later there were only three of them left. One of the crew was the great-grandfather of this author we took down. She came looking for her history one hundred and fifty years later.'

'Did she find it?'

'She found the old man's diary.' He looked sideways at her then. 'She spent a night on Enderby Island and when she woke up in the morning she saw nine men standing in the mist just watching her. They didn't speak, they just stood there looking, and they were wearing the kind of clothing seamen wore in the nineteenth century.' He paused. 'At first she had no idea what she was looking at: they were so still they looked like part of the mist. But then one of them moved, took a pace and stopped. Then, as she watched, they just vanished into the mist.'

EIGHTEEN

Libby and Tom checked into a motel in the centre of Invercargill, then headed down to Bluff Cove to see if the Korimako had docked yet. Tom drove past the new aluminium smelting works close to the harbour. A massive factory ship from Scandinavia was unloading and Libby stared at the height of the superstructure as they skirted warehouse buildings and covered dry docks where vessels of various shapes and sizes were being repainted. The Korimako was berthed alongside a high wooden jetty with loading bins built along the top. Libby could see Jonah on deck as they parked the truck and he waved at her.

The boat seemed to sit low, the hand-painted bell-birds on her bows close to the waterline, and Libby squinted, not quite understanding why she looked like she did.

Tom nudged her and smiled. 'The boat's not low, the wharf is high,' he said.

John-Cody came out of the wheelhouse on the starboard side and pinched the end of a roll-up. Libby watched: she had noticed he was smoking more than he had been of late. His face had a grey sallow quality that spoke of weariness entrenched rather than transient. Something about his general demeanour disturbed her: it had done since the meeting with Ned Pole.

'Hi,' she said, as she climbed on deck.

'Did everything go all right with Bree?'

'Just fine, thank you.'

John-Cody looked up at Tom. 'You got gear to bring aboard?'

Tom nodded. 'There's a fair bit, aye.'

'It's mostly my equipment,' Libby said.

'No worries: there's only the four of us. You can store what you want by the chart table, so long as the gangway is clear. The rest you can put in the for'ard cabins. Try and keep it on the floor or the bottom bunks, though. The weather's likely to be interesting when we get south.'

'Have you heard a long-range forecast?' Tom asked him.

John-Cody nodded. 'She's blowing nor'nor'east right now. It's going to stay that way for another twenty-four hours then gradually fade westerly. If we leave tomorrow morning we should be all right for the next thirty-six hours, which is how long it ought to take us.'

'That's good?' Libby asked.

'It's four hundred and sixty kilometres, Lib. At seven and a half knots thirty-six hours is very good.' John-Cody gripped one of the wooden wharf posts and hauled himself up to the dock. 'Let's have a look at this gear.'

Between the four of them they transported all the expensive equipment Libby had acquired over the years and stowed it on the deck of the *Korimako*. Then Jonah helped her put what she wanted in the for'ard cabins and she arranged the rest by the chart table.

Later that afternoon they moved the boat round the wharf and set the diesel pumps into the twin fuel tanks. They took over half an hour to fill and Libby watched the dials clicking round.

'Will that be enough?' she asked Tom.

'Plenty. Even if things turn nasty.' He smiled at her then. 'A successful Subs trip is all about preparation.'

John-Cody was poring over the chart table, scanning an expert eye over a sheet which showed the southern tip of New Zealand at 46 degrees and ran south beyond the Auckland and Campbell Islands to a latitude of 56 degrees. He had the way-points in his head and would enter them in the global positioning system as they got under way. Some skippers set just the one waypoint, but experience had told John-Cody to break it up. He and Tom had always used three: Bluff Leads, Reef Shelter Point and finally Port Ross. The GPS calculated the longitude and latitude and as long as they stuck pretty close to the rhumb-line they would get where they wanted to go.

The wind rocked the boat where she lay at her mooring: Libby came out of her cabin and steadied herself. She had brought her computer and it was set up on the table. John-Cody had shifted the chart to one side.

'Sorry. Am I getting in the way?'

'No,' he said. 'You're fine.'

She stood behind his stool and he was aware of the scent of her hair. Libby looked over his shoulder, very conscious of him: she could feel a tingling sensation in her limbs, a fluttering across her skin as if every sense was heightened, every pore alive to this man seated before her.

'That's where we're heading,' he told her, pointing, 'out of the Foveaux Straits and skirting Stewart Island. We keep the Snares well to starboard and run almost due south for Port Ross.'

'And it'll take us thirty-six hours?'

He nodded. 'We sleep in the motel tonight and sail with the morning tide.'

'Why not just stay on the boat?'

John-Cody smiled at her. 'Because my room's got a jacuzzi and a big bed. I need a lot of sleep, Lib. I might have to be up for the next thirty-six hours. You won't see me after seven this evening.'

'We'll all take our watches, though.'

'Of course, but she's my boat and I hear every sound she makes, which makes deep sleep a little difficult.'

He folded the chart away and helped her set up the equipment she might want to use on the way down.

'How's your seasickness?'

'I should be fine.'

'This can be a rough trip.'

'So I keep hearing.' She told him what Tom had told her.

'The *Invercauld*, huh, just one of many before they made decent engines.' He tapped the carpeted deck under their feet. 'Don't worry about getting ship-wrecked. That's not part of the agenda. The sea can be rough as hell, though. If it gets really bad I'll tell you to strap yourself in your bunk and stay there.'

That night Libby did not sleep well: the room was

comfortable, but there was a lot of traffic on the main road outside and she had been spoiled by the silence of Supper Cove. She tossed and turned and in the end she had to get up and make some tea. She thought of John-Cody asleep next door, the quietness of his mood. She wondered about his sudden decision to go south, a marvellous opportunity for her but surprising nonetheless. She was glad that Tom and Jonah were with them: Jonah always lightened the atmosphere and there was something about Tom that instilled confidence. She needed to sleep; there was much preparatory work to be done during the trip south. Before they got to where the dolphins were normally seen she wanted hydra-phones in the water in readiness. They had to be calibrated to the computer, and there was the underwater video camera she had considered using too. Libby knew only too well that seasickness and fatigue ran together and it was with this in mind that she finally fell asleep.

Tom woke her with a knock at the door, telling her that everyone was up and the owner of the motel was going to drive them to the docks. Breakfast would be taken on board and all Libby had to do was jump in the shower and throw her things in a bag.

As she dried her hair she could see Tom and Jonah in the car park outside and she was filled with a sudden sense of excitement. This was an adventure: at the end of it possibly a new pod of bottlenose dolphins and, if what John-Cody had said was correct, the tribe of southern right whales.

Downstairs she loaded her bag in the back of Tom's twin cab and hunched between Jonah and

John-Cody. Tom rode up front with the motel owner who would bring the truck back. There was an air of expectancy over everyone. Jonah was in a fine mood: he had never been to the Sub-Antarctic before and had the same feelings of anticipation as Libby. The two of them laughed and joked in the back seat. John-Cody sat next to them, eyes hooded, looking out on the world as it flashed by, acutely aware of the removal order stuffed in his back pocket.

At the boat they loaded the last of the gear and the stores, Jonah taking over the galley and putting away the dry goods and the stuff for the fridge. He handed Libby milk and bread and pastries to put in the freezer below deck. Jonah had secured the freezer bunk, telling Tom he was far too old to climb the one step it required to swing himself up at night. Tom took the library bunk opposite the diesel heater and his bags were laid on the floor with his wet-weather gear, which was ready to step into.

Ten minutes later John-Cody lifted the handset on the VHF. 'Bluff Radio, this is the *Korimako* requesting permission to leave the harbour. Do you copy?'

A woman's voice answered him. 'This is Bluff Radio. Switch to channel 14 please.'

'Going over, Mary.' He switched channels. 'Permission to leave the harbour?'

'As you go, Gib. We'll talk to you this evening.'

'Roger that. *Korimako* out.' He hung up the handset, switched to autopilot and turned on the GPS. Libby knelt on the seat facing the front windows and watched him setting the waypoints. He took his woollen seaman's cap from where it was housed over the compass and set it on his head.

'Now you really do look like a sea dog,' she told him.

He smiled briefly, stepped into his wet gear and slid open the port door. Moving along the rails, he made sure that the dive bottles were secure in their cage and then went port and starboard to check the aluminium weather shields they had fixed over the side windows. Tom was washing the deck down and he stuffed the hose through the scuppers, while John-Cody hauled on the sheet and unfurled the jib. Libby watched him, saw the sail unwrap itself from the drum on the luff spar and was reminded of Ned Pole's words. John-Cody worked quickly, secured the sheet on the winch and set the tack, which they should keep all the way south. Libby watched him through the blurred front windows: she watched Tom and imagined the two of them fishing together all those years ago.

Jonah was making bacon sandwiches, toasting them under the grill before the waves got too crashy and the galley was secured. He had already prepared a basket full of sandwiches and cold pizza: there was fruit in abundance and plenty of fresh water to drink. He sang Maori songs as he worked and gradually the roll became swollen under their feet and the waves lit up the prow as they headed for Stewart Island. Next stop the Sub-Antarctic, Libby thought, and if we're lucky a harbour full of whales.

Before they left Stewart Island behind the weather closed in, bruised and angry clouds dipping against the horizon west and east of them and ahead just the greyness of sky meeting sea. The swell lifted to three metres as they crossed the strait and Libby stood by the starboard door, shifting her weight from foot to foot with the barrel roll. John-Cody stood across the bridge from her, his arms folded, gazing ahead, cap set high on his head and the sleeves of his sweater rolled up to the elbow. His face was lined and had the same greyness in the skin she had seen yesterday.

'Are you OK, boss?' she asked him.

He glanced sideways at her. 'Fine. You?'

'Yes.'

'If you want to work, go ahead. Treat the chart table as your own.'

'Thanks. I'll stay up here for a bit.'

He went astern and sat inside the glasshouse to smoke a cigarette. Libby watched him and felt just a little bit queasy: she was not normally seasick, but this was a relatively small boat and they were entering water as rough as any she had seen. The sea was washing over the bowsprit now, flooding the white steel of the deck before draining through the scuppers. The boat pitched into deep and foaming troughs before lifting to punch holes in the following waves.

She went below and switched on her computer and within a few minutes the activity and focus settled her stomach. She felt the chill as the door was opened upstairs and she heard John-Cody ask Tom to light the heater. She brought up the noise evaluation program she had been running in Dusky Sound and knew she had nothing conclusive enough to stop Pole obtaining his water activity permit. She sat back on the plastic stool and rested her fists on her thighs. John-Cody descended the steps behind her and ducked into his cabin for a moment. He came out with a book and hooked the curtain back to stop the build-up of condensation, then he clipped back

411

the door to Libby's cabin for the same purpose. She swivelled round and looked at him, bending her head to see the cover of his book.

'Just some trash,' he said. 'Passes the time, though.' He looked beyond her to the computer screen. 'Still working on that then?'

She nodded. 'I'm not finding anything though. Well, I am, but not as quickly as we need to.'

'Pole.'

She nodded.

'I'm not holding my breath either.'

She looked out of half-closed eyes at him. 'That doesn't sound like you.'

He didn't say anything.

'Tell me if I'm wrong but I thought I heard a hint of resignation in your voice.'

'Realism, not resignation.'

'You don't think you'll win the hearing, do you?'

He made a face. 'I don't even know when the hearing is.'

He went upstairs where he spread himself on the bench seat behind the table and tried to bury himself in the cheap detective novel he had picked up in Invercargill. Jonah had the galley shut down, the gas turned off, and they were using the electric kettle to make tea and coffee. Tom was drinking tea-tree oil and hot water as it was supposed to calm the nerves: not that he suffered from them overly. He liked the taste when it was mixed with honey and what was good enough for Captain James Cook had always been good enough for him.

The day dragged on, hour after hour with the roll of the sea their constant companion. Libby came up top again and took her favoured position by the

412

starboard door, watching the ever-dimming line of the horizon through spray-spattered front windows already dulled by perspex. She looked sideways and saw a Gibson's wandering albatross riding the air currents in and out of the wave troughs. He was alone and he used no wing-beat as he disappeared and reappeared steering expertly on the wind, now close to the boat and, a matter of moments later, far in the distance.

The swell deepened as Stewart Island was left behind and the Southern Ocean current began to bite. John-Cody told her it didn't really kick in till they were south of the Snares, but this far east they could feel it. The wind was still from the north and hit them straight up the stern, causing the jib to luff so much John-Cody considered taking it in again, but just when he thought he would the breeze shifted and the sail billowed from head to clew.

He went below as darkness fell, and lay down in his cabin. They had agreed on two-hour watches, which gave them six hours' sleep at a time, and John-Cody closed his eyes and slept. That was rare, but he was taken by a weariness he had not felt since those first few days after Mahina died, and with Tom on board he felt easier about the boat. Tom was arguably a better skipper than he was though his Sub-Antarctic experience was not so great. He had sailed in many different seas, however, and was steeped in marine lore. He took the first watch.

Libby stood part of it with him; the saloon was dull with the side windows blocked out and the atmosphere rarefied with condensation. He told her of the time he had been fishing off Banks Peninsula when he saw a boat called the *Jailer* suddenly take definition in the mist. It was Friday 13 May and a bitterly cold day. He was on a trawler, the youngest member of a crew of seven, and he had been on watch when the boat appeared. They sailed by very close, too close, and he had not seen them come up on the radar, which had jarred his nerves to begin with. He rushed on deck and yelled at the hands he could see working, who seemed oblivious to the near collision. They ignored him and the boats steamed apart, then the *Jailer* was lost in the fog.

They hit port two weeks later and he sat drinking beer at the bar reading an old copy of the *Otago Times*. The drink stuck in his throat and the hairs crawled on his scalp when he read about the loss of the *Jailer*, sunk with all hands on Tuesday 10 May.

Libby was silent after that, watching Tom's eyes in their wrinkled pockets of flesh as he saw that ghost ship again.

'You always keep your eye on the radar at night,' he told her before she went below. 'And watch the horizon. It's dark out there, but the sky is a lighter grey than the sea. You watch the radar and the horizon. Open the door if you want to see better.'

Libby went down to her cabin, weary all at once after her semi-sleepless night and the constant wallowing of the boat. The diesel hummed in her head, its rhythm punctuated every now and again by the sound of waves slapping the steel hull. John-Cody's light was off and his head turned towards her. His eyes were closed and one naked arm hung over the edge of the bed; his jeans were crumpled on the floor together with his sweater and she could see his T-shirt at the shoulder. She stood a moment and watched him by the pale light from the bridge, the

414

edge of his bunk propped up by spare pillows as there were no straps on the double berths. His features looked ravaged and again she wondered about him: something had changed, but he hadn't said what it was and she didn't want to question him. She glanced at the chart table where his brief-case stood, securely closed; it was made of leather and very old, the sort of thing a college lecturer might carry. She looked down at him again and the light cast shadows on his face so she could no longer see his eyes and she was filled with the desire to cup that face in her hands and very gently kiss it.

Amazed at her feelings, she stepped into her cabin in sudden embarrassment: for all she knew, he had been watching her then. But he did not stir, and the only sounds she heard were those of the engine and the sea. Leaving her door hooked back, she peeled off her jeans and sat down on the bunk. The boat rolled harshly, almost tipping her onto the floor. The next thing she knew, John-Cody was up on the bridge wearing just his underpants and T-shirt. Libby moved to the bottom of the steps and heard Tom telling him that everything was fine; the current had shifted, that was all.

Libby watched the two men in silhouette against the for'ard windows. John-Cody was tall, stiff-backed, the muscles standing out in his legs. She found herself looking up and down those legs and again desire set her senses tingling. She went back to her bunk and was swinging her own naked legs under the duvet when John-Cody slid down the steps.

'Everything OK, Lib?' He paused, leaning in her doorway as she arranged the duvet around her.

'Yes.'

'You seasick?'

'No.'

'Good on you.'

She heard him climb back into his bunk and within seconds all was as it had been, nothing but the rumble of the engine and the hissed thrashing of the sea next to her head. Unlike his berth, she had her head to the stern, which had felt more comfortable. She had never tried to sleep with the sea crashing against the side, however, but to her surprise even the really violent swell was actually quite soothing. She found herself lying on her back and rolling from side to side, sometimes with such force that she rolled right over, but sleep crept up on her and her eyes closed with the darkness and the next thing she knew John-Cody was shaking her awake.

'On deck, seaman: your watch.' He disappeared above and Libby sat up, rubbed her eyes and looked at the luminous hands on her watch. It was midnight: she'd had four hours' sleep. Tom would have finished his watch at ten and John-Cody would have taken his from ten until now. She was due to wake Jonah at two and then sleep until eight. She pivoted with one foot on the floor and one on the wall to John-Cody's cabin, feeding a sweater over her head.

All was quiet in the saloon, the only lights the one over the stove and the flickering green from the radar. By the starboard door the GPS glowed in dull white lines like the wash from the palest moon.

John-Cody splashed boiling water into two mugs and passed her a cup of tea, which she almost spilled as the boat suddenly shifted.

'Cram it into that space between the radar and the autopilot.' John-Cody pointed to where he normally placed his own mug. 'I'm going below,' he said. 'All you need to do is keep an eye on things.' He tapped the radar. 'This is set in eighth-of-a-mile rings so you'll have plenty of warning of other vessels.'

'What about rocks?'

'There are no rocks between here and Port Ross. The sea's a hundred and fifty metres deep; it'll drop to six hundred and fifty when we cross the continental shelf.' He pointed to the revs and the temperature gauge. 'Dead easy,' he said. 'She stays just below forty degrees and the revs are at nine fifty. Don't touch the throttle unless you have to. If the revs drop even by one I'll be up here. If you have to wake me, come down and call. Don't shake me. OK?'

Libby nodded. 'What about our position?'

He led her across the bridge to the GPS and indicated the rhumb-line. 'Don't let her drift more than half a mile either side. The wind and current combination will knock her off course now and again, so keep an eye on things. If you need to alter course, use the autopilot.' He showed her the three settings, auto, power steering and compass. 'She's fine as she goes right now, but tweak her if you have to.' He smiled at her then. 'Can you handle that?'

'I think so.'

'Good girl.' He took tobacco from his pocket. 'I'm going to hang out the leeward door for a smoke. She's your boat.'

As soon as he said that Libby concentrated. She checked the dials and the radar, then their position on the rhumb-line and stepped back to the radar again. The wind was coming across the starboard quarter nor'west now and John-Cody smoked his cigarette out of the port door. He stood with his back to her and the wind rushed in his hair, spray licking round his feet from waves which had fallen below three metres for the first time. Libby peered up at the sky and saw stars between the clouds: the greyness of the afternoon had threatened storms, but thankfully they hadn't materialized. The last thing she needed with such tiredness in her limbs was standing watch while waves swamped the deck.

John-Cody came back inside and checked to make sure she was all right before disappearing down to his bunk. Libby had hoped he might stay with her, but he didn't. Whether it was fatigue or just a further indication of his distance she couldn't say. But as soon as he was gone a strange sense of loneliness overtook her and she stared at the bow lights, where waves soaked the prow and chain locker, shattering like spurs of diamonds in the sudden incandescence.

She put the skipper's stool down and sat for a while, but could not see over the dashboard. It was more comfortable to stand up and lean against the back of the seat behind her. The quartz clock was set on the wall to her left along with the barometer, which indicated a change of pressure and rain in the air. Libby listened to the hiss and crackle through the otherwise silent radio speakers. The wheelhouse creaked and groaned, wood and metal and plastic all moving under the alternating pressure on the hull. Jonah and Tom were asleep up for'ard. Libby ducked her head to look down the steps and she saw the diesel heater was still and cold and the loneliness came upon her again.

A massive wave hit as the *Korimako* dipped into the chasm of a trough and spray thundered across the bows. Libby was thrown against the dash so hard she had to grip the edge and she felt sure John-Cody would be standing next to her any moment. He didn't appear though, and she smiled to herself as she figured that crashing waves must be in his repertoire of acceptable changes in the boat's behaviour. She stood and braced herself but they rode the next one and she settled back into what Tom called the Southern Ocean roll, one leg bent, one leg straight, alternating as the swell threw them from port to starboard. She was aware of a weight in her gut that she associated with seasickness, but she didn't actually feel nauseous and over time the responsibility of keeping watch alone was enough to banish the feeling.

For two hours she shifted along the bridge like a crab, moving from radar to temperature gauge to rev counter, then across the gangway to the GPS. John-Cody had two of them: one doubled as a depth sounder for work in the fiords, but only one was switched on at a time. Caution and safety were his watchwords. There were two of everything, including the single-side-band radios mounted over the chart table, and three separate mast antennae above the deck. The chances of their being out of communication for very long were remote. That gave her comfort. Earlier she had spoken to Bree, who was at the office, and they had fixed on four thirty each day as the time to speak.

Libby made herself some tea and risked half a smoke on the leeward side, but still got covered with spray. The doors were stiff from the salt and she vowed she would follow John-Cody's example and lubricate the runners with washing-up liquid in the morning. She was due to wake Jonah at two, but he came up the steps of his own accord, his hair untied and his dark face pinched with sleep. 'Cup of tea,' he said to her and made a beeline for the kettle. 'Anything happening?'

'Nothing.'

'That's the way I like it.' He took a sandwich from the basket, stripped off the polythene and ate it in two bites before taking another. He bit into an apple at the same time and crunched and chewed in unison. He told Libby that she could go below again now, but she was not sleepy yet and fancied some company. The boat, she had discovered, could be a lonely place despite its size and the proximity of one person to another. It was partly to do with the incessant hum of the engines, which made you feel isolated when you were below decks. So she stood some of the watch with Jonah and her mood brightened as he put music on low and cracked the odd joke.

He told her about his life, how he had grown up shifting all round the South Island with his parents and elder sister. His father had held all manner of jobs, from fisherman to tradesman to travelling salesman and Central Otago miner. They had lived part of the time where the old man lived now, in the tiny borough of Naseby. He recalled Sundays when all the pubs were shut save the one at Danseys Pass, and how the people of Naseby travelled the twenty miles or so of dirt road for a lunchtime session. If the police came the people in the last house they passed would phone the pub, which gave everyone enough time to leave and to bolt the doors. While their parents were busy socializing with their friends, he, Mahina and the other children would be left to their own devices. The pass was walled with hills and gulches, a river running through the middle of it. In summer they splashed in the water and played hide-and-seek in the bush to keep out of the heat. In winter they brought home-made sleds and ran the gauntlet of rock and tree stump and sheer drops on the hillside.

He talked with a fondness for his childhood that Libby couldn't remember. Hers had been much like Bree's, being hauled round the world with her parents. She was seven years younger than her nearest sibling and had been used to her own company before she went to boarding school. She ran away three times, till her father read her the riot act and told her that unless she knuckled down to work, he would disown her as soon as she reached sixteen. For some reason that had penetrated where other threats had failed and Libby buried herself in work. She ended up taking and passing her 'A' levels two years before everyone else.

Jonah told her that even at a really young age Mahina could name the birds from their calls, the trees from their seeds and the flowers from their scent. As soon as she was old enough to pilot a dinghy she persuaded Southland Tours to ship it into Deep Cove, where she had an agreement to tie up with the fishermen. He smiled broadly at the memory. 'She was good at things like that, getting what she wanted.'

Libby looked up at the calm presence of memory on his face. 'You've got over her death,' she said. 'You talk with fondness and love.'

'That's how I remember her.' Jonah leaned on his elbows and smiled through the gloom at her. 'Mahina's gone, Libby. She left the day John-Cody scattered her ashes.' His eyes shone then. 'In a rush she would have dived, down into the depths, swimming with the dolphins for a while then out to sea and the north. She wouldn't have rested till she came to Rerenga Wairua, the most northern point of Aotearoa, which the pakeha calls Cape Reinga. The place is Tapu to all the native peoples and she would have rested there: one last look south and then gone, climbing down the promontory and into the world of our ancestors.' He paused and a light burned in the back of his eyes. 'She wanted to be allowed to go, to forget and not look back. Now, she doesn't remember. We're not even a fleeting memory. She's gone, lost to this world and dancing her way through the next.' His features darkened then and he glanced over his shoulder at the steps aft. 'Unless Gib hasn't let her go yet.'

Libby felt suddenly troubled. 'You mean he might trap her here?'

'Crowding his thoughts with her. Yes, it might trap her. She loved him so much. It might hold her back. That's why she gave him the year to get over her, enough time to let go and get on with his life. That man has so much to do. He knows so much more than anyone else; that's why he was left behind. In the end he knew more about this place than Mahina did herself.'

'About Fiordland?'

'Not just Fiordland, Aotearoa, all that is Tapu, the soul of things.' He shook his head. 'It's been awful watching him this last year. That's why I spent so much time up in Naseby. I thought the worst would come when he let her go. I thought he might fall apart then without his promise to hold him together.' He gestured across the galley. 'But then you and Bree came over and he was different.'

'Until now.'

Jonah nodded. 'Yeah, until now. What happened, Lib? He's worse than I've ever seen him.'

'I don't know what happened.' Libby shook her shoulders. 'He had a meeting with Ned Pole and then went over the hill for a week. When he came back he went to Dunedin and then this trip was suddenly on.'

'What did he do in Dunedin?'

She shook her head. 'I don't know, Jonah.'

John-Cody lay in his bunk, aware of the murmur of conversation coming from the bridge. The illuminated hands of his watch told him that Jonah was on watch now but Libby hadn't yet come down to her cabin. He lay on his back, his eyes on the pattern thrown by the curtain on the ceiling. The diesel sound was so familiar he normally never heard it and the rushing of the sea was ingrained in his veins. Yet tonight he heard it all, the slow hum, the rumble of water on steel. It resonated through his head as if just to remind him, to plague his memory and chew at his emotions. He was going to the place of desolation and solitude, where the dawn chorus resounded with the myriad voices that Fiordland once had echoed. He was going where southern right whales courted one another, where they mated and gave birth. He was going where Hooker sea lions commanded the beach and the albatross the sky. He was going where a history of man and the sea grew up like nowhere else, where one had battled the other and often perished trying.

He should be contented. All was familiar, yet he didn't feel contented; he felt alone and lost and confusion stalked his mind like a restless unwelcome guest. He tried so hard to think of Mahina: since this new situation reared its head he had done nothing but focus on Mahina. She was his past, his link to everything they would take from him. But she was dim now, dimmer than she had ever been, and that feeling disturbed him more than any other.

He lay there trying to think about her, trying to recall lost moments of love, the passion between them, but Libby crowded his mind. He had sensed her earlier, lying so warm and close in the berth just a pace away. He thought of her then like he had before, in the homestay when he imagined her naked under the shower. He thought of her when he'd sneaked a glance as she dried off in front of the heater or came out of the aft shower with a towel covering her breasts. Shoulder, arm, thigh, glimpses of nakedness that set something moving in him he thought he would never feel again. In twenty-five years he had never once thought of being with another woman. They had been so complete, he and Mahina, so utterly drawn to each other that the thought of another woman's body, another woman's scent, was anathema. But now, even with all this hanging over his head, he found himself drawn to Libby physically: he wanted to sit near her, stand near her, watch her, bathe in her aroma when she occupied his air space. He was conscious of the movement of her mouth when she spoke, the animated gestures with hand and arm as she articulated one thought or another. He watched the line of her nose, the smooth beauty in her cheeks, the way her neck arced into clavicle. During the summer he had found himself appreciating the strength in her limbs, the line of muscle in hamstring and calf. He listened when she spoke, recognizing the same authority with which Mahina had spoken.

Shivers had run the length of his spine when he listened to her talking of Supper Cove at night and the whisper of the Tuheru in the darkness. Never in his life had he heard them or imagined he had, but Mahina spoke of them all the time and here was matter-of-fact Liberty Bass replicating what she said without knowing she had said it. He thought of the way she had moved barefoot in the bush that time on Sealers Beach, the way the dolphins accepted her almost as one of their own. The parallels were scary: he had no idea whether they were real or whether he was just seeing them because he wanted to. Did he want Mahina back in the form of another? Was that what this was about? Did it matter? How could it matter? But if it didn't matter then why was he going through this pain, allowing these thoughts to course in his head like a river that had burst its banks?

He heard her coming down the steps and he wondered for a second if she would pause and gaze at him as she had done before. Her back had been to the light and he had not been able to see her eyes and felt sure she could not see his: she wouldn't stare so openly without speaking if she could. There had been a silent beauty in that moment. He thought about what Alex had said to him about Libby, how it was a girl thing to recognize when he had been oblivious. He had watched her more carefully after that and had seen nothing to change his initial opinion until she stood and gazed at him tonight.

She came down the steps now and glanced in his direction, but this time she didn't pause and he could hear Jonah moving about on the bridge. Libby went next door and he sat up to listen as she undressed, but the engine thundered in his ears and he heard nothing else. But he counted the seconds, imagining the time it took to wriggle out of jeans, socks and T-shirt and slip into the comfort of that bunk. He lay back against the pillow, throat suddenly dry and amazed at himself.

NINETEEN

John-Cody took over the watch at six and Tom went back to his bunk. At seven Libby stirred and, wrapping herself in her dressing gown, she climbed the aft steps and found him sitting at the table drinking coffee. The boat dipped and rose against the horizon and the swell kept the sideways motion even, but the sea was not rough and Libby had found her sea legs.

'Morning,' she said.

'Morning. The coffee's still hot if you want some.'

She poured herself a cup and reached down into the cold store for some milk.

John-Cody had a bilge pump switch in bits on the table before him. Libby held the coffee mug to her breast and stood by the starboard door.

'You like it there, don't you?' John-Cody said to her.

She looked round. 'It seems like a good place to stand and I get to keep my balance.'

He came and stood next to her. 'You didn't need to get up. Tom and Jonah won't be about for a while yet.'

'I was awake.' Libby flicked the hair back from her face. 'How far away are we now?'

'Fourteen, fifteen hours or so.'

'Will the weather hold?'

He leaned on the dashboard and peered at the horizon. The light was growing and the sky remained clear. 'It should do. But you never know down here. The closer we get to Port Ross the worse it will be. The currents have a habit of running opposite to the wind, which makes for interesting seas. Storms can blow up really quickly.' He smiled again. 'But we'll be fine once we're actually in Port Ross.'

'Do you think the whales will be there?'

'They'll certainly be on their way. We might bump into one or two as we go south.'

'And dolphins?'

He made a face. 'You never can tell with the dolphins. I'll let you know when we reach the area where I generally see them.'

He poured more coffee, crossed to the business side of the bridge and glanced at the autopilot, then moved it a few degrees to port with the changes in the current. Libby watched him, noting the cat-like balance in his movements. He was at home in his domain; this was his turf and he was more comfortable here than anywhere else. She imagined him being calm in the foulest, most treacherous weather. She realized then just how safe she felt. There was a sense of security that was not just about his being skipper of this boat. It was strange to contemplate: she had not thought much about security in the past; it was not something she had felt she needed, having lived pretty much hand-to-mouth for as long as she could remember.

428

An hour later the radio crackled and she heard Bree's voice through the speakers.

'*Korimako, Korimako, Korimako*. This is the *Kori*-base. Do you copy, Captain?'

Libby glanced at John-Cody. He was smiling but his eyes were tight at the corners. He went down to the chart table and picked up the transmitter. 'Reading you loud and clear, Bree. How are you?'

'Good, thanks.'

'You sound like a Kiwi, love.' He chuckled to himself. 'You've obviously been hanging out with Hunter too long.'

'I could never do that. What time is it there?'

'Same as it is with you. Are you waiting for the bus?'

'Yes. Where are you?'

'Fourteen hours north of the Auckland Islands.'

'Wow. You'll be there tonight then?'

John-Cody looked at his watch. 'Yep, we should drop the old flounder bomb at about nine o'clock.'

'You mean the anchor, the old Bruce.'

He laughed again and he said he missed her. 'I'll get your mum. Stand by.'

He handed the transmitter to Libby and went back to the bridge. The jib was luffing badly so he clambered into his wet gear and slid open the port door. The deck was slippery, washed by the sea with each belly roll in the troughs. John-Cody bent to the winch and checked the tension in the sheet. The wind howled in his ears, the chill chewing his flesh and the engine vibrating through the deck at his feet. He loosened the sheet a fraction: the wind kicked out the luff and the sail billowed full. He glanced at the sky and thought about running up the mizzen, but he would need Jonah for that. It could wait. He stood up and crabbed his way across the rolling deck to the chain locker where the claw was rattling. He stowed it behind the winch wheel and made it fast.

Then he stood up and the wind was in his hair and the spray licked his face as the boat plunged into another trough. Waves broke over his boots and washed the length of the deck. He stood for a long moment staring ahead and feeling suddenly very alive: he could taste the salt in the air. He could smell the special scent of the sea, more than just salt – the richness of it, the depth, the moisture and the cold, indescribable in any exact terms. A cry to the port bow made him look up, both hands gripping the pulpit rail, and he saw a black-browed mollymawk bank into the wind like an aircraft turning sharply. The bird descended low to the waves, dipping in and out of the troughs, then lifted close to the bows and soared over John-Cody's head. He stood and watched and marvelled at its perfect dynamic flight and its ability to use the differing wind speeds to carry it. The bird could stay in the air for five thousand kilometres and still gain enough weight to feed a chick.

He faced the horizon again. Their course was due south till land was in sight, then a fraction east – they would need to skirt the squalls that raged along the North East Cape. That was ages away yet though, another full day's sailing.

A whale blew off the starboard bow and he looked round to see if Libby was watching; he saw her standing in the doorway, holding on to the rail. He turned again as the whale blew a second time: two separate streams of air expelled fifteen feet above the waves in a distinctive V shape. The whale rolled in the water, the waves breaking over its back in blue and green and whitened foam like surf thrashing rocks on a beach.

Libby joined him, pulling her jacket around her, picking her way across the middle of the deck. The boat bucked and rolled and John-Cody held out a hand for her, clasped her fingers and drew her to him as she stepped over the chain locker.

'A southern right,' she yelled. 'V-shaped blow.'

He nodded. All baleen whales had two blowholes as opposed to the single one of the dolphins. But the right whales and their cousin the bowhead were slow-moving and the twin blow came up as distinctive streams, whereas the rorquals, blue, fin and sei, tended to blow in a single coalesced stream. The V-shaped blow was how you identified a southern right from a distance. Together Libby and John-Cody watched as the whale dived, then a few minutes later surfaced again, blowing harder this time. Libby thought about the power in those great breaths. The whale replaced 90 per cent of the air in its lungs during respiration; humans used only 13 per cent. She turned to John-Cody and tugged her hair back where it was whipping about her face.

'You know, every time I see a whale I always think the same thing,' she said. 'I can't help remembering they once lived on land.'

John-Cody made a face. 'Maybe when we've messed things up completely we'll evolve the same way.'

He stayed on deck when she went back inside. He lit a cigarette, cupping his hands round his petrol lighter against the wind. He remembered the last

431

time he had seen a southern right whale in the open ocean, when he and Mahina came south with a film crew who were making a documentary about the town of Hardwicke at Erebus Cove. The town that never was, Hardwicke had been a whaling settlement designed to hunt the very creatures that now returned to spawn in safety one hundred and fifty years later. For four hours they had watched a pair of southern rights courting just north of Port Ross. Later when the crew was filming in Davis Bay the two of them had wandered beyond the boat shed and the World War II depot, where the lookouts were posted, to the cemetery. There they had stood in the rushing of the wind to remember all those who had died trying in vain to tame the islands.

He pinched out his cigarette and put the butt in his pocket, then he turned to go back inside and saw Mahina at the port door leeward of the wind. He stood for a moment, the shock standing out on his face. Then he realized it wasn't Mahina but Libby.

Inside with the door closed the wind was quieter and the constant hum of the engines took over. It was almost eight o'clock now and John-Cody could hear Jonah below decks. Libby had gone to take a shower and he glimpsed her as she stepped out of her cabin with a towel wrapped around her. For a moment just now he had been unnerved, mistaking her for Mahina like that. And all at once a terrible thought struck him. What if he hadn't let Mahina go? She had stayed to watch over him for a year, so much longer than she should have, but after that he had to let her go: that was their agreement. What if he'd broken that agreement? What if he still held her – a

432

prisoner between two worlds, unable to enter either?

That thought was still with him as he sat at the chart table checking by radio for other vessels in the area, when Libby came out of the shower. He could raise no-one locally, but Bluff Harbour told him the *Moeraki* was heading south in the next twenty-four hours. Libby clipped the door back and he turned and saw her, wrapped in the bath towel, hair wet and her skin crimson from the heat of the water. Her shins were smooth and her tiny feet arched like a ballet dancer's. She rubbed moisture off her nose and sniffed the smell of cooking in the air.

'Jonah's making breakfast,' John-Cody said. 'How does bacon and eggs sound?'

'Wonderful. I could eat a horse.' She went into her cabin and he turned back to the charts. She sat on the edge of her bunk, one foot against the wall to keep her balance, and rubbed at her hair with the towel.

'Thank you for all you've done for Bree,' she said suddenly.

'That's OK.' John-Cody swivelled round on the stool and caught sight of the underside of her thigh where her foot was raised to the wall.

'She loves being with you.'

'She prefers Hunter.'

'That's different, John-Cody. You know what I mean.' Libby blew out her cheeks. 'I still feel so bad about those letters. God knows how long she's been writing.'

'Don't feel bad.' John-Cody stood up. 'I told you before, Lib. We make our choices, stand by them and do the best we can. You love Bree. That's obvious to anyone. You've done the best you could for her.

433

Besides, maybe writing the letters like that was actually good for her: maybe it helped her deal with stuff. It's upsetting for you, I can see, but I don't think it does any harm.'

'You really think that?' Libby looked troubled, disturbed, and the disturbance was in her soul, echoing perhaps his own. 'There's lots of stuff I'd like to have done differently.' She sat back so the towel fell a little lower, exposing the swollen tops of her breasts.

'We can all say that. We do what we do, Lib. We just do what we do.'

He lifted the top of the chart table and cursed lightly under his breath. Libby got up and came over.

'What is it?' She leaned next to him, keeping the towel in place with her free hand.

John-Cody was holding a rubber-encased compass with the needle spinning wildly. He shook his head. 'I meant to replace this. I even laid it out the last time I was on board.' He sucked breath. 'That's what comes of walking round with your head stuck up your ass.'

Libby wanted to ask him what he meant, ask him about his mood, this new and terrible silence that had come over him. But he tossed the useless compass aside and climbed the steps to the bridge.

The dolphins were not where John-Cody had hoped they would be. He, Tom and Libby all scanned different parts of the horizon but couldn't spot them. The waves were too high to see them blow, and they were relying on sighting the animals themselves. But they didn't and Libby was filled with a sense of disappointment, which was odd considering her

434

background and her knowledge that there was nothing as unpredictable as a marine mammal. She was quiet for a while and went below to consider what implications this new situation had, if any, for her research.

An hour later John-Cody called her back to the bridge and pointed through the for'ard windows. Libby stood and stared and the excitement bubbled again in her breast. The day was dying slowly and black clouds pressed the horizon, jagged at the edges and heavy with threatened rain: but the rays of sun still burned, cascading in ribbons of frayed light. Three huge rocks thrust skyward from the ocean and beyond them she saw the broken height of a coast-line.

'That's the northern coast of the Auckland Islands,' John-Cody said. 'Welcome to the Sub-Antarctic.'

The darkness gathered now and Libby felt the swell shifting again under their feet. John-Cody was watchful, moving between GPS and radar like a leopard pacing a cage. The clouds unleashed their rain, which fell at an angle of forty-five degrees, buffeted and blistered by the wind, rattling over the *Korimako* like firecrackers. Jonah battened down the hatches in the galley and he and Tom brought in the jib, their wet-weather gear running with water when they came back inside. Libby took both sets down to the engine room and hung them up on the line. Behind her the massive Gardner engine thundered on relentlessly. She could smell diesel and oil and salt mixed in a cocktail that made her feel suddenly nauseous.

Back on the bridge John-Cody was steering east of the north coast, where fur seals bred at Three Cave Bay and shags nested south of the North East Cape. Libby opened the starboard door a fraction and could hear the booming of the waves as they rolled in breakers twenty feet high to crash against the crags and send columns of water racing vertically up the cliff face. The sea boiled white and grey and yellow as black ridges of rock sharp as serrated knives broke open the waves. John-Cody moved behind her, almost touching her; she could feel the warmth of his breath on her neck.

'Powerful, isn't it?'

'Incredible.'

'The *Derry Castle* was wrecked on the northern reef in 1887. There were twenty-two crew members and one passenger and they all went into the sea.' His voice was deep but soft in her ear. 'Fifteen of them drowned.'

Libby shivered and closed the door again. 'I tell you what,' she said. 'Why don't you just get us into Port Ross?'

He did, steering the *Korimako* east and south of the currents that plagued Pebble Point, and in darkness they entered the natural harbour between Enderby and Ewing Islands. In the lee of Enderby the sea grew calmer; the wind still howled but they were moving into sheltered waters and Libby felt the Southern Ocean roll fading under her feet.

They anchored in Sandy Bay, lying short of the swathes of bladder kelp that grew a metre a day, and Jonah fired up the gas stove. 'Who's for mutton stew?' He placed a pot he had cooked ashore on the work surface and prised off the lid. Libby sniffed and smiled.

436

'It smells good even when it's cold.'

'That's because it is good, Libby, especially when it's cooked the way I do it' – he winked at her, a glint in the black of his eye – 'with roasted kumara on the side.'

'Sounds even better.' Both Libby and Bree had acquired a real taste for the Maori sweet potato since they had been in New Zealand.

She opened a bottle of chilled Montana Chardonnay and poured four large glasses, then put another bottle in the cooler. She called John-Cody and Tom up from where they were checking the engine and they drank a toast to the safe passage south. The main engine was off, only the auxiliary running. Libby swallowed wine. Then she heard a rumbling noise, long and drawn out, burred at the edges, a sound that was almost vibration. 'That's a southern right whale,' she said.

They went on deck wrapped up against the winter night; rain clouds hid the stars and the water was coal black. The mountains lifted in grey shadows above Sandy Bay and Libby heard the bark of Hooker sea lions on the beach.

Water shifted behind them and they crossed to the other quarter where a great dark shape lifted like a bank of oiled mud from the sea. Black and shiny with running water, the great whale rolled on its side and slapped the surface with a shovel-like flipper ten feet long. They were soaked. Libby stepped back, caught her breath then looked down again as the whale lifted its head and she could see the paler colour of the callosities that covered its jaw like barnacles. They heard the weighted rubber-like explosion of sound as another whale blew some

437

distance from the boat. 'It seems they're already here in numbers,' John-Cody said.

The whales were early; it was only May and the majority would linger till almost November, mating in groups, the males fighting for the continued path of their genes, coupling with a female en masse, one set of sperm displacing that of her previous lover. The pregnant cows would give birth throughout the period, and as spring shook off the ghosts of winter they would leave the harbour on their migratory path north.

Libby lay in her bunk that night and listened to the whales in the water, roars and grunts and vibrating sounds so deep they rattled the hull. It was nothing like the song of the humpback; these whales communicated at a much lower frequency and could send sound many miles through the ocean. They did not echolocate like dolphins, but it was generally accepted they used their low-frequency pulses to navigate great distances.

The southern rights were a gentle race, inquisitive and slow-moving, preferring shallow water, which had almost been their downfall. The Basques hunted the northern breed to virtual extinction during the Middle Ages. The same had occurred with the whales here in the Southern Ocean. Libby knew from previous research that many New Zealand scientists believed these whales were the descendants of those driven to the very brink back in the nineteenth century. Their colouring was different: they had a greater area of white or grey skin, and were more mottled on the underside of their bellies. That would be a sign of inbreeding, which was bound to occur if their numbers had been vastly reduced. There were only a couple of thousand of them left in the entire ocean. Tomorrow, if it was possible, she planned to dive with some of them.

John-Cody woke in the night. The wind had dropped to a whisper and perhaps it was the sudden stillness that disturbed him. He got out of bed and pulled on his clothes, then made his way up the steps in darkness. The clouds had rolled back and moonlight illuminated the wheelhouse on all sides. As soon as they dropped anchor he and Tom had unfastened the aluminium shutters to relieve the feeling of claustrophobia that developed on any voyage south. He stood a moment to gather his thoughts, listening to the huge variety of sounds the whales were making outside.

Feeling in his pocket for tobacco, he made himself a cigarette then stepped on deck to smoke it. There was a chill in the air, but nothing compared to the ice when the wind was blowing, which it usually did: in fact he could not recall such a calm night in the Sub-Antarctic. He moved to the bows and leaned on the rail and made out the dulled shapes of sea lions on the beach beyond the kelp. Another whale called from behind him and the sound was eerie, ringing out in heavy discordant chimes against the night. He thought then of the shipwrecked sailors, ancient colleagues who had been lucky enough to make it ashore when their vessels foundered. He thought of those who had not been so lucky and were taken by the sea or dashed against rocks till the life was beaten out of them. He thought of the Moriori Maori who had survived on these islands for almost fourteen years, the longest anyone had lived down here. But even they left in the end and it was a fact that nobody had ever tamed the islands; perhaps that was why he and Mahina had loved them so much.

The whalers didn't last, neither did the sealers, but they left only when they had savaged the respective populations almost to nothing. Charles Enderby's town of Hardwicke lasted only three bitter years and was abandoned in 1852. Now the islands were abandoned to the giant megaherbs, the tangled forests of rata and the wildlife, which thrived in abundance unhindered by man.

John-Cody paced his boat, moving quietly in his soft-soled shoes so as not to disturb the three sleepers beneath him. From bow to stern along both quarters he checked the ropes, the sail sheets, the lifebelts and the dive locker. He stood resting against the glasshouse and smoked his cigarette, then cupped his hand to the fresh-water barrel and drank. Again a bull called from the depths and the sound reverberated in his soul. He looked up into the night where the blackened firmament rang with a million stars. He got his bearings and located the ones he knew: Lyra and Vega, Aquila; the constellation of Hercules almost due north, Corona Borealis to the west and Serpens Caput west again. Silently he trusted that Tom knew them as well as he did, then he went below deck.

Libby lay awake in her bunk. She had heard John-Cody moving about earlier as if he was troubled by dreams, tossing and turning in the bunk next door. When he got up she could see him through her open door, silhouetted by the moon at the top of the steps. She had wanted to get up too, but didn't. Quite why, she was not sure: she heard him go on deck and she lay there deliberating. He was gone only ten minutes then he was back in his bunk with his reading light still switched on.

Libby rolled on her side and tried to sleep. But sleep wouldn't come. Her head was crammed with emotions, disparate thoughts that cluttered her mind till it hurt. She thought about Bree and the two of them being in New Zealand, she thought about Nehemiah Pole and Dusky Sound and the difference in John-Cody since that day he had gone to meet him. There was a terrible distance in his eyes, as if he was there on the boat with them and at the same time somewhere else. The fun had gone out of him, as if he was right back where he had been when she and Bree first arrived. Why was she so bothered about it? Her concern was Dusky Sound and the reality that a resident pod dwelt there and what might happen to them.

But John-Cody crowded her thoughts: he had done for a while, at home, when she was alone in Dusky and here and now on this boat. She sat up and watched the light from his cabin still creeping across the chart-room floor. Slipping out of bed she went to the toilet and when she came out she saw him lying on his back, his face still and closed, sleeping the sleep of the dead.

TWENTY

That first morning Libby was on deck as soon as it got light. The cloud drifted low and purple with thunderheads, the wind skating the surface of Port Ross. It lifted in foaming caps of white and whipped the tangled mass of rata where the tree trunks grew only so high and then bent at right angles. The branches massed together, forming a web of foliage that scarred the flanks of Enderby Island. She could hear a thousand birds, the combined weight of their song piercing the wind with a strangely mournful timbre. John-Cody moved next to her.

'What birds live down here apart from albatross and mollymawk?' she asked him.

'There's flightless teal on Adams Island. That's found nowhere else.' He smiled. 'It's a duck though. Those you can hear over the wind are bellbirds, and at night you'll hear white-headed petrel. The New Zealand falcon preys on them both. *They*'re pretty tough little guys. They've been known to have a go at people if their nests are disturbed.'

Across the bay a whale breached. They both watched as it came high out of the water then landed on its side, smashing into the surface with a sound

442

like glass shattering. Libby narrowed her eyes: the whale was much lighter in colour than most southern rights she had seen. Its back was a powder blue/grey with ivory patches in places. It rolled, flippers out of the water, and showed them the mottled cream of its belly.

'Moby Dick,' John-Cody said.

Libby stared. 'You've seen him before?'

'Oh yes, every time I've been down here. He's always one of the first to arrive.'

Libby looked again at the huge pale creature breaking the waves by the boat. 'The white whale,' she murmured.

He smiled, leaning on the rail with his hands clasped together. 'Not white, but as close as I've seen in a southern right.'

They watched as another whale joined Moby Dick, slightly smaller and much darker in colour. The pair swam slowly towards the boat, keen to investigate this new arrival in the harbour. Libby felt her excitement building. She had been in the company of whales many times before, but the feeling was always the same: an almost childlike sense of expectancy. She and John-Cody stood side by side at the rail as the pair came closer, massive, rolling together so the water sloshed against their hides, sending out a wake big enough to rock the *Korimako*. Moby Dick lifted a great flipper and slapped the water again, then he eased himself closer and caressed the back of the other whale, which Libby assumed was female. Gently Moby stroked her and they heard the low grunting and a higher-pitched calling, catlike almost in quality.

The two vast mammals moved with incredible

grace till they were right up to the boat. Libby could make out the callosities, white and fibrous like drying battery acid, tattoos almost, round the huge shovel-shaped lower jaw. The female lifted her head, a quarter the length of her body, spy-hopping beside the boat. Her jaw was very black and she had four round callosities running back along her skull. With a low guttural moan she sank beneath the surface and turned her flukes to brush the hull so the boat bobbed like a top. Moby Dick followed her and they swam together before she dived deep. He lob-tailed for a moment, just his great grey flukes visible against the backdrop of Sandy Bay, then they too disappeared beneath the surface: and Libby watched, the image of his caress, so vast and yet so gentle, imprinted on her mind.

After breakfast they went back on deck and saw Moby Dick breach close to them once again. He was alone this time and playing, slapping the water with his flippers, then whacking his flukes with such force the deck was showered with spray. The wind had died a little but the cloud was still low and grey, curling like wisps of smoke against the hills.

Moby Dick approached the boat and Libby lifted the lid on the dive locker where she had stowed her drysuit. John-Cody watched through the galley window for a moment then he went on deck.

'You can't dive alone, Lib.'

'Then come with me.' She already had her jacket off and was laying out her under-suit. He hesitated. He had intended to dive, but not quite yet and not with Libby.

'You've dived here before, haven't you?' she said.

444

He nodded. 'In a seven-mil wetsuit: it was bloody freezing.'

She laughed. 'You're a tough guy and we won't be in for long. I've got underwater video gear, John-Cody. This is a great opportunity.'

'DoC doesn't allow you to swim with the whales.'

She wagged her head at him. 'DoC isn't here. Besides, I work for DoC, remember?'

She pulled down her jeans, revealing white knickers and brown legs, sitting back on the top of the locker to ease the jeans over her ankles. He gazed at the smoothness of her thighs and she felt that gaze and goose pimples that were nothing to do with the cold lifted on her skin. It was as if his eyes physically stroked her, caressed her as Moby Dick had caressed the female he courted. She folded the jeans and stood up and John-Cody found himself staring at the apple cheeks of her bottom. The muscles stood out against the skin of her legs and she worked her fleece over her head and stood there in T-shirt and knickers, her nipples suddenly hard against the flimsy material.

'Are you going to get changed or just stand there gawping?'

John-Cody flushed red. 'Sorry. I didn't mean . . .'

'It's OK.' She laughed. 'Let's get in the water.'

Still he stood there, unsure what to do, unsure of so much all at once. Jonah tapped the window and John-Cody looked round to see him grinning widely. He coloured still further and bent for his own suit in the dive locker.

Libby pulled the under-suit on and zipped it up. Now she looked like an overgrown child in a Babygro. John-Cody helped her into the cumbersome rubber drysuit and zipped it across the shoulders. He wished he had one: he knew these waters and just how chill they were at this or any other time of year. He would last twenty minutes at most before the blood froze in his veins. But he couldn't let her dive alone: he had dived alone once, but only for a short while. The sea lion colony sometimes brought in the odd mako shark or white pointer, and black-suited divers had the unfortunate habit of looking a lot like sea lions. A few years ago a scientist had lost an arm to a white pointer off Campbell Island. Only the bravery of a twenty-one-year-old girl had saved his life.

He changed quickly, peeling on the rubber suit, then lifted his harness out of the locker and watched Libby checking hers. His wrist-mounted dive computer was in the cupboard under the wheel and he went in to get it, asking Tom and Jonah to let the dinghy down from the transom. On deck Libby was checking compressed air bottles with the attention of an expert. She hoisted two out and John-Cody rechecked them, then he picked up his mask and fins and they made their way to the back of the boat.

The *Korimako* was the only vessel in Port Ross but habit made him run up the dive flag anyway. He fastened his air tank then wriggled into the straps, the sudden weight bending his back. Libby was already set and she was checking her air supply through the demand valve. The dinghy was in the water and Tom was making a few circuits to empty the bottom through the plughole. Plug back in place, he came up to the dive platform where Libby and John-Cody clambered aboard.

They moved very carefully through the water. There were a lot of whales and they were

446

slow-moving and kept close to the surface. Both Libby and John-Cody had their masks dangling at their necks, fixing them only when John-Cody spotted Moby Dick spy-hopping once again.

Tom cut the revs and Libby slipped over the side and surfaced again, then Tom passed her camera down. The water was blue green and clear as crystal. John-Cody took a breath and fell backwards, feeling the sudden rush in his lungs as the cold hit him. For a moment he could do nothing but concentrate on his breathing, harsh and ragged in his chest till he surfaced and cleared his mask, then trod water until he could slow his breathing again. The water was freezing, colder than he remembered, and he thought of the chill and darkened places where only whales were prepared to dive. Libby gave him the OK signal then they sank below the surface and worked their way down to ten metres.

Libby kicked round in a slow circle, fully three hundred and sixty degrees. John-Cody tapped her on the shoulder. She faced him, eyes bright through her mask, and he pointed over her shoulder. She looked round as an enormous black shadow drifted out of the hazed light which penetrated from the surface. Again John-Cody touched Libby's shoulder then pointed down and they descended till they were underneath the whale as it swam. Libby was filming. John-Cody watched her and also kept watch on the apparent emptiness of their surroundings.

They were still close to Sandy Bay and a couple of big bull sea lions flew by with a wing-beat of flippers. One of them spun round, sallied in close and barked in his face. John-Cody looked in its eye and blew bubbles. The sea lion barked again, then ducked away and was gone. Above him the passing of the whale, as big as a locomotive, blocked all light and the sea went from green to grey in a moment. The familiar thrill brought on by proximity to such size, power and intelligence washed through him. He felt a calm descending and he worked the water with gentle fins as the whale disappeared into the new green of the sea.

Libby had lowered her camera and was signalling to him. He swam over and saw her eyes were shining with excitement. For a long moment they looked at each other and then she reached out with fingers encased in rubber and gently squeezed his arm.

A whale had turned and was moving round them in an arc: not Moby Dick but another smaller one. John-Cody could make out her genital slit and the swollen lactation grooves on either side. He frowned and looked at Libby, who had seen what he did. The cow was heavily pregnant. She must have conceived last July; there would be a ten-month gestation period with twelve months more before the infant was weaned. Southern rights gave birth once every three years and the pregnant cows would seek shelter in the shallow bays, often alone but sometimes with another whale in attendance, like a midwife.

The expectant mother swam in slow circles and Libby filmed her carefully, looking at her markings; she was mottled like a painted horse on the underside of her belly. Obligingly the whale came close, face on so Libby could document the definition of her callosities, jaw line and eyebrow and the tip of her snout: these would be unique and years of practice had enabled her to identify individuals quickly.

The pregnant cow moved away and two bulls came towards them, pushing another female ahead of them. John-Cody signalled Libby to dive deeper. These were courting whales and as many as six or seven bulls could mate with the same cow; that meant a lot of turbulence and fluke movement that could easily drown them. Libby finned down, filming the males circling the female who swam on her back now, flippers breaking the surface. They caressed her with muzzle and flank and flipper; later they would try to roll her over if she didn't turn to breathe, then one after the other they would dive beneath her and mate.

But now there was nothing but gentleness, fore-play, two males vying for the same female, each trying to show his prowess, moving around her in playful rolls, gliding his body against her, touching her with fin and belly and the underside of his jaw. John-Cody felt the cold of the sea working its way into the layer of air that had been built up by the suit. He checked the dive gauge and knew he was at saturation level. The courting whales moved off again leaving them alone and he indicated the gauge to Libby. She acknowledged and slowly they began their ascent.

On deck Libby was bubbling with excitement. She had dived with whales before, but never had she caught the mating ritual on film. She peeled off her drysuit and half unzipped the under-suit. She cleaned her camera and took the film out, stowing it carefully in a zip-lock polythene bag. Jonah and Tom were on deck and they looked on and smiled as she chattered away nineteen to the dozen.

John-Cody leaned on the rail in his dripping

wetsuit, hair soaked against his skull, sipping coffee and smoking a roll-up cigarette. He stared across the open harbour where the sea lifted to batter the cliffs of Ewing Island. The sounds rushed in his ears, the howl of the wind, the slap of water against the hull, the creak of the shrouds above his head. A gale was raging along the coast and all at once the utter desolation of this place hit him. A chill ran through him and with it a sense of loneliness that no amount of company could compensate. He heard Libby and he heard Tom and Jonah, and yet he heard nothing but the shriek of the wind, the mournful cry of an albatross and the fury of sea on rocks.

He stared at the great forest of rata where he and Mahina had walked then crawled as the branches bent closer and closer to their heads. Peat-laden soil under bare feet: they had made love beneath the canopy where interwoven limbs could still the wind for a moment.

He felt eyes on him and looked round to see that Libby had stopped talking and was watching him from her perch on the dive locker. He looked at her and she looked at him and there was gentleness in her eyes that recalled understanding. And through all this desolation he felt an urge for her, a sense of yearning that moved from his breast to his loins like a bridge between the spiritual and the physical. It was a weird feeling, one he didn't understand: one that smacked of betrayal in an incomprehensible way.

'That was wonderful,' Libby said. 'Thank you.'

John-Cody felt the rocking of the boat underfoot. 'We need to get to an all-weather anchorage. I've let us stay here too long.'

He peeled off his wetsuit and stood freezing in just his boxer shorts and T-shirt. Tom had read his mind and already started the engines. Jonah was flaking the anchor chain and John-Cody and Libby went inside to shower.

'This is going to be a storm and a half,' John-Cody said to Tom. 'Take us right into Laurie Harbour.'

He heard the final rattle of the anchor chain and felt Tom engage the gears as he stepped into the for'ard shower. He was very cold, his flesh bitten by sea and wind, and it took a while before the heat of the water began to penetrate. The life slowly returned to the skin though and he stood for a long time with water falling over his shoulders, chilblains in toes and fingers. He took the shampoo, massaged his scalp and tried to push away the memories he knew would surface. Seeing Moby Dick had brought them all back: the courtship ritual before mating, that pregnant cow burgeoning with new life. It disturbed him. It was not what he had expected.

They steamed beyond Erebus Cove and dropped anchor in Laurie Harbour. The depth varied between twelve and sixty-seven metres and John-Cody, dressed and warm once again, supervised their position using the radar and depth sounder as well as the ever-dimming visibility. The wind was less ferocious here but still it howled at them through the glasshouse, flapping the transparent plastic door and rattling the wire shrouds so they hummed and sang and vibrated.

Libby was busy working at the chart table. She had her computer set up and linked to the digital video camera to revisit the images she had filmed. They were good, very good, as good as any she had ever got and it was only now, back in the warmth of the boat, that she was able to freeze-frame and really study the state of the pregnant cow. She ran a hand through her hair and sat back. John-Cody came down the steps and bent over her shoulder.

'She's very close to her time,' Libby said. 'Maybe we could film the birth. Nobody's ever done that.'

John-Cody looked at her, mouth twisted down at the corners. 'I told you we tried once. It was night and the lights attracted great shoals of krill.' He shifted his shoulders. 'Birth's a very private thing, Libby. Maybe whales don't want to be filmed.'

'Maybe not. I'd like to try though. If we *could*, just think what a breakthrough that would be.'

John-Cody looked at the ceiling as the wind rocked the boat again. 'You might have to wait a while. This is going to blow and blow.'

'You think so?'

'I know so. The wind is coming from the north-east. It's right on top of us and it's going to stay that way for a while.'

She lifted one eyebrow. 'You're experienced enough to know that?'

'No, I just listened to the forecast.'

He was right. The storm kicked into a fury and did not let up for three full days. Libby worked as much as she could at the chart table and dangled low-frequency hydra-phones over the side of the boat so she could listen to the mating calls of the whales. She sat for hours wearing her headphones and monitoring the different patterns of sound, isolating some and saving them in different programs so she could evaluate them later. There were low-frequency

452

pulses, tones that lasted between half a second and twenty seconds, vibrations like snores, and deep guttural moans. They were forms of communication, a language system about which humans knew nothing at all except that the whales could hear one another over great distances, depending on conditions in the water. It was at times like this – during the hours she would spend listening to them talking to one another and considering the great migrations they undertook – that Libby felt very small and insignificant in the great scheme of the universe.

John-Cody lay in his bunk and listened to the wind in the shrouds on the afterdeck. He stared at the ceiling and remembered looking at another ceiling nearly thirty years ago, when he had made a decision that altered his life for ever.

He was with the band in the upstairs room at Big Daddy's on Bourbon Street, his draft papers in his hand. They all held their draft papers. Dewey was staring at his and telling the others again how he didn't even know where Vietnam was.

'It's in South East Asia, Dewey, where it's hot and wet and people like us are getting killed or maimed every day.' John-Cody looked at the paper, the US Army calling him to serve in Vietnam: to shoot people, get shot maybe.

'What's maimed?' Dewey said.

'Getting bits blown off you.' John-Cody looked at him. 'Arms or legs or your head maybe. You've seen the pictures on TV. They try not to show us that stuff but this is America, they can't not show it.'

'So what happens to the band?' Jimmy Tibbins

asked him. 'I mean we were just getting good.'

'I know.' John-Cody strummed a few chords on his guitar then laid the Fender down. It had taken him three years of delivering newspapers to save up enough to buy it. The rain leaned into the shutters so they rattled and bounced in their housings.

'Hell of a storm,' someone said. 'It's blowing all along the gulf coast. They reckon there's flooding at Mobile.'

They went their separate ways, each as subdued as the others. The draft notices gave them dates for their medical examination and after that it was training, then the jungles of South East Asia. John-Cody stowed the Fender in its case and walked home. This part of the city could be dangerous at night, but he had grown up here and had a route that kept him out of trouble.

He lay in bed, listening to his father snoring through the wall. His sister got up and went to the toilet. Earlier she had asked him how long he would be in Asia. He had no answer for her. Now he lay with his hands behind his head and stared at the wrinkled cracks that littered the ceiling.

His father had handed him the unopened letter when it came: both of them knew what it was and they sat together at the kitchen table and looked at it. His mother left them alone to talk.

'Did you fight, Dad?' John-Cody had asked him.

His father shook his head. 'Your granddaddy got killed in World War II, but the army never took me.' He slapped his thigh as he said it. He had been injured in an accident when he was thirteen and the surgery on his right leg had left it an inch shorter than the left.

'Would you have gone?'

'I wouldn't have had a choice.'

'Just like I don't.'

His father said nothing, merely looked at him, his gaze steady and even across the space between them.

'I want to play music, Dad. I don't want to kill anybody.'

His father nodded. He was a harmonica player and a good one, working at the railroad station in the daytime and playing Cajun clubs at night. There was nothing either of them could say. An edict from the government had fallen through the letterbox and John-Cody was summoned to serve his country. He wasn't in college, had no remote chance of going to college and was banking on a career in music. The band was good enough to get noticed, playing rock 'n' roll as well as the blues-type stuff expected in New Orleans.

He lay back in bed later with sleep far from him and he made a decision, perhaps not even consciously: he didn't remember it being conscious. Early the next morning he got up and packed a small bag, took his guitar and stole out of the house. He had a few hundred dollars saved from the money he earned on Bourbon Street and he went to the Greyhound terminal and took a bus heading west. He told no-one, just crept away without looking back and left New Orleans for ever.

He got off the bus in Dallas and played music on the street for a few extra dollars before moving out to the highway again and extending his thumb for a ride. Two months later he got out of a truck in McCall, Idaho, right by Payette Lake. He liked what he saw, lied about his age and got a job, tending bar in Hogan's Hotel. He had been working in various clubs for three years already and had watched some of the best bartenders in the world mix cocktails. He knew more about alcohol than most of the customers who frequented Hogan's over the weekend, and on top of that he had a fancy guitar he could pick at. He had cultivated his father's limp to avoid too much scrutiny. He was mature for his years and could grow a good beard by the time he was seventeen: his hair was thick and long and with the limp he looked like he had already been to Asia. Some people commented on it, but he avoided that kind of conversation and after a couple of months his weekend guitar-playing had doubled Hogan's takings.

Then one day the FBI showed up and arrested him. He had been watching Hogan's back as they paid in at the bank. A sedan pulled up and two agents jumped out and challenged him. Sweat on his brow, though there was the hint of fall in the air and the leaves were beginning to turn russet on the cedars that lined the sidewalk. One agent watched the street while the other handcuffed him then pressed his head down like a felon and forced him into the back of their car. People stood and stared as they drove him out of town.

TWENTY-ONE

Those two FBI agents plagued John-Cody's mind for the next week. Three days of storms and they hunkered down in Port Ross with the atmospherics so bad they could barely raise Alex on the radio. John-Cody, Jonah and Tom worked on maintaining the boat while Libby monitored whale activity via her system of hydra-phones. When the weather allowed, John-Cody took the dinghy across to Erebus Cove where they dropped a hydra-phone mounted on a buoy. Libby could see the awesome power of the Southern Ocean as it battered Friday Island and Rapoka Point between Enderby and the main Auckland Island. The noise was terrific, a continuous booming roar that lifted above the howl of the wind. She thought about the *Derry Castle* and the *Grafton* and the wreck of the *Invercauld*. 'This must be a terrible place to die,' she said.

John-Cody squinted at her from his stance in the stern.

Back on board the *Korimako* he thought about Libby's words and the sky glowered at him as if his very thoughts had angered the gods. That brought him back to Mahina and the new confusion that reigned in his head: so many mixed emotions, such tangled thoughts. His head echoed with it and he had to go outside to breathe, but when he did the weight of the storm seemed to push him down to the deck. He stood against the rail, rain and spray streaming off his oilskins, alone with his thoughts and this place and the voices of whales lifting through the tempest.

The FBI took him to Boise where he was locked up for the first time in his life, a weight like a stone in his gut as the key turned in the lock. There was one window in the cell, a narrow slit high in the wall, and the bars covering it were like bars across his soul. He could feel the first fingers of claustrophobia beginning to probe and he stood up and paced the floor like an animal. He worked his hands at his sides, loosening the joints as he did when he was getting ready to play. His guitar had been left in the upstairs room he rented at Hogan's bar and it was all he could think about now. There was no air in the cell or that was how it felt and he had to fight to get some movement in his chest. A stitch developed and he could neither sit nor stand in any degree of comfort.

He heard people moving about in the corridor on the other side of the wall and only then did his confinement really hit him. Freedom, the thing he valued above all else, the ability to come and go as he pleased, had been taken away from him. His wrists still chafed from the handcuffs, having been forced to sit on his hands all the way from McCall. He looked at the door with no handle, touched its flatness with his fingertips, ran his palms over its smoothness as if requiring a sense other than sight to convince himself that he couldn't get out. His whole future, whether he lived or died, lay with those on the other side of that door. If they did not open it he would die in here like some skeletal wreck lying underground in chains.

He sat on the bed and considered his actions. He had skipped the draft, run off hoping they would never find him. He would not fight. He had known that as soon as the draft papers landed. He had known it as he picked at his guitar in that upstairs room when a silence descended on the band the like of which none of them had ever known before. Even now he knew it. He was scared in a way he had never been scared before and he had no idea what they would do to him. But he knew he could never put on fatigues, pick up an M-16 and aim it at another man. It was beyond him, as beyond him as waiting to mug somebody in the dark places of the French Quarter.

Finally they opened the door and he looked into the face of another special agent, a small but well-built man in his mid-twenties, hair clawing the back of his skull and hacked to a fuzz on top. In his hand he held a sheaf of papers and he shook his head in a dismissive sort of way, stepping back from the door. 'Haul ass, cowboy.'

John-Cody stepped into the corridor and the trapped air broke from his throat in a cough. The agent looked back at him. 'Does get kind of airless in there, doesn't it?' He took John-Cody to an inter-view room, stark and bare with just a thin-topped table and two chairs. John-Cody sat down, resting both hands in his lap and trying to keep the quiver from his limbs. The agent could smell his fear and his eyes darkened as if the weakness sent a charge right through him.

'You ran away from the draft. That makes you a coward, Mr Gibbs.' He sat back, resting one elbow on the chair back. 'It makes you unpatriotic. Your country needs you and you're letting us down.' He shook his head. 'If I had my way we'd shoot people like you. You see, to me you're a deserter, you just haven't done the training yet.'

John-Cody was aware of every breath that climbed from his lungs and sank back again. He said nothing, kept his eyes averted, concentrating on keeping those breaths going because if he didn't he thought he would die as he sat there.

'The army is a little bit more flexible than me, though, Gibbs.' The agent sat forward. 'Fortunately for you. You see, they get a lot of people running off like you did, thinking that nobody would come after them.' He made a face. 'Maybe because you're young they give you the benefit of the doubt.' He stood up. 'I'm going to drive you up to Fort Brett where they'll ask you again to join up. Nice of them to give you a second chance, don't you think?'

John-Cody stared at him and in that moment a sense of calm descended. The trembling ceased and he looked the agent squarely in the eye.

'It won't make any difference.'

'Excuse me?'

'I still won't go.' John-Cody screwed up his eyes. 'You may think it's cowardice, special agent, but I could no more shoot someone in Vietnam than take your gun and shoot you.' He made an open-handed gesture. 'You see, I'd be useless to the army.'

'Are you being a smart ass?'

'No, sir, I'm just telling you how it is.'

The agent laughed. 'Then get used to the cell back there, because you're going to be seeing another one just like it. Only you won't have it all to yourself.' He leaned on the table and leered. 'You understand what I'm saying?'

Libby took a cup of coffee to John-Cody who was in the anchor locker scrubbing the wooden boards the chain rested on. They had been in Port Ross a while now and he'd worked out there were eleven days to go till he would be deported. The storm had shaken the sea for more than a week and only today had the wind dropped and allowed the waves to settle. Libby had spent the entire time working from the *Korimako*; the surface of Port Ross was too rough to accomplish anything in the dinghy and the eddies cutting in from the sea made it far too dangerous to dive. She crouched by the locker and he smelled the coffee before he saw her and looked up, wiping grime from above his eye with the back of his hand.

'The wind's dropped,' Libby said.

He nodded. 'Finally. That's how it is down here. It's why we have to carry extra stores in case we get stuck. The longest I've sat here is two weeks waiting for a window in the weather.'

'You can't get home until it changes?'

'You've seen the waves, Lib. You'd be punching into a wind that was doing nothing but driving you back again. One time me and Tom were two thirds of the way to Stewart Island when the wind shifted to the north and there was nothing we could do except turn tail and run.'

461

Libby warmed her hands on her own coffee cup. 'I want to dive again. I want to try and find that pregnant cow.'

He placed his mug on the deck and hoisted himself out of the chain locker. The wind *had* lessened considerably: it still ruffled his hair where it frayed out from under his cap, but the grey weight of the cloud had gone and the sky was blue crystal, the winter sun strong all at once overhead.

'She's probably given birth already.'

Libby shook her head. 'I don't think so. She was close, but not that close. I can read the signs,' she added when he looked doubtful. 'It's my job, John-Cody. Believe me, I know what I'm doing.'

He rested one arm on the rail. 'I've seen you, Libby. I don't doubt it.' He was quiet for a moment, watching pillars of sunlight fall against the rocks, casting them with slivers of silver as if someone had thrown glitter over the roughened edges. A silence that dulled the senses had descended on the landscape. He spoke without looking round.

'Tomorrow. We'll take the dinghy and see if we can find her.'

His voice was hollow and small and Libby tried to see the expression in his eyes, but he had turned his gaze from her.

That night Jonah cooked pork and apple with kumara and Libby ate with the expectancy of the morning in her breast. She had spent the remainder of the day working at the chart table before she and John-Cody took the dinghy and made a circuit of Port Ross, calm and flat now, only crusted in white caps close to the rocks. They counted thirty different whales and John-Cody told her that this was merely

462

the vanguard: many more would arrive through-out the winter. They picked their channels carefully, John-Cody standing in the stern of the dinghy, ever watchful of where the sixty-foot giants were moving. They cruised just beneath the surface, lifting their heads to blow with a sound like a compressed air hose. Libby took countless photographs, of tail flukes predominantly; the whales were rarely at the right angle to get good shots of callosities. Together they sought the pregnant cow but could not locate her.

John-Cody told Libby not to worry, she would still be around. There were a number of cows with calves already, but none small enough to have just been born. She was probably feeding at sea but would return to the sheltered waters for the birth. Tomorrow they would get into their dive gear and trawl the harbour again.

After dinner John-Cody answered a radio call from the *Moeraki*, fishing north-west of Port Ross outside the management area. They told him they had been having a few engine problems and asked if he had any spare oil filters on board. He always carried spares and told them if they sheltered in Port Ross they were welcome to some.

Later Libby called Bree, the first clear conver-sation in days, and was relieved to hear that everything was all right back in Manapouri. Bree seemed to be having an excellent time up at Blackmount with Hunter and his family. She said that school was fine and she had discovered she was much better at rugby than she thought.

'I'm a good passer, Mum,' she said. 'I can get the ball to spin really well.' She also told them that she'd had two more riding lessons with Ned Pole and he had set up a series of jumps, which she cleared without any problems. Hunter had gone along with her and put Barrio through his paces.

'Mr Pole was really thrilled, Mum. I think Hunter being on Barrio reminded him of his son.' She paused and sighed. 'I wish you and John-Cody liked Mr Pole, he's actually really nice.'

Libby listened and nodded. 'It's not that we don't like him, Bree. We just don't agree on Dusky Sound, that's all.'

'Yes, but surely there's a compromise? That's what you're always telling me: to compromise. There must be some way. It'd be so cool if you all got on.'

John-Cody stood quietly on the bridge and listened to Bree's voice through the speakers.

He did not sleep at all that night. He lay in his bunk watching the moonlight reflected in the water through the porthole. The boat creaked and moaned as metal expanded and contracted under the varying pressures against the hull. Tonight he could hear every sound with a clarity that normally eluded him. Every creak of the wooden steps up to the saloon and bridge, a pencil rolling on the chart table, the metal pinging on the oven, the shivered rattle of the shrouds, the hollow slop of water against the hull, the rhythmic burr of Libby's breathing in sleep. His eyes were wide: the hours ticked past and yet he had no concept of time.

The pencil rolling became an irritation and he got up and put it in his briefcase, which stood by the side of the chart table. He lifted it to the desk and fumbled inside for the familiar feel of the envelope,

464

then read again the letters from the immigration service without switching on the light. He stood in the half-darkness, then put the letters back and wandered up top where he watched the black surface of the water through the side windows. A whale blew further up Laurie Harbour and the vapour sprinkled like a fountain in the moonlight. He heard grunts and groans and long throaty ridges of sound: he heard muttered moans and thin tonal mewling coming from the main group beyond Erebus Cove. Sound travelled far in the quieter nights where the acoustics bounced through the water. On deck he rolled a cigarette and looked up at the moon.

Night began to grey into day and again he was aware of just how alive he felt. He stood by the rail where the cage held the compressed air bottles and selected which one he would use. The water shifted below the scuppers, thick and black and cracked by chinks of light where the moon and stars broke upon it. Laurie Harbour gave him only twenty-seven metres in the deepest part, but it was littered with forests of bladder kelp and he could lose himself in those. He smoked his cigarette, rolled and smoked another and then quietly, just as dawn was breaking, he lifted the compressed air bottle, checked his watch with the gauge and let half the air out. What was left gave him twenty minutes at best.

His wetsuit was in the dive locker, which he opened quietly so as not to disturb anyone. Carefully he worked the lycra over his limbs. He pushed his hair back so the hood would cover it properly and selected a weight belt with fifteen kilos on it. He carried the gear to the afterdeck where he stacked it against the glasshouse and then went back for his mask and fins. He buckled the buoyancy control device, tightening the tension straps across his chest, demand valve and spare dangling on the end of their hoses. He had his dive computer strapped on his wrist as he always did, habit more than anything else today, and he washed his mask carefully after climbing down to the platform. The wind was fresh and cold against the exposed skin of his face and the water felt like ice on his fingers.

Before he pulled on his gloves John-Cody took the tangi-wai, the teardrop stone Mahina had given him, and held it in his palm. The tightly woven material of the glove pressed it against the skin. Strapping the mask over his eyes he secured it and checked the air supply.

Libby woke up with a strange feeling in the pit of her stomach: not quite fear but something akin to it. She was acutely aware of the silence. The wind seemed to have died away completely, something that never happened here; she had grown used to the rushing sound in her ears as part of daily life. But she did not hear it now and the silence had an eerie quality about it. It was accentuated by the silence from John-Cody's cabin and all at once she got up, pulled on her robe and looked at his empty bed. Again the sensation plucked at her and she stared at the bed for some sign of his passing. She glanced at the chart table: his briefcase stood on top whereas last night it had been underneath. Dressed only in her robe, she climbed the steps to the saloon and bridge but he was nowhere to be seen. The port door was open a fraction, however, and Libby could feel the chill breaching the crack.

John-Cody slipped into the icy water and it

knocked the breath right out of him. He hovered a moment, still holding the wooden slats of the dive platform until he could calm the rush in his lungs and get used to the cold. He could see the hull of the *Korimako* through the haze of his mask and with it her port of registration. The memories flooded back: the day he quit fishing for ever when he and Mahina decided to try to bring some understanding of the fragile ecology to those visiting Fiordland; the day he flew to Australia after seeing the *Korimako* advertised. That was the catalyst, when the pair of them went for broke and sank every penny they had and a great deal they didn't into the purchase of the boat. Before then they had chartered other boats to use but it was only when they bought their own that they had finally taken their efforts seriously.

Gradually his breathing settled into a rhythm and he relaxed, his mind wandering now, almost in a dream. He turned and kicked away from the dive platform, swam a few yards on the surface then slipped quietly beneath it with only the line of bubbles as evidence of his passing.

Libby went on deck, hugging the robe about her, barefoot against the chilled metal. John-Cody was not on the foredeck so she picked her way down the narrow gangway beyond the wheelhouse. He was not on the afterdeck either and she screwed up her face and then heard the slap of fins and saw a dark shape drifting below the surface fifteen yards off the stern. She was about to call out but knew he wouldn't hear her and she leaned over the rail and watched the bubbles as he descended. Dread cramped her gut. Why would he dive so early and on his own when all the time they had been down here he refused to let her enter the water without a buddy? She remembered his moods, the terrible silence that had enveloped him since that meeting with Ned Pole: she stood on the stern, watched the flat of the water and the line of bubbles gradually moving away and felt totally and utterly helpless.

John-Cody swam straight down, kicking laconically with his fins and feeling the chill of the water rush over his body. He could hear no sound save the rasp of his own breathing, giving him life still so evident it filled every pore of his being. The water was cold and clear and empty: he saw a handful of silver-backed fish swimming away, and clawing up at him from where it was rooted to the bottom near the shore, line after line of vertical bladder kelp, yellow and brown like the tentacles of some gigantic swaying sea monster or the billowing hair of a goddess fallen from heaven. The whales liked to swim among the kelp, gently rising to the surface where they would lay the massed fronds over their sensitive blowholes.

He dived and as he did so his life unfolded before his eyes in a way he had not expected. He saw the faces of his parents who had died years ago back in New Orleans. He had seen them only once after he left that morning, when they came to McNeil Island for a visit before he was paroled. He saw Bourbon Street in the rain, could hear the strains of his own guitar above the sound of his breathing. He saw the roads through Texas, dust-blown, desert edging the blacktop and tumbleweeds kicked around by the wind. He saw the ice sculptures in McCall, Payette Lake frozen where the really keen fishermen drilled holes in the winter. He saw the ice-bound highway on the Camas prairie and the back of the FBI agent's head, just before they ran off the road.

He saw the car wreck and himself standing ankle deep in powdered snow on the road above the scene, like some shivering sculpture of his own in the moonlight. He remembered the frost-bitten chill in the air and the weight of his breath as steam. He remembered just how silent that Idaho night had been before the headlights from the truck lit up the bend in the road and the chattering diesel engine broke open the stillness. He remembered the bar in Bellingham and the first mate's stare: the vessel steaming up the strait and his belly bilious as they hit the open sea. He remembered Hawaii and then the second and third boats and the New Zealand coastguard's scrutiny and how he determined he would jump ship as soon as the skipper informed them they were landing their catch at Bluff Cove. He saw his deer trap at Yuvali Beach and he saw Mahina for the very first time, mud climbing naked ankles where she hopped out of the dinghy.

He finned down and heard the first whale grunting loud and higher pitched, almost like threads of humpback song coming through the depths like a warning.

Libby stood at the stern rail for a few minutes before the cold and her sudden fears drove her inside once more. The sunshine of yesterday was broken now with patches of mist mottling the tangled land south of the Hooker Hills which seemed to mass against the boat, rata and scrub, and all at once a thousand black petrels were leaving their nests for the sea. They startled her, the scavengers of the Sub-Antarctic lifting into the air with one combined shriek, massive wings beating the air as they took off towards the ocean. She watched a pair leave the main cluster and fly high in courtship, the male with his wings pinned back, breast thrust out and his beak open, calling to her in black silhouette against the sky.

She went below and dressed quickly, then she looked again at John-Cody's cabin, seeking some sign of his intentions. Call it woman's intuition, she had no other name for it, but she knew something was wrong. She had half a mind to wake Tom and Jonah but for some other reason, not quite apparent, she resisted. At the chart table she paused, eyeing John-Cody's open briefcase standing where it had not stood last night. She looked inside and her gaze settled on a battered brown envelope. She did not remember seeing it before, and she furrowed her brow when she realized it was from the immigration service. There were three letters in all and a handful of words assaulted all of her senses.

Forty-two days to leave the country or face arrest and forced removal.

TWENTY-TWO

The whale was a young male under ten years old,
barely an adolescent: dark on his back, almost the
black of his ancestors but mottled at the fluke and
tips of his flippers. Sea lions were hounding him,
darting at him, nipping his tail flukes and torpedoing
off his flanks. John-Cody finned down past them,
watching for a moment as two of the young sea lions
came right up to him, circling with a grace which
belied their movements on land. They barked at him
as if they knew his purpose, but his resolve was fixed
and he finned slowly on. Swathes of bladder kelp
rose up from the seabed to greet him, yellow and
brown and interspersed with other varieties of weed.
Two yellow-eyed penguins flew past after krill, probably taking him for a sea lion and giving him a wide
berth. The water was clear and blue with the sunlight falling in incandescent shafts that glittered
below the surface. There was no evidence of a
current; the only wash he felt was from the tail flukes
of a whale passing some distance away. Whales
weighed upwards of seventy-five tonnes and could
move with surprising speed, and getting in the

way of the flukes meant broken limbs at least.

John-Cody was no longer aware of how cold the water was. His head felt clear for the first time in a long while, almost at peace, and yet way at the back of his mind was a nagging sensation, not enough to disturb his purpose but there all the same. Tom would get them home: that was why he had brought him. Jonah was good crew and Libby knew what to do in a boat.

His thoughts centred on himself again. As soon as he had seen the bald facts of the letter from immigration he knew he couldn't go through with it. Fiordland was the only home he wanted: the boat, the sounds and this place where the wind was so strong it pushed columns of water back up the cliff face. The fight was lost, Pole and his backers were too strong and they held a trump card he could not play against. He wondered again how the man had managed to find out about his past. But Pole was a Vietnam veteran and proud of it, his wife was an American lawyer and a good private detective could find out just about anything. None of that mattered any more. They wanted the *Korimako* but the skipper of the *Korimako* wasn't bringing her home.

Libby stuffed the letter into the back pocket of her jeans and thought about waking Tom. It seemed the obvious thing to do but still something stopped her. She could not identify what that something was, but she might be wrong about the whole thing and worrying Tom would not endear her to John-Cody when he surfaced. Didn't she mean if he surfaced? The letter said it all. It answered the question of why he had brought her here in the first place. There was

472

no chance of finding a resident pod of dolphins this far south: they had both known that. She had jumped at the chance of seeing the lost tribe of southern rights. John-Cody had come here to die.

That thought twisted like knotted cord in her stomach and she went back on deck. Standing in the stern she looked for his bubbles, the tell-tale line of rising air pockets that would indicate where he was and that he was still alive. She couldn't see any. Moving to the port quarter she looked the length of the boat and saw the dive flag still twisted in its lowered position round the shroud. He hadn't raised it. He always raised the dive flag: it was habit, even down here where there were no other vessels. She gripped the stern rail with freezing fingers, and desperately she scanned the flattened surface of the bay for any sign of him. There was no sign and she knew she needed to be higher. The jib mast had a crow's nest at thirty feet: without another thought she rushed for'ard and climbed.

Moby Dick moved through the water with the poise of an animal half his size, a grey and silent ghost probing the depths with gentle strokes of his tail flukes. Like the younger male he too had been harried and hassled by sea lions at play, but they had left him quickly and now he eased his massive bulk deep below the surface.

John-Cody saw him out of the corner of his eye and eased back to witness the great whale's approach. He had first seen him seven years previously and every time he had been down here in winter since, the grey whale had sought out the boat, coming alongside to roll and play and slap the surface as if greeting an old friend. During his quiet periods he would doze on his side with his eye closed to the sky, while Mahina leaned over the rail and sang to him in her native tongue. Now he swam above the thickened layers of bladder kelp heading straight for John-Cody.

Libby stood on the spreaders with her back to the bows and used binoculars to scan the surface for any sign of bubbles. Tom came on deck scratching his head and muttering. She heard Jonah banging about in the galley.

'What're you doing up there?' Tom called to her.

She didn't answer him immediately: she was watching Moby Dick as he dived one hundred yards beyond the *Korimako*'s stern. She saw him lob-tail for a moment, then his flukes disappeared with barely a ripple in the surface.

'John-Cody's diving.' She lowered the binoculars and looked down at Tom. The sun was bright; it burned holes in the mist and reflected off the white steel of the deck.

'He's what?'

She climbed down the mast and dropped to the deck beside him. 'I know. It's weird. He's told me not to dive here alone. He's only got a seven-mil wetsuit and he hasn't run the flag up the shroud.' She pointed. 'I'm worried about him, Tom. He's a stickler for every tiny detail on this boat and he hasn't run up the dive flag.'

'He's been quiet lately, I'll give you that.' Lines furrowed deep in Tom's brow and Libby followed him back inside. Still she hadn't mentioned the letter though it was in her back pocket. Tom told Jonah what she had just told him and Jonah lifted the weight of his hair from where it hung in his face.

'Bloody cold to be diving.'

Libby looked in his eyes. 'We can't see any bubbles.'

John-Cody held his position as Moby Dick approached him. The whale was silent, moving very slowly with barely a downstroke from his tail flukes; at just under seventy feet he was one of the largest whales in the bay. John-Cody was tiny, insignificant, no more than a dot in the water and yet the whale approached with caution, concern almost, and for the first time since they came down here John-Cody's resolve began to weaken. He stayed where he was, conscious all at once of his airtime. The whale moved round him in a circle, twenty feet above his head, blocking the light from the sun and casting the seabed in shadow.

The sea had gone dark and John-Cody felt the chill in his bones. The darkness lifted from inside him and he imagined this place with rain and howling winds, storms whipping the land for days and days at a time and Libby's words echoed in his head: *a terrible place to die*.

Moby Dick drifted closer and all at once his bulk was so huge it was overpowering. John-Cody felt a sense of fear, panic in his throat that almost made him kick for the surface. But the whale, perhaps sensing his disquiet, wallowed and slowed and eased gently down to eye level as if deliberately seeking him out. John-Cody kicked back with his fins, the whale so close now that everything else was lost, a great grey wall that stretched the length of his boat and three times his own height. Moby Dick's eye was wide and pale like an albino, lifted in rolls of blubber so it extended slightly from the side of his head, the pupil huge and dark and round. John-Cody could make out every mark in the callosity, every line in the raised flesh of the socket. The eye fixed on his and John-Cody looked directly into it, as if he was being allowed a glimpse of the whale's soul: a sharing between old and young, the wise and suddenly foolish.

The sea washed cold: enclosed in his suit, the only sound was the rasp of his breath and the gentle rising grunts coming now from the whale. John-Cody stared into the whale's eye and Mahina stared back at him. He started, almost forgot to breathe then looked again and she was there still: not pale and wan and dying with her features ravaged by cancer but young and vibrant with fire in her hair and the darkness in her gaze he witnessed the first time he saw her.

He went limp in the water, looked again and saw only Moby Dick looking back at him. He was close enough to touch the great whale and unconsciously he stretched out a gloved hand and laid it on the puckered hillside that was the callosity. For a moment the two of them remained like that, sixty feet under the sea, then John-Cody checked the dive computer on his wrist and realized he had just enough air to make it back to the surface.

Libby climbed to the spreaders once more, binoculars dangling from her neck, and settled herself in the crow's nest. Tom was in the stern with Jonah standing on the wheelhouse roof. All of them were looking for the same thing, bubbles rising some-where on the surface. Libby scanned the bay; she had the best vantage point. Slowly she moved the glasses over the water, ignoring where whales blew or penguins darted and sea lions broke to bark at one another. She had seen Moby Dick dive one hundred yards off the stern and she concentrated on that area, heart high in her chest, a morass of thoughts clogging her mind. She stared and stared, conscious now of the time, glancing from the bay to her watch and back again. She saw a patch of bubbles break fifty yards off the stern.

She cried out and the others looked where she looked and she put the glasses to her eyes again, saw the bubbles more clearly and knew he was ascend-ing. She watched, biting down on her lip, and then she saw the black of his suit and more bubbles, geyser-like now: his hood broke the ripples and he spat the demand valve from his mouth.

John-Cody felt the sun on his head as he rose the final few feet after decompressing the last stage; he spat his mouthpiece and saw the white of the *Korimako*'s stern in the distance. He pulled down his mask and for a moment he floated on his back, the tank much more buoyant now with the lack of air in it. He looked at the cumulus curling thick and white, grey still at the edges, stretching like a blanket across the expanse of the sky. Tears fell freely though he made no sound and he didn't know why he was weeping, only that he had seen Mahina in Moby Dick's eye and knew she had been trying to tell him something. He felt weak, weaker than he had ever felt, resolve fractured now. He lay with his arms wide in a crucifix, fins sticking out of the water, and then he gazed towards the boat and saw Libby watching him from the spreaders. Instinctively he lifted a hand to the top of his head indicating that he was all right.

Libby saw the movement and exhaled heavily. She could feel her heart racing in her chest and all at once she had to hold the ring of steel that formed the crow's nest for support.

'He's OK,' she called down to the others. 'I'm going to take the dinghy and pick him up. Jonah, heat a kettle of water and pump up the auxiliary for the shower. He's going to be freezing.'

Tom cast the dinghy off and she stood in the stern, opened the throttle and powered across the bay to John-Cody.

He lay where he was, looking at the sky and seeing Mahina all over again. Why had she come? What was she trying to say to him? For the second time since they had left Bluff Cove he was visited by the feeling that she was trapped still, unable to return home, suffocated within his own consciousness.

His thoughts were interrupted by the buzz of the Honda engine that drove the dinghy. Righting himself in the water, he saw Libby coming for him, a strange mix of fear and relief on her face. Slowly he swam towards her, mask loose at his neck. She circled him, came up on the port side and flicked the gears into neutral. They looked at each other for a few moments, eye to eye, her standing in the boat and him in the water, getting colder by the minute. He didn't speak, just unbuckled his empty tank and hoisted it over the side.

TWENTY-THREE

Libby talked to Bree on the radio later that afternoon. The *Korimako* was still anchored in Laurie Harbour and earlier she had seen the heavily pregnant cow wallowing like a hippo in the shallows. John-Cody had been quiet all day, more distant than ever. He had sat in the dinghy after she helped him aboard, holding his fins, mask and snorkel and watching the water as it slipped by the gunwales. He had said nothing about what he had been doing or why he had dived alone, and she had felt unable to ask. Libby had gone below and it had been a great relief to make contact with her daughter.

'Mum, I think I'm in love with Hunter,' Bree told her.

'Bree, you're not even thirteen.'

'So what? What's age got to do with love?'

'Nothing, I suppose. Have you kissed him yet?'

'I might've done.'

Libby laughed then, realizing just how much Bree was growing up.

'How do you know you're in love?'

'I can feel it, Mum. Hunter, he's so mmmmm. I get all sweaty when I'm near him.'

'Mmmmmm? What's mmmmmm?'

'You know what I mean. Anyway I'm not going to talk about it on the radio. I'm having a great time at the farm. Hunter's mum and dad are so nice to me, and now Mr Pole's been teaching me I'm much better on a horse and Hunter and me help with the sheep. We took the horses over the hills on Saturday. It was cold but I felt like a cowboy, the world seemed so big all of a sudden. I'm so happy here. I want to stay in New Zealand. Not just for the two years, I want to stay for ever.'

'We'll see.'

'No, let's not see. Let's settle, Mum. I'm in school. You can't keep dragging me away all the time.'

'Bree, I don't do it on purpose. It's all to do with . . .'

'I know, *work*. But try and stay, Mum. I love it here. I'm so happy. I've never been happier. There's Hunter and Sierra and the hut and the lake and you and John-Cody.' Bree paused then. 'How is John-Cody? He was so quiet when you left. I know you fancy him, Mum. How is he?'

Libby laughed out loud.

'I'm sorry, but I can see it when you're around him, the way you look at him. Don't worry, I feel the same about Hunter. It's love, Mum. You shouldn't try to fight it. There's nothing you can do.'

'So you're the expert all of a sudden.'

Bree laughed. 'John-Cody fancies you too, I can tell.'

Libby sat up straighter.

'But he hasn't let go of Mahina yet, not properly.

480

He needs to. She's gone. Maybe you can help him. He needs to let go of her, that's what makes him sad and she wouldn't want him sad.'

Libby thought about that and considered the wisdom she heard in her daughter's words. 'You think so?' she said.

'Yes. I do.'

Libby considered the letters she had read from the immigration service and her mood darkened. 'Bree, you just take care,' she said. 'We'll be back soon.'

'No, Mum: you take care. I'm safe here on land. You've got four hundred and seventy kilometres of ocean to cross, remember.'

'Don't worry, John-Cody's a brilliant skipper and there are no icebergs down here.'

'Mum.'

'What?'

'I'm serious about staying here. I thought I'd hate it, but I love it. I don't want to move anywhere else. I want to stay here and for you and John-Cody to get married.'

Libby stared through the porthole at sea lions swimming on their backs, one flipper raised and bent at right angles. She had seen the fur seals do that in Dusky Sound but had no idea why.

'I think you should ask him. He'll never get round to it.'

'Bree!'

'Why not? It's a new millennium, Mum. Girl power, remember?'

Libby laughed again. 'I'll bear that in mind. Just don't *you* go asking Hunter.'

John-Cody was standing in the prow smoking a

481

cigarette when Libby went back up to the bridge. Both the wheelhouse doors were open and a chill filled the saloon from the harbour. Tom came in from astern and closed the windward door. Libby could hear Jonah down in the engine room. The boat smelled of diesel from the heater and coffee standing cold in the pot. John-Cody straightened and clipped his cigarette: the wind caught his hair and scattered it about his face. He looked at the clouds and his gaze tightened, then he came back into the wheelhouse and studied the barometer. Libby saw that the pressure was dropping.

'Is there another storm blowing in?' she asked him.

'Yes.'

'Have you any idea when?'

'Less than twenty-four hours.' John-Cody squinted at her. 'Why?'

'Because I saw that pregnant cow again today: she's due any time, John-Cody.'

He looked at his watch and then out of the window into the gathering gloom. The days had grown shorter still since they had been down here. 'Forget trying to film at night,' he said. 'We won't stand a chance. If we can find her tomorrow, I'll dive with you.'

For a long moment they looked at each other and Libby thought about what Bree had said. It was true she did care about him, she found herself thinking about him all the time: she loved his smell, his maleness close to her. She loved the seams in his face, the blue vein that lifted against the skin under his eye. She loved the fractured lines about his mouth and the tanned sinew of his forearms. 'I spoke to Bree just now,' she said. 'She's in love with Hunter.'

John-Cody smiled then, for the first time in a couple of days. 'Did she tell you that?'

'Yes.'

'Then she told the whole fishing fleet in the Southern Ocean. How's she doing?'

'She misses you.'

His eyes dulled once more and he looked beyond her. 'Is that what she said?'

Libby nodded. 'She wanted to know why you were so quiet when you left. She asked me if you were still quiet.'

'What did you tell her?'

'I said that you were.'

He looked at the floor.

'Why did you dive alone this morning?'

He didn't reply. Libby waited. He could sense her expectancy; feel how close she stood to him, scent her hair, the texture of her skin. He moved past her to the aft steps.

'I need to raise the *Moeraki*,' he said. 'See if they've fixed that oil filter.'

That evening after dinner Tom and Jonah went down to the engine room to make some checks. It was a habit of Tom's to make sure the Gardner was cleaned and oiled and all the gauges were working properly. Jonah was learning about marine engine maintenance and Tom was an excellent tutor. The storm had not grown into anything yet and Libby sat in the saloon and read a book, aware of the creak of the wind in the shrouds on the afterdeck. John-Cody had tried in vain to raise the *Moeraki* before he contacted Bluff Radio for news. According to them the boat was still fishing

483

but had missed one check-in. He came up the steps looking troubled.

'Is that very bad?' Libby asked him.

'Not very bad, there could be lots of reasons why a boat doesn't check in on time. You've seen the atmospherics: sometimes you can't get a proper signal. It's happened to us lots of times down here.' He shrugged. 'Jack Mackay is a good skipper. The *Moeraki*'s a sound vessel. They'll be all right.'

He was silent after that, then got up to make some coffee and placed a mug before Libby. He put some music on very quietly and they sat in the stillness without talking. Libby thought about what Bree had said about her and John-Cody and wondered if anyone had been listening. She wondered also if she cared. John-Cody looked beyond her, staring through the darkened for'ard windows.

'What're you thinking?' Libby asked him softly. 'I'll give you an English penny for your thoughts.'

He looked sideways at her. 'I don't think they're worth that much.'

'I'm buying. Why don't you let me judge?'

'There's nothing to tell you.'

'I think there is.' Libby wanted to bite the bullet but suddenly she was afraid. 'Why did you dive on your own like that this morning?'

'I've dived alone here lots of times. It's different with you. While you're on my boat you're my responsibility, Libby. I've had one death. I don't want any more. That's why I tell you not to go without a buddy.'

She nodded. 'But why didn't you run up the dive flag? You always run up the dive flag.'

He could feel her probing; picking at him,

484

demanding something of him in a way that he didn't want to acknowledge. He didn't answer her. Libby watched his face, the darkening about his eyes and the concentration that dipped his brow in heavy lines.

'I saw the letter from the immigration service. What's going on, John-Cody?' It just came out, she hadn't intended it to but it did. She heard the words, did not associate them with her voice and then he was looking at her from under hooded eyes.

'I'm sorry. I didn't mean to pry. You were in the water and I was worried. You've been so quiet, so distant. I didn't know what to think.'

John-Cody sat and looked at his fingernails. The music drifted softly and Tom and Jonah's voices came to him now and again from below deck. He bit his lip and looked at Libby.

'Come out to the glasshouse,' he said.

Libby followed him outside and she took two cigarettes from her pack, broke off the filters and handed one to him. He lit it with a trembling hand, then they sat either side of the table with the door partially rolled up and the stars chill and bright as diamonds overhead. John-Cody smoked in silence then he looked across the table.

'I'm wanted by the FBI in the United States,' he began quietly. 'I told you I didn't go to Vietnam when I was drafted but I didn't tell you why.' He paused and sucked on the cigarette. 'I refused to go. I got my papers in New Orleans and just skipped out. A few months later the Feds turned up and arrested me. They drove me to an army base near Seattle.'

*   *   *

485

They didn't handcuff him though he thought that if the young agent in the passenger seat had had his way, he would have been bound and gagged and dumped in the trunk for the duration of the journey. He sat in his own silence while the two agents talked in low voices about subjects that didn't concern him and the countryside rolled by and the army drew nearer and nearer. He had no idea what was going to happen; the agent had talked about a second chance, whatever that meant. But inside he was scared, not blind fear but a gnawing trepidation stalking him quietly, darkly, from all directions and there was nothing he could do about it. He thought of New Orleans, his father and mother and sister, the other members of his band, in training maybe or already in Vietnam or occupying a body bag perhaps. The chances of a grunt getting killed on his first foray into those jungles were pretty good, he figured. There would be nothing like taking out the fresh faces first; the longer you were there, the more chance you had of surviving. The man in you would become a soldier: experience would give you no choice.

Late that night they drove into the base, stopping at the gate where two marines with pistols and M-16s checked the car and the ID of the two FBI agents and shone a torch into John-Cody's face. The car was directed into the complex and the agents got out and handcuffed John-Cody then marched him up the steps of a wooden building and handed him over to the military police.

A very tall, very well-built officer with no hair and a thin moustache took his details. Then he was marched in silence to a cell at the far end of the wooden block, where the door was closed and locked and John-Cody sat down in the silence of the night and listened to his heart beating. The cell was tiny, seven feet by four: he paced it. With the bunk along one wall he almost had to turn sideways to get in. It reminded him of old television footage he had seen of Sing Sing Prison in New York. He sat on the bunk with his head in his hands and tried not to cry. Maybe he should just go, get himself killed or kill some other people and get it over with. He tried to evaluate why he hadn't gone: was it not wanting to have a gun in his hands or was it just the cowardice the FBI agent called it?

He must have slept because the sound of bolts being drawn woke him in the morning and he looked up into the face of another military policeman. 'Good morning, soldier. This is your lucky day. You got a "get out of jail free" card.'

John-Cody looked at him and said nothing.

'Jump to it, soldier. Let's go.'

The officer marched him into the glaring sunlight where a group of marines in fatigues were being drilled on the parade ground. John-Cody stood with his hair to his shoulders and rubbed his eyes like a sleepy child. He was marched across the ground where the drill had stopped and the marines catcalled to him: part of the psychological process no doubt. He surprised himself by thrusting back his shoulders and holding his head high like some innocent prisoner on his last walk to the gallows. He was marched between two huts and came face to face with a drill sergeant, smaller than he was but broad and stocky with a face that looked like it grew up in a boxing ring. The MPs stood down and the sergeant marched him towards the gates and John-Cody saw a group of twenty or so recruits in civilian clothes standing in line at the polished steps of the guard house. He breathed deeply through his nose and looked directly ahead as the sergeant moved him into line. When the sergeant spoke his voice was a hoarse whisper in John-Cody's ear.

'Don't embarrass me, asshole.'

John-Cody's heart beat faster and the sergeant stepped away, wheeled to attention then parted his feet, hands behind his back. He looked at the raw young faces ten yards in front of him, John-Cody at the far end of the line.

'Gentlemen,' he said. 'I am Sergeant Oslowski. You fine young specimens of American manhood have been summoned to fight for your country.' He paused, licked his lips and his eyes fixed on John-Cody. 'Now, take one pace forward and accept the honour you've been accorded.'

They all stepped forward: all except John-Cody who stood his ground, hands behind his back, breathing hard but with his chin in the air and his eyes fixed on a red-tailed hawk drifting in silhouette against the sky. He waited in the silence that followed, then heard the sergeant stamp over to him, come alongside and hiss into his ear.

'I said, step forward and accept that honour.'

John-Cody held his ground.

'Did you hear me?'

'Yes, sir.'

'Step forward.'

'No, sir.'

'Gibbs.'

'I will not, sir.'

488

The others were staring at him, some with ridicule and some with awe in their eyes. Oslowski stepped in front of him and nodded to the two military policemen waiting off to the side. He told them to cuff him and throw him in the glasshouse till he cooled off. Just before he was marched away John-Cody turned to Oslowski.

'It won't make any difference, sir,' he said. 'I'm not going to Vietnam.'

'Don't you count on it, boy.'

He was locked up for a week: no contact with anyone, just meals and water pushed through the slit in the door. He had a bucket for his toilet with one roll of paper and the bucket was not emptied for three days. The stink lived in the back of his throat, making him feel permanently nauseous. At night it seemed to be worse. The cell was airless, with one tiny window through which marines and raw recruits alike called him all the names he had ever heard and a good many he hadn't.

And his resolve hardened and he grew calmer, knowing now that he could take whatever they threw at him. His isolation inspired him in a way he would never have thought it could. He allowed his mind to wander, back to Louisiana and the bayous, the big river and New Orleans in summer rainstorms, the heat and the smell of hosepipes washing the streets of the French Quarter early in the morning. He wondered what his parents were doing, if they even knew he was here, if anyone had told them. They had not been in contact but no doubt they were aware of the situation. He had not called them, but home would have been the first place the FBI looked when he didn't show up for his physical.

At the end of the week he was allowed to empty the slops in his bucket, then he was locked in the cell for another couple of days. One evening, not long after it got dark, the door swung open and two military policemen with shadowy faces marched him into the night. They ran him round the camp, one either side, trotting him round the perimeter then weaving between the billets and the mess halls so everyone could see him and he was verbally abused in every way imaginable. He ran with a smile on his face though, and his eyes on the horizon, never once looking left or right, even when a half-empty beer can struck him below the ribs. The MPs slowed to a march then delivered him to two others at the steps of a long low building. Here he paused to get his breath, but his arms were pinned and he was hauled up the steps and marched into a room so dark he could not see his hand in front of his face. The door was slammed behind him and he stood there, having no idea where he was and unable to get his bearings.

He did not know how long he stood in the darkness, but all at once music began to play from either side of him: at first he didn't recognize it and then he knew it was Glenn Miller, the big band sound of the 1940s. The music washed over him and images took definition on the wall at the far end of what he now realized was one long room. Film projections, GIs from World War II in landing craft in the English Channel. He heard a voice talking about the military, about how the armies of the United States were a beacon for the free world against the advance of communism. Words to engender fear, a warning about the red peril that marched through South East Asia catching everyone off their guard. He saw John

Wayne in action, a clip from a war movie about a war he didn't fight in. He stood with his arms folded while image after image, voice after voice, assaulted his senses through the darkness. It lasted twenty minutes or more, like a presentation, a sales pitch almost, and when it was done a solitary voice rose above the strains of the band.

'John-Cody Gibbs, you've been chosen to serve your country. Step forward and accept that honour.'

John-Cody stood where he was.

'Step forward, son. Your country needs you.'

'No, sir.'

'Step forward.'

'No, sir.'

'Gibbs, step forward and serve your country.'

'No, sir. I will not, sir.'

'I'm going to ask you one more time. Step forward, Gibbs.'

'No, sir,' bile on his lip now. 'I will not do it, sir.'

John-Cody gazed at Libby through the darkness. Another cigarette burned between his fingers and he was aware of Jonah moving on the other side of the galley window.

'They sentenced me to three years in the state penitentiary,' he said. 'I was released after eighteen months and told to stay in Washington State. But I couldn't get a job, the parole officer saw to that. So I skipped over into Idaho. They caught up with me again and were taking me back when the car was wrecked in the snow. I got out and headed for the coast. I got passage on a trawler in Bellingham and went to Hawaii. From there I came here. You pretty much know the rest.'

Libby stared at him. 'And you're illegal here.'

He nodded. 'I never married Mahina, never got my citizenship.'

'But it's been twenty-five years, John-Cody. Surely they can't deport you after twenty-five years?'

'Under any other circumstances, they told me. But my character's in question. The FBI has a file on me.'

Libby sat with her arms folded. 'I thought there was an amnesty for people who refused to fight in Vietnam.'

'There was. They received pardons from the government.'

'Well, there you go then.'

He shook his head slowly. 'I'm a parole jumper, Libby. I'm technically a felon.'

TWENTY-FOUR

Libby woke up, aware of a slight movement under the hull: the boat was silent save for the sound of water shifting against steel. She lay on her back with moonlight breaking the tiny porthole, casting shadows on the louvred door that was pinned back to the wall. She could smell cigarette smoke, which was odd, as John-Cody didn't allow smoking inside the boat. Getting up, she reached for her robe and slipped it over her T-shirt and knickers. John-Cody's bed was empty.

He was leaning in the half-open port door smoking and listening to bull whales grunting at one another through the darkness. Clouds hung over the mountains and draped almost as low as the shore, but the bay reflected the moon in the surface of the water. The wind had dropped and with it the needle on the barometer and it was only a matter of time before the storm blew in.

John-Cody heard Libby's feet on the steps, the even creak of wood as she came up from below. He remained where he was, watching the horizon, catching a great plume of vapour as a whale blew close to the boat. The harbour was alive with sound, moans and grunts and in the distance the deeper rumbling roar that he had found no reference to in any textbook. Libby moved behind him. He didn't look round, didn't see her, just felt her presence and scented her like an animal, nostrils flared slightly. He drew on the cigarette and pinched the end and when he turned she stood on the bridge behind him. Her face was oval and pale in the moonlight and he gazed at her, roving her features with suddenly hungry eyes. Neither of them said anything.

Strange thoughts scorched his mind and he didn't know what he was feeling. Behind him a whale rolled in the surf, setting the water to boil. Libby looked into his face and he could see the light in her eyes, searching his own with a desire he had never witnessed before.

Libby looked into his ravaged features, the hunted look in his eyes, the way his steel-grey hair was chipped and frayed at the ends. She studied the lines round his mouth, the dull red of his lips in the half-darkness, the slight hook of his nose and the great strength in his jaw. She gazed at his chin, his neck, his chest where it was exposed by his shirt. She looked at the shape of his shoulders, broad and strong still, his torso tightening to trim and narrow hips. She gazed at him and she knew that she saw now what Mahina had seen when he was young, the lighted tunnel into a man's soul. She saw the fear in his eyes, the confusion and sudden trembling that the future had brought him. She didn't speak: she felt her stomach cramp with an ache she had never experienced before and she knew then that she loved him.

John-Cody stood straighter and Libby rested the flat of her palm against his chest and he was aware of how his heart pounded and that she could feel it and that made him suddenly vulnerable and he wanted to pull away. But he didn't pull away and she moved closer and again he trembled. She reached up and cupped her palm to the back of his neck: her fingers were cool against his flesh and she coaxed his lips to hers.

At first he didn't respond. He couldn't. He tried to think of Mahina, but Mahina wasn't there and he was filled with a sensation of the sea, rushed suddenly and coursing. Mahina was loose like a dolphin, kicking spray from the waves and racing north to the last resting-place before the world of her ancestors. And then he knew he *had* held her back, broken his promise and trapped her. He felt suddenly weary but Libby took him in her arms and the weariness bled through him and in that moment Mahina was gone, free to chase the stars and taste the breath of eternity.

Libby wrapped her arms about him, aware of his weakness. She pulled him towards her and held him, her face in his neck, skin rasped by his stubble. He eased his body against her, holding her, wanting her and drawing her deeper and deeper into his being. Libby plucked at the buttons of his shirt and one by one they popped. John-Cody rested his back against the dashboard, his feet slightly apart, head thrown back as she caressed his skin: eyes closed, he felt the pressure of her fingertips, the sharp kneading sensation of her nails as she dragged them to his belly and the belt buckle of his jeans.

There was a fire in him now, a fire that had been

put out with Mahina's passing but had begun to smoulder with Libby living next door and now it burned with a new and sudden fury.

Stepping away from him Libby dropped her robe and peeled her T-shirt over her head and the cold that came from the open port door lifted her flesh in goose bumps. John-Cody felt the weight all at once in his throat. He stepped out of his jeans and took a pace towards her. Libby took him in her arms and pressed herself against him, one leg climbing so her foot was on the edge of the bench and he could feel the warmth of her thigh against his own.

He took her standing up, pressing her against the wheel and lifting her. They made love frantically, in a wild and savage silence with Jonah and Tom just a few feet away below deck. The air was chill and cold and their breath came as clouds of steam but sweat rose on their bodies, matting their hair, faces close, lips touching, pushing against each other. John-Cody buried himself in the heat of Libby's love, her breasts against his flesh and the scent of her thick and heady in his nostrils.

Afterwards they remained coupled as they were, Libby holding John-Cody as tightly as she had held anyone in her life. Gradually though, she released her grip and stood with her head against his chest, resting the fire in her cheek while the passion that had risen became a quiet tenderness between them.

John-Cody bent for Libby's robe and placed it round her shoulders, then stepped into his jeans and buckled them. Neither of them said anything. They stood and held each other, watching the moon resting over Laurie Harbour and listening to whales talking to each other in the night.

496

*   *   *

In the morning John-Cody woke early and alone and lay in the half-darkness. Libby had come to bed with him and they made love again and then he had slept with her close beside him. He could hear her breathing through the thin wall between their two cabins and he assumed she had gone back to her own berth for the sake of Jonah and Tom. He closed his eyes and saw her naked on the bridge, her body half in shadow, and desire grew up once more. He saw her eyes and heard her voice and he could smell her. For a moment he let his feelings run riot and then he tried to think of Mahina as the old stirrings of betrayal and remorse came over him again. But he couldn't see her and he knew she was finally gone. He was glad for her, but his own future was as bleak as it had been yesterday, complicated still further by this new situation with Libby.

Sadness descended like a weight, something he knew he couldn't shift, so he threw off the bed-clothes and got up. Dressing quickly, he felt the rocking motion of the boat and went up to the bridge, where he watched the early morning mist drifting over the water. At the edge of the harbour he saw swirls of rising spray, twisters on the sea, little whitened squalls indicating the strength of the wind. He sipped coffee and saw a whale breach, leaping high and smashing the water like concrete. He thought briefly of his future, the one he didn't have, and wondered how he could possibly face what was coming. The first storm had eaten into his forty-two days and they would have to leave soon if he was to have any time at all for preparation. His gaze drifted to the dive locker and he wondered if he could summon the strength to try again now that he knew Mahina was finally free.

In the shallows across the bay he saw the pregnant cow roll and he went down to wake Libby.

Tom and Jonah lowered the dinghy, easing it down on the hand winches till the aluminium bottom slapped the surface of the harbour beyond the dive platform. Libby and John-Cody, ready in their dive suits and with the camera equipment between them, clambered into the little craft.

'We don't have long,' John-Cody said. 'The wind is really lifting and if it's this far into sheltered water it's serious.'

The water was even colder than yesterday and John-Cody rued the fact that now he could finally afford a drysuit he still didn't have one. His old bones would not last long in this temperature and he hoped the cow was close to her time. They finned away from where the turbulence dragged from the open sea, to where the water was quiet and empty save for the forests of bladder kelp that climbed up from the seabed.

The cow was thirty yards from them, close to the shore in relatively shallow water. John-Cody could see the swelling in her belly and he knew the birth was imminent. A strange sensation crept up on him as first he trod water then followed Libby's lead, finning below the great black whale as she blew hard on the surface: he had come here to kill himself and yet finally, through Libby, he had let Mahina go and now he was underwater again, only this time for birth, not death.

The cow bellowed, the sound loud enough to make him wince, vibrating through the water as a cry of pain: the whale eased over on her side and then back again, rolling in the water so the wake washed out to knock both Libby and John-Cody backwards. They steadied themselves and saw another whale making its way through the depths. The two animals greeted each other, easing their flanks together, stroking with flippers and rolling. Libby was below them, treading water and filming. John-Cody held back slightly as she moved in closer, watching to see how the whales would react and if their presence would be tolerated or not. The helper, aware of them both, turned and swam towards them like a giant black wall filling the sea before them, then she stopped and hung where she was, the line of white callosities running the length of her jaw. She picked them out visually, her eye working round in its blubber-encased socket, and then she rose once more to attend the pregnant cow.

John-Cody finned over to Libby and her eyes were wide and shining behind her mask. He indicated they should descend a little further and swim round so they were behind the two whales. They swam hard, finning down quickly, John-Cody checking the depth gauge and the time they had used already. The two whales were off Beacon Point, not far from the Hardwicke site, and John-Cody could feel a new and disturbing current working its way through the bay.

Libby slowed and righted herself, camera ready and focused on the two whales. The attendant was swimming round the pregnant cow whose genital slit was expanded now, and Libby felt a rush of adrenaline as she realized the birth was upon them. The cow rolled again and moaned and Libby could feel her discomfort woman to woman. All at once she thought of Bree, wondering what she was doing at that very moment. The cow moaned again and slapped the water so hard the reverberation almost took the camera from Libby's grasp. But she held on and as she did she saw the tail flukes of the calf appear through the expanding genitals.

John-Cody stared at the unfolding drama. For a split second he saw Mahina again in Moby Dick's eye telling him this was not his appointed time, that there was new life in the world; and he felt a sense of things ongoing, life and death, rebirth.

The newborn calf was immediately attended by the midwife, then the mother herself turned to look at her baby. John-Cody watched and felt that something was wrong. Then Libby was clutching his arm and pointing: he looked again and realized that the baby was just lying in the water, not rising instinctively to the surface for that first vital breath.

The midwife had backed off and now the mother swam below her calf, gently lifting it on her snout, coaxing it to the surface. But the infant did not move. It had to move in order to breathe, and needed to swim constantly until it developed enough blubber to keep it buoyant and close to the surface.

But there was no downward sweep of new flukes, no thrust of the head with its array of whitened callosities. The mother lifted it, pressing the baby to the surface, and John-Cody watched with every muscle tensed. The calf didn't breathe and when the mother let go it sank like a stone. He stared at the mother, underneath her baby once more and easing it back to the surface: still it would not breathe and the water enveloped it again.

The mother tried repeatedly, but every time she let

go the baby sank, the flukes were still and the infant sucked no life. *Come on.* John-Cody voiced the words in his head. *Come on. You have to breathe.*

The mother nosed the calf to the surface again but when she left it, it sank. John-Cody felt Libby's gloved hand on his arm and he tightened his own fist round the tangi-wai in his palm. *Breathe. Goddamn you. Breathe.*

But the baby wouldn't breathe, wouldn't swim. Its flukes were still like old rubber, its flesh puckered and wrinkled and peeling, very pale in the blue green of the water.

The midwife returned, nuzzling the mother and in her turn guiding the infant towards the surface. Between them the two whales tried again and again and again, the calf lying across their snouts at an odd limp angle as they eased it above the surface. The midwife backed off and the mother tried again on her own: but the calf rolled off her snout and began to sink. John-Cody stared and stared and felt the emptiness in his soul as the mother remained where she was, no longer moving in.

And the calf jerked, swept down with its flukes and rose to the surface as if it had woken from sleep. The mother swam underneath as if she was unsure it could make it, but the calf swam and breathed and blew and dived and blew all over again. John-Cody clenched his fist round the teardrop stone. Libby swam up, still filming the whales but looking directly at him. She brought her face close and through her mask he could make out the tears in her eyes.

A glance at his wrist told him it was time for them to ascend and together they rose, drifting in a cloud of bubbles till their heads broke the surface and they saw the calf blow from above. John-Cody tore his mask from his face and gulped air himself, lying on his back with Libby beside him, their gloved fingers entwined.

He heard the whine of the dinghy's outboard and saw Jonah tearing across the bay towards them. Instinct told him something was wrong. He and Libby swam towards the dinghy, drawing Jonah away from where the calf was now enjoying its first moments of life. Jonah spotted them and slowed and when he drew alongside John-Cody already had his tank unbuckled.

'What's up?'

'The *Moeraki*.' Jonah's eyes were dark. 'They called for help on the radio. Mayday and then nothing.'

John-Cody hauled himself over the side.

'Tom saw smoke on the other side of the point.' Jonah gestured north across the bay and John-Cody gazed at the tendrils that lifted beyond Rapoke Point on the ocean side of Enderby Island. He had seen the like many times before and knew it could just be cloud, as it so often was down here. He stood up and shaded his eyes and saw the spirals moving on the wind and knew there was no way he could say for sure whether he was looking at wisps of cloud or smoke from a burning boat. Jonah was helping Libby over the side: John-Cody stepped to the helm and guided them back to the *Korimako*.

In the wheelhouse he stripped off his wetsuit and stood in a soaking T-shirt and underpants. Tom came up from the engine room and John-Cody threw a towel round his shoulders and took the wheel, whipping it hard to starboard and piling on the revs.

502

They could afford to drag a little so long as the anchor chain didn't rake the hull. He stared at the sky, dark and brooding now above the harbour, and he knew the storm was gathering force. Libby frowned as they headed east out of Port Ross, looking at the gaps between the land that lay directly to the north.

'Wouldn't it be quicker to go straight up there?' she asked.

John-Cody spoke without looking at her. 'Too dangerous, Libby, there's no safe passage. We have to go the long way round.'

His face was suddenly still as he felt the current surge westerly beneath his feet.

'Which way is the wind blowing, Tom?'

'From the east.' Tom's voice was grave and John-Cody looked at him, aware he felt it too, and the two men regarded each other and said nothing. John-Cody stood at the wheel and Libby passed him his jeans, which were lying on the bench.

'What is it?' she asked as he worked them over pale and frozen legs.

'Get below, Lib. Try to raise the *Moeraki*.'

Libby dropped down the aft steps and lifted the handset on the single-side-band radio. '*Moeraki*, *Moeraki*, *Moeraki*. This is the *Korimako*. Do you copy, over?'

On the bridge John-Cody steered the *Korimako* at full speed towards the entrance to Port Ross and the North East Cape. Tom stood beside him and Jonah also and none of them spoke as they saw the squalls baiting the sea to a fury beyond the point.

'Any joy, Libby?' John-Cody yelled down the steps.

'No.'

'Keep trying.' He looked ahead then glanced at Tom. 'Your boat,' he said, left the wheel and stepped onto the deck. He stood a moment by the dive locker with the wind full in his face and watched the white-tipped waves dancing on the horizon. Experience told him the storm was off the North East Cape, running out a mile or so east and up the coast of Enderby Island. If they could skirt it they would be OK, but by then the *Moeraki* and her crew might be lost. He chewed his lip and considered. They had not got the aluminium shields up on the side windows and there was barely time now. He looked through the fuzzy perspex at Tom and their eyes met and held. John-Cody knew they were both thinking the same thing. They would have to risk the eye of the storm with a westerly current under their feet and an easterly full in their faces.

The first big waves crashed over the bows as they hit the choppy water out of the lee of the point and John-Cody went back inside, worked his way to the aft steps and called down to Libby.

'Brace yourself down there, Lib. This is going to be rough.'

She glanced up at him and for a moment they just looked at each other and then she turned her attention back to the radio.

John-Cody set the autopilot and signalled for Jonah to give him a hand with the aluminium shields. Tom joined them and they managed to secure the leeward side, then made their way round the stern to the windward, which would be far more difficult. They were beyond the North East Cape now and the sea swamped the deck. John-Cody slipped and slithered in his rubber boots and Jonah gripped the rail as they tried to manhandle the shield into place.

'*Give it up!*' Tom had his hand cupped to his mouth and screamed at them through the wind. Between them they managed to get the shield back leeward and stow it.

The wind tore at the tussock grass on Enderby Island, so powerfully that it ripped great clumps from their roots, and they caught in twisters which carried them out to sea. The water was black and foaming and it crashed between the rocks lifting like scarred and broken teeth beneath the cliffs.

The *Korimako* was tossed like a spinning top, barrel rolling from side to side as she ploughed into the wind and dipped into troughs where the waves reared above the deck and broke with a sound like gunshots. Below deck, Libby sat at the chart table, gripping with one hand and her knees while she tried in vain to contact the *Moeraki*. In the end John-Cody appeared above her.

'Give it up, Lib. You won't raise them now.'

She came up to the bridge still wearing the nylon inner she wore under her drysuit, gripping the handrails on the steps for all she was worth as the boat lurched from side to side. The front windows were awash, opaque almost, and John-Cody was steering by the radar, the current running the keel like a switchback. Jonah had everything battened down in the galley, but the boat rolled and crockery shifted and stores rattled the doors of the lockers, pots and pans striking one another with a metallic clang that set Libby's teeth on edge.

They were approaching the eye of the squall now

and Libby stared out of the starboard windows at the white-dusted whirlwinds twisting up from the wave tops: ghostlike and spectral they rose, swarming across the ocean as if in battle with one another. She moved next to John-Cody where he stood at the wheel with every muscle tensed, and gripped the top of the bench for support. Tom was in her place by the starboard door, resting his weight on the lip of the dashboard, feet rooted against the edge of the cold store behind him. Jonah sat at the table and held on.

John-Cody peered through the water-washed windows and thought about the crew of the fishing vessel in trouble north of Enderby Island. He looked sideways at Libby.

'When you were on the radio, did you hear any other vessel trying to make contact?'

She shook her head.

And then her eyes balled in their sockets and she stared past him and through the window at the massive wall of water rising right in front of them.

John-Cody saw the look in her eyes and he twisted round and the breath stuck in his throat.

'Oh my God.' Then he was yelling, 'Standing wave. Standing wave. Get back from the windows.'

He had barely got the words out when Libby saw the white crust flake at the summit as the wave began to topple. Fifty feet or more it rose, obscured by the weight of the storm, and then it was rearing right in front of them.

She had no time to move: the wave hit with a sound that split her eardrums. A great tearing crack, a rumble like thunder right overhead and she felt the rush of the wind and then explosions across the

506

bows and tonnes and tonnes of water splintered the reinforced windows. For a second all she heard was a great rending sound, then the windows gave and she was slammed against the wall to the right of the aft steps. Gallons of water sucked the breath from her body. She was picked up, held for a second in fingers of ice, then tossed below with the sea pouring over her in a blast that raked her bones. She hit the floor and the water enveloped her in a darkness that filled her mouth, nose and lungs, stopping up her ears and blinding her so she floundered, kicking like a diver, hands out to protect her face.

John-Cody dropped to his knees just before the wave hit and he grabbed the spokes of the wheel and held on. He felt Tom crash against him then he was gone and he held that wheel for all he was worth. The sheer volume of water dragged at him like decompression in an aircraft, hauling and clawing and tearing. It sucked and boiled, rushing in his ears, filling his mouth: he tasted blood and salt and thought for a moment he would drown. He felt the *Korimako* roll badly and for a terrifying second he feared she would capsize, but then she bobbed and he was thrown bodily sideways, hands torn from their grip as he crashed into the starboard door.

The boat righted herself and instinct took over as he scrabbled for a handhold: grabbing the door to the switch locker, he held on. The water hissed around him as it poured back through the smashed windows and washed out of the scuppers. John-Cody got to his feet, freezing cold, the sea to his waist, and looked for the others. Tom was below deck for'ard and he bobbed at the top of the steps, the cabins full of water. John-Cody grabbed him by

507

the hair and hauled him up and he opened his eyes and coughed and spluttered, vomit mixing with the water. Jonah reared up from behind them, a cut above his eye, and dived for the bilge-pump switch. John-Cody heard it click and hum and thanked God as the pumps began to work.

He looked for Libby but couldn't see her and in the same moment he spun the wheel to port and turned the *Korimako*'s stern into the wind, pointing them back the way they had come. He stood as the water level dropped and they ran for shelter at full speed. He yelled at Jonah to hunt for Libby and moments later he appeared at the top of the aft steps pushing her before him. John-Cody stared at her, pale and shivering, the shock etched in her eyes.

'Are you all right?' he shouted above the noise of the pumps and the wind battering them now in the stern. Dumbly she looked back at him and then she nodded and her eyes fluttered, closed then open again and focused.

John-Cody steered by the wheel, fighting both the current that was against them and the wind that was behind them now. They heeled and rolled, taking on more water: he lost his footing and dropped to one knee before righting himself. Below decks they were awash, the pumps barely able to cope. Speed was what they needed and he flattened the throttle and the engine rattled and hammered under his feet.

'What on earth happened?' Libby came alongside him.

'We took a standing wave. A westerly current meeting an easterly wind, it pushed the water into a wall that built and built till gravity toppled it over.'

Then he noticed that the compass head was gone,

ripped away from the gimbal that mounted it on the dashboard. He stared at the global positioning system and the radar and both the screens were blank. The breath dried in his throat as he looked at the autopilot, where the bearings were spinning out of control.

TWENTY-FIVE

Ned Pole listened to the radio reports in his office and chewed on a fingernail. He had heard the distress call go up from the *Moeraki* and Tom Blanch answer on the *Korimako*. That was all he had heard; checking with the skippers of his crayfish boats, he learned that that was all anybody had heard. He sat at his desk and gazed absently out of the window. Jane was on the phone to the US, discussing John-Cody Gibbs's imminent departure. He heard her talking about the *Korimako* and the wharf and how the price ought to come right down. He wandered to the window where the rain was sheeting and stared at the back paddock where the three horses took shelter under the trees. Barrio whinnied, pawing the sodden ground: Pole had not ridden him since he had witnessed Hunter Caldwell on his back and memories of his son were fresh and raw and painful.

Behind him Jane put the phone down. 'All's well,' she said. 'They want your plans on e-mail as soon as possible.'

Pole squinted at her.

'Your plans, Ned: for the sound. How it's going to work. This is your baby, remember, your big chance to prove you can be a businessman after all.' She looked at him with her head to one side, a little mockery in her eyes.

'No-one can make contact with the *Moeraki*.'

Jane lifted one eyebrow.

'She's a fishing boat, last position given as north of the Auckland Islands.'

'So?'

'So she raised a Mayday call and was answered by the *Korimako*. Nobody's been able to raise either boat since.'

'So?' Jane said again.

'They could be lost, Jane.'

Jane shrugged. 'Oh well, that'll save immigration the bother of deporting Gibbs.'

Pole looked at her then and finally knew he hated her. 'You've never been to sea, have you?' he said.

'No. And I don't intend to go.' Jane sat down at her desk and indicated his. 'Perhaps you better get the plan on e-mail, Ned. We've got a home to save, remember?'

Alex was on the telephone to Bluff Harbour. She too had heard the *Moeraki*'s distress call and Tom responding to it. Ever since then she had been trying to raise the *Korimako*, had got nothing and was asking if Bluff had picked up anything she had missed. They hadn't but told her they would come back when they heard any more. There were no other boats within the immediate vicinity; the closest was beyond the Pukaki Rise, three hundred kilometres north-east of Port Ross. Alex went back to the inner office and sat down. She glanced at her watch: it would soon be time for Bree to come home and she wondered what to tell her. Bree would want to talk to her mother as usual and would worry if she couldn't. She looked out of the window, a little knot of fear in the pit of her stomach: storm clouds were gathering over the mountains.

John-Cody dropped anchor in Port Ross and Libby listened to the terrible metallic clanking that resounded through the boat. The bilge pumps were working overtime and the water level was down to their knees below decks. On the bridge everything was saturated, weed and debris from the sea pasting everything in a green and brown sludge; it was freezing and there was no chance of any heat with the diesel stove knocked out. Libby suggested lighting the oven to try to warm things up but John-Cody wanted the gas conserved. He was staring at his dashboard and his face was thin and grey and pensive. Libby looked where he looked. Already she had noticed the compass was wrecked, but she saw him working at the radar and the twin GPS consoles where all the screens were blank. Tom came alongside her, hair plastered against his head, clothes wringing wet. He stood there shivering. All the cabins had been swamped and there was not a stitch of dry clothing anywhere.

John-Cody was twisting knobs and pressing buttons on the GPS, but still the screens were blank. He eased the monitor forward and looked at the back, then cursed lightly under his breath.

'Is it dead?' Libby voiced everyone's fear.

John-Cody looked over at her. 'Dead as: both of

them.' He slapped the top of the monitor with the flat of his palm. 'Tom, keep the pumps working, I'm going to try and raise somebody.' He slid down the steps and splashed into freezing water up to his knees. 'Libby,' he called, 'put on a wetsuit. It's the only way you're going to stay warm. Jonah, as soon as the pumps are clear, make us something to eat.' He lifted the handset on the first radio, twisted the dials to 4417 and heard the buzz of interference.

'*Kori*-base, *Kori*-base, this is the *Korimako*. Do you copy, Alex?'

Nothing.

'*Kori*-base, *Kori*-base, *Kori*-base, this is the *Korimako*. Do you copy?'

Still nothing: not so much as a change in the tone of interference.

John-Cody put the handset down and tried the second radio but still he got no answer. He swung back up the steps and went on deck. The wind was dropping, which was something, as the storm blew itself around the North East Cape. He looked at his watch: five o'clock and almost fully dark. He went astern and checked the aerial masts for the radios. One was gone, the other buckled halfway up. The third, the spare high on the mizzen, looked intact. He wondered what had become of the *Moeraki* and a chill ran through him. Amazingly he found a dry cigarette in his pouch and lit it, letting the smoke escape his lips as a whale breached further down the harbour. He could have kicked himself for not getting the hand-held compass fixed.

Tom came astern and they looked at each other for a long quiet moment.

'We've got no navigation,' John-Cody told him.

'We can still make it.'

John-Cody looked at a sky heavy with cloud. 'Yes, but we need that lot to shift first.'

Tom leaned on the rail: he had a soggy blanket round his shoulders.

'Put a wetsuit on,' John-Cody told him.

'Can't get one to fit.' Tom patted his stomach. 'I'll be all right.' He looked longingly at John-Cody's cigarette. He offered it to him but Tom refused. 'I mean to give it up, Gib. If I can get through this kind of stress, I reckon I've got it beaten.'

'We need to fix boards over the holes in the windows,' John-Cody said. 'Let's get on with it and then we'll see if we can't get that heater working.'

The three of them went below while Libby took over making soup. Ripping the mattresses from bunks, they lifted the plywood boards and carried them upstairs. The three central windows had been fully breached and there were cracks in the others where the perspex had given and raked across the glass. John-Cody fetched a saw from the engine room and they began to cut the boards to size. They had to be fixed to the wooden struts on the inside because the housings on deck were fully moulded with no fixing point available. Tom shaped them as best he could and Jonah screwed them in place. First, though, they cut a small hole in each so they had some forward vision. When they were finished John-Cody wiped sweat from his brow, drier and warmer now. Tom's clothes too were drying. Libby had already been up for'ard and laid some of the sodden blankets over the line in the engine room. The diesel heater was still soaking, however, and they could not get it to light.

John-Cody looked at the wooden windows and sipped the soup Libby passed him. 'These will have to do,' he said. 'We'll leave the side shields off so we can see.'

'Won't that be dangerous?' Libby looked startled.

He moved his shoulders. 'I guess if we were really unlucky we could take another wave, but we've got no compass or GPS or anything, bonny lass. We need to see so we don't hit anything.' He looked at her over the rim of his mug. 'We've also got no autopilot so we'll have to get home with the wheel.' He paused and glanced at the others. 'That'll mean lots of watches, spelling one another in short bursts. It's the best way to stay alert and try to maintain some kind of course.'

'But how can we set a course?' Libby asked him. 'You make it sound like we can.'

'We don't have a choice, Libby. We need to get home.'

'Why can't we just sit and wait for a rescue?'

'Because the boat's seaworthy apart from navigation: I've been on fishing boats that put out every day in a much worse state than this. Floating coffins, some of them.' He touched her on the shoulder. 'Listen, it takes twenty-four hours to reach the Snares from here. That's if the weather's being kind. Right now the wind's blowing from the north. The squall is probably localized to the area round the North East Cape. We can sail round it and then head north. When the wind changes it'll blow nor'west then westerly and sou'west, all of which we can use.'

'Sails?' Jonah said.

'Jib only. The *Kori*'s wounded, Jonah. I'm not going to risk both sails.'

515

All at once John-Cody felt alive: he had passed his point of no return; whether it was making love in the wheelhouse or the birth of the whale or Mahina's final departure he didn't know, but he was alive and the energy pulsed in his veins. Whatever was coming he would face and he had promised Bree he would get her mother home safely.

'Have we got enough fuel?' Libby asked him.

'We've stayed longer than I wanted to and used more, given our little excursion today, but so long as we get a few breaks now we'll be fine.'

'But how do we navigate?'

'Dead reckoning.'

Libby arched one eyebrow and he crooked his index finger at her. She followed him on deck and he stood with his arm about her shoulders and pointed at the cloud-wrecked sky above them. 'Somewhere up there is the Southern Cross. I showed you, remember? If I can see the Southern Cross I can find due south between the pointers and the stem. If I know where south is I can guide the boat north. And that's the way home.'

The word *home* echoed in his head as he said it. Libby heard it too, like a bell tolling between them, and she looked into his face then reached out a hand to calm the hair where it flew in his eyes. He held her for a moment and then bent his head and kissed her, face chill in the wind, smelling of the sea. He looked in her eyes and saw the questions rising. He brushed her lips with his fingers.

'We need to get some sleep now. We leave at eight o'clock in the morning.'

'Not earlier?'

He shook his head. 'I want to get to the Snares in

daylight. God help us if we come across them in the dark with no compass or radar. We leave here at eight. I reckon twenty-six hours to get there, given we'll have to skirt the squall. That means ten a.m. when we hit.'

The night was very cold and they all stayed in the wheelhouse, Libby and Tom draped round the C-shaped bench at the table, John-Cody stretched out on the floor along the bridge and Jonah lengthways between the aft and for'ard steps. They had managed to get the diesel heater going and it burned with a flickering orange flame. The water had been pumped out but the boat was sodden and dank and cold, dark below deck with moisture into everything. Libby lay in the half-darkness with a damp blanket over her, listening to Tom's laboured breathing and thinking about Bree. She hadn't been able to talk to her today; there was still no radio contact. She wondered what Bree was doing, what she was thinking, whether she was worried or whether Alex would have told her it was quite normal to have difficulty contacting a boat in the Sub-Antarctic. Atmospherics. Since she had been here Bree had learned a lot about atmospherics.

She looked at her watch: only nine o'clock and yet she felt the weariness of the day envelop her. Sleep would not be long in coming despite the discomfort. She thought about John-Cody then, how much she loved him now and the fact that she would have him for only a few days longer. God only knew how long it would take them to get back to the South Island. That was if they got back at all. He had talked about the Southern Cross, but stars didn't come out in the daytime: nobody had told her how they would

517

navigate in the daytime. Those thoughts chilled her and she closed her eyes and tried to think of happier times.

Her mind drifted and she thought about the calf they had seen being born, and prayed her video equipment had withstood the battering from the standing wave. She had locked it in the aluminium cases as soon as they got back on board so it ought to be all right. She saw the calf again in her mind's eye, heard the voice in her head willing it to live when it seemed it would surely die. She remembered the mother's attention, her fevered attempts to lift it to the surface so it could draw breath for the first time. The instinct of millions of years of evolution had been summed up in a moment between life and death. For a while the outcome was balanced on a knife edge, then all at once there was life: and within minutes of that victory Jonah was telling them that men might be lost north of Enderby Island.

Opening her eyes, she looked at the shadows cast on the ceiling by the reflected light from outside. One thing she had learned about the sea: it was never pitch black. You could always see the horizon, unlike the darkness on land. The sea was darker than the sky and you could pick things out in the gloom. That would aid their passage north; they ought to be able to see any other boats before they hit them. Maybe in the morning the radios would work.

Bree held Hunter's hand, the two of them sitting in the house in Manapouri. They had got off the bus and gone to the office to call her mother on the radio, but hadn't been able to get through. Alex had tried hard to hide her fears, but Bree saw through her. She asked and Alex told her the truth: a boat called the *Moeraki* was missing and the *Korimako* had answered her distress call. Bree had heard that distress call before, watching a film on television. Mayday. Mayday. Mayday. It sent a shiver through her now and she tightened her grip on Hunter's hand. Alex was sitting in the other chair with Bree and Hunter squashed into one, listening to the conversations between the boat skippers on fisherman's radio. Nobody had been able to raise either the *Moeraki* or the *Korimako*.

Bree could hear the distress in the depth of the men's voices: comrades possibly lost in the Southern Ocean, it was what they all feared the most. She looked at Hunter and he squeezed her hand more tightly. Sierra, sensing the mood, sat with her chin resting on Bree's thigh, her dark brown eyes gazing up. Bree heard the rumble of a diesel truck outside and then the sound of a door slamming. There were footsteps on the path and Sierra gave a low growl and someone rapped on the door: Bree jumped up to open it and saw Ned Pole, tall and lean in the porch light.

'G'day, Bree.'

'Mr Pole. Come in.' Bree turned to Alex. 'It's Mr Pole, Alex.'

Pole came inside and Sierra lay down again. Pole held his hat in his hands, working the brim between his fingers. He nodded to Hunter and looked at Alex. 'Just thought I'd pop by, Alex. The weather reports reckon the storm'll blow itself out north of Port Ross. They're sending a plane in the morning.'

Alex got up to put the kettle on. Pole sat in the chair she had vacated and stretched out his legs.

'Have you still not heard from the *Korimako*?'

Alex shook her head. 'I heard them answer the Mayday and that was it.'

'It'll be the storm. Don't worry. They're probably jammed up with static rain. It'll be right in the morning, you'll see.' He looked at Bree then. 'Don't you worry about anything, Bree. Gib's a good skipper and he's got Tom with him. I don't know a better seaman in New Zealand than old Tom Blanch.'

'Tom hasn't been to sea in years,' Alex said to him.

'That doesn't matter. He can't unlearn what experience has already taught him.' Again he looked at Bree. 'Don't worry: they'll get your mother home. They're probably just sheltering out the storm.'

Hunter looked at him then. 'Do you think they reached the other boat in time, Mr Pole?'

Pole's face was grave, his eyes narrow and dark. 'I don't know, Hunter. I hope so.' He looked at Alex then. 'The *Moeraki*'s out of Dunedin: I know the skipper pretty well.'

'They'd reported some engine trouble,' Alex said.

Pole nodded slowly and stood up again. 'Thanks for the coffee, Alex, but I have to be going. I just thought I'd check on the young folks.' He twirled his hat again. 'If you need anything you know where to find me.'

Libby woke to the sun on her face and sat up, almost banging her head on the table. The others were already awake and within seconds she heard the auxiliary fire and the familiar comforting rattle of the diesel engine sent vibrations through the deck. John-Cody and Jonah went outside and began to haul on the anchor wheel. Libby frowned and then she realized the standing wave had knocked out virtually all the electronics. Tom came up from the engine room still dressed in his normal clothes. Jonah was wearing a wetsuit but John-Cody wore the jeans and sweater that Libby had half dried out for him. She went on deck and asked if she should cook breakfast. Jonah called that there were bacon and eggs in the cold store. Libby caught John-Cody's eye and a glance passed between them. He worked with sweat on his brow, the muscles standing out on his arms and veins bulging at his neck.

Ten minutes after eight they were steaming south of Ewing Island to put some distance between the boat and the storm, which was still blowing for all it was worth around the North East Cape. As they entered the open sea on the eastern side of the island Libby watched the spray licking up the walls of the cliffs with such ferocity the high tops foamed in white. Tom moved at her shoulder. 'Hard to believe we were in the middle of that yesterday.'

Libby shivered. 'Maybe we should've gone round.'

Tom shook his head. 'A Mayday's a Mayday, Libby: grave and imminent danger. We had to try and get there as fast as we could.'

John-Cody was at the wheel with Jonah down below. The boat stank now, with soaking mattresses and carpets and bedclothes, weed and kelp draped across the lockers in front of the windows. Jonah turned on the deck hose to wash it down. Libby watched him, standing across the bridge from John-Cody at the starboard door. It was dark in the wheelhouse, the windows blocked with wood, holes cut in the middle to see by. The holes let the wind whistle through and the chill was ever present. John-Cody had the heater working full blast below but it was nowhere near enough to dry the boat out. The seats they had slept on last night were damp and rancid and already mould was setting in. Libby's wetsuit squelched and was very constricting: she considered taking it off.

'Take your choice between freedom of movement and warmth,' John-Cody told her.

'You're not wearing one. Tom's not either.'

'Jonah's got mine and Tom reckons he can't find one to fit.' John-Cody cracked a smile. 'Don't worry about us, Lib. Just keep yourself warm.'

'If my drysuit inner wasn't soaked I'd wear that. I'm going to try the radio again,' she told him.

'Be my guest.'

She went aft and sat on the plastic stool at the chart table: she tried both radios in vain for nearly twenty minutes then came up to the saloon once again. John-Cody stood square at the wheel, feeding it back and forth through his hands to right the course in the current, which he could feel shifting under his feet. He glanced over his shoulder.

'Try again later, when we get round the squall. It's probably blocking the signal. We've still got one good aerial left so it ought to work.'

Libby came alongside him and peered at the sea through the hole in front of her face. The wooden boards were crudely cut but securely screwed down in case the boat took another wave. Jonah stepped inside, his hair tied back in a ponytail.

'Deck's clean, boss.'

John-Cody nodded. 'Give Tom a hand, will you, Jonah? The dinghy's got a loose shackle on the transom. I don't want that coming away if we hit some more weather.'

Jonah disappeared on deck once again and John-Cody glanced at Libby. 'Take the helm, Lib, and keep her as she goes.'

Libby took the wheel and brushed her hand over his. He gripped her fingers for a moment then eased a loose strand of hair behind her ear. 'Your boat,' he told her.

He stepped on deck and she watched him by the mizzen through the hole in the wooden board. He stood with his back to her and shaded his eyes from the sun, which peeped now and again through sucker holes in the clouds. He lifted his left hand and glanced at his watch, then he looked across the port bow towards the storm. He came back inside and took the wheel again.

'What were you doing?'

He looked sideways at her. 'Have you got any dry cigarettes?'

Libby shrugged. 'In the wheelhouse?'

'Why not? The wheelhouse is wrecked anyway. It'll ease the smell of old seaweed in the nostrils.'

Libby checked her gear and found a pack of dry cigarettes; they had been wet but were dry now and the paper was yellowed. She lit one for him and he puffed smoke from the side of his mouth.

'What were you doing just now?' The *Korimako* pitched in the swell and Libby shifted her feet, gripping the back of the bench for support.

'Taking a bearing from the sun.' John-Cody worked the wheel through his hands as the boat bucked and punched into waves that washed across the bows. 'The wind's changing,' he muttered.

Tom came in through the starboard door. 'The wind's moving round to the west.'

John-Cody nodded. 'As soon as I turn us north I want you to hoist the jib.'

'You sure just the jib?'

'I reckon. We're limping, Tom. Let's not take any chances.' He looked at Libby again. 'When we head north we'll be away from the squall. Your job is to man the radio.'

'How do you know we're heading north?'

'You can find north with a watch,' he explained. 'All you do is point the twelve at the sun or where you think the sun is if there's cloud cover, then look where the hour hand is and midway between the hour hand and twelve is north.'

Libby's eyes were suddenly shining. 'So we can find north in the daylight and south at night. That's brilliant,' she said.

'That's if the stars are out: they're harder to locate than the sun.'

John-Cody took them about four nautical miles east of Port Ross and then turned the boat north, slightly favouring the north-west as far as he could gauge it. Jonah and Tom raised the jib and set the tack. Libby went below and started again at the radio. Immediately she heard voices through the crackle of static and twisted the knob till the crackle subsided and she distinctly heard somebody calling the *Moeraki*. She yelled above for John-Cody, who slid down the steps. Together they listened and then John-Cody frowned. 'They've got a plane up searching.' He snatched the transmitter from her hand and called the aircraft. 'Foxtrot Tango Alpha 1-7, this is the *Korimako*. Do you copy, over?'

They heard a hiss and a whistle over the speakers and then a voice drifting in and out of the static.

'Reading you just, *Korimako*. What is your position, over?'

John-Cody pressed the transmitter again. 'Exact position not known: we've lost all navigation. I reckon we're a few miles due east of Port Ross. I'm trying to skirt the squall. Is there any sign of the *Moeraki*, over?'

'Negative, *Korimako*: we're sweeping the area, but so far that is negative.'

John-Cody looked at Libby and for a moment he thought about all the ships that had ever been wrecked on the savage shores of the islands: he knew them by heart, had listed them years ago and had never ever forgotten them.

'Copy that, Foxtrot Tango Alpha.'

'Are you OK? Do you require assistance, over?' The voice was weaker now.

'We're seaworthy, but the instruments are out. Over.'

They heard no more, the static took over and John-Cody twisted the thumb wheel down then transferred the switch back to the speakers on the bridge. They went up top where Tom stood at the wheel and Jonah was busy with the stove.

Libby again debated whether or not to swap her wetsuit for the regular clothes she had laid out in the engine room. Jonah still wore his, however, and the wheelhouse was cold and draughty. She checked to see how dry her other clothes were but they were still damp so she left them where they were and went back to the bridge.

The sea was rougher now, their horizon the height of the swell immediately around the boat. The water was grey blue, flecked in spittle with flint-like breakers slapping against the hull. The wind was blowing nor'west to west and the sail was full and billowed hard at the seams. The engine was static at seven and a half knots and even Libby could tell that if the wind shifted the wrong way they would be going nowhere fast. John-Cody must have read her mind because he came and stood next to her, his back to the cold store, arms folded across his chest.

'The swell is only about four metres, Lib. It looks worse when we're in the troughs, but we are making progress. The wind is good from this direction and it should shift behind us. If it keeps up we'll see the Snares tomorrow morning.'

'And after that?' she asked him.

He laid a hand on her shoulder. 'Let's make the Snares first.'

But her words stuck in his head. If they made the Snares unscathed then they only had four hours of ocean and they would come to Stewart Island or somewhere along the South Island itself. If they made that he had only a handful of days before he left Aotearoa for ever. As they lay at anchor last night he had told Tom and Jonah what was going on and afterwards they were silent. That silence was with him now and once again he questioned whether or not he could get through it. He had vowed that he would get this boat and her crew home safely, but that's all he had vowed. What came after, leaving the country, America and the FBI, prison again after twenty-five years – would they do that to him? He had no idea, but the thought chilled him more than the wind that broke the wooden boards and he concentrated on looking forward, the bow pitching and punching into waves that washed the deck.

His thoughts were broken by the radio, a voice loud and clear beside him.

'*Korimako*, *Korimako*, *Korimako*: this is *Kori*-base. Do you copy, boss?'

John-Cody leaped down the aft steps, Libby close behind him. 'Alex, this is Gib. Reading you loud and clear.'

'Thank God. What the hell's going on?'

'We took a standing wave answering the *Moeraki*'s Mayday. Is there any sign of her?'

'None.'

John-Cody bit his lip.

'What's a standing wave?' Alex said over the speakers.

'You don't want to know. Suffice to say we've no radar or GPS or compass.'

'You're kidding me.'

'No, I'm not, but it's OK. We've skirted the storm and are heading nor'nor'west for the Snares. What's the weather forecast?'

'It's good for the next twenty-four hours.'

'Sweet as.' John-Cody gripped Libby's hand. They heard Bree's voice and he handed the transmitter to Libby.

'Bree, it's me, Mum. Are you OK?'

'Oh, Mum. We've been so worried about you.'

'It's OK. I'm fine. I'm in very good hands.'

'Is everything all right, though? They said you answered a Mayday. Is everything all right?'

'Everything's just fine, Bree. Don't worry. We'll be back at Bluff Cove just as soon as you know it.'

'Thank goodness. Mum, I don't want you to do this again. Just come home, please. We thought you were dead. I thought the boat had sunk. I thought I'd

527

never see you again.' She broke off then. 'Let me speak to John-Cody.'

'OK, darling, I love you.'

'I love you too, Mum. Be careful.'

Libby passed the handset back to John-Cody.

'Hey, Bree. How are you?'

'Will you look after my mum for me, please?'

'Of course.' He leaned closer to the radio. 'You trust me, don't you?'

'Of course I do.'

'I'll bring her home, I promise. You just be waiting, that's all.'

'OK. Thank you. I love you.'

'I love you too, Breezy.' John-Cody handed the radio back to Libby and went up the steps. Libby felt his pain acutely, like it was pain of her own. 'Take care of Alex, Bree, and call whenever you want. If you can't get through it'll only be because of the weather. We'll be just fine here. Don't worry. John-Cody knows exactly what he's doing.'

'You love him, don't you, Mum?'

'Yes, Bree, I love him very much.'

'Then marry him. I want us to stay in New Zealand.'

Libby closed her eyes, knowing that John-Cody could hear through the speakers up on the bridge.

'I've got to go now, Bree. I have to stand my watch.'

'Have you told him, Mum? You know you need to tell him.'

'Bree,' she said, 'don't worry. Everything is fine.'

Libby climbed the steps to the saloon and the silence hit her: the engine chattered and the boat had its familiar metallic hum, but everyone was silent.

528

John-Cody stood with his back to her, shoulders square at the wheel. Libby could hear the hiss of static once more through the speakers; she stood for a moment and wondered how she could break the news to Bree. She moved alongside John-Cody and he stared, gaze fixed, through the hole directly in front of his face. The wind chipped at his skin, drying it, making him screw up his eyes. He held the wooden wheel in both hands, easing gently to port or starboard whenever the current shifted. Libby stood at his shoulder, looking where he looked, then reaching out she entwined her fingers with his. John-Cody eased the wheel to starboard and Libby steered with him.

TWENTY-SIX

Darkness fell early in the Southern Ocean winter. Land had been lost to them a long time before and John-Cody checked the course as best he could every hour or so with Tom echoing him at odd intervals. Every minute, every wave they punched through, each sheet of spray littering the deck in pearls of white took them closer to the Snares. Libby, at the wheel, kept ducking her head to look up at a sky still smothered in cloud. She felt anxious; the worry had been growing with every moment as the world dulled outside. How could they hold their course if they couldn't see the Southern Cross?

Both John-Cody and Tom were quiet, John-Cody resting on the bench and Tom squatting on the skipper's stool with his hands gripping his knees. Jonah had slept for a few hours, somehow finding some comfort among the dank and rancid bedding, and now he came up from below, hair loose, muttering darkly as if his sleep had been stalked by dreams.

They were running low on food and he rummaged in the cold store for something to cook for dinner. Libby stood at the wheel, weariness in her limbs as the light faded and the waves ahead grew dimmer. Jonah rustled up some tinned food and Tom took his turn at the helm. Libby ate at the table, the smell of salt and rubber in her nose, looking over her shoulder now and again for any sign of the stars. There was none and she looked at John-Cody, half seeking a hint of concern in his eyes. He ate slowly, methodically lifting his fork to his mouth then chewing mechanically. His face was closed, his thoughts his own, and now and again he would sip from a glass of water. The boat reeled in a sudden eddy and the crockery slid so they had to grab it to stop it crashing onto the floor. Libby watched Tom work the wheel through his palms, endeavouring to hold their course. John-Cody had told her that the current continually kicked them off their crude rhumb-line and they had to keep the right speed and make corrections with the wheel. He had no way of knowing whether they were succeeding or not as they had no compass bearing to check.

Libby was aware of a dull clunking sound coming from somewhere in the stern and John-Cody's face told her he had heard it too.

'What's that?' she asked him.

'A loose shackle on the transom winch.' He looked at Tom. 'I'm thinking we're going to lose the dinghy, Tom. That wave pretty much ruined the transom.'

Tom looked over his shoulder. 'You reckon maybe we should just drop and tow her?'

John-Cody made a face. 'I'll go and check the shackle.'

The wheelhouse grew colder as he hauled open the leeward door. Libby shivered, wriggling her shoulders as she watched him disappear into the night, yanking the door to in his wake. The darkness was almost complete now: she could no longer see anything of the horizon and the waves were walls of black.

John-Cody worked his way astern, holding tightly to the rail as the *Korimako* jerked and rolled with the swell. He gauged the waves to be close to four metres and the wind was up in the west. It was moving as he had anticipated, however, which was a good thing. They had been travelling for almost ten hours now and he hoped the bearing they were on was a good one. The wind coming across the bows from the port side indicated they had not strayed very far if it had indeed turned westerly; there had been too much interference on the radio to check the weather forecast, but his instincts told him it had.

One look at the transom and he knew Tom was right, they should drop the dinghy onto its line and tow it. He stood for a moment watching the waves pitch and roll, rising on all sides, the boat bucking like a horse, and he held on to the rail with both hands. He couldn't do anything about the dinghy on his own, not with the shackle in the state it was, so carefully he made his way back along the starboard side and ducked into the wheelhouse. Libby was at the helm and Tom sat on the moist bench, eating. John-Cody touched Libby on the shoulder and took over. She sat down next to Tom and worked the heels of her palms into her eyes. John-Cody peered at the sky through the holes in the bunk boards. Wind and spray combined to lick his face and he saw no break in the clouds. That disturbed him: it was a long time since daylight and now he needed the stars.

Behind him Tom pushed away his plate and stood up. 'Gib, I'll go and drop the dinghy.'

John-Cody looked over his shoulder. 'You can't do it by yourself.'

'I'll give you a hand, Tom,' Libby said.

Tom glanced at her and then at John-Cody. John-Cody looked at Libby. 'OK. But be careful, that little boat is heavy.'

Tom stepped into his wet-weather gear, tying the pants with the waist string. Libby was still wearing her wetsuit and she zipped it to the neck and pulled on sodden gumboots. John-Cody felt the current shift underfoot and he turned the wheel a few degrees to port; again he looked at the sky and still there were no stars to guide him.

Libby closed the door behind her and followed Tom, one hand on the rail, working her way to the stern. The deck lights were switched on so they could see what they were doing, but the sea was dark, the swell rolling in massive black flakes and the wind howling in her ears. She held on to the rail and waited while Tom looked at the shackle, holding it in one hand while supporting himself with the other.

'We'll just lower her as she is, Lib,' he yelled across the wind. 'There's nothing I can do about this.' He indicated the rope twisted round the cleat on the transom. 'Take the leeward side.'

The wind tore at him and Libby watched his baggy wet-weather gear shiver and luff like a sail. Tom dragged the hood down so he could see but it lifted and buffeted the back of his head. Libby wound her hand round the rope, readying herself to unhook the twist from the cleat. Tom stood a moment, cupped his hand to call to her and then a wave crashed over the stern.

Libby braced herself, tightening her grip on the rope as the water washed over her. It filled her mouth and nose, blinding and choking her in the same moment. Balance gone, she lost her footing and slipped on the greasy deck. She screamed as she felt the wave suck her through the rail, but her legs caught either side of a strut and her grip on the rope kept her from being dragged overboard. She scrabbled for a foothold, panting for breath, eyes blurred, then lost her footing again. Finally she regained her feet, one hand on the rail, the other still clutching the rope. She looked over at Tom, but Tom was no longer there.

For a moment nothing registered. Then it hit her, and she suddenly found her voice.

'*Man overboard!*' She screamed the words, but they were lost to the wind. Her heart thumped in her chest and she gripped the rail, desperately searching for Tom. But she couldn't see anything and she raced up the starboard side and yanked open the door.

John-Cody stared at her, seeing her face framed white against her soaking hair.

'Tom's overboard.'

He reacted instantly, dropping the revs and slamming the gears into reverse.

'Jonah, your boat. Libby, get back astern. You shouldn't have taken your eyes off him.'

'I couldn't see him at all.'

'Dammit. Get astern.'

Libby ducked back into the wind as the boat pitched into a new trough: water crashed over the stern and raced the length of the deck to boil around her ankles.

Jonah was at the wheel now. 'Hard astern,' John-Cody told him. 'Keep her hard astern.' He dived for the door but Jonah's voice checked him.

'The jib.' He pointed through the boards and John-Cody hesitated for a second.

'No,' he said. 'Leave it up. It'll keep her steady. Hard astern, Jonah: keep her as she goes.'

Libby gripped the quarter rail for all she was worth, eyes on the blackened surf, desperately searching for any sign of Tom. Terrible thoughts went through her head: he hadn't worn a wetsuit and he hadn't worn a life jacket to go on deck. Her mouth dried and the sweat stood out on her brow and all at once she was burning. John-Cody was beside her: he tossed a red and white lifebelt into the water and a light started flashing amid the waves.

They were going full astern now and the boat dipped so they had to hold on as the waves battered the quarters. John-Cody peered into the gloom and as he did fear gripped his heart like a fist. Memories, Bluff Cove twenty-five years ago and the first time he set his eyes on Tom. The crayfish boat, deer traps, the grin on Tom's face when he saw Mahina and John-Cody together at Deep Cove.

'*Tom!*' he yelled into the night, but the night took his voice and swallowed it. 'Libby. Help me with the dinghy. We need to get it down. He might be able to grab it.'

Again Libby wound the rope about her hand and between them they dropped the dinghy into the surf.

Still they went astern and John-Cody looked to port and starboard, then he gripped Libby's arm.

'Tell Jonah half revs now. I don't want Tom chewed up in the prop.' Libby worked her way along the deck to the wheelhouse and John-Cody moved port and starboard, eyes wide, skinned right back, seeking some sign in the shifting wedges of sea. The spray lifted to soak him and salt stung his eyes, dried his mouth till his lips felt cracked and old. He stared at the waves, the rising swell, the blocks of black and the troughs: there was no sign of Tom. The lifebelt moved with the waves and he could see the light blinking on and off. The dinghy was tugging on her rope, pushed up against the starboard side as the *Korimako* went astern. He felt the revs drop and then Libby was next to him again.

'Any sign?' she yelled.

'None.' John-Cody moved back and forth across the quarters, leaning right over the rail, wondering whether he should get in the dinghy itself and look from there. But the sea was swollen to four metres and the dinghy was already half full and swinging.

'*Tom!*' he yelled. '*Tom!*'

Libby joined him and together they called and called. But there was no reply: the sea shifted mercilessly and gave up nothing of Tom. The lifebelt came in and out of vision and the light blinked on regardless. John-Cody pushed Libby out of the way and went back to the wheelhouse.

'Take her full ahead, Jonah.' He hesitated. 'No, my boat. Go astern and help Libby.'

Jonah was out of the wheelhouse like a shot and John-Cody took over. He put the *Korimako* ahead again, hauling the wheel to port until he gauged sixty degrees. He was going to bring her about using a Williamson turn, which big ships performed to get them back on their exact course when a man went overboard. He steamed forward until he judged the distance to be right, then he brought the wheel four full turns to starboard and the *Korimako* leaned into the wind.

Astern Libby and Jonah held on as the boat heeled and dipped so the rail was washed in the swell. Libby kept staring at the sea. Now she thought she saw something and now she didn't: a flash of white – Tom's hair? – no, only the cresting white cap of a wave.

They came about, bows into the current so the boat listed badly till they were head on once more. Libby moved for'ard and gripped the rail on the starboard side of the wheelhouse, Jonah on the port, still desperately searching. But time was running out: Tom had no means of staying afloat and the sea was ice cold. Libby's knuckles were red raw and she could no longer feel her hands where they gripped the metal rail. On the bridge John-Cody had the boat back on what he thought was their original course and he left the wheel for a moment to grab Jonah.

'As she goes now, half revs: keep her steady, Jonah.' He scrabbled in the locker beneath the dashboard for the torch. It was the most powerful one he had on board, with a wrist loop tied about the handle. He looked at Jonah again. 'Keep her really steady, I'm going to get some height.'

On deck he slithered where the water flooded the scuppers and almost lost his footing, then he was at the jib and climbing hand over hand, thirty feet to the spreaders.

Libby watched him, swarming up the mast like a monkey despite the savage roll of the sea. She dare not let go of the rail for fear of disappearing over the side and there was John-Cody climbing the mast. At the spreaders he hauled himself through the metal loop of the crow's nest and stood up. The boat rocked, the deck bellying from side to side below him as he shone the torch on the sea. The world was greyer up here and the sea less black. But it was vast, running to the horizon in all directions, and nothing moved except flecks of white like spittle on a giant's jaw. He looked for'ard and aft, port and starboard, the torch casting a yellowed glow across the waves, but there was no sign of Tom. The panic lifted in his throat, burning him like bile. What could he do?

There was nothing he could do. Just as with Elijah Pole there was nothing at all he could do. He looked at the deck and saw Libby's face in the torchlight, upturned to his, the same fear in her eyes. Jonah stepped out of the port door, hand cupped to his mouth.

John-Cody did not hear him, did not try to reply. He kept the torch on the water, the light spreading round the boat, but he saw nothing. There was nothing to see and in that moment he knew Tom Blanch was lost. And then, as if in acknowledgement that the fight was over, the current all at once felt weaker. He could tell from the swaying of the mast, and the wind was lighter in his face: it was westerly still but not as strong, and as he looked above his head he saw patches of sky through the cloud.

Back in the wheelhouse he hesitated for a moment, deliberating. Jonah was below, trying to raise any other vessels in the area. He received nothing but static and came up, face grey and shaking his head. Libby stood on deck still, holding the rail and staring into the sea with the shock seizing her body. She saw it again in her mind: the wave hitting, almost being lost then regaining her feet only to find that Tom was lost instead, as if the sea had looked for a sacrifice and been prepared to take just one. She didn't know how long they had been searching: it was as if time had stood still. But Tom was fifty-seven years old and the sea was freezing: he had no life jacket and no wetsuit.

John-Cody appeared at her side. 'He's dead, isn't he?' Libby said, not really hearing the words, her voice half lost to the elements, but the wind had dropped and the tone echoed in her head like a bell.

John-Cody leaned on the rail and said nothing. He stared at the water and his heart didn't believe what his head told him. For a long moment he was conscious of each individual breath, then he straightened up and stared at the grey horizon.

'Yes,' he said. 'He's dead.'

Silence in the wheelhouse: John-Cody looked at the clock. They had been sailing for fourteen hours, but he had no idea how long they had been here and still he was turning the *Korimako*, trawling the empty sea for any sign of Tom. He knew there would be none: too much time had elapsed. They had to go on; he had to get Jonah and Libby home, but he didn't want to leave. Libby moved next to him where he stood at the wheel.

'I'm so sorry,' she said. 'We took a wave. I almost went over. By the time I regained my feet he was gone.'

John-Cody bit his lip. 'A man can go overboard very easily here. Tom should have put a life jacket on.' The hypocrisy of the comment struck him: he had just climbed to the spreaders with no life jacket in a four-metre swell. But he was still right: Tom should have protected himself; both of them should.

'Why don't we stay till it gets light?' Libby said.

'Tom's dead, Libby.' John-Cody knew it in his heart: he knew it with the same certainty that he knew Mahina was dead and Eli Pole had been dead when he peered over the pulpit rail and saw him tangled up in the halyard. He bent to look through the holes cut in the boards. The wind had slackened right off now and the swell was much lower. He stared at the sky and saw stars against the blackness.

He took a bearing from the Southern Cross and steered them back onto a course of nor'nor'west. He had no real fix on where they were now: they had lost time and although he knew how long they had been sailing and at what speed, he had no idea how much the current had knocked them off course. All of which worried him.

Tom was gone and there would be time enough to mourn him later: right now he had two other lives in his care; they had lost radio contact again and he had no help. He had no handle on their position other than the bearing he had taken, and ahead of them lay the Snares and before the islands themselves the Western Chain, five major rocks spreading in a line some two miles into the sea. He stood at the wheel as the clock ticked beyond eleven and Libby dozed on the bench behind him. Jonah brought him a mug of black coffee and set it down.

'See if you can find me a cigarette, Jonah, will you?'

Jonah hunted in Libby's rucksack, stowed against

540

the window to the glasshouse, and found a crumpled pack. John-Cody fished in his pocket for his lighter. The smoke was good in his lungs and it calmed him. Jonah sat down on the bench and laid his head in his hands. He closed his eyes and was still.

John-Cody guided the *Korimako* on into the night with the breeze freshening his face through the holes in the plywood board that made up the for'ard windows. It kept him awake and eased his mind as he realized the weather was getting better. That could only aid their passage north; it also meant they would be back in radio contact shortly and he twisted the volume wheel on the speakers to make sure anyone trying to get them would be heard. He thought of Bree and his promise to get her mother home: he thought of the wisdom in those twelve years, the wealth of experience tucked away already and trickling out now and again to surprise them.

Glancing behind him, he looked at Libby sleeping, sitting upright on the sodden bench with her head thrown back and her eyes shut fast. She breathed silently through her nose, breasts rising and falling under the 7mm suit. Her hair looked very black against her face, which was pale and drawn, purple bags of flesh shadowing the skin under her eyes.

He looked for'ard again and pulled on the cigarette, holding the smoke in his lungs for as long as he could before exhaling. Jonah slept in little snores and John-Cody raised a smile, then he thought of Tom and the smile died on his lips. Opening the port door he flipped away the last of the cigarette and felt the wind on his face but much less strong than before. It was shifting sou'west as he had thought it would, but the fury was gone and he estimated the swell to be down to three metres and falling.

The world was grey and black in equal measure, the sky softer and less dense than the sea. A royal albatross drifted on currents of wind close to the boat, lifting over the bows and banking into the east. John-Cody watched its passing and for a moment he thought of how short his time was now and how the decisions he had made would place him back in custody and the chances of his ever seeing this place again were slim to nothing at all. So he stood by the wheel and watched the world through the side windows and took in the grey and black and silver of the sea when the moon washed over the waves as if to cast them in metal. He took in the scent of the sea, the tang in the air, the salt and the moisture on the wind. He took in the flecks of spray that crested the *Korimako*'s bows and the way the moonlight shimmered in the spreaders. He took in every shifting shape on the horizon and he closed his eyes and saw Moby Dick in the depths of Port Ross.

Jonah relieved John-Cody at 1 a.m. and then Libby relieved Jonah at four. John-Cody slept on the bench directly behind her, half slumped against the window with his arms folded, his age showing as grey lines in his face and his hair loose at his shoulders. His mouth was open a fraction and the stubble gathered in salt and pepper across his jaw. Libby thought of Tom's white hair and sparkling blue eyes, and she wept silent tears for him as she stood there at the wheel. She felt an ache in the pit of her stomach, half fear, half longing, and she looked to port and starboard, astern and for'ard to make sure they were not gaining on any other boats and none was gaining on them. She felt the ache for the future, not being able to recall how many days John-Cody had left and knowing that the future without him would not seem like any future at all. It was the first time in her thirty-two years that she had felt anything similar and she wondered about Bree and what her reaction would be when they broke the news to her.

She thought of Ned Pole and his plans for Dusky Sound and she couldn't help but wonder at him. He had stopped the school bullies in their tracks, bullies Libby didn't even know were there. He had transformed Bree's life at a stroke and yet in another he had ruined John-Cody's. The same man had barely raised his voice in anger when his only son was drowned, yet a handful of years later he was responsible for having John-Cody deported. None of that made sense: the deal at Dusky was so important it had made him that callous, and yet he could display a gentleness to Bree that was reminiscent of John-Cody himself.

The *Korimako* steamed north-west and the wind dropped still further till the sail luffed and flapped like a sheet pegged on a clothes line. Libby thought the jib ought to come in but Jonah and John-Cody were sleeping and she had to stay at the wheel. It would not impede their progress, the revs remained at 950 and the boat headed on at seven and a half knots. She gazed through the hole in the board and felt a new dampness on her face; fog was lifting from the surface of the sea, spectral like smoke. Slowly she shook her head: that was all they needed, with no navigation. She looked at the sky and the stars were hidden, dawn was on its way and the world was grey and bleak and a silence descended that stifled the sound of the engine.

John-Cody was dreaming: he and Tom were in a storm in the Foveaux Strait west of Dog Island. They were running with the sea, the decks awash, seeking shelter from a wind that howled from all points of the compass. Just the two of them on board, Tom's face white with fear, and he could feel the tension in his own as he fought with the spinning wheel. The sea raged about them like thunder in his ears, waves curling and lifting, standing for what seemed an age before dashing against the windows with a sound like cracking whips. He stared at the glass and wondered how long it would be before it gave and both he and Tom were swept overboard to their deaths. The current shifted violently under his feet and he hauled the wheel round, but it shifted again and he opened his eyes, saw Libby wilting at the helm and Jonah with his head in his hands. The storm was gone and Tom was gone and he realized he had been dreaming.

Carefully he prised himself away from the table, trying not to disturb Jonah. A grey light bled through the windows and he looked at the clock above the barometer: eight almost and getting light. Eight o'clock: the current was silent under his feet and sweat crawled in his hair. He hauled open the port door and stepped out on deck.

The *Korimako* moved through water as still as glass and he could barely see the bows for the fog. For a long moment he just stood, head high like a hunter, and then he felt movement and a shiver worked the length of his spine.

544

'*Libby!*' He snapped her from her doze at the wheel.

She cried out suddenly. 'Sorry, I'm sorry. I didn't mean to—'

'Turn the engine off.'

'What?'

'Do as I tell you. The black handle.' He jabbed a finger at the dashboard in front of her. 'Pull it up.'

Libby did as she was told and the engine shuddered and died: John-Cody stepped back on deck and waited till the vibrations left the metal. The boat rocked gently, water smacking steel, the shrouds creaked but apart from that there was no sound: except . . . and he heard it and a weakness went through him that all but took his legs. A slow rushing, a sound that had sent terror through generations of sailors; like moist breath, hollow, long and drawn out, then a moment of silence before the boom of waves upon rock.

He stepped inside, pushed Libby away from the helm and twisted the ignition key. He hauled the wheel to starboard, turning them full about.

'What's going on?' Libby picked herself up where she had fallen against the door. Jonah was next to her, eyes bright and questioning.

'Rocks.' John-Cody squeezed the word between clenched teeth. 'Waves on rocks we can't see.' He looked at Jonah. 'Get on deck. I'm going to run south and kill the engines. Tell me when you can no longer hear anything.'

Jonah went on deck and Libby stepped alongside John-Cody. 'If it's rocks it's land.'

He looked sideways at her. 'How long has the fog been down?'

'I don't know. I must've dozed off.'

'If you were tired you should have woken me.'

'I'm sorry.' She looked up at him. 'But if it's land . . .'

'I don't think it is land. I think it's the Western Chain.'

Libby frowned.

'Tahi, Rua, Toru, Wha, Rima: five massive rocks, Libby, rocks stretching into the ocean. If we run aground on them we're dead.'

They steamed south for a few minutes then he killed the engine.

'Your boat.' He stepped on deck while Libby held the wheel and he listened along with Jonah. 'Hear anything?' he asked as the vibrations died once more. Jonah looked at him and nodded.

Back on the bridge he started the engines again and they steamed south. The sound was on the starboard side now and he went on for a few more minutes before trying again. He stood with Jonah, both of them at the starboard rail and looking west into the gloom.

'Hear anything?'

Jonah shook his head.

'Me neither.' John-Cody pushed fog-damp hair from his eyes and went in to start the engines. Now he turned the boat east and they steamed for a mile or so and then he hauled the wheel to port. Libby was watching him. He could still feel the roll of the ocean current though the wind was nothing and the water looked flat as a millpond.

'What're we doing now?' she asked him.

'Going north again. We do that and we listen.'

They steamed ahead and he cut the engine and

gazed through the holes in the board till Jonah shook his head. John-Cody started the engine. Again they went north and again he cut the engine and still Jonah shook his head. He started the engine once more and they went north and this time Jonah nodded.

John-Cody left the wheel to Libby and went out on deck. He stood and listened and again he heard the rushing sound off the port bow. He still felt the current under his feet and nodded slowly at Jonah. 'Western Chain,' he said. 'That's the Southern Ocean roll.'

'What now?' Libby asked when he went back inside.

John-Cody put his arm round her shoulders. 'Now we go east for an hour then north very gently. We're east of the Western Chain and in a couple more hours we'll be in the lee of the Snares. We sit there till the fog lifts and then we'll see the islands.' He broke off and stared through the holes in the boards. 'After that we've got four hours at sea till we reach Stewart Island, and from Stewart Island we can see Bluff Cove.'

TWENTY-SEVEN

Bree and Alex met the boat at Bluff Cove. With the Snares left behind and Stewart Island all but in sight, Libby had spoken to them on the radio and told them roughly what time they would be in. John-Cody kept the news of Tom's drowning to himself. Tom had a widow in Manapouri and he didn't want her to learn of her husband's death over the air-waves. Alex had parked her car on the wharf and Libby stood in the bows and watched Bree waving frantically as the boat steamed into harbour. John-Cody was at the wheel, steering his course through the holes in the boards. They were almost out of fuel and the Korimako limped in, having lost a crewman. John-Cody was as drained as he had ever felt and it was all he could do to bring the boat alongside. He would have to leave her there at Bluff with Jonah to organize repairs before driving Tom's truck back to Manapouri. It would take another two days to steam to the wharf at Deep Cove and John-Cody had only four days till he had to leave New Zealand.

Bree leaped on board as they docked and Libby scooped her up and held her. John-Cody threw on the stern line while Jonah secured the bows. Bree kissed her mother, then wriggled from her grasp and made her way astern where she flung herself on John-Cody. 'Thank you. Thank you. Thank you,' she said.

'Hey, Breezy, no worries.'

Silent tears ran on Bree's cheeks then she grinned broadly and wiped them with the back of her hand. 'She can be a pain at times, John-Cody, but she's the only mother I've got.' She looked the length of the boat to where Libby was talking to Alex.

'Where's Tom?'

John-Cody held her by the shoulders. 'I'm afraid Tom is dead, Bree. We lost him overboard in the storm.'

Bree stared at him, then the tears filled her eyes again and she clung to him and this time she sobbed and sobbed. John-Cody held her very close, feeling the sobs rack her body and staring at his reflected image in the oily black of the water. Libby walked the length of the deck and laid a hand on Bree's shoulder. For a moment the three of them remained like that, John-Cody looking into Libby's face with Bree buried in his chest.

Alex drove them home. When they pulled up outside the house John-Cody was almost dropping with fatigue, so weary he could hardly prise himself from the car.

Libby took his hand and guided him towards the door but he held back and asked Alex for the keys to his truck.

'I've got to go and see Ellen Blanch. I can't let anyone else tell her about Tom.'

'Then let me drive you,' Libby said.

'No.' He shook his head. 'Stay here with Bree.'

Alex said she would drive him and John-Cody got back in the car and they drove the short distance to Tom's house on View Street. Wearily he climbed out and fumbled for the comfort of the tangi-wai stone in his pocket. His grip tightened around it as he saw Ellen waiting for him in the doorway, white-haired and suddenly very frail: he realized then that she knew.

Bree made her mother a cup of tea and she sat and held it with both hands, letting the steam play over her face. Bree watched her from where she leaned against the kitchen work surface and Sierra trotted over and rested her head on Libby's lap. Libby stared at the crackling fire that Bree had laid in readiness and was aware of a fatigue deep in her soul. She was still sitting there when she heard a car pull up and then the front door opened and John-Cody stood there. His face was the colour of old parchment, faded and lined, seamed in veins of blue. He leaned in the doorway as if unsure of his legs.

'Did you see her?' Libby asked him.

He nodded.

'You need to sleep.'

Again he nodded. Libby rose from her seat, set her cup down and held out a hand. 'Come on,' she said. 'I'll help you.'

John-Cody stumbled like a blind man, taking Libby's hand and following her to the bedroom he had shared with Mahina.

Libby sat him on the bed and tugged off his boots. He pulled his sweater and shirt over his head and she unbuckled his jeans and slipped them down his legs.

He stood naked before her and she looked at the smooth hardness of his body. Then she eased the duvet back and he sank into the bed and was asleep before his head touched the pillow.

Libby watched as he lay motionless, his face like death. When she picked up his jeans the green stone that Mahina had given him fell out and she held it, working her fingers over the edges, and then laid it on the dressing table. Looking round, she saw Bree watching her from the doorway.

'You do love him, don't you?'

Libby nodded. 'Very, very much.'

Bree smiled then. 'I'm going to meet Hunter. You should sleep too, Mum. You look exhausted. I won't disturb you when I come in.'

Libby smiled and nodded and when Bree had gone she sat down on the bed. John-Cody lay silent before her, unmoving. There was no sound, just the faintest rise and fall of the duvet.

Naked, she slipped into bed next to him and rested on her elbow, feeling the softness of his breath on her flesh. Leaning lower she moved her face over his, her nose, mouth, the weight of her cheek: just touching lightly, tracing the contours of his features with her own, not kissing but smoothing herself against him. He lay like stone, lost somewhere far from her. She watched him for a while then sleep began to weigh against her eyes and she kissed him on the mouth and lay back, her head against the coolness of the pillow.

TWENTY-EIGHT

Libby woke before him in the morning: she had no idea what the time was, only that it was late and there was no sound from the living room next door. Getting up, she slipped on a robe and went through. Bree's room was empty. She had got herself up, had breakfast and headed off to the bus without waking them. The clock on the cooker read nine fifteen. Libby looked at the sky through the window: low cloud, very white and threatening snow. There was a chill to the air and she banked up the fire with coal and went back to the bedroom. John-Cody lay on his side, still sound asleep, and Libby climbed in next to him. He stirred and mumbled something and she whispered in his ear and smoothed her palm across his brow. She slept again and when she woke he was sitting on the edge of the bed in a bathrobe, holding a cup of tea. She rubbed her face and sat up and the duvet slipped below her breasts and she saw the desire all at once in his eyes. Taking the cup from him she set it down then reached for the collar of the robe and drew him to her. He eased the duvet aside and neither of them spoke as he climbed on top of her, pushing her legs apart and slowly, gently, entered her.

They lay in the moisture of their bodies and held on to each other as if their lives depended on it. John-Cody stared at the ceiling, at the wood panelling on the walls.

'What do you see?' Libby asked him.

'I see you.'

'Are you sure?'

Raising himself on one elbow, he looked round the room. 'Mahina's gone from here. I kept her longer than I should have, but she finally left at the Aucklands.' He let the breath seep from between his teeth and then he told her what she already knew, how he had dived to kill himself: how he had dived with only twenty minutes of air and Moby Dick had sought him out in the depths of Port Ross. He told her how the whale had looked into his soul and as he did so Mahina had risen in his eye. He lay back in the bed, Libby in his arms with the weight of her breasts against him.

'I wasn't sure then. I'd been challenged. Cracks in my armour, I guess. I wasn't sure of anything. But when we saw that calf in the water the following day, I was so desperate for it to live I knew I had to go on.'

He thought about it all then. Three days and he would be back in the United States.

'I've got to leave,' he said. 'I haven't even bought a plane ticket. I can't afford for immigration to provide me with one.'

Again Libby smoothed his face. 'I want to come with you.'

He took her hand and kissed it. 'Stay here. You've got the Dusky Sound research to work on.'

'I don't want to do my research without you.'

'I want you to. With me gone, you're the only person between Pole and those hotels. You must go on.'

'What will you do?' she asked him.

'I don't know. I have no idea what's going to happen when I set foot back in the US.'

Tears glistened in Libby's eyes. 'I want to be with you, John-Cody.'

'You can't. Stay here. Live here. Get the *Korimako* fixed for me. Bree wants to stay here, remember. She deserves some stability.'

'Bree wants me to marry you.'

He smiled then. 'I know.'

'You heard her on the radio. She wants it more than anything.'

'She'll be OK.'

Libby looked at him, hand fisted in the sheet. 'And what about you?'

John-Cody sighed. 'I have to face the past. Whether I want to admit it or not it's been there at the back of my mind for a quarter of a century. Maybe Ned did me a favour.'

'I don't think so.'

He shrugged. 'I don't either. But I don't have a choice. If I'm not out of here by Thursday they'll arrest me and I won't be allowed anywhere near the place for five long years: I can't have that, Libby, not if you're here.' He got up. 'Help me pack, would you? We don't have much time.'

Bree cried and cried when they told her. She went to her room and for a while she was absolutely distraught. Libby and John-Cody sat in the living room by the fire and waited till she had calmed down then John-Cody went through to her room.

'Hey, Breezy.'

Bree looked up at him, her face red with tears. She smudged a hand over her eyes.

'I don't want you to go. Why does this always happen to me? Just when I think for once everything is going to work out, something happens to ruin it.'

He sat next to her and she took his hand and traced patterns on his palm with her fingers. 'I don't want you to go.'

'You'll be OK.' John-Cody lifted her chin so she looked at him. 'You'll have your mum and Alex and Hunter. You'll have Sierra and your schoolmates.'

'I want you.' Bree hugged him then, holding very tight.

'And I want you. But I have to go back to America.'

'But why? Why did Mr Pole do this?'

John-Cody shrugged. 'I don't know, Bree. I've been trying to figure it out myself.' He stood up. 'Maybe this is revenge, finally, after what happened to poor Eli.' He blew out his cheeks. 'Don't think badly of him. He helped you out big time, didn't he?'

'I wish he hadn't.' Bree's eyes smarted. 'I wish I'd never ridden his horses. I never will again.'

Bree went to school the next day and at lunchtime she joined John-Cody and her mother for Tom Blanch's memorial service in the church on Mokonui Street in Te Anau. The building was packed with fishermen and townspeople and they spilled out into the yard. Bree saw Ned Pole head and shoulders above most of those paying their respects, with his wife standing next to him. Afterwards everyone went to the cemetery to bless a stone John-Cody had commissioned and when the blessing was over they all filed away. Bree had watched John-Cody and watched Ned Pole and noticed that neither man looked at the other all the time the service was going on. After it was over John-Cody guided Ellen Blanch to her car and travelled back with her and Libby. Bree told them she would walk back to school to meet Hunter at the bus stop. She stood for a while by the memorial, which was simply inscribed: *Dearest Tom Blanch: cherished husband and friend.*

The cemetery emptied quickly. The people of Te Anau were well used to funerals after the helicopter wars and all the fishermen who had been lost over the years. Bree was one of the last to leave and she was about to go when she noticed a figure crouched by a grave at the top of the hill. Picking her way between the stones she drew closer and recognized Ned Pole. He was laying fresh flowers on Elijah's grave.

He must have heard or felt her approach because he looked over his shoulder and their eyes met. His gaze was stern for an instant as if she had interrupted a precious private moment and then his eyes softened and he beckoned her.

'How are you, little lady?'

She stood with her hands behind her back, eyes sharp, jaw trembling all at once. She could feel the pounding of her heart, thinking just how tall he was when he stood up. She had to do this though and she screwed her courage to the sticking point.

'Why did you do it?'

Pole frowned. 'Do what exactly?'

'Tell the government about John-Cody.'

Pole was silent.

'Was it because of him?' Bree pointed to Elijah's headstone.

'Bree . . .'

'Was it? I don't think he would have wanted you to. From what you've told me – he wouldn't have wanted you to do that.'

'Bree, I didn't tell the . . .' Pole stopped himself. How could he explain?

'John-Cody said you did. My mum said you did.'

'It's not as simple as that.'

'He was going to marry my mum. I know he was.' Bree bit down on her lip.

Pole took a pace towards her. 'Bree, there's things you don't understand.'

Bree stepped back. 'You mean like Dusky Sound. I do understand. You want to put hotels there and they don't want you to. That's no reason to get rid of John-Cody.' Tears fell from her eyes now.

'Bree, don't cry. Please. Look, it's not like you think it is. Nothing's ever that simple. There's business to think about and people's lives.'

'But it's so unfair. He's been here such a long time. This is his home. He's such a good man. He hasn't done anything wrong.'

Pole wrinkled his eyes at the corners and he looked beyond her, into the future and back into the past. 'You're right. He hasn't done anything wrong.'

'Then stop it. Stop what's happening. Tell them to leave him alone.'

'I can't.' Pole lifted his hands, dropped them at his sides again. 'I'm sorry, but there's nothing I can do now.' He stepped towards her again, but she backed away from him.

'Bree.'

Bree was trembling. 'You've ruined my life. I thought it was getting better but you've gone and ruined it.' She walked away, stumbled and then looked back at him. 'I never want to ride your horses again. I'm never coming to your house. I'll tell Hunter the same. You shouldn't have sent him away.'

'Bree.'

'He could have been my father!'

For a long time after she was gone her words echoed in Pole's ears. The wind lifted and he could sense the snow in the air. He drew his coat around him and looked back at the headstone and the grass and the flowers where the wind had already scattered the petals. Slowly he drove home and, parking the truck, he sat in the cab smoking a black cigar and watching the horses in the paddock. This place would be saved now, but all at once he was weary of it. He could see Jane on the telephone in the study, standing at the full-length window overlooking the balcony. He stared up at her and he thought of Mahina, as he always did, like a shadow that no amount of sunlight could penetrate. He saw her in his mind's eye naked in the bush: and the breath caught in his throat and he smelled the blood of the deer and the resinous tang of death.

John-Cody stood with his bag in his hand and looked at Libby. She had driven him to Christchurch airport and he was about to board a plane for Los Angeles. He could not quite believe it. Everything had been so rushed. His palms were moist and his brow hot, sweat running off him as if he had a fever. He looked at Libby now and realized just how deeply he was in love with her.

'I don't know what to say to you.'

She looked into his face. 'Just don't forget about me.'

'Forget?' He shook his head. 'God, Libby.' Dropping his bag he caught her up in his arms. 'How could I forget?'

She was soft and smelled of womanhood, hair in his face the very scented essence of her. John-Cody felt the weight in his gut and he held her a moment longer then gently eased her away. 'Say goodbye to Bree again for me,' he said. 'And get the boat fixed, please.'

Libby cupped his cheek. 'I need to know what happens as soon as anything does.'

John-Cody managed a smile. 'Lib, they'll allow me one phone call, whether they'll let it be long distance I don't know.' He saw the fear break against her eyes and he smoothed her hair. 'Don't worry. I'll figure it somehow.' He wanted to be alone: he didn't want to prolong this. 'I'll call you.' He stood a moment longer. 'Go and see Ellen Blanch for me. She was married to Tom for almost forty years. She's really going to miss him.'

'John-Cody.'

'Yes?'

'As soon as my work is done I'll come and find you. I'll bring Bree.'

'I don't know where I'll be.'

'It doesn't matter. I'll find you.'

He looked at her and she looked at him, then she kissed him one more time and turned. She walked with a straight back and didn't look round: he watched her go until she passed through the automatic doors and stepped out into the night. He reached in his jeans pocket for the familiar comfort of the tangi-wai stone, but it wasn't there. He searched the other pocket and then he cursed under his breath: he'd left it lying on the dressing table at home.

He paid his airport tax and was about to go through to the departure lounge when a row of telephones stopped him. There was something he had to do; something he had to know before he finally left New Zealand. Taking a handful of change from his pocket he picked up the phone and dialled.

It was late and Kobi was probably asleep, but John-Cody knew the old man had the phone by his bed and he answered in three rings.

'Kobi, it's me, Gib. Sorry to wake you.'

'That's OK, mate, how you going?'

'I'm at the airport.'

The old man was silent for a moment. 'It's really happening then.'

'Yes, I'm afraid it is.'

'I'll miss you, you old joker. Another one of you leaving me.' He hissed breath through his teeth.

'Kobi, I don't have much time but there's something I need to know.'

'What?'

'Mahina. I know she used to confide in you after her mother died. I need to know something I think she might have told you. Did she ever have a relationship with Ned Pole?'

Kobi was quiet for a moment then he cleared his throat. 'You asked me that already. The answer is no, mate, she didn't.'

'Are you sure, Kobi? Would she have told you?'

'She told me everything, Gib. I would've known.'

John-Cody felt the relief in his veins. 'Thanks, Kobi, I'm going to miss you.'

'Likewise. You take care of yourself.'

'I will. Bye, Kobi.'

'Goodbye, Gib.'

Kobi put the phone down and lay back in the darkness for a moment, then reaching above his head he pulled the cord for the light and climbed out of bed. It was ice cold in the room and his bones ached, but he went across to his chest of drawers and sought the letter he'd received from Mahina.

Libby stayed at the airport hotel and cried long into the night, something she had never done before. It was grief, a loss, the tears just flowed and there was nothing she could do to stop them until she was all cried out. She woke in the morning, looked at the clock and wondered if he would be there yet. She worked out the hours and decided he wouldn't. She got up, settled her bill, bought a cup of coffee from the petrol station and drove back to Manapouri. The drive took all day, through Central Otago down to Queenstown and on from there. She counted thirteen hours from when his plane took off and tried to imagine the feelings he would go through when he touched down in the United States.

John-Cody landed at Los Angeles with a trembling sensation in his limbs. It wasn't so much fear as deep-seated trepidation: memories shifting restlessly through his mind all the way from New Zealand, thoughts, fears, wondering whether he would ever see Libby again, whether he would ever sit on the dive locker aboard the *Korimako* and listen to the silence of Doubtful Sound. He dozed and slept fitfully, but bad dreams disturbed him, dreams dominated by Elijah Pole's face and Tom's white hair barely visible among the waves. He had a window seat and the buildings of Los Angeles lifted in squared blocks of stone from the desert floor. Smog hung round the buildings where the sun couldn't burn through, and as the plane got closer he picked out the freeways jammed with cars.

He saw the two FBI agents as he walked up the closed gangway to the gate: grey suits and cropped hair, their badges open in the breast pockets of their jackets. He was back in McCall after he jumped parole and they were the same men, though they couldn't be because both were young and twenty-five years had elapsed. He had told the New Zealand authorities his departure date and they must have informed the FBI. The two agents spotted him and came over. He waited, his canvas grip the only baggage he had, his hair long and not brushed and still frayed at the ends.

'Mr Gibbs?' The smaller of the two, with dark hair and bright blue eyes, spoke to him. 'I'm Special Agent Thomas. This is Special Agent Givens.'

John-Cody looked at the other man who smiled a little awkwardly. Both of them seemed uneasy, almost embarrassed. He set his bag down on the floor.

'You want to cuff me?'

'No, sir,' Givens said quickly. 'Just as long as you don't run away.'

John-Cody shook his head. 'Son, I just quit running.'

They flanked him through immigration and customs and he ignored the glances he received from other passengers. He said nothing and they said nothing, other than telling him they had to take an internal flight to Seattle and hoped another journey wouldn't be too tiring.

On the plane they occupied three seats with John-Cody in the middle. They told him that the Seattle field office had dealt with his case back in the 1970s and that's why they were taking him there.

'What'll happen to me?' John-Cody asked Thomas. 'I do my other eighteen months – that and the time they add for parole jumping?'

'Sir, to tell you the truth, I don't have a clue. I've never been involved with anything vaguely like this before. Not with Vietnam and all.'

Givens smiled then. 'Hell, I wasn't even born.' He looked at John-Cody. 'You were a boat skipper in New Zealand?'

'Aotearoa,' John-Cody said. 'That's what the Maori call it. It's good enough for me.'

'Aotearoa then. What kind of boat?'

'Buck-eye ketch.' John-Cody looked at him. 'You sail?'

Givens nodded. 'Out of San Diego for a while.'

'That'd be good sailing.'

'We thought so.' Givens squinted at him. 'New Zealand immigration told us you just got back from the Sub-Antarctic. Pretty rough down there, I bet.'

John-Cody stared into space. 'Yes,' he said, 'pretty rough.'

The conversation died after that and when they landed at Seattle another agent was there with a car to meet them. John-Cody sat in the back with Givens as they drove downtown to the field office. The building was square and flat, three storeys and guarded by black-uniformed FBI cops. Thomas flanked him on one side and Givens opened the doors and they walked him the length of the hall to a door at the end. John-Cody saw the lock on the outside and the saliva dried in his mouth. Thomas opened the door and he saw a bench with a white pillow and grey blanket and his mind rolled back. For a moment he just stood there.

'Inside please, Mr Gibbs.'

He looked at Thomas and fought momentarily for breath.

'Please, sir. It's just a holding cell.'

John-Cody stepped into the cell and they closed the door and he heard the lock tumble and he was trapped again like an animal. He shut his eyes and saw Hall's Arm with stands of rimu and kahikatea beyond the toi toi and jointed spear grass. He saw the massed forest of beech and heard weka calling and high above it all there was snow on the peak of Mount Danae.

Jonah sat with his father in the converted room in the general store in Naseby. Kobi lay stretched out on the bed, his head propped against pillows with a bag of sweets at his elbow. The TV was on in the corner and Jonah sat at the table and stared at a photograph of Mahina with John-Cody just after they got together. His mother had taken it and now she was gone and Mahina was gone and as of this morning John-Cody was gone also. He looked at his father and saw he was staring too.

'Hotels in Dusky Sound.' Kobi shook his head, let

go a breath and closed his eyes again. 'I used to fish in Dusky Sound. Your sister loved that place. Even when she was tiny.' He lay for a few minutes more and then sat up. 'Ned Pole, eh. Always was the joker.' He took his wallet from where it lay on the shelf beside his bed. 'Go and get us a beer or two, Jonah. Better still, go over to the pub and set them up. I feel like a drink tonight.'

Jonah stood up and fished in his pockets. 'I'll shout you the piss, Dad.'

'No, boy.' Kobi shook his head. 'I'll shout you. You just go on ahead and set them up.'

Jonah took the wallet and stepped out of the room. Kobi waited till he heard the sliding door close at the back of the store then he slipped a hand under his pillow and took out Mahina's letter. She had written it when she knew she was dying and when he read it and took in the implications she was already dead. He held it to him now, hands trembling slightly, then he slipped it into his jacket pocket and reached for his hat. He would get Jonah to drive him to Te Anau in the morning.

Libby sat with Alex in the office. She was due back in Dusky Sound but hadn't the heart to go. She had been on the phone to the Green Party all morning, trying to get them to look into the boundaries of the national park more quickly. She told them that Pole's hearing was imminent and unless somebody did something the fiords would never be the same again. They understood of course and the House of Representatives were looking into the matter, but there was no way they could hurry the parliamentary process. The hearing was less than a week away and she was trying to prepare a submission of her own. She would cite the dolphin pod and the Department of Conservation would back her, but she was not in a position to prove that the pod was resident and the argument about an acoustic model was a non-starter. There was neither the funding nor the time needed to provide such a model and the economic pressures on the area were significant. Fiordland depended on tourism and all Pole was doing was adding to the tourism revenue. He would win: something in her heart told her he would almost certainly win. With John-Cody gone, the way was much clearer.

She sat on the couch reviewing the videotapes she had made in Port Ross and her fears were replaced by a sudden rush of excitement: all that had happened, the tragedy of Tom's death and John-Cody having to leave the country, had overshadowed what she had achieved. She was the first person on the planet to film a southern right whale giving birth: not only the birth, but the drama that followed when the calf would not take its first breath. Alex watched with her. When the film was finished they both sat there in amazement.

'My God, Libby, that's powerful stuff,' Alex said. 'You could make a fortune with it.'

Libby glanced at her and stood up. 'I don't know about a fortune but I might get something for it. I think I should show it to Steve Watson in Dunedin.'

John-Cody sat in the cell for an hour, sixty minutes that felt like an eternity: the sweat ran on his palms and moistened his hair and he went through every emotion he had ever experienced going back twenty-five years. When a key finally turned in the lock he didn't quite believe it, but Thomas smiled at him and stood aside, indicating for him to come out.

'The Special Agent in Charge wants to see you, Mr Gibbs.'

John-Cody followed him down the hall and up to the next floor where they came out in a foyer with a leather chesterfield and armchair in FBI blue. The Fidelity Bravery Integrity shield was emblazoned on the wall and a secretary looked on as Thomas led him to a spacious office with a big desk and a twin set of couches against one wall. Windows dominated one side and a big man dressed in a blue suit stood with his back to them, hands in the pockets of his trousers.

'Mr Gibbs, sir.' Thomas withdrew and closed the door and John-Cody stood there in his jeans and denim shirt and the agent still stood with his back to him. His hair was white, cropped like a marine and shaved above the wrinkles that lined the back of his neck. He turned and his face was flat and square-jawed and there was something familiar about him.

'Sit down, Mr Gibbs.' He gestured to a high-backed chair in front of the desk then sat down himself. For a moment they looked at each other without speaking then the agent cocked his head to one side.

'You still play guitar?'

John-Cody frowned.

'You don't remember me, do you?'

'Should I?'

The agent sat back. 'The last time we saw each other was a mother of a night on the Camas prairie. Agent Muller. I arrested you that night.' He half smiled. 'I remember you telling my partner and me it might not be such a good idea to drive that road at night. I figure that maybe we should've listened.'

Recollection now: his face, his eyes and the square, almost carved features. John-Cody nodded slowly. 'You were in the passenger seat.'

'That's right.'

For a moment they looked at each other and then John-Cody looked at the desk and the office and the SAC's card in the tray. 'You made it up the ladder then.'

The agent laughed. 'It took me twenty-five years, Mr Gibbs, but yes, I'm the boss in this field office. What've you been doing since I last saw you?'

'Skippering a boat in New Zealand.'

'I heard that. Sorry we had to bring you back.'

'So am I.' John-Cody ran his tongue round the inside of his mouth. 'What happened to your partner?'

Muller's face darkened. 'He died in that car wreck.'

Again John-Cody was standing by the road with his breath coming in clouds of steam. 'I'm sorry.'

'Not your fault.' Muller sat forward then. 'If you hadn't got to Grangeville and told the sheriff I wouldn't be sitting here myself. I want to thank you for that.'

For a long moment they looked at each other. 'What happens now?' John-Cody asked him.

Muller pushed back his chair and stood up. 'Right now I give you a ride to a hotel. You get some rest and we talk again in a day or two.'

'Will I go back to jail?'

'Not if I can help it.'

TWENTY-NINE

John-Cody stayed the night at a hotel in Seattle. Muller made the reservation from the telephone in his office and then drove him downtown in his own car.

'You're all set,' he said. 'I've got to talk to the prosecuting attorney about your case and as soon as I have some news I'll send a car for you.' He smiled then. 'Promise me you won't go walkabout.'

John-Cody returned the smile. 'You have my word.'

'Good enough.' Muller leaned across him and opened the door.

John-Cody checked into his room then went to the bar and ordered a beer and a shot of whiskey. He sipped the beer and slammed the shot then ordered another. He slammed that one, ordered a third and sipped it.

'Winding down, uh?' the bartender said to him.

'Something like that.'

It was warm outside still, summer in the northern hemisphere, incongruous to John-Cody after all those years of having the seasons the other way round. He ordered food at the bar then went to his room and slept through till morning.

He stayed a full week in the hotel waiting for Muller or somebody else from the FBI to contact him. With too much time to think, he kicked his heels and wandered the city aimlessly. Two days running he took a cab to the docks and sat for hours drinking coffee out of styrofoam cups and watching the fishing boats leave and return to the harbour. Gulls cried and it was good to smell the salt in the air, feel the wind on his face and, above all, gaze out to sea.

When he got back to the hotel on the evening of the seventh day Agent Thomas was waiting for him.

'I need to take you to the field office right away, sir,' Thomas told him.

John-Cody narrowed his eyes. 'That sounds ominous.'

Thomas's face showed no expression but he gestured to a car parked in one of the bays outside and John-Cody stepped across the asphalt ahead of him. His heart jarred his ribs and he could feel the sinking sensation once again in his stomach: he was glad he had spent some time at the harbour.

Thomas hardly spoke on the way across town to the field office. He left the car in the underground car park and they went up in the elevator. Muller was on the phone when Thomas showed John-Cody in and he waved him to a chair. John-Cody sat and tried to concentrate on keeping his breathing easy. Outside he could hear the howl of the traffic, horns blaring, engines roaring, and he knew it was a sound he would never get used to again. Muller swung back and forth in his chair as he spoke into the phone and every now and again he would glance at John-Cody, but he didn't smile. In the end John-Cody could sit still no longer so he got up and paced to the window. All he could see were buildings, the street below and hundreds of vehicles choking the life out of the place. Behind him Muller finally put down the phone.

'How you doing?'

John-Cody turned. 'I don't know. Maybe you could tell me.'

Muller picked up a folded sheet of paper from his desk and moved to the window. He gestured outside. 'Not much of a view but better than some, I guess.' He passed the sheet of paper over.

'What's this?' John-Cody took it gingerly.

'It's a letter of declination, Mr Gibbs. From the prosecuting attorney's office.'

'What does that mean?'

'Why don't you read it?'

John-Cody looked in his eyes. 'Why don't you tell me?'

'OK.' Muller put his hands in his pockets, hunched his shoulders and then he smiled. 'In a word – your freedom.'

For a moment John-Cody didn't say anything, then carefully he opened the letter.

'Basically what they're saying is that they agree with what I told them,' Muller went on. 'What happened was twenty-five years ago and to do with your conscientious objection. You're not a felon, Mr Gibbs. In my book you never were. They've pardoned you in the same way that everyone else was pardoned.'

'What about the parole violation?'

'Forgotten. Written off. Never happened. Your slate is clean. You're free to go where you please.'

John-Cody looked at him. 'Except New Zealand.'

Muller's face clouded. 'I'm sorry about that.'

'So am I.' John-Cody held out his hand. 'Anyway it's not your fault. Listen, thank you for what you did.'

'I didn't do anything other than exercise a bit of common sense.' Muller shook his hand. 'Good luck, Mr Gibbs.'

Outside John-Cody stood on the sidewalk, where Thomas was waiting by the car to drive him back to the hotel. He was free but he was trapped. His home was thousands of miles away and there was no way he could go back to it. The traffic whizzed by and the sound drummed in his head and for a moment he closed his eyes, but it was no good, no amount of imagining would take him there again.

'Mr Gibbs?' Thomas's voice broke in on him.

John-Cody squared his shoulders and walked over to the car.

He phoned Libby from the pay phone in the hotel lobby the following morning.

'So your record is clean?' she said.

'Yes. I'm still stuck here though. I can't come back to New Zealand.'

Libby was silent. He could tell she was fighting with tears. 'What're you going to do?' she said at last.

'I don't know. Pretty soon I'm going to need some money though. How're the repairs going on the boat?'

'They're under way. I've supervised them myself,

but Jonah's on his way back from Naseby. He's going down to Invercargill to check.'

'How's Bree?' John-Cody asked.

'She's OK. A bit morose. She misses you terribly. She wants an address so she can write to you.'

John-Cody was still for a moment. 'She hasn't written any more of those other letters, has she?'

'No. I let Jean in on it, John-Cody. She said she'd tell me if Bree posted any more.'

John-Cody leaned against the booth. 'Look, as soon as I get settled I'll call you with an address. But right now I have no idea what I'm going to do or where I'm going to do it. I'm lost, Libby, and I've never been so lost in my life.' He paused for a moment. 'Look, my money's running out. I'll call you as soon as I know where I am. In the meantime you better put the boat up for sale, the wharf too. I'm going to need the money.'

He hung up and Libby stared at her open palm where she held the tangi-wai stone that Mahina had found at Anita Bay. She had kept it with her ever since she discovered it still lying on the dressing table. Getting up, she wandered outside where snow lay along the branches of the trees and not a single bird was singing. She hugged her arms to her chest, closed her eyes and imagined him standing there with her. The ache lifted against her breast and she had to fight the sobs that rose in her throat.

She phoned Steve Watson at the Marine Studies Centre in Dunedin and arranged to see him the following day. Watson was in the lab when she got there and they went through to the lecture area

573

where a TV and video was set up. He watched the film and his jaw dropped.

'My God, that's fantastic.'

'I thought so.'

'Who was with you?'

'John-Cody Gibbs.'

Watson frowned then. 'Hey, I'm really sorry about that. I heard you two were an item.'

'We were, yes. Well, about to be. Yes, you can say we were.'

'I've met him a few times. There are very few people who have done more to protect Fiordland. He's a good man, Libby.'

'It's a pity the immigration authorities didn't think so.'

'I heard he was wanted by the FBI.'

'He was.'

'Not any more?'

She shook her head. 'He phoned from Seattle yesterday. They cleared him, pardoned him, whatever. Anyway the slate is clean now.'

'Legally? You mean officially?'

'Absolutely.' Libby stared at him. 'Why?'

Watson got up and switched off the TV. He ejected the video and passed it back to her. 'This is worth money, Libby. I'd say a lot of money. Either by sale to a TV company or on the lecture circuit, both maybe.' He paused for a moment. 'Have you considered what you're going to do?'

'Right now?' Libby nodded. 'I'm going to prove there's a resident pod of dolphins in Dusky Sound.'

'And after that?'

'Use whatever I make from the tape to fund an acoustic model.'

574

'Of Dusky?'

'And Doubtful: if they put hotels in one, they'll put them in the other.'

Watson furrowed his brow. 'That'll take years.'

'Perhaps, but that's my plan.'

He sat down again and folded his arms. 'Libby, there's something I need to tell you. I'm leaving the university. I've been offered a post with the World Wide Fund for Nature.'

'That's great, Steve. Congratulations.'

'Thank you.' He pushed his glasses higher up his nose. 'It means there's a vacancy here now: head of cetacean research. Ph.D. required, of course.' He smiled at her then. 'I don't know what you think but I reckon I'm looking at the best possible candidate.'

'My work's in Fiordland, Steve.'

'I know. But you've done more work on dolphin communication than anyone I've ever met, Libby. Not only that, you know more about baleen whales than I ever will. The university would benefit hugely from you being part of the team.'

'Would I get the job?'

'Of course you would. You know that already. They want continuity and a smooth transition. You would provide both.'

'But why would I want it?'

Watson looked closely at her then. 'For two reasons, I think.'

'Which are?'

'Number one, you could administer the acoustics study from here if you brought in the funds to do it: and you've already told me you can do that.'

'And number two?'

'You could apply for New Zealand residency.

575

Citizenship eventually if you wanted it.'

Libby looked up sharply.

'That means your husband could as well,' Watson went on. 'If he was of good character and had no criminal record.'

Libby stared at him. 'I'm not married, Steve.'

'No, you're not, are you?'

Kobi drove to Te Anau with Jonah.

'Where does that joker Pole live these days?' he asked.

Jonah looked sideways at his father. 'By the golf course. Why?'

'Take me there, would you?'

'Ned Pole's house?'

'Yeah, Ned Pole's house.'

Jonah turned off the main road and trundled down the track to Pole's house. His red and silver twin cab was parked in the drive and Kobi looked at his son as they pulled up.

'Just leave me here, Jonah. Ned'll drive me back to Manapouri.'

'You sure, Dad?'

'Course I'm bloody sure. Go on with you.' Kobi struggled out of the car and straightened his back. He stood leaning on his cane and watched as Jonah turned the car around then headed down the drive. When he was gone Kobi surveyed the log-style house.

Pole watched from where he was dumping hay into the feeders for the horses in the barn. They were stabled for the winter and Barrio kicked at his door in anticipation of eating. Pole did not hear him; his attention was fixed on the wizened old man who

576

shuffled towards the house. Kobi Pavaro, Mahina Pavaro's father: he hadn't set eyes on him in twenty years, but he would recognize that face anywhere. For a moment he leaned on the stable door. Then Barrio kicked again and the impact jarred his bones.

'Enough,' he snapped and tossed hay into the feeder.

Kobi heard him shout from where he stood in the yard and he looked across at the barn and waited. Moments later Pole appeared in the doorway and the two men regarded each other.

Kobi cleared his throat. 'I want to speak to you, Pole.'

Pole walked towards him, silently thanking God that Jane had gone back to the States for a few days. He looked at Kobi's bent back and Kobi looked at him.

'Kobi,' he said. 'It's been a long time. Good to see you.'

The old man's eyes were pale slits. 'Is it? You may not think so when you've heard what I've got to say.'

THIRTY

Pole stared at the old man as he spoke: Kobi's voice soft, barely louder than a whisper but with a sense of menace that chilled Pole to the bone. Kobi was diminutive and frail but his eyes were like razors and his words cut to the quick. Pole looked beyond him, beyond the lower paddock to the copse of manuka, and he was back in the bush cutting entrails from a deer ready for the helicopter.

The sound of somebody approaching came to him long before he saw them: he had spent two years with special forces in Vietnam and lying hidden in jungle while detecting any approach was his business. He could tell the person was barefoot by the way the sound lifted from the forest floor, softer than booted feet, the sticks straining before they broke, a subtlety not noticed by the untrained ear. He looked through the branches, saw a flash of naked skin and his throat slowly tightened.

Silently he watched now, sweat on his face as she moved between the beech trees, the staggered growth of fuchsia, supplejack like lianas strung across the forest. She moved with care and poise, disturbing no leaf in her passing; she eased aside a crown fern and paused to watch a yellowhead. Birds called around her as if they knew who she was and her presence was as natural as their own. She was Maori, not yet nineteen and naked as the day she was born.

She was heading straight for him and Pole crouched, aware of the deer's blood on his hands and arms, matting the hair to the elbow. He was aware of the scent of death, the black vacuum in the eye of the stag he had brought down with a single shot. Little bubbles of blood crusted the deer's lips and Pole looked from their blackness to the black of the girl's hair: Mahina Pavaro, John-Cody Gibbs's new girlfriend.

His eyes bunched as that truth hit him. Pole had coveted Mahina; wanted her from the first moment he saw her in the bush, naked as she was now. That had been three years ago. She had been roaming around like this since she was fifteen and he had seen her often, had been a silent witness content just to watch her with a tightening in his throat and a stirring in his jeans. Never once had he thought of allowing her to see him, knowing how wary she would be in the future if she thought someone was watching. But he knew the paths she trod and when he was with the helicopter crew he made sure he was the one to drop into the bush to hook up the fallen carcasses.

He was married and he had a son and often when he watched her he thought of his wife, and when he did guilt clouded like fine mist in his head. But that guilt had eased of late: since Eli was born his wife's interest in him had diminished to all but nothing. As if she had desired his presence inside her to procreate and no more: she was fertile, she had her child and Pole felt more and more marginalized within his own family. But he had these secret times when he watched Mahina and in his heart he loved her, wanted and desired her. Yet he had remained content just to watch, till that last time in Gaer Arm when he was after a stag and his hunt had been disturbed by the sound of a dinghy on the Camelot estuary. Curiosity brought him to the clearing and the waterfall and his world caved in when he saw her naked with John-Cody Gibbs.

Those thoughts haunted him while he hid behind a rock as she stood ankle deep in ice water and stripped off shorts and T-shirt, not for him, but for Gibbs. And Gibbs had taken her, not just then but for ever. In that moment she was lost to him: and that loss served only to deepen the darkness he walked in at home.

And yet there she was, moving into the clearing and heading straight for him: he could see her between the ferns and secondary growth trees, a glimpse of thigh and stomach, of black pubic hair shadowy under her belly. If she kept on this path she would step on him. Closer and closer she came. He caught sight of her breasts, her full dark nipples; he watched the way her hair washed against her shoulders as she ducked between the trees. Just a few more feet and she would see him. There was no way to avoid it now. He crouched a moment longer then stood up from his hiding place over the fallen deer.

Mahina jumped back with a cry: shock in her eyes then fear. They stood there a moment, Pole looking down at her, so much taller, throat working as the lust grew in his eyes. He said nothing, just looked on like an animal and then slowly, blood encrusting his fingers, he reached out and touched her. Mahina recoiled, trying to cover her nakedness. From somewhere above them a falcon shrieked. Pole gripped Mahina's shoulder, fingers pinching her flesh. He bent and tried to kiss her.

Mahina jerked her head away, writhing under his grip: her foot caught in some roots and she toppled over. Now Pole stood above her and his hands hung loosely at his sides, blood still drying on them, blood on the side of his face where he had wiped away sweat. The sun peeped between the tops of trees and shone on the smooth darkness of Mahina's skin. She wriggled back on the forest floor, thighs rubbing against each other. He just stood there gazing down on her, didn't move, didn't speak, tongue swollen inside his mouth. Again the falcon shrieked, closer this time, and again he ignored it. Mahina tried to get up but fell back a second time and Pole dropped to his knees beside her. He grasped her hand, but she lashed out and began to thrash with her legs. The movement exposed her further and Pole's eyes dulled. He held her ankle with one hand, the other on her thigh, a crude rough stroking, fingernails like a claw.

The falcon hit him with the force of a punch, a stinging pain at his left eye. He threw up both arms to protect himself and saw the bird beating the air with steel-blue wings and screeching at him. Mahina rolled away, got to her feet and disappeared into the bush. The falcon dive-bombed Pole again and he flailed at her with his fists. Only then did he see her nest scraped under a ledge at his feet.

The spell was broken and his heart thumped

his ribs. He leaped to his feet and called after Mahina.

She ran naked through the bush, the sound of Pole's voice echoing across the valley, the fingers of beech trees scraping her flesh. She ran blindly, hands out in front of her, down the hill, crashing through the undergrowth, then she heard him coming after her. A scream lifted in her throat but she stifled it and ran on, ducking through the trees, stumbling on roots and fallen twigs, feet sucked by mud and soaking vegetation. She ran and she ran. She ran until she saw water glinting beyond the final tree line and all she could think about were her clothes and her boat and just getting away.

'Mahina.' Again he called from behind her. 'Mahina, wait. I didn't mean anything. Wait. You've got it wrong. Wait.'

But she hadn't got it wrong and she ran and stumbled, face scratched by branches, nicks in her naked flesh, cold though sweat covered her body.

Pole stumbled blindly, fear and panic and sudden self-loathing welling up in his breast. What was he thinking of? What on earth was he doing? Again and again he called her. But his only answer was the cry of the forest birds rising as one against him. Finally he stopped running. In the distance he could hear the whump-whump of the helicopter rotor blades. He caught his breath, bloodied hands on his knees, then he scoured the bush ahead. She was gone, vanished as mist in the trees.

Instinctively he fingered the scimitar-shaped scar at the corner of his eye and Kobi's voice brought him back to the present. He looked down at the old man

582

and then beyond him again to the paddock and the lake and the mountains.

'Mahina wrote to me,' Kobi said. 'She told me what you did. We never spoke of it; she just wanted me to know and told me to say nothing because she feared what John-Cody might do, or worse, her brother. John-Cody's a peaceful soul, but Jonah is a warrior.' He paused and looked at the house. 'Where's your wife?' he said. 'She'll be the first one I tell, then I'll publish the letter and when that happens your precious American backers will drop you like hot coal.'

The colour was gone from Pole's cheeks. 'That's not how it was, Kobi.'

'That's exactly how she wrote it.'

'That's how she would. I can see that's how she would. But it wasn't like that.' Pole looked beyond him again, unable quite to look him in the eye. 'I didn't do anything to her, Kobi. I didn't hurt her.'

'You were about to.' Kobi indicated Pole's scar with the end of his walking stick. 'A falcon: what would have happened if she hadn't been guarding her nest?'

Pole was quiet, kneading the knuckles of one hand in the palm of the other. He looked beyond Kobi, back to the bush and Mahina's nakedness.

'Nobody will believe you,' he said quietly.

Kobi laughed, his voice cracking like a dry twig. 'Won't they? What would I have to gain – an old man from Naseby? At worst they'd believe the rumour. Jonah would kill you. Even if he didn't, who would want to go hunting with a rapist?'

The word stung and Pole closed his eyes. Strange

583

feelings clashed inside him, a mixture of fear, self-loathing and, in a way – relief.

'I only found out when Mahina was dying,' Kobi said. 'This was her last hope. Humiliation for her in memory, but that was all right if it would stop you ruining Dusky Sound.'

'Kobi.' Pole's voice was a hoarse whisper. 'My backers will get someone else.'

Kobi shook his head. 'No, they won't. I've lost count of the times I've heard about the big man, the original Aussie bushman, the best hunter and guide in Fiordland. Their plans won't work without you. The scheme is in your name. Besides, the whole thing will be tainted. Walk away, Pole, or I'll expose you for what you are.'

He turned then, towards the barn where he could hear a horse stamping. He stood for a moment looking at the house and the paddocks then he moved back to Pole. 'Drive me to Manapouri,' he said.

Pole drove in silence. The sun came out and warmed the tops of the mountains and the Lake of the Sorrowing Heart glinted in icy blue. 'I'm not a bad man, Kobi,' he said as they pulled up outside the office.

'Aren't you?' The old man stared ahead through the windscreen.

Pole grasped him by the shoulder. 'Haven't you ever wondered why I didn't go after Gib when Eli died?'

'Eli's death was an accident. If it appeased your conscience that's up to you.' Kobi shook off his grasp and opened the door of the truck.

Pole watched him shuffle across the little wooden bridge into the office then he turned his truck and

584

drove home. When he pulled up in the yard he sat for a moment and heard birds in the trees and the breath of wind through the grass and he felt strangely liberated. He climbed out of the truck and went indoors, into his bedroom where Jane's things littered the dressing table. He wandered up to the study and looked at his rifles and the fax machine and the two computers; then he sat in his leather chair and swivelled back and forth. His son smiled at him from the photograph. Pole looked at him for a long moment, then he picked up the telephone and dialled the regional council. When he was finished he wrote a letter to Jane and pasted it to her computer screen. Then he went to the bedroom, threw his clothes in an old grip bag and snapped it closed. Finally he took his Bible and Eli's picture from his desk and went out to his truck.

John-Cody was in New Orleans, renting a battered room in the French Quarter and waiting tables in a restaurant on Decatur Street. He had been there for a month and still Libby hadn't sent him any money from New Zealand. It concerned him; the cost of living was not what he remembered and he had to rely on tips to get by. He had bought a guitar and on his days off busked for a few extra dollars, playing guitar blues on the stone steps of Washington Artillery Park across the street from Jackson Square.

He had not intended to come back to New Orleans: he hadn't experienced city life since he left it the first time and had doubted whether he could stand the hustle and bustle again. When Agent Muller had given him the news he had not known what to do: back at the hotel he had packed his bag then stood on the sidewalk with nowhere to go. A week and a half later he arrived at the same Greyhound bus station he had left twenty-five years earlier. He walked familiar and yet unfamiliar streets, went to his parents' old house in mid-city and watched the new family who lived there, from across the street. Quite why he had come back he didn't know; perhaps it was just that it was the only familiar place in the United States, except maybe Hogan's bar in McCall. He thought about going back there a third time, but the previous trips had been less than successful and Hogan would be long dead anyway. He felt the restlessness in his soul, however, and the road beckoned as it had done all those years before and he took a bus heading south.

New Orleans baked with the heat of summer and most of the tourists had given up and gone home. The French Quarter sweated day and night and the only relief was the frequency of the rainstorms that swept in from the gulf. He sat on the steps of the park now, guitar across his knees, picking at the strings, one of his own compositions that he hadn't played in a while. He was waiting on a call from Libby and he was thinking about Dusky Sound. There was nothing he could do now and he probably wouldn't see it again, but that didn't make it any easier. If he closed his eyes he was on the bridge of the *Korimako*, sails up, weaving between the islands with the wind blowing across Five Fingers Peninsula.

He played with a bent head, glancing up every now and again to watch the human statues and the artists and tarot readers in Jackson Square. Some of them he knew to talk to now, sitting here as he did

586

on his days off, an upturned hat at his feet. He chewed an unlit cigarette and played and thought back to the days gone by when he and the band headlined at Big Daddy's.

Libby pushed open the door to the restaurant on Decatur Street and glanced at the waiters, white aprons tied about their waists, waiting for the lunchtime rush that wouldn't come. One of them picked up a towel and walked over, a broad smile on his face.

'Lunch for one, mam?'

Libby smiled and shook her head. 'Actually,' she said, 'I was looking for John-Cody Gibbs.'

'He's not working today.'

Libby's face fell. 'Do you know where I could find him?'

'Well, he might be at home. But you know what – you might want to look in Jackson Square. He sometimes plays guitar down there when he's not working.'

Libby thanked him and left the restaurant, walked a couple of blocks to Royal Street and headed for Jackson Square. She had never been to New Orleans before but the hotel had provided her with a little street map outlining the grid that was the French Quarter.

She came to the square and a clown on stilts walked around her in circles till she fished in her bag and handed him a couple of dollars. He made a great show of bowing to her and Libby moved between the rows of portrait artists and fortune-tellers and hobos lying against the railings. She walked right round the enclosed patch of grass but couldn't see

John-Cody anywhere. She crossed back to Decatur Street and could smell the boiled mud of the Mississippi River just across the train tracks. She looked towards the old Jax Brewery and back towards her hotel, then across the street where concrete steps rose to a pair of cannons. She saw him sitting there with a guitar across his knees.

She watched for a long time, aware of butterflies in her stomach: his hair hung long and ragged still at the ends where he had cut it nine months previously. Two mule-drawn carts rolled past in front of her and she crossed the road to the steps.

John-Cody played softly to himself, not looking up, not looking for any custom, just lost in memories that were private and special and old. He picked at the strings, voice very low, and a shadow fell across him as someone blocked out the sun. Still he didn't look up. Behind him one of the riverboats blew its whistle, long and loud and edged with the heat of the day.

'How about some South Island blues?'

He stopped playing.

'Something from Aotearoa maybe.'

He shaded his eyes and looked into Libby's face. For a moment he just stared then he stood up and reached for her. They kissed for a long time, lightly first then more deeply till they broke. Libby sat down on the step next to him and he gazed at her, still not quite believing that she was there. She pointed to the guitar.

'You could make a living with that.'

'I might have to. Unless you brought me some money.'

'I brought you something else.'

588

From her purse she took the sliver of green stone and placed it in his palm. John-Cody stared at it and his mind rolled back to Fraser's Beach and Mahina and the blue gum tree. He closed his fingers over the stone and it bit into his flesh. Then he took Libby's hand and placed it in her palm. 'It belongs to you now,' he said.

She looked in his eyes and looked at the stone and then she kissed him again. Across the road two of the clowns were clapping and John-Cody lifted a finger to his temple in mock salute. Libby sat and held his hand: she laid her head on his shoulder, closed her eyes and knew that she was home.

'What happened in Dusky?'

'That's partly why I'm here.' And then she smiled. 'Ned Pole withdrew his application.'

'He did what?' John-Cody stared at her.

'He withdrew his application. I have no idea why, but he withdrew and the whole thing folded. He took off somewhere, the bank foreclosed on his house and his wife is coming back to the States.'

'I don't understand.'

Libby moved her shoulders. 'Neither do I, John-Cody. Jonah took Kobi over to see him and the next thing I knew the council was phoning the office to tell us the application had been withdrawn. I immediately stuck in a request for a five-year moratorium.'

'Five years?'

She nodded. 'That's how long it will take for me to complete my research.'

He furrowed his brow. 'To prove there's a resident pod?'

'No, to create an acoustic model.' Again she took his hand. 'You see, John-Cody, you're looking at the new head of cetacean research at the University of Otago. I've sold the film we made in the Aucklands and the money is more than enough to fund the research. It's enough for me to charter a boat full time.'

'That's terrific, Lib. So you're staying in New Zealand. Bree must be over the moon.'

'Bree misses you badly. She's not the same without you.'

John-Cody bit his lip and gazed across the square where the sun reflected off the white stone of the cathedral.

'I have a boat in mind that I'd like to charter,' Libby went on, 'but at the moment it doesn't have a skipper. You don't happen to know anyone, do you?'

He sat back and smiled. 'Lib, it's a wonderful thought but I can't go back to New Zealand.'

'Can't you? Your slate is clean, John-Cody. You can prove good character.'

'I wish it were that simple.'

Libby took his hand between both of hers. 'John-Cody, listen, the job at the university is permanent. It means I can apply for residency and in time New Zealand citizenship.' She paused then, trembling slightly, and cupped his face with a palm. 'So can my husband.'

For a long time John-Cody stared at her, the breath caught in his chest. He could hear the clopping of mule hoofs and the rattle of engines, the laughter of clowns and the slap of the river on the boardwalk at their backs. The sun beat on his head and the breeze was hot and humid. Libby touched his hair, fanning the tattered ends between her fingers. 'Don't you think it's time I fixed this?' she said.

John-Cody stood on the open deck of the boat that took them across Lake Manapouri with Bree beside him, her hand in his. They crossed the mountains in the bus and at Wilmot Pass he looked out on Deep Cove as if for the first time. The driver pulled over and he climbed out with the tourists then crouched with his arm resting on his thigh and looked at the silence of the sound, snaking towards the sea. Libby moved next to him and Bree and Hunter and they all stood together and gazed into the stillness. John-Cody thought of Mahina and Tom Blanch and all the years he had fought for this place. He looked at the wedding band in gold on the third finger of his left hand and caught sight of Libby's glinting in the sun.

He saw glimpses of the *Korimako* through the bus window as they pulled up at the wharf. The breath was tight in his chest and his heart jumped as he stood looking down on his boat. Libby picked up the bags while Hunter and Bree unloaded the food boxes and John-Cody left them to it. Slowly he walked down the iron steps to where she lay against the wharf in brilliant white, the sun reflecting off the scrubbed steel of her deck. The port door was open and he could hear music playing softly, then Jonah appeared with a smile splitting his features.

'Good to see you, boss. Welcome aboard.'

They shook hands then embraced and Jonah almost crushed him. He indicated the gleaming windows with brand new perspex covering them. John-Cody stepped onto the bridge, ran his fingers over the polished wood of the dash and smelled the smells he had thought would be nothing now but memory.

Jonah cast off for'ard and Hunter astern then Libby threw off the spring. Bree stood next to John-Cody hauling the wheel to starboard: she gave three blasts on the horn and they backed away from the wharf.

They steamed up the sound where Commander Peak dominated the entrance to the narrows with no waterfall brushing its flanks. John-Cody stood at the wheel and steered by hand till they entered the Malaspina Reach and then he switched on the pilot and joined Libby on deck. North of Seymour Island Bree yelled from the port bow, and they saw dolphins blowing close to the wall: moments later they were surfing the bow wave led by Quasimodo. They rode the wave all the way up Bradshaw Sound, leaving the boat only as it entered Gaer Arm. John-Cody took the *Korimako* in close to the estuary at Shoal Cove, where the Camelot River swept down from the mountains. He checked the depth and dropped the anchor, backed up slightly till the boat was secure and then cut the engine. As the shadows lengthened he stood on deck and Libby took his hand: together they leaned on the pulpit rail and listened to the song of the sound rising from the stands of kahikatea.

THE END